Hidden Moon Bay

A Pelican Pointe Novel

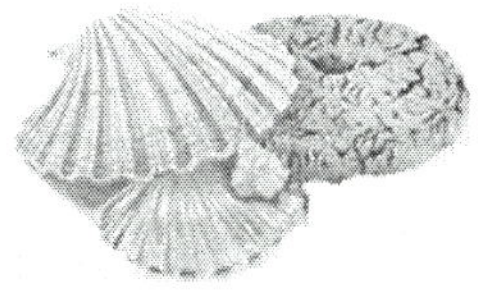

VICKIE McKEEHAN

beachdevils
PRESS

beachdevils
PRESS
ISBN-13: 978-0615723051
ISBN-10: 0615723055
Printed in the USA

Cover design by Vanessa Mendozzi
Pelican Pointe map designed by Jess Johnson

Visit the author at:
www.facebook.com/VickieMcKeehan
www.vickiemckeehan.com/

For Marty, who taught me imagination
and creativity could pay the bills.

Acknowledgements

Thousands of years before the Spanish arrived in California, a Native American people called the Chumash, or "shell people" lived and thrived along the state's rugged coastline, canoeing back and forth among the Channel Islands, specifically Santa Cruz Island. For years these native people fascinated me, so much so, that I wanted to bring a Chumash descendant to life in a contemporary story. To do that in a creative way, there's a lot of research and support involved. My thanks to Nakia Zavalla, Cultural Director of the Santa Ynez Band of Chumash Indians for providing me with translations, and for the Santa Barbara Museum of Natural History. Your combined efforts ensure the Chumash are not forgotten by future generations.

"Three things cannot be long hidden:
the sun, the moon, and the truth."
Buddha

Hidden Moon Bay

A Pelican Pointe Novel

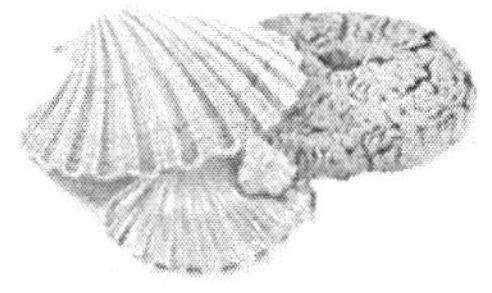

VICKIE McKEEHAN

beachdevils
PRESS

Welcome to Pelican Pointe

Prologue

Four months earlier
Chicago, Illinois

Trouble was about to overtake Emile Reed. The interview had not only been a disaster but had run longer than expected. The parking garage had almost emptied out, leaving behind the dim glare of cheap fluorescent lighting.

Not paying attention, her mind on her ruined career, she failed to hear footsteps come up behind her. An arm jerked her back into a hard, muscled chest. Then a huge, sweaty hand covered her mouth. Despite stiffening her body in response, he yanked her backward then sideways, dragging her toward the stairwell.

She fought. She kicked. She did her best to scream, moving her head wildly back and forth, but the huge hand refused to budge. By sheer force he dragged her in the direction of the stairwell. She resisted the only way she could. She dug her heels into the cement to try to stop his progress. But ultimately he was too powerful and manhandled her into the stairwell, shoving her face up against the concrete wall.

The hand over her mouth was replaced with a cold piece of steel at her throat. He slowly turned her around. The knife he held came into focus. A pair of icy, silver eyes stared back at her through the slits of a ski mask.

The second she felt the point of the knife prick her skin, felt liquid trickle down her neck, it crossed her mind if she didn't find a way to fight she was going to die.

Her assailant tightened his grip.

A raspy voice threatened, "I'm here to make sure you don't testify. Once I give you a Colombian necktie, no one will come forward to squeal."

The man stood so close, Emile smelled his stale, cigarette breath. Tattooed knuckles held the shiny weapon with one hand while the other reached to unbuckle the snap of his jeans.

His mouth curled into a sneer. "But first, what do you say we have ourselves a little fun?"

The blade left her throat long enough to slice at the buttons of the Oxford shirt she wore.

She gaped in terror as the plastic bits dropped in soundless flight to the cement. The steel made another sweep toward her chest while his free hand squeezed hard the tip of her right breast through her bra.

Emile brought her knee up, connecting to his crotch. The instant she made contact, the second he doubled over in agony, she closed her fist and with an uppercut to his throat, punched him harder than she'd ever hit anything before in her life.

The man staggered backward.

The second she heard the metal of the knife clang to the concrete, she reached out and shoved him with everything she had the rest of the way down.

She grabbed for the handle on the door. The door came back hard, hitting him in the side of his head. He crumpled to the pavement.

Emile didn't wait for him to land. She shot out of the stairwell running in three and a half inch Jimmy Choos until her feet protested and her lungs burned. All she could think about was getting away from the stairwell.

And the man sent to kill her.

Now, as she sat inside her little BMW 323, stopped at the light on Lake Shore Drive and the ramp to the expressway, she did her best to stop shaking and catch her breath, tried to calm down.

Absently, she clutched at her tattered shirt with no buttons. She shuddered. Even though it was mid-May and a warm muggy night, she felt like she'd landed on an iceberg. She turned the car heater up to high.

She'd fought. God help her, she'd gotten away.

But for how long? The man sent to kill her, sent to deliver the message, had gotten through. Big time. How long had he been following her through the parking garage? Why hadn't she noticed him sooner?

Because she'd been too deep in thought about the stupid interview she'd blown not twenty minutes earlier. It was too late now, she realized. No sense beating herself up. But from now on, she planned to be more careful, a lot more careful.

When the light turned green, she breathed out a ragged breath and pressed down on the accelerator, screeching onto the 55 ramp, gaining some serious speed. She spared a nervous glance in the rearview mirror. It didn't look as though anyone had followed her, at least, not yet. Since she couldn't be sure, as soon as she could, she merged into the steady stream of traffic, changing lanes until she'd reached the farthest one.

And simply drove and drove and drove.

She wouldn't be going home. At least not any time soon. They'd be waiting for her. She thought of her cozy little condo she'd owned for four years and how she'd painstakingly picked out every stitch of furniture there one piece at a time. She let out a sigh, knowing how much she'd miss it.

But it was too dangerous to go back.

Her mind raced with options. She could head east to New York State where her mother lived. But that was a fairly obvious destination for anyone looking for her. Same with going south to her sister's in St. Louis.

She couldn't go to them; she couldn't risk putting the people she loved in harm's way.

No, she'd already made too many mistakes and bad decisions for that. She could head north to Toronto where an aunt lived. But anyone who knew her might be able to find out about any relatives she'd used on past employment applications for personal references.

Still gripped by panic, she tried to think.

She couldn't stay in Chicago. If she had to, she'd drive clear across the country.

She knew one thing though. No matter what she'd promised the feds, she couldn't go through with it, wouldn't put her family and herself in danger any longer.

If she'd been worried about testifying, appearing in court before today, before that maniac in the parking garage, she was absolutely terrified now.

Because she was certain of one thing: Jeremy Dochenko had no intentions of giving up until she was dead.

Chapter One

Present day
Somewhere along the California coast

Hayden Ryan kept her eyes on the road and her hands firmly locked on the steering wheel in the ten and two position while the rain bashed against the windshield and the wind battered the Mini Cooper as though it were no more than a pesky bug, slapping at it with such force she was afraid she might lose control and end up in a ditch.

She'd taken a wrong turn sometime after dark, after she'd left the 101 in search of a gas station. She needed to find some place to stop—and soon. But a place to spend the night was starting to sound unlikely.

If she didn't find a convenience store that sold gas pretty soon, she'd be forced to pull over and wait out the storm on the side of the road, something she really didn't want to do.

As if to prove a point, the Pacific storm threw another blast of water in her path and rocked the Mini. The wind practically tossed the car off the road. She was pretty sure she was somewhere near Santa Cruz, but at this point couldn't be certain.

She hadn't seen a road sign in forever.

She never should have veered off I-80.

If she'd gone into the Bay area, she'd be someplace by now, at the very least tucked into a cheap motel room with a bed and bathroom.

But she'd read about the high cost of living in San Francisco and didn't think she could pull it off under her current set of circumstances. She'd headed south instead.

Santa Cruz had sounded a lot more affordable and she hoped would prove to be a decent place to find a job. She wanted to check out the picturesque town, its boardwalk, and the sandy beaches there, and all the points of interest she'd read about on the Internet while sitting in the Denver library.

Maybe when she got there she'd send out postcards to everyone and let them know she'd reached the Pacific Ocean.

Okay, maybe that wasn't practical, but the thought was there.

She slanted a wary glance at the gas gauge. The Mini got a stingy thirty-seven miles to the gallon, but at the moment, it was woefully hovering close to the E, and had been for miles.

Running out of gas would leave her stranded and without options.

Her system jolted at the thought of that.

Why oh why, had she ever left the interstate? She should have just taken I-5 north and headed straight into Canada. She had a new passport and new ID, why hadn't she tested both?

Because when push came to shove she was a big, fat, old chicken. She let out a huge sigh. Indecision wasn't her friend, couldn't be. She'd make this work.

But at this rate she'd be out of gas soon and maybe out of luck. When that happened…no, no, she wouldn't think like that.

Hayden might have thought she had put plenty of miles between her and Chicago and the man that wanted her dead, but she wouldn't risk getting found now. She'd gone through too much, left too much behind to give up now.

Her mother and sister understood she was on the run and why. Hayden made certain she found a way to call them once a week using a prepaid wireless cell phone she'd purchased just to keep in touch and let them know she was okay.

But she couldn't ignore one fact. That night in the parking garage Dochenko's messenger had made it clear.

There was no way she could testify against him now no matter how many times the feds promised to keep her safe. She knew they couldn't. For months now the government had pressured both her mother and her sister. Repeatedly. They had begged and pleaded, cajoled and even threatened her to enter the witness protection program. But the minute she'd discovered what that meant, what doing so entailed, that she would lose all contact with her mother and sister for good, forever, Hayden had turned them down—flat.

Despite the shows on TV, Hayden knew the feds weren't infallible. As long as Jeremy's minions were out there somewhere, she could still be vulnerable. Nothing was foolproof.

And she would have lost control over her own life. Something she refused to do.

Instead of all that, Hayden had created her own kind of protection program. She had ceased to exist as Emile Reed.

It had taken patience and cunning and spending time in places like Sioux City, Iowa, and then Lawton, Oklahoma before moving on to Lincoln, Nebraska, where she'd hung out long enough with a friend from college, Kate Michelson, who also happened to be an attorney.

Kate had helped her obtain a new social security number right along with a new name. Emile Reed had morphed into Hayden Ryan, a name she'd purposely chosen because, more often than not, it could just as easily belong to a male as a female.

In Kansas City she had gotten rid of her sporty little BMW and bought a used Mini, opened a checking account using a wire transfer from her mother in upstate New York who had sent it through the aunt in Toronto who had in turn sent it to a friend of the friend in Lincoln before it had made its way to Hayden in the form of a money gram.

She had stayed just long enough in Denver to turn her platinum hair into a silky shade of black, shorten the length to a straight spiky cut in the back with sides that angled sharply below her chin. That was about the same time she had exchanged her Nebraska driver's license for a Nevada one and changed the tags on the Mini…yet again.

So far, she had been living on her savings from the last four years but she was about out of money. She had already decided on taking care of that by trying out her new ID and getting a job once she landed in Santa Cruz.

Through it all her poor mother had been left to deal with some very angry and upset feds. Hayden was truly sorry about that. Because those same people were no doubt deeply disappointed in Emile Reed's decision.

She took heart in the fact that her mother kept reminding the feds that her daughter had every reason to fear Jeremy Dochenko and had gone on the run because of it. Hayden was grateful that at least her mother had supported her decision.

At least her loved ones understood the situation.

After all, the man had killed before, a fact that the feds had a tendency to gloss over. Of course Emile hadn't known that little tidbit when she'd gone to work for the wealthy Russian stockbroker four years earlier. It certainly hadn't come up in the interview.

She remembered being so fresh and green right out of college, hoping to be a part of something grand in the business world that she'd been sucked in by the smooth talking conman.

How was she supposed to know her boss had been hard at work defrauding and bilking thousands of investors out of billions before she'd ever drawn her first paycheck?

But it was what went on after she was hired that she had a hard time getting past.

In four years, Jeremy had been the one who had dealt with the bank officers. Had she known that he was altering the financial statements she so painstakingly handed him each month she would have gone to the authorities herself. Maybe if she had bothered following up with the bank, she would have caught on sooner. Why hadn't she known he kept a second set of financials for the bank's eyes only?

By the time she had started to question the client accounts, by the time she realized Jeremy's "investment" acumen was one big lie, the SEC was already knocking on the door. They'd stepped in to investigate, which left the justice department not far behind in prosecuting him.

She might've worked diligently on a daily basis, even avoided taking vacations, but she had to admit now, she'd been a bit full of herself back then. She'd put her all-important job ahead of everything else including personal relationships.

Even though she'd done absolutely nothing illegal, she felt guilty. How could she not have realized what Jeremy had been doing? If nothing else, she obviously hadn't followed through enough to catch on sooner. She might even be guilty of sloppy oversight, and remiss in her fiduciary duties.

So when the government knocked, she had cooperated fully, agreed to testify in detail to Jeremy's business practices and his schemes, even going so far as to explain how he had managed to cover his tracks for so many years without getting caught. But all that was before the judge had allowed Jeremy to post bail, before he had vanished, disappeared like the snake he was and before that thug had attacked her in the parking garage.

To Emile, the in-your-face attempt on her life had changed everything.

Emile Reed's life had died four months ago, shred by Dochenko's greed. So Hayden Ryan had come into existence and with it, a chance to put everything behind her.

But every now and then she thought about that time immediately after losing her job. She'd tried to make the transition work. She'd never been without a job before even in high school. She had been in the process of hunting for another one, going out on interview after interview. But she hadn't counted on the fact that no one wanted to hire an accountant who had ties to the likes of Dochenko.

Okay, so that part hadn't exactly worked out. That day in the parking garage, she had been coming from yet another job interview where it had gone downhill the minute they had discovered the depth of her association with the con man and his fraudulent past.

Then the swine had shown up in the parking garage, brandishing a knife, making it clear what Jeremy wanted, clear what Emile Reed's options were. As long as she lived, she'd be able to testify against Jeremy at his trial and might be the difference between his spending a lot of years behind bars or whether he got off scot-free.

Either way, it wasn't her responsibility, losing her life wasn't part of the bargain. She knew very well there were other ways the government could make their case. Because she refused to accept life in a witness protection program that meant she had to give up her mother and sister. There was no way she would put her life in the hands of the government when they obviously couldn't guarantee her family's safety, or hers.

Just this week, the last time she'd talked to her mother, she had reminded Hayden that Jeremy's business partner had already turned up dead. Just a day before the attack in the parking garage, a co-worker had been found shot to death in his high-rise condo off the downtown Loop with a gunshot wound to the back of his head. The newspapers had called it an execution style slaying. Of course, no one could prove Jeremy had anything to do with that death, either. But it didn't take a genius to figure out why his partner had ended up dead. He'd known too much just like she had.

The feds had also promised to protect Saul Raymond. And look how that had turned out.

So much for keeping one of their key witnesses safe and sound, thought Hayden. More than once she had counted herself lucky that the man in the parking garage that night had carried a knife rather than a gun. If he had, she didn't doubt for a minute she'd be dead by now with a bullet to the brain.

With that image in her head, she shivered and turned the heater up a notch. To get her mind back on the situation at hand, she fidgeted with the CD player and concentrated on Eddie Vedder's voice extolling the fact he was still alive.

In a very real way, she could relate, couldn't she? Even if she had been forced to take matters into her own hands to make it happen.

If she ever found the 101 again, she swore she'd kiss the pavement. Right now though, she was grateful there wasn't much traffic. She hadn't seen another car in over an hour, which did not bode well in her favor. No traffic meant she was probably on a back road somewhere which meant no chance for a gas station or a convenience store or food or a damned restroom for that matter.

Her bladder was starting to give off the warning signs that soon she'd have to pee. Her stomach joined in with a rumble or two to let her know it was time to eat. Absently, she wondered if she had any more power bars left in her backpack for dinner. She sighed. Her fuel wasn't going to last much longer either.

Maybe she should pull over and hope the rain let up.

On impulse, she eased the car to the shoulder. At least she thought it was a shoulder. Hayden could see nothing but rain and darkness outside the car's windows.

Reluctantly, she killed the engine to save her precious gas fumes and grabbed her fleece lined jacket from the backseat. After shrugging to get it on, she dug into her backpack. Hoping to find a too-skinny protein bar that would have to last until morning, she realized she should've bought more at her last stop. If only she had a cup of hot coffee or tea to wash it down. She reluctantly picked up the cup that held the soda she'd bought at the same time as the bar and now held nothing but caramel-colored water. She sucked a disgusting sip through the straw. It was better than nothing. She should've bought more water for the road, too.

Hunger had her biting into the chewy concoction with gusto. Sitting there in the dark, it didn't take long for exhaustion to overtake her and she soon drifted off to sleep to the sound of rain still pummeling the car.

Ethan Cody had seen better nights. Not only was he hungry and tired, but the September storm was wreaking havoc with what should have been his night off.

It had already washed out a bridge near San Sebastian causing several accidents, which in turn, had forced him to play traffic cop for damn near two hours clearing up the mess. Then he'd decided to stay until Caltrans showed up to close off the bridge and set up a detour.

After that, he had been asked to take an elderly woman whose power had gone out over to Watsonville to spend the night with her sister.

That was before he'd gotten drenched to the bone when he'd had to get out in the downpour again helping old man Taggart jump-start his truck, which had given out in the middle of Main Street, loaded down with organic produce.

It was all in a day's work for a deputy sheriff, he supposed. Despite the fact Ethan worked for his brother, Brent, who had been elected county sheriff four years earlier, he enjoyed the work, most times, except on nights like tonight when people didn't have the good sense to come in out of the rain.

And now, some poor idiot schmuck had left his car parked practically in the middle of the road making it a damned road hazard. What was it about rain that deadened people's brains and left them without the ability to drive on a slick street? he wondered as he hit his emergency flashers and the overhead lights for the fourth time in as many hours.

Resentful about the situation before he even crawled out of his truck, he decided to ticket the driver no matter what his excuse just to make a point. Out of habit, Ethan ran the Nevada plates, waited until he got the results. For some reason he pictured the driver of the little car squirming at the prospect of law enforcement sitting behind him for so long.

Reluctant to crawl back out into the freaking weather, he listened as the radio crackled to life and the dispatcher told him, "Plates are clean. Car's registered to a Hayden Ryan."

Okay, that's a start, thought Ethan. When his headlights revealed movement inside the car, he decided Mr. Hayden Ryan was about to get a very unwelcome-to-California memento to go with his out-of-state plates.

Hayden woke to flashing lights in her rearview mirror. Damn. Despite the fact she'd done nothing wrong and knew for a fact her registration would come up clean, a fist of fear clogged her throat at the prospect of dealing with law enforcement.

It was the first time she'd encountered a cop since leaving Chicago, which was a miracle in itself considering how many miles she'd covered. As she sat there waiting for him to crawl out of his vehicle, she wondered what was taking him so damn long. She pulled out her registration from the glove box, dug in her wallet for her driver's license. And waited. What felt like five minutes ticked by before she watched the truck door finally open and a rain soaked man dressed in a yellow vinyl slicker step out onto the road and make his way up to the driver's side window.

She waited for him to tap on the glass.

When he did, she rolled the window down no more than three inches because of the pouring rain and cold wind.

Ethan peered into the car. His first surprise came in the form of a female driver with huge, wary green eyes. Those green pools pulled him in. But then, the letters ER flashed at him like a neon sign, making him think this might be an emergency situation. She might be experiencing more than car trouble. Maybe she had taken ill behind the wheel and that's why she was blocking the road.

Cautious, he shined his flashlight into the car's interior, checking out the passenger seat, then the backseat, and let it slowly illuminate the inside of the small car, telling him she was indeed alone.

Automatically he shifted into cop mode. "Evening, ma'am. Nasty night tonight. Is everything all right? Could I see your license and registration, please?"

"Sure," Hayden replied, trying to make her voice sound calm. "Is there a problem?"

Despite the cold rain, she did her best to stop shaking long enough to hand off the piece of plastic that was her brand-new driver's license and the registration, hoping it wouldn't get soaking wet.

As soon as Ethan's hand touched hers in the exchange, however briefly, a series of images bombarded him again.

Danger seemed to surround this woman. The letters ER kept coming at him so fast he finally had to focus on studying her ID. Ethan relied on the flashlight to read, first the driver's license, and then the registration. The name Hayden Ryan matched both. The Nevada license read SEX: F, HAIR: BLK, EYES: GRN, HT: 5-07 WT: 125.

Everything seemed in order, nice and tidy. No doubt the photo ID matched the driver behind the wheel. But something was off. He just didn't know what it was. With nothing concrete, he couldn't very well hold her based on dangerous vibes.

He had to almost shout over the wind and the rain. "You're blocking the roadway, ma'am. When you pull off onto the shoulder, make sure you're all the way off otherwise you're a road hazard. On a night like tonight somebody could easily speed up behind you, try to brake, lose control, and slide right into you. The road narrows some here, anyway."

"Oh. Well. I didn't think of that. I couldn't see very well in the pouring rain, so I tried to pull off for a bit. But I didn't want to get stuck. I must've gotten turned around after dark looking for a gas station. I'm almost running on fumes."

"You got lost. No car trouble?"

"No car trouble. I was trying to make Santa Cruz tonight. But I don't have the gas for that unless Santa Cruz is right around the corner." She smiled nervously. She'd never been very good at flirting and tonight was no exception.

He smiled. "Ah. Well, you're not even close to Santa Cruz. Pelican Pointe is where you landed and out in the middle of nowhere at that. But lucky for you there's a bed and breakfast just down the road. You can stay there for the night if they aren't sold out." Since it was past tourist season Ethan doubted they'd be full up. "Place is called Promise Cove. If you'll follow me I'll show you where it is. I know the owners."

Of course you do, Hayden thought, mildly irritated, as she did an automatic calculation of how much cash she had on hand in her backpack. She knew B & B's could be a tad on the pricey side. But with her name change she'd also gotten one credit card for emergencies which she had tucked away in her wallet. It had a five thousand dollar credit limit. She had yet to use it for anything. She supposed she could break down and indulge herself for one night at a cozy B & B. She really didn't want to spend the night in the car on the side of the road.

"All right then, Deputy. You lead the way," she finally managed to tell him.

Ethan nodded and climbed back into his truck. He immediately reached for his cell phone to dial Promise Cove. Wouldn't do any good to lead the woman to the B & B if they didn't have an available room.

But tourist season usually ended with Labor Day and it was now the middle of September. As soon as Jordan Harris picked up, Ethan got right to it. "I got a stranded motorist, Jordan, about a thousand yards from your front door. Female. Name's Hayden Ryan. She needs a room for the night. Can you help me out?"

"As a matter of fact, we can. You on your way?"

"Yep. We'll be there in five. Thanks, Jordan." Ethan disconnected. He didn't add that Hayden Ryan had acted skittish for some reason. No need mentioning the gut feeling he'd gotten to Jordan. Probably nothing to it anyway, he decided, more like, alone on a dark stretch of road in the pouring rain and edgy about running out of gas.

His brother, Brent, would have said the gut feeling was the shaman in Ethan, a gift from their father's Chumash heritage passed down through the Santa Ynez.

Like his father, Ethan had an intuitive side about him. He'd known early on he had a certain something that frequently allowed him to "read people" he'd sometimes rather not.

Like the time in the ninth grade he'd picked up on Janie Sullivan wanting to get all hot and sweaty after the basketball game. Okay, maybe that had been a good vibe and one that had eventually led him to losing his virginity that very night on a sandy spot of beach where the two of them were so green they hadn't even had the good sense to remember to bring a blanket.

But for every positive instance there had been twenty others that had made him feel just plain weird because he really didn't care to know his little league coach had been getting it on with Ruthie Ann Jenner, the mother of his ten-year-old best friend, Todd.

In his line of work, though, using his intuition or his gut feeling or reading people sometimes served a useful purpose every now and then when things got dicey and he needed to figure out how best to handle a crisis situation with a volatile subject.

As soon as Ethan hung up the phone with Jordan, he cut the flashing lights and put the truck in gear. He pulled around the Mini Cooper in order to lead the way and waited for her to start her car.

Hayden followed him down the dark road and suddenly wondered if she might be following a serial killer to her death. Had he been wearing a uniform? She tried to remember if he'd been dressed in official looking clothes.

All she'd been able to make out was the man's dark eyes and obvious Native American good looks, his strong chin with its slight cleft indentation and his hair worn longer than what one might expect from a member of law enforcement.

She'd been so shaken at seeing those emergency lights she hadn't been able to think straight. Maybe she should have asked to look at his ID, she thought now.

Just when she was working herself into a good panic over it, the headlights of his truck coupled with her own, highlighted an apple green sign that read, "Promise Cove Bed and Breakfast, established 2009 by Scott Phillips. Jordan and Nick Harris, Proprietors."

Okay, so maybe he was no serial killer.

When he took a left, thanks to her headlights, she caught a quick glance at the official-looking seal on the driver's side door that signified the vehicle was indeed a county police car.

She breathed a sigh of relief and continued to follow him into the turn down a long driveway that seemed to go on and on till they reached an old Queen Anne Victorian that stood large and looming in the dark. That is, until the front door flew open letting out a burst of light from inside the house.

The deputy motioned for her to go around him and park at the side of the house.

As soon as she'd pulled the Mini up beside a Ford Explorer, the deputy got out, shouldering the weight of the wind and the pouring rain to walk her to the front door and make sure she got safely inside. From somewhere he'd found an umbrella.

Hayden grabbed her backpack, purse and suitcase and prepared to step out into the wet, chilly night. She flipped the hood up on her jacket, opened the car door and found the deputy holding the open umbrella for her, and waiting with his arm stretched out for her to hand him her suitcase. Reluctantly she handed off the luggage and together they walked up to the wide massive wooden front porch where the deputy closed the umbrella and set it down by the front door.

Another black-haired man, this one with lake blue eyes, stood waiting, holding open one of the twin front doors and stepped aside so they could both come in out of the weather. Briefly they all three stood in the wide entryway until the man said, "Ethan, good to see you. Nasty storm. Been busy?"

"Hey Nick. Yeah, it's been a bad one. You and Jordan doing okay out here? No problems with the power?"

"So far, so good. And the new roof's holding like a gem, too."

To Hayden, he stuck out his hand and introduced himself. "Nick Harris. I'd say it's a pleasure, but getting stranded on the side of the road in the dark in the middle of a Pacific storm is not much fun."

When a woman with long honey blond hair appeared in the foyer carrying a little girl on her hip, Nick turned in their direction, beaming, and said, "This is my wife, Jordan."

Fogged brain from the nap in the car, Hayden struggled to remember the new name. The harder she tried the more it slipped away. She'd never been the type of person to wake easily and now the hours spent behind the wheel seemed to be catching up with her.

Glancing at the good-looking couple, the innkeepers, who all but gave off warm and cozy, home and hearth, she felt a bit drained and a lot disheveled.

Nerves hit her all of a sudden. She stumbled over her words. "Um, uh Hayden…uh, Ryan. Hayden Ryan." It wasn't every day she introduced herself using her new name. Damn, she'd have to work on that. As she tried to overcome her jitters, Nick took her coat and hung it on a peg by the front door.

"Well, let's get you set up," Nick offered. "I'll take your things on up. You'll be staying in the Sand Dollar Room. It's one of our best with its own bathroom."

Ethan handed Nick her suitcase and noticed Hayden's teeth chattering.

Jordan saw it too and ushered them both into the living room toward the roaring fire, blazing in a gigantic stone fireplace. Chatting all the way, Jordan told Hayden, "The Sand Dollar has a view of the ocean and access to the back balcony. As Nick said it's our best. We ate dinner at seven, but I can fix you a plate. Roast beef with baby carrots and potatoes. Apple pie for dessert. Do you prefer tea or coffee?"

"Tea, please. That all sounds heavenly," Hayden finally managed. "I've been starving for hours."

"I bet you have. You were so close to us, too. But I bet you couldn't see a thing in all this rain. Now you come over here and sit by the fire, get warm." Jordan turned to Ethan. "And you stay for a plate as well, Ethan. There's plenty. Even though the tourist season is pretty much over I still haven't adjusted my recipes. Still cooking for a houseful of people."

"I could eat. Thanks, Jordan. And I'd love a cup of coffee. Looks like it's going to be a long night. Let me just radio in." Ethan stepped back out into the foyer to make his call.

"Where are you from?" Jordan asked casually, as she drifted closer to the stone fireplace, hoping her nervous guest would follow. She eased the baby down on the floor to toddle. "Since we opened last May, we get people staying here from all over the world. Last summer we had a couple from Scotland, another from France, and a family visiting California for the first time from Sweden."

Hayden's mind raced trying to memorize what she'd practiced a dozen times. She walked closer to the fire, not to get warm but to take her time as she desperately tried to recall her story. But her mind went blank. Never a good liar, she couldn't pull her made-up history out of her fog-brained head fast enough. For no apparent reason she blurted out, "Nebraska."

The minute the word left her mouth, she realized her mistake. Her driver's license had read Nevada the same as the registration on her plates, not Nebraska.

God, could she be any dumber or any more nervous.

If she'd been hoping the sheriff's deputy had been distracted enough to pay no attention to her blunder as he carried on a conversation with his dispatcher, she was in for a major disappointment. Because suddenly she noted he eyed her with open suspicion.

His dark, cop eyes sent out contemptuous daggers loaded with distrust. Damn it. She visibly winced. Nothing said hostility like the deputy's furious stare.

His face said it all. She was raising felony red flags faster than Charles Manson.

Two seconds later, Hayden tried for damage control. "Nevada, I meant Nevada." She thunked her own forehead with her palm. "Tells you how out of it I am. I've been driving since this morning. The nap in the car must have fogged my brain more than I thought."

She forced herself to look into Ethan's mistrustful eyes. "I didn't live long in Nevada. It didn't suit me."

For a distraction, Hayden bent down to pet the multicolored mutt of a dog that had wandered over to lean against her leg. The furry thing hung out his tongue, appreciating the attention and rolled over on his back to let her stroke his belly.

Hayden put more into the gesture to buy more time.

But Ethan simply watched her with cop interest, as if he thought she might wait until everyone went to bed and murder them all in their sleep.

Without leaving Hayden's stare, to make sure Jordan understood just how much he regretted bringing this woman to their doorstep tonight and to make his point, Ethan offered, "Ms. Ryan here was on her way to Santa Cruz. It was Santa Cruz, wasn't it? Or maybe it was some other place?"

The implication came through loud and clear. The "some other place" comment hinted he didn't buy her name any more than he did the Nevada address on her driver's license. "Yes, it was Santa Cruz. And it's just Hayden," she said flatly, as she stood up from petting the dog and crossed her arms over her chest in a defiant gesture.

Jordan ignored Ethan's accusing tone and made her own assessment. The woman looked worn out and defeated. "So you're looking to stay in the area? Maybe you're looking for a job, maybe you'd consider settling in Pelican Pointe instead of going all the way to Santa Cruz."

"Well...uh, I do need a job. But that's why I thought I'd check out Santa Cruz. I'd heard good things about it. You know, a bigger job market there." She'd read up about the coastal town while sitting in the library, figured it was better than the Bay area on her budget. "Before it got dark I saw some very pretty woods and rolling hills off the 101."

"There are plenty of both around here. Pelican Pointe isn't as big as Santa Cruz that's for sure. And it's off the beaten path, which means there aren't a lot of jobs to be had here, but there are business opportunities. I know Drea Jennings opened a florist shop in town last month. Her family owns The Plant Habitat, the local nursery in town. Drea's Flowers are all grown locally, even the orchids. It's kind of an extension of the family business, a vertical, I think they call it. But with Homecoming approaching, and the holidays, Drea might need an extra pair of hands. And Murphy's been talking about adding another cashier at the store. And Margie might need a waitress down at the Diner. She's always complaining she can't keep wait staff on the evening shift. What do you think, Ethan?"

"My guess is Miss Ryan is probably looking for a bigger place to lose herself in than Pelican Pointe."

At the deputy's cold tone, Hayden's temper uncharacteristically sparked as she pointed out, "If I'd wanted to lose myself, Deputy, I would have headed to

San Francisco. Last time I checked San Fran is infinitely larger than Santa Cruz by a few hundred thousand people."

Ethan leveled his eyes on her and countered, "The name is Ethan Cody, Ms. Ryan. And I have no problem remembering my name, or where I've lived."

Of course you've never had to remember a lie Hayden thought. Your life is probably nothing short of perfect. And you don't happen to have an angry Russian trying to murder you either.

But when Hayden opened her mouth to make a catty comeback nothing came out. She bit her lip instead. Great, she thought, I've been here two seconds and already made an enemy, an enemy wearing a uniform. One more reason to move on first thing in the morning, she decided.

That is, if she could just get through tonight.

When Nick reappeared, sensing sudden tension in the air, Jordan, ever the hostess, turned to Hayden. "Nick will show you to your room, where you can get settled while I get the food ready. Take all the time you need to freshen up and unpack. There's no hurry. Dinner will be waiting for you when you're ready."

"Thanks," Hayden muttered wearily, as she glanced back at Ethan.

"This way," Nick offered as he started back up the stairs.

As soon as they'd disappeared, Jordan headed off into the kitchen with Ethan trailing behind. "What was that all about?"

"Don't know, but there is something off with that woman."

"How so? You mean that Nebraska/Nevada thing?"

Reluctant to sound harsh but knowing Nick and Jordan deserved to know who they would be sharing their home with for the night, Ethan explained, "Yeah. Her license and tags read Nevada. And were both dated just two weeks ago. Now, here she is in California looking for work. I get the sense the woman might be on the run, Jordan."

Knowing Pelican Pointe wasn't the friendliest of towns Jordan eyed Ethan and calmly pointed out, "That suspicious nature, Ethan, is exactly what keeps newcomers away from Pelican Pointe. And could it be that maybe Hayden Ryan is tired because she's been behind the wheel all day, just like she said, and got a little anxious because she got lost and feared she might run out of gas on a strange, dark, unfamiliar road out in the middle of nowhere. Or it could be she's suffering from some type of head injury or illness."

Jordan cocked her head and smiled knowingly. "I believe in giving people the benefit of the doubt, second chances, Ethan. But then, I'm not a deputy sheriff," she added, as she went directly to the cabinet and took down two huge matching mugs. She turned to the ever-present coffee pot and poured Ethan a cup of steaming liquid, handed it off.

Ethan grinned as he took the cup and looked around for the sugar. "You're probably right. Force of habit. She did look tired. I think she might have been asleep in her car when I found her."

"There you go. Disoriented. You woke her up, surprised her." As she started setting out food from the commercial fridge, she reminded him, "You never know what problems a person has just by looking at them, Ethan. There are all kinds of people out there having rough times for various reasons." She thought of her own Nick and how troubled he had been when he had first arrived in Pelican Pointe.

And at the time no one in town bothered to give her a chance let alone the time of day. Plus, she knew if Nick hadn't shown up when he did there would be no B and B now. "Try not to judge her too quickly, Ethan. That's all I'm saying. If she is running from something, she probably has a good reason."

Jordan thought of her friend, Lilly Seybold, another newcomer who had divorced her husband after several incidences of domestic violence and was now in a relationship with Wally Pierce who owned the gas station and auto repair shop in town.

Small towns were full of people with problems and their own secrets.

"When people get to a new place, a new town, they need friends just like anyone else, a new start, not a bunch of intrusive questions and suspicions upfront."

Because Ethan knew how difficult life had been for Jordan living in Pelican Pointe since losing her first husband in Iraq, he held up his hands as if in surrender and said quietly, "When you're right, you're right. I know you and Nick are trying to recruit people to give Pelican Pointe a chance, to get fresh faces in here, some new blood and all that."

He remembered how badly the town had treated her up until last spring when Nick had shown up and shamed the whole town into helping her open up her B& B on time.

Knowing that, he promised, "Okay. I'll give her the benefit of the doubt and chalk it up to her being tired after a long day of driving. How's that? Now, will I get my share of that roast beef I smell?"

Jordan's mouth curved. "You're sweet, Ethan, now help me set the table."

By the time Hayden came back down, they were all waiting for her, gathered around the dining room table. Ethan had shed his rain slicker. He sat there with his longish jet black hair still glistening with rain and poking out of his collared uniform shirt while his soulful dark chocolate eyes seemed to watch her every move.

Picking up her napkin, she realized he still looked as though she planned to abscond with the good silver first chance she got. So she decided to ignore him. And she was certain this particular man wasn't used to being ignored by women, not with a face like Johnny Depp, that dimple in the chin, and a long lanky frame making him a good six-one. His prominent Native American features, the nose and dark eyes stood out on his face in a stubborn set, no one could mistake for genial.

And all that exotic damp hair gave him the look of a fierce warrior who'd weathered the elements on his own and knew how to survive.

She forced herself to look away and focused on the darling little blonde sprite who looked about two, and sat peacefully on her father's lap eating a dish of vanilla ice cream covered in fudge sauce. She had the sticky stuff all over her mouth as she desperately tried to work the spoon.

When Jordan saw Hayden staring at her daughter, she made the introductions. "This is our daughter, Hutton. She's learning to use a spoon. And the dog's name is Quake."

"Cake," Hutton repeated, sending everyone a messy grin. Jordan interpreted the comment. "That's what she calls Quake. It's a step up from Dog, which is what she used to call him."

Hayden laughed out loud but couldn't help notice again how Nick seemed to glow in the direction of his wife. "She's adorable. How old?"

"She'll be two in December," Nick answered like a proud father.

Ethan tried not to stare at Hayden. But much to his dismay, he couldn't help himself. She had the most brilliant shade of green eyes he'd ever seen. Probably contacts and as fake as her Nevada license, Ethan reasoned.

But it looked as if she had been crying. Puffy, red-rimmed eyes, stood out of a too-pale face which made her look exhausted. Her black hair was now drier and sported a bit of a cowlick in back. She'd changed from jeans and shirt into a one piece, thick midnight blue colored dress that showed off her legs. And the woman had fine legs, Ethan decided, as he cut into his roast beef.

Hayden concentrated on her plate as Jordan attempted to make conversation. "What a lovely woolen dress, Hayden. You didn't have to dress up for dinner. We're pretty casual around here," Jordan commented, before adding, "How's your room? Is everything okay?"

Hayden didn't want to admit to Jordan that her wardrobe was rather limited these days. The dress had been a gift from her friend, Kate, before she'd headed west. Nor did she want the woman to know that she desperately needed to do a load of laundry. "The room's wonderful. Thanks. You have a beautiful home here."

And she couldn't help but wonder whether or not she'd ever have anything or anyplace as nice to call home ever again. She sighed out loud, remembering her cute little condo and how much she missed the one thousand square feet of space. How long would she have to hide out, keep running?

Her crying jag upstairs had only made her feel worse about her circumstances, about the decisions she'd made. But she couldn't go back and erase the last five months or for that matter, four years of working for a sleazebag.

She forced a few more bites of food down and thought glumly that she would have loved nothing better than to have stayed buried in her room for the rest of the evening to wait out the storm until morning, alone.

But she had figured these people would be down here waiting for her to eat. And it looked as if Deputy Ethan Cody was chomping at the bit to interrogate her at the first available opportunity. Right now, Hayden just wanted to eat her meal in peace then spend some serious soak time in the tub upstairs before falling into bed.

Lost in her reverie, Hayden realized every eye was on her. Manners had her straightening her spine and posture, remembering to tell her hostess how much she appreciated the meal. "You're a very good cook. It tastes as good as my mom's."

A slew of questions formed in Ethan's brain. It was on the tip of his tongue to pursue that line of inquiry about her family. But as if sensing Jordan's disapproval, he kept his mouth shut.

When he saw the little smile form on Jordan's face, he knew he'd done the right thing and was just about to comment on the food himself, when Hayden surprised him by adding, "I always wanted to learn to cook."

Jordan went into cheerleader mode. "It isn't that hard really. You just have to take the time. Problem is, people are so busy with their jobs, commuting back and forth, raising families, they don't have time to cook anything except what can be popped in the microwave. Or, they rely on fast food and take out. It's the way of the world."

"I know I relied on speed dial and every takeout joint within a five block radius," Nick added just as jovial as his wife.

"That just about describes my life since college and why I haven't bothered with learning how to do more than boil water." There was something about these people and their friendly, upbeat nature that drew Hayden into conversation. "Although, I do make a mean chocolate chip cookie—and fudge nut brownies."

"Had a busy life, have you?" Ethan's war with curiosity won. "Doing what?"

While Jordan and Nick were the epitome of gracious, the Deputy on the other hand, was the antithesis. Hayden gave him a cool stare before she retorted, "Accounting. But I'm looking to change careers. It was a boring way to spend sixty hours a week inside a cubicle." She'd had a corner office. And boring? Her job had been many things, but boring hadn't been one of them, especially with the SEC and the feds to deal with, and certainly not with Jeremy wanting her dead and Saul Raymond already there.

"I agree," Jordan declared, "I could never spend eight hours in a cubicle."

"I tried that," Nick agreed. "I got tired of the seventy hour work-weeks in L.A., the lengthy commute, the stress-filled day, the sleepless nights. Since I left all that behind, my stress level is almost nonexistent. Of course, marrying Jordan might have had something to do with that."

"They're newlyweds," Ethan explained with a nod of his head. "What's it been three months now?"

"Four," Jordan said with a blissful little sigh. "Happiest four months I've spent here in Pelican Pointe."

"Well, that explains it," Hayden said matter-of-factly. Although it didn't explain how they had an almost two-year-old toddler.

"Explains what?"

"The goofy way you two look at each other."

Jordan blushed. "Oh that. Yeah, we're still in the honeymoon stage."

"Thank God," Nick said, as he leaned over and kissed his wife on the mouth, completely oblivious to their guests.

Ethan decided to change the subject. "If you're heading out to Santa Cruz, are you waiting for your stuff to catch up with you? Or do you still have your furniture in Nevada?"

More questions. Hayden wanted to strangle the guy. She was relieved when Jordan patted him on the arm and said, "Ethan, don't interrogate our guest. Hayden is entitled to her privacy and to enjoy her meal without being grilled. Can't you see how tired she is?"

"Sorry," Ethan muttered and took another bite of meat. "Just making conversation."

Jordan stood up from her chair. "Now Ethan, you behave yourself while I get the apple cobbler. Nick, you and Hutton referee these two while I'm getting the pie." She disappeared into the kitchen.

Picking up the light conversation, Nick wanted to know, "How do you like your Mini?"

Finally a safe topic, Hayden decided. "I love it! It's on the small side, but hey, it's just me. The gas mileage is incredible though. If I'd been driving anything else today, I would have run out of gas long before I ever left the 101."

"Running that low, huh? Well, don't worry about it," Nick assured her. "We'll get you taken care of before you head out. If the storm is still with us tomorrow, you can always stay here another day."

"Oh. Well. Thanks. I…uh… What time exactly is check out?"

Nick laughed. "We're not that formal around here, Hayden. You check out when you check out. If that's noon or three p.m. it's no big deal." Sensing she might have money worries, he added, "And the room rate is off season. At the moment we have no other guests, although we do have two couples scheduled to arrive Friday to stay the weekend. But if some other traveler happens our way tonight and needs a room, we have five other guest rooms."

"Thanks. I feel like I could sleep for a week."

"It's the lousy weather," Ethan said. "Makes a person want to crawl into bed and snuggle up tight."

At that moment his radio crackled to life as another emergency call came through from dispatch, something about a one-car accident out on the 17. Hayden watched him stand up to leave, realizing for the first time how difficult his job must be on a night like tonight. "Well, it looks like I gotta head out. Nice meeting you Hayden Ryan. Good luck in Santa Cruz." He turned to Nick. "Tell Jordan I'll have to take a rain check on that cobbler."

Nick slapped Ethan on the back. "Next time then. I'll get you a to-go cup for the coffee. And walk you out."

"Appreciate it, Nick."

With Hutton on his hip, Nick got up and headed out to the kitchen.

Hayden wasn't sure why after the hard time he'd given her, but she decided to say something nice. After all, she did have him to thank for not having to sleep in her car tonight.

Because of him she had a soft bed waiting upstairs and a nice soak in a tub on her agenda. She lifted her cup of hot tea and gave him a little salute. "You stay safe out there, Deputy."

Before Ethan could respond, Nick came back carrying a large to-go coffee cup. "Black. Plenty of sugar, right?"

"Right. Thanks."

As Ethan turned to go, Hayden added, "And thanks for rescuing me from the side of the road. I appreciate it."

"No problem. You be careful on your way to Santa Cruz. It's a cruel world out there."

"Don't I know it?" Hayden said miserably.

Chapter Two

Yawning and stretching like a cat, Hayden woke to bright sunshine streaming through the double French doors. She looked around at the soft lavender painted walls with the beach-themed photographs hanging there, the stencils shaped like little sand dollar shells, hand painted along the border, and the old antique furniture. What had Nick and Jordan called it? The Sand Dollar Room? She'd been so tired when she'd gotten out of the tub last night she hadn't really appreciated the décor. But now, the combination of old and new, the modern mixed with old-fashioned seemed to work. And she had to admit, for twelve hours the place had sheltered her like a silky cocoon.

She hated like hell to have to leave it.

Leaning over she picked up her watch off the nightstand. Nine-fifteen! She'd slept like the dead. Kicking off the covers, she crawled out of bed and wandered into the bathroom.

A few minutes later she came out wearing a soft fuzzy white robe she'd found hanging on the back of the door.

Curious about where she was, after not being able to see much of the area last night in the rain, she wandered to the balcony doors. Throwing both doors open, she strolled out onto a long wide deck. The view went on and on until the sea met up with the horizon.

She'd finally done it. She'd reached the Pacific Ocean. After more than three thousand miles of traveling including all the detours she'd taken, she stared at the water. Ripples of surf glistened in the sun. It spread out before her like a vast, dark green emerald as it met a pale-blue cloudless sky. No storm clouds on the horizon today, she decided.

The ocean air felt crisp and clean after the rain. Birds darted back and forth as if it were spring and not autumn. All kinds of fragrant smells filled her senses. Flowers, Hayden realized. Groups of pink and purple, red and yellow blooms dotted the landscape below the deck.

She stretched her neck over the railing to get a better look at the grounds. An assortment of blossoms dotted the courtyard just beyond the deck where tables and chairs offered an outdoor eating area. There were winding paths meant for long walks and woods for exploring.

Everywhere she looked the tops of cypress, magnolias and maple trees swayed in the breeze, their leaves already flushed golden with the ripe colors of fall, while abundant tall pines dropped their needles scattered every which a way on the lawn below.

What a beautiful day, what a beautiful place.

Was all of Pelican Pointe this gorgeous, she wondered? If so, maybe she could find a place to live in town. Even though small towns tended to be cliquish and filled with people who sometimes used any excuse to get into everyone's business, she couldn't deny the allure of living in one.

Would Pelican Pointe be like living in Mayberry? Could she fall off the radar more effectively in a small town this size rather than a bigger place like Santa Cruz?

But then, Deputy Cody's words from last night came back to haunt her. *My guess is Miss Ryan is probably looking for a bigger place to lose herself in than Pelican Pointe.*

What did he know about it anyway? Hayden thought bitterly. No, it would definitely be better if she got as far away from Pelican Pointe and Ethan Cody as possible.

She reached for her clothes.

As she dressed in the berry-colored turtleneck and jeans from last night she'd hung in the bathroom to dry, she wondered if Jordan would mind if she used her washer and dryer before she checked out.

Remembering the mistrust she'd seen in Ethan Cody's eyes had her changing her mind. She decided what she should do is get on the road to Santa Cruz as quickly as the road could take her south. The less time she lingered here the better.

But first she'd eat breakfast and get directions to a gas station.

She opened the door to her bedroom and ventured out into the hallway. The old Victorian seemed massive. She hadn't wandered its rooms last night but now she was sorely tempted to do just that. If her stomach hadn't rumbled she might have taken the time to look around.

Hayden discovered the back staircase leading down to the kitchen where she found Jordan sitting at a long kitchen table thumbing through a newspaper while Hutton sat on the floor trying to work the pieces of a giant toddler puzzle into place. Nick and the dog from last night were nowhere in sight.

As soon as Jordan spotted Hayden though, she called out, "Good morning," in that peppy, cheerleader voice of hers. "Did you sleep well?"

"I'll say. My head hit the pillow and I was gone. I'm sorry I missed breakfast. There was a schedule on the dresser upstairs that mentioned breakfast ended at nine-thirty…"

Jordan didn't let her finish. "Don't be silly. Ethan practically dragged you here last night. By force. I'll fix you bacon and eggs or sausage or whatever you like. Just name it."

Hayden shot her a grin. She picked up an upside-down mug from the counter and helped herself to a cup of caffeine from the coffeemaker on the counter. Jordan went to the fridge and took out a small pitcher of cream. Hayden poured in a generous amount before taking a long soothing drink of what smelled like a hazelnut blend.

"It was no hardship, believe me. The bed was a lot more comfortable than my car. A muffin and this coffee will do me just fine."

"Are you sure? It's no trouble to fix you a real breakfast."

"Thanks, but this muffin looks delicious, better than the stale donuts I've picked up from a convenience store." She took her coffee to the bank of kitchen windows that looked out onto the courtyard. "It's so beautiful here. I had no idea what I was missing in all that rain. You're so lucky to be able to live here."

"Yes, I am," she agreed wistfully, thankful she had Nick in her life now after two miserable years of living out here by herself.

"You should take some time and see the cove before you decide to head out." She hesitated before adding, "You know, Hayden, Nick and I were talking last night after you went to bed… If you are serious about putting down roots in a new place, why not give Pelican Pointe a chance instead?"

Surprised at hearing her earlier thoughts voiced out loud, she said, "I don't know. Small towns don't usually take to newcomers."

Jordan grinned knowingly. "Yeah, I wish I could tell you Pelican Pointe is different. But it's not. It has its own problems. But the town sorely needs some fresh blood, new residents and new businesses to keep it thriving and growing. We need people with new ideas so that the town keeps going, keeps changing, doesn't die off."

Jordan stared at one of Lilly's paintings, a watercolor of the Pelican Pointe fishing pier. Since the B & B had opened in May, Lilly had sold at least fifteen of her framed artworks to Jordan's guests.

By working the full summer season for the B & B Lilly had saved enough money to officially put an end to her dependency on county welfare. By the end of the summer season she had moved out of Derek Stovall's trailer and into a rented two-bedroom cottage bungalow two blocks from the wharf, known locally as Smuggler's Bay.

Jordan knew Wally Pierce had been instrumental in helping Lilly find her little house to rent since she and Wally had been seeing each other steady for several months now. Lilly's life had infinitely improved over the past six months.

Jordan liked to think she'd had a little something to do with that.

If Ethan was right and Hayden was in trouble or running from something, Jordan knew for certain an outsider like Hayden could use a friend. Anyone could use a friend. And Jordan personally knew something about needing one. She had spent too many lonely months out here by herself not to appreciate how important friends could be. So she intended to nudge Hayden toward a friendship—and to staying.

"Is there anything besides accounting you've always wanted to do, maybe a hobby you really liked, something that interested you enough to spend time doing? It's just that I'm not sure an accountant could make a go of it in Pelican Pointe. Most people own small businesses and tend to do their own books." She knew Murphy did. And Lilly kept Wally's. And Margie had a head for numbers.

Jordan spread out the county newspaper to make her point. "The thing is, as you can see there aren't a lot of help-wanted classifieds. This is a pretty depressed area right now, and that includes Santa Cruz."

Hayden turned from the window and stared at Jordan. She'd been afraid of not being able to find a job even with her accounting background what with the economy so dead.

"You're suggesting I stay in Pelican Pointe and…what, open a business? But…"

"That's exactly what I'm suggesting. Before you say no, hear me out. There are plenty of vacant storefronts along Ocean Street and Main that need a tenant. Right now they're dirt cheap, leasewise."

"But you just said it's a depressed area."

"For jobs. But Pelican Pointe needs some—local flavor, new businesses to keep locals and tourists interested in the town. I'm not saying that we get a lot of tourists here, yet. But with the opening of the B & B, we're getting more than we used to. I'm not suggesting it'll be easy. It won't be. But…"

It was sweet of this woman to want her to stay but Hayden had to make her understand. "Look Jordan, I appreciate the thought, but I don't have the kind of capital needed to start a business. I'm stretched a tad thin right now." And couldn't get a loan as Hayden Ryan even if she begged. But she couldn't tell Jordan that.

"It wouldn't take much. Look, I have a friend, her name's Lilly. See that painting over there on the wall, the one of the fishing pier? That's one of Lilly's. She too, was a newcomer to Pelican Pointe. Not six months ago she took a hobby and turned it into her own little business.

"Now granted, she still works here three days a week, helping me. And she has a part time job at Wally's service station running the counter, keeping the books, ordering parts, that sort of thing, while Wally concentrates on the repair side. She also paints signs. Lilly is hardworking and industrious because she has two kids to support."

Jordan took a breath before going on, "The point is if you're looking to set down roots, looking for a friend or two, we could put our heads together and see if we can find something for you here. Maybe think outside the box. God knows, it worked for Lilly."

"Why on earth would you do that, for a complete stranger? You don't even know me."

Now where had she heard that before? "Because at one time or another everyone could use a friend and I wasn't kidding when I said the town needs new blood. Those storefronts are sitting there wasting good space because Pelican Pointe's been dying for years. Nick and I think it's time we brought it back."

"It's an intriguing idea. I'm just not sure I have any potential. Accounting came easy for me in college so I really never strayed far from my major. It was what I did for four years." She thought back to all those job interviews she'd had in Chicago after her career was destroyed by her association with the Ponzi King.

People hadn't exactly been warm and fuzzy at the prospect of hiring someone who had been associated with the likes of Dochenko. Nor would they be so inclined anywhere in the USA. for that matter because she had no real references except Kate.

Okay, so her career was in the toilet, DOA even. So what was she going to do to earn a living now? When she saw Jordan waiting for further explanation, Hayden sighed. "As for hobbies I'm not sure I have any to speak of that I could turn into a moneymaking proposition. I like to ice skate, go hiking when I have the time, used to love the outdoors. But I don't think that's what you mean." Hayden gave her a wry smile.

"Well no." Jordan chuckled. "Not exactly what I had in mind."

"I was a camp counselor in high school, a life guard during the summer. I worked my way through college as a waitress. The tips were pretty good. And I spent some time working in the university day care center as an assistant. See the problem?" She eyed the newspaper on the kitchen table. "Could I take a look at those classifieds?"

"Sure." Jordan slid the paper across the table, watched as Hayden ambled over and sat down, began to peruse the want ads. She already knew there wasn't much in them for a career woman like Hayden.

"It isn't like it has to be decided right now. Stay here another day or two, enjoy the sights, go into Pelican Pointe, maybe check out the town and see what you think. Maybe seeing it up close and personal something will inspire you."

Jordan laughed. "Okay, that might be setting your expectations a tad high. But make sure you go down to the wharf though. Check out Smuggler's Bay. That's the area of town with the best view. And the best place to get a feel for what the town has to offer, get the most local flavor. You know a bar for the locals, a gift shop for the tourists, the bait and tackle shop, that sort of thing."

"Okay. But I need gas. I'm running on fumes. Oh, look here's something," she said, as she read over the ad. "Springer Real Estate needs a receptionist. It's part time but…"

"You stay away from Springer Real Estate," Jordan warned. "Kent Springer, the owner, will more than likely be serving jail time soon, probably before the holidays." At least she hoped he didn't get off after getting caught trying to set fire to Promise Cove. "I don't see how his real estate business will be able to stay open if he's convicted and is serving time in jail."

"Really, what did he do?"

"A very long list of bad things, each worse than the last. Kent Springer's a snake in the grass and shouldn't be trusted. Don't go near that place." She took a breath before going on, "And you have enough gas to get to town. Ethan put five gallons of gas into your car early this morning. You'll have to return the gas can to Wally's service station it's on the corner of Main and Beach Street, you can't miss it."

When Hayden's jaw dropped open, Jordan added, "You left your car unlocked. Ethan just popped the gas cap and bingo."

Left her car door unlocked? Sheesh, could she get any worse at this security thing. "He didn't… He shouldn't have bothered."

"That's the thing. I think he felt bad about being so hard on you last night. Ethan's a good guy but…"

"He's a cop," Hayden finished.

"That too, but he's kind of—psychic."

Hayden's mouth dropped open again. "Get out." "People say Ethan takes after his dad. His father is one of those people who helps law enforcement out every now and then, finds missing people, and uh—you know, dead bodies. Markus Cody has had some success at that. He has a fair rep up and down the West Coast from Washington State to Baja."

"Wait a minute, I've heard of him. Markus Cody was the one who helped locate that little girl, the one who went missing from Eugene, Oregon, two years back."

"That's him."

"He lives here?"

"Santa Cruz. Ethan's brother, Brent, lives there too. Brent's the county sheriff. Ethan lives… Gosh, I don't know where exactly, somewhere near the pier, I think. But Pelican Pointe is part of his assigned patrol area. We see him around town all the time."

"Great. I don't think the deputy likes me very much."

"I'll be honest, Hayden, he thought you were running from something, someone."

Hayden's eyes went wide. "For chrissakes, am I that transparent?"

"Not to me. Are you in trouble?"

Hayden sighed, propped her chin on her fist and looked away, not meeting Jordan's eyes.

Jordan wasn't surprised. It wasn't the first time Ethan Cody had nailed someone's particular circumstance. "Okay. Here's the deal. Everyone's entitled to their secrets. Everyone has troubles."

She thought of Nick and how he had come to her so unhappy. "Everyone's entitled to privacy. But like I said, in my experience, most people could use a friend. You don't owe me an explanation. Not until you want to talk about it, that is. But, I could be your friend if you need one. You have no reason to trust me, but if you want to talk…it sometimes helps."

Hayden finally managed to squeak out, "It's behind me now. I hope. I don't want to talk about my problems though. You sound like you've had your fair share." She couldn't imagine that. This house, this place, seemed so perfect.

"If you stay, I'll tell you about it some time," Jordan promised.

Ethan Cody might be a sheriff's deputy but it hadn't been his first choice as a career. He'd wanted desperately to write.

As in, earn a living at it. From the time he was eight years old he remembered listening to his grandfather tell stories about the shamans and all the folklore from his Chumash heritage.

He'd been captivated enough to begin his writing career with his own one-page newsletter, reinventing the stories his grandfather told him before he'd moved on to events and activities in his own little Santa Cruz neighborhood. Sometimes he'd come up with fictional stories of his own enough to entertain the family and close friends until he landed an actual paper route at twelve.

In between playing junior high basketball and baseball in high school, he'd made good enough grades to get into community college where he'd taken every writing class they had offered. By the time he enrolled in UC Santa Cruz he had quite a few of his own manuscripts under his belt.

But after college graduation, bills had to be paid. During those years afterward, he'd knocked around playing lead guitar in a local band, something he still did on an occasional Saturday night at a little dive near the boardwalk in Santa Cruz, not far from the house where he'd grown up. He'd tended bar there, even worked as a waiter.

When his brother Brent had been elected sheriff four years ago, he'd offered Ethan a steady job. Because bills still had to be paid, Ethan had reluctantly taken the position, not because of his love for law enforcement or the vocation, but out of necessity.

Some days Ethan felt like he'd sold out, given up his quest without so much as a struggle. He hated to think about spending the rest of his life sitting on his ass in a patrol cruiser hauling drunks to the county jail.

But paying the rent couldn't wait for a writing career to take off.

Even though he worked sometimes a sixty-hour work week, he still managed to dabble with his stories, murder mysteries mostly, a few espionage thrillers.

Once a month or so he'd send a few off to agents and those publishers who happen to still accept unsolicited manuscripts. After all this time, he still had yet to be published. But in his time off, he loved spending time reading other people's work, reading other people's books. And Ethan loved reading books almost as much as he loved to write.

But after so many years of rejection he had to admit the truth. Maybe he just didn't have what it takes to be a writer.

As he made his rounds from San Sebastian down to Pelican Pointe, the way Ethan saw it he'd already done his good deed for the day. He'd brought gas out to the lady with the big green eyes, the one hoarding a secret, the one who couldn't remember where she came from.

He never deliberately set out to use his ability. Unless someone gave him reasons to travel down that path. The vibes usually just poured out before he could put up a roadblock to stop them.

That's how it had been the minute he'd locked eyes with Hayden. He'd gotten a serious reaction from the woman and not the kind that itched at his libido. He'd gotten that one of course. You couldn't look at a woman with her body and that face, not to mention those long lanky legs, without getting a pull in that direction.

But even though the woman was a looker, it didn't cancel out the fact that she remained shrouded in mystery, hiding some dangerous aspect about herself. She all but reeked with secrecy.

The two-week-old driver's license and registration were a dead giveaway she was on the run from something. And even though he might not be in love with what he did for a living, he took his job seriously.

You couldn't wear the uniform every day to work, strap on a .45, crawl into a police cruiser, and not. So when he'd seen *'Miss-I-can't-remember-where-I'm-from'* his law enforcement radar had gone off full tilt along with his second sense.

He might be a writer at heart, but being a cop paid the bills. And like most cops, he had trust issues, especially when it came to placing a certain amount of confidence in a total stranger, one that couldn't remember where she hailed from.

So as long as Hayden Ryan stayed with Nick and Jordan he planned on keeping an eye on the woman. And if she did happen to end up over in Santa Cruz, he'd get his brother to do the same there as well.

Because of Jordan, Hayden stayed on another day.

She told herself it was because she wanted to check out the town, but it wasn't true. At the reduced, off-season rate they were giving her, she figured she could afford one more day to indulge herself before she had to face Santa Cruz.

And Promise Cove was so lovely, her bed so comfy, her room so homey and cheery, it was the closest thing in months she'd found that reminded her of what she'd left behind in her own house, the one she'd so reluctantly placed on the market. It hadn't sold yet and might not. The way the shaky real estate market was right now she had to prepare for the fact it could be six more months before the agent found a buyer. And when it did sell, all the details and paperwork would be handled by her sister, Sydney, who now had power of attorney for Emile Reed.

There was no denying her life right now was a complicated mess.

And it shouldn't have been. She hadn't been the one to swindle and defraud thousands of people out of billions of dollars. Yet because of someone else's greed her life had infinitely changed for the worse.

Hayden had to admit she certainly hadn't found a motel since she'd gone on the lam that offered the same type of amenities Promise Cove did. Where else could she chow down on Jordan's home-cooked cuisine, dry off wrapped in luxuriant Egyptian cotton towels, and sleep burrowed into twelve-hundred-thread-count sheets?

She really didn't want to think about leaving just yet.

Around ten-thirty, telling Jordan she wanted to wander around town, she set off for Pelican Pointe with directions from the pretty innkeeper. She enjoyed the twenty-minute scenic drive, as she gawked at the wooded landscape, the chunks of wildflowers along the way, and the fields of plumping ripe strawberries growing next to the road. All kinds of towering trees grew in the area, junipers, oaks, noble firs, and Douglas. Christmas trees maybe? Hayden wondered, as she spotted the mountains to the east in the distance.

When she passed the city limits sign she thought Pelican Pointe looked like any typical small town along the coast. Ancient trees lined Main Street as did neatly trimmed houses that mingled with the business district.

There was the Snip 'N Curl, the First Bank of Pelican Pointe, Murphy's Market, Knudsen's Pharmacy, and Drea's Flowers, which looked as if the woman named Lilly had been busy creating a brand-new, hand painted sign that hung smartly from the overhang.

Unlike the one over the Hilltop Diner, which looked like the design hadn't changed since the sixties. Then there was Ferguson's Hardware, Springer Real Estate and finally, Wally's Pump-N-Go.

She pulled up to fill the tank with gas and return the gas can. An old-fashioned ding announced her presence. She opened the door to crawl out, but before she'd taken two steps, a gangly man came out of the garage area, wiping his hands on a red rag. He wore his sandy-blond hair long, and pulled back in a squat ponytail. With a wave of his hand he offered, "I'll do it. Pop the gas cap for me, wouldya? Don't worry, there's no price difference."

In one smooth motion, he tugged on the pump, twisted off the cap to the tank, and stuck in the nozzle. "Nice car. I don't see many of these. Does it get as good a gas mileage as they claim?"

"It does. I drove almost four hundred miles yesterday without having to fill up."

He whistled. "Impressive. So you've put some miles on her lately, huh? I'll check the tire pressure for you then and the oil just to be on the safe side." Wally couldn't help but note the woman's Nevada plates. What they had here was an out-of-towner, he realized.

"That'd be great, thanks," she said as she wondered how long it had been since anyone pumped gas in her car and checked under the hood without having to take it to a garage for that very purpose. "Where I come from this kind of service is—nonexistent."

He grinned. "Let me guess, big city. Welcome to small town USA. Usually, I let the guys pump their own, but the women—whether they're young or old or in between, if I'm not too busy putting in a new engine or carburetor, I try to make it a point to pump gas for 'em."

Hayden smiled. "Well, thanks." Wally seemed friendly enough. If the rest of the town was like him, maybe she'd decide to stay.

When the pump clicked off, he thumbed the air over his shoulder and told her with a wink, "You pay the good-looking brunette inside."

Hayden made her way into a narrow, cramped elongated convenience store where a counter held a cash register and all kinds of displays for lighters, candy and gum, breath mints. Packages of cigarettes, a huge assortment of brands, filled the slots behind the counter, along with cans of smokeless tobacco.

A young, petite woman with glossy chestnut-brown hair punched some buttons on the register and announced, "That'll be forty-two dollars, please."

Hayden cocked her head. "By any chance are you Lilly?" At that moment two little towheads popped up from behind chairs in the waiting area that emptied out through a door to the garage. The little girl held a naked Barbie doll in one hand and waved a miniature purple outfit in the other, while the little boy ran two matchbox cars around on the floor.

Hayden handed the woman some bills to pay for her gas.

"How'd you know that?"

"Jordan Harris mentioned you were a friend of hers. I'm staying out at Promise Cove for a couple of days. She showed me your watercolors. You're very good."

"Oh, that. Jordan is fantastic. Nick's pretty good, too. They've both turned out to be such great friends to me and the kids. Are you down from the Bay? We get a lot of tourists here from the San Francisco area." Lilly tilted her head to study Hayden. What she saw was a tall, stylish woman in trendy jeans with one of those celebrity-flattering, angled bobs that only a couple of women on the planet could pull off. This one definitely had the hairdo working for her.

When Hayden saw Lilly staring, she asked, "What? Do I have something on my face?"

Lilly laughed. "Sorry. I was admiring your hair. I'd love to wear mine like that but it wouldn't look as good on me as it does on you. That's the same way Katie Holmes wore her hair when it was short."

"Good eye. I'm pretty sure hers was the photo I brought into the salon to show the stylist what I wanted. I'm Hayden Ryan by the way," she managed to toss out, a lot smoother than she had the night before.

"The look definitely works on you. Are you just passing through or here to stay?"

"That's the million-dollar question. If I stay I'll need a job, a place to live, and a whole lot of luck finding both. I'd planned on heading to Santa Cruz, maybe I still will."

"Hmm, I'll be honest. It took me a while to find work around here. You have to have a ton of patience and be willing to think outside the box. As it is, I have two part-time jobs because I couldn't find a full time one. I almost packed up and went back to Monterey, that's where I'm from, but my kids have moved around a lot.

"And after my mom died, there's really no one there that I'm close to anymore. I decided to tough it out here. And you know what? I'm glad I did. Pelican Pointe isn't the friendliest town, but Jordan and Nick are out to change that. Wally and I are, too. But because of Nick and Jordan I'm off state assistance. Believe it or not, Jordan has turned out to be my closest friend. She's had a rough time of it, too."

"Jordan?" Hayden asked in surprise. That must be what she had alluded to earlier.

"Yeah, but it isn't up to me to tell you about it. You'll have to ask her."

"I'll do that. Well, it was nice talking to you, Lilly. If you hear of a job or a house to rent, could you let Jordan know? I'll be at the B & B until the weekend."

"I'll ask around. Wally grew up here. He helped me find my house within walking distance just a few blocks from here. If anyone knows what's going on around town, it's Wally. Good luck to you, Hayden. I hope you stay and I'll see you around town."

"Maybe," Hayden said as she waved goodbye to the kids. She left Wally's and drove up Beach to Ocean Street, which ran north and south along the old wooden pier. Across from the wharf she found a parking place on the street in front of a row of cute little bungalows with well-maintained lawns, some decorated with little whirly windmills with neatly manicured flower beds.

This area reminded her of the little town in New York where her mother lived.

She got out and walked along the road admiring the houses with their neatly trimmed shutters and coats of colorful paint, their homey front porches and wondered if she could find one for rent, But after walking the length of Ocean and back again, there were a few that sat empty with for sale signs in the yards, but not a single one available for rent.

Feeling somewhat deflated, she crossed the street determined to check out the shops, though most of them looked as if they were either geared to the local fishermen or tourists.

There was the bait and tackle shop, which was a little too smelly and messy to her mind to stay for very long. But then she'd never had the desire to fish.

She checked out the boat rental place and decided she might rent a canoe and go kayaking if she stayed in the area. When she came to the bar called McCready's, it was a little too early in the day to go inside for a drink. She skipped that, and headed into a tiny T-Shirt shop that also stocked tacky souvenirs. There were shot glasses, ash trays and all kinds of sea shells crammed into plastic bags, along with beach essentials for the tourists who might have forgotten to pack their sun tan lotion, flip flops, or swim suits. The beachwear looked as though it was about three years behind in style.

When she got back outside on the sidewalk, it didn't take long to discover what Jordan had meant. Hayden passed plenty of vacant storefronts. There were as many here as she'd seen along Main. Some were in such bad shape though it would take a ton of money and plenty of elbow grease to bring them back to life.

But something about the area appealed to her. Maybe it was the fact that it wasn't Chicago and what she was running from. Maybe it was the quaintness of the narrow streets, or the tree-lined neighborhoods, or the row of small independent retail shops.

But looking out at the spectacular view of Smuggler's Bay and the ocean beyond, stretching out as far as the eye could see, she decided this was what lured her. The idea of living this close to the water.

She couldn't help it; she wandered down to the little strip of sandy beach below the retail area and began to gather seashells. Soon she had enough to fill her pockets. The sand along this stingy part of beach might not have been the most pristine like the kind she'd seen during the one trip she'd taken to Cancun. No, this beach contained a dirty brown top layer from too many tar balls washing up on shore. But then, no area was perfect.

When her leg muscles started to burn from all the walking, she sought out one of the benches at the far end of the pier that looked out over the Bay and sat down to watch the boats bobbing up and down in the water.

There was no denying how ancient the town looked or how much it needed a serious makeover. Rising from the ashes or coming back from the dead might be expecting a little too much.

Sitting there taking it all in, Hayden simply wasn't convinced she had anything to offer, or to contribute to the town's resurrection.

If she landed here instead of Santa Cruz what was the downside?

She'd have to deal with the curiosity that she was sure to garner about any newcomer in a town this size. But then wasn't that true no matter where she ended up. Could she handle the eventual Spanish Inquisition from Deputy Cody? Now there was a dilemma, she decided. But who was to say she wouldn't face the same thing in Santa Cruz.

All Cody would have to do was make a phone call to his brother and bam! Hayden Ryan would be on some other member of law enforcement's radar. Maybe she should head to San Francisco after all. But the exorbitant high cost of living there prevented her from even seriously considering that for longer than ten seconds. She reminded herself, once again, that Santa Cruz was an unknown.

She sighed. Decisions, paths, forks in the road, whatever they were, it was time to take one and stick to it. Because what it boiled down to was that she really liked Jordan Harris. The woman added a big plus sign in the Pelican Pointe column.

Hayden sat there a little while longer trying to shore up her courage to head over to the Hilltop Diner and fill out an app. The Hilltop Diner needed a waitress. It had been the only other employer in town, other than Springer Realty, that had advertised under the help-wanted section of the newspaper. Technically there had been three, but Hayden didn't think she qualified to work on a fishing boat.

She'd already decided somewhere between leaving Wally's and talking to Lilly and walking around that it was time to dig deep and muster the nerve to start over somewhere. And it might as well be here in this little speck of a town. She wasn't sure what appealed to her. It certainly wasn't the town itself. Jordan Harris on the other hand, seemed nice and genuine. So did her husband, Nick. Add to that, she had met Wally and Lilly, who had been friendly enough to put a dent in that outsider resistance veneer. Lilly had even admitted to taking help from the state. Real people with real problems. Of course, none of those problems included a crazy Russian snake who wanted them dead.

Letting out another sigh, she got up to walk back to her car and go back to Main Street and the Diner.

Margie Rosterman had scraped together her savings and bought the Hilltop Diner in 2001, a '50s malt shop knock-off that had been a Pelican Pointe staple since 1965.

Margie was tall, almost six feet, with a wild head of graying red hair and huge blue eyes. Dressed in jeans and a white shirt, the woman looked sixty, but Hayden had learned within the first ten minutes her basic life story and that she happened to be ten years younger.

"I haven't had time to get a resume together," Hayden explained. "Coming in here was impulse." Hayden sat in one of the four red vinyl booths that lined the front wall with window views of Main Street and started having second thoughts. "I just got into town day before yesterday. For now, I'm staying out at the Promise Cove B & B. But I have references." And Kate had lined every one of them up for her.

"Good to know. Jordan's good people. But resumes don't matter much with me. Half the time people lie on them anyway. And don't take this the wrong way, but I've run my own place for so long references don't mean a thing to me either. Half the time people get friends to say pretty much anything good about them when the opposite is true. Believe me, if you have what it takes to waitress I'll know it, if you don't, well, I'll know that too. It doesn't take a rocket scientist to wait tables, but it's no piece of cake either. I've had people think they could waltz in here and do the job with a blindfold, only to discover before the end of the day, they can't cut the mustard. It's harder than it looks."

"It is that. I have waitressed. It's been a while, but I figure I can get the hang of it again."

"Good, 'cause I need someone to work the late shift, five days a week. That's four to nine, Tuesdays through Saturdays. Twenty-five to thirty hours to start. That's all I can offer for now, no benefits either, but you get a fifteen minute break and meals thrown in before your shift starts if you get here early enough to eat. Plus, the regulars tip real good. You get Sundays and Mondays off, which Abby Pointer covers 'cause the Snip 'N Curl is closed those two days."

When Hayden looked confused, Margie went on, "Abby works there the rest of the time for her older sister, Janie. Abby's got a little girl. Most times it takes two jobs in this town to make ends meet. But it ain't a bad place to live and this ain't a bad place to work.

"I open up at six in the morning, run the morning routine for two hours on my own until Eileen Faraday comes on at eight when business starts to pick up. She works until two. Eileen's been with me six years come next spring. Two to four I cover myself 'cause the lunch crowd usually tapers off about that time of day. Still, we can get a few stragglers coming in to grab a cup of coffee and a piece of pie or cake, or get a burger to-go. I run a real nice place, clean, and I'm fair. Just ask Max, that's my cook, Max Bingham. Been with me since I opened this place up ten years ago.

"Truth is I have three reliable employees I can count on, Max, Eileen and Abby. The 4 to 9 shift is the one I can't seem to keep filled. Every person I've hired comes and goes like this is some kind of a stopping off place for most of them. No one's itching to spend their nights slingin' hash their whole lives, believe me, I know."

Hayden looked around. The place wasn't large. It had a black-and-white-checkered floor that was far from spotless. In fact, there were yellowed stains on the linoleum, maybe decades old that had worked permanently into the pattern. The black marble-looking counter was just as faux as the décor, which tried for retro but came off a bit on the tacky side instead.

The eight padded red stools under the counter had seen a lot of wear and tear and at one time someone had tried patching a few of them with red tape, but the color was a tad off and some of the ends of the sticky stuff had long since curled up in protest.

The dining area consisted of eight mismatched square tables and an odd assortment of chairs, plus the four booths along the front windows. At the end of the counter Margie had somehow managed to squeeze in a Wurlitzer juke box, which at the moment was blaring out Clint Black's Killin' Time.

Hayden couldn't imagine making much tip money here. But she was desperate. And she'd decided that a small town might be better than Santa Cruz for keeping a low profile. After all, who on earth would believe straight-laced accountant Emile Reed would ever end up here?

"When do you want me to start?" Hayden asked, as her stomach jingled with nerves.

"Tomorrow would work for me."

Hayden reached across the table to shake hands with Margie. "Thanks. I'll see you tomorrow afternoon then."

The minute she parked her car in the driveway at Promise Cove, Hayden went in search of Jordan. She found her where she'd left her, in the kitchen preparing dinner, spreading marinade over some type of fish.

"Guess what? I found a job!"

"The Hilltop Diner, I know."

Hayden plopped down on one of the tall bar stools in front of Jordan at the counter. "Wow. News travels fast. Is that some kind of record even for a small town?"

Jordan chuckled. "Margie called, said she forgot to mention you have to wear a uniform."

"A uniform? But…" Hayden frowned. "Margie wasn't wearing one. She wore jeans and a button-down white shirt. I just thought…"

"She's the owner. She said you could stop by and pick it up in the morning before your shift. Seems like the last waitress left one behind."

"Ewwww. Someone else's uniform? I'm not wearing that."

"Don't blame you. We'll figure something out. Why don't you pick it up, see if we can come up with something similar? We're about the same size and I have an outfit I used to wear when I catered, traditional black slacks white blouse. Oh my God, I just had a thought. Seems to me the few times I've been to the Hilltop, the waitresses there wear these God-awful, hot pink outfits."

Hayden's face fell. "Hot pink? You're joking."

Not wanting to heap anymore disappointment on her than was absolutely necessary, Jordan decided to change the subject. "What did you think of Pelican Pointe?"

"I saw a lot of empty buildings."

"The town's fallen on hard times."

"I walked up and down the neighborhood near the pier, drove through town, and didn't see a single for rent sign either. Which brings me to ask, I was wondering if you could discount one of the rooms for me? You know, like staying here thirty days or longer might get me a better price, at least until I can find a place to rent."

At that moment, Nick came through the back door, catching the last part of the conversation. "You didn't tell her?" he asked Jordan.

"I was waiting until dinner. Why don't you do the honors?"

Nick nodded. "We have a studio apartment over the garage. You're welcome to rent it. It isn't much. There's no phone line and if you need to use the Internet you'll have to make use of the computer here in the house for guests. There's no AC, but with winter coming that shouldn't be a problem. But hey, the shower works, the bed's comfortable. Why don't you go take a look and see if it will work for you until you find something better?"

Hayden sat there with her mouth gaped open. "Just like that? I...I...don't know what to say." Tears glistened in her eyes. "Why? Why are you guys so nice to me?"

Nick and Jordan saw the emotion on Hayden's face about the same time. They exchanged looks. It was Nick who explained, "We're a big believer in second chances, Hayden. And being good neighbors, helping one another out through difficult times. Times are tough for a lot of people right now, it might be financial, but then again it might be something harder to define, harder to talk about. Get Jordan to tell you about our situation sometime."

With that, he tossed his keys on the desk in the corner and walked around the counter to where his wife stood, placed his arms around her waist. "I didn't kiss you hello, did I? Let me fix that," he said, as if Hayden wasn't even in the room. Hayden stuck her chin on her palm, leaned on the counter and watched the show as Nick gave his wife a killer smile before going in for a long deep kiss.

Newlyweds, thought Hayden, as she cleared her throat, slid off the stool and started for the back door. "Do I need a key?"

When the couple came up for air, it was Jordan who answered. "Door's unlocked. It's across the courtyard. Take the stairs up."

When Hayden had gone, Jordan looked up at her husband's lake-blue eyes and said with concern, "She's in trouble, Nick."

"Yeah, I figured as much."

Hayden followed a walkway through the flower-filled outdoor quad and up a set of stairs next to the garage. As soon as she opened the door, the smell of lemon polish hit her along with the scent of the sea. A bank of windows on the ocean side had been left open to let in the breeze, as a result newly hung curtains fluttered in the air.

The old hardwood floor gleamed in the sunlight that drifted in from another pair of windows flanking each side of the bed. The one-room studio was bright with plenty of natural light but had very little furniture. An ancient, sagging green sofa divided the living area from the bedroom space. The old, urn top Maplewood was covered with a goose down comforter, a set of over-sized, plump pillows along with crisp white sheets. At the foot of the bed sat an antique blanket box for extra storage. She looked around for a closet and realized a 1920s era armoire in the corner substituted for a place to hang clothes.

She poked her head into the bathroom. There was a shower stall, but no tub. No problem, she could work with that as long as the water got hot. A small polished mahogany table next to the shower held a stack of fluffy, white towels.

One of those soft, thick hotel robes hung on a wall peg by the glass door.

The tiny kitchenette took up one wall and consisted of a two-burner stovetop, a twelve-inch sampling of counter with a stingy overhead cabinet, the only place to store groceries, and a built-in under-the-counter mini fridge.

Parked underneath the bank of windows was a white three-piece wrought iron table set with two matching chairs with bright green cushioned seats.

Hayden peered inside the little refrigerator, found a miniature bottle of wine chilling along with several little packages of cheese wedges. Tears wet her eyes again. She shook her head. These people were incredible. They didn't know her from Adam and yet had shown her nothing but kindness since she had walked through their front door. For all they knew she could be a grifter looking for easy marks.

She wasn't sure what to think. The cynic in her, created by a con man named Jeremy Dochenko, couldn't help but wonder if they had some kind of an angle she might be missing. Were they trying to convert her to some weird cult while they waited for their spaceship to trail after the next great comet?

But the pre-Jeremy, Emile Reed, who'd been raised in the Midwest by honest, hardworking people, thought Hayden Ryan might have hit the mother lode when Ethan Cody had plucked her from the side of the road and led her here to Promise Cove and to Nick and Jordan's front door.

Over dinner, the talk was all about Hayden's new digs. "So when can I move in?" She asked as excited as any ten-year-old would before walking through the gates at Disneyland.

Jordan looked over at Nick affectionately. "I sure don't remember you being this excited about living in that old place."

"At the time I just wanted to be close to you." He grinned, wiggling his eyebrows up and down. "And it worked too. I'd have slept in a tent just to be here," he said warmly. "And I never once complained."

"Aww, you romantic."

"Uh, guys? Could we focus here?"

"Sorry," Jordan said. "We have a hard time keeping our hands off each other."

"So I've noticed."

"You could move in tonight if you want. I know you said you didn't cook but if you want to boil water for tea, we'll have to replace that old stovetop. That thing hasn't worked since the eighties. Otherwise, I'm sure there's an extra microwave somewhere out there in that stuffed-to-the-gills garage we brought with us from the Bay. A microwave will come in handy until we can switch out the range. And I have an extra coffeemaker you can use."

"Thanks. And the rent?"

Nick tossed out a ridiculously low number. "A night?"

"A month," Nick confirmed. "I stayed there rent-free as I recall, got meals thrown in, as a matter of fact. At the time, I might have felt like I'd lived in better, but I found it comfortable. And Jordan has it fixed up nice, even brought up a little table and chairs we found in the garage. There's also an old TV I found in the garage. No matter what I tried I couldn't get anything but snowy reception, so I hooked it up with a DVD player. Feel free to watch as many movies as we have in our inventory. Like I said before, the bed's not bad, although it's not as good as the one I'm in now." He paused long enough to wink in his wife's direction then take her hand in his, place a kiss on the palm. "The ghost, however, is free."

"Now, Nick," Jordan admonished, when she saw Hayden's eyes go wide. "He's kidding."

"She says that now," Nick said casually. "After the fact...I still see him sometimes when I'm digging around in the garage or mowing the grass or when I'm down at the cove. Hayden might not be able to see him."

Okay, now Hayden was just plain curious. "A ghost? For real? Who?"

Jordan sighed. "Scott Phillips. My first husband. He died in Iraq. He was Nick's best friend. This was his childhood home. It's so strange how Nick sees him walking around the grounds, or down at the cove, or walking along the path in the courtyard." She shook her head. "Scott never shows himself to me. Maybe he's mad at me or something for falling head over heels in love with his best friend."

Jordan tilted her head in Nick's direction. "But somehow, I don't think that's why. I lived here for a year after he died and not once during that time did Scott ever manifest, or whatever, to me."

Although Hayden liked to think she kept an open mind about most things, ghosts were one of those gray areas she'd never actually considered existed. "But...that's..."

"Crazy?" Nick offered. "Yeah. Maybe. But I know what I see. I thought maybe after everything had settled down, after everything we'd been through, after Jordan and I got married, he'd leave me alone. But... I used to think I was nuts. Now I think it's just Scott's way of telling me he's here to protect the place he loves so much, maybe oversee things, keep an eye on things."

"So Hutton is..." She glanced over at the little girl with blonde hair sitting in her booster chair practicing scooping up macaroni and cheese with a spoon.

"Scott's," Jordan said, glancing lovingly at her daughter. "But Nick is in the process of adopting her. And we're trying to have a baby."

"Every chance we get," Nick added without a trace of self-consciousness.

"Well," Hayden said, not knowing what else to say to that. She changed the subject. "That price is incredibly low… for the apartment, I mean. Are you certain?"

"It's a room over a garage, Hayden. Not the Taj Mahal," Jordan pointed out.

"But it's a roof over my head when I really need it and is incredibly generous. Not to mention perfect for me right now. You couldn't possibly know how grateful I am. To both of you."

"And just so you know," Nick assured, "we have no plans to check your references or your rental history."

Hayden nibbled at her lip to keep from misting over again. She had to say something to these people to reassure them she didn't have a checkered past. "I just don't believe you guys. I won't let you down. I'm not a risk. I don't do drugs or abuse alcohol. I'm not a grifter looking for an easy mark no matter how suspicious Deputy Cody is. I'm not running from the law. I own my car out there. I don't have a lot of money, but then I don't have a lot of bills." She'd paid them all off with her savings before she'd changed her name. Kate had helped her take care of all the details when she'd spent time with her friend in Nebraska.

"Glad to hear that," Nick said, smiling.

"Uh, I looked around town…made a list of all those empty storefronts along with all the things Pelican Pointe doesn't have. There's no coffee shop in town, or bakery. Nor is there a bookstore, a gym, or a day care center."

Nick looked at Jordan. "Well, I don't know how Jordan feels but I think a coffee shop wouldn't work because the Hilltop would be stiff competition. And Murphy sells coffee to-go, too. Most people buy theirs at Murphy's though. Same with baked goods. Margie bakes her own pastries, pies, that sort of thing. And they're pretty good. I think she buys her donuts from the Costco over in Santa Cruz though."

Jordan nodded. "Margie doesn't make her own donuts. I know the Methodist church has a day care program for working moms. Lilly uses it whenever things get crazy at the service station. But when she's working here she usually brings the kids with her. I'm not sure the church has enough of an overflow that a day care center would make it. But we could check it out. As for the gym…"

"There isn't a big following around here for people who want to work out, at least not at a gym," Nick finished. "The locals jog, surf, hike or have some other kind of workout routine on their own. A gym, down the road, might make a good investment but I don't see it happening now."

"But a bookstore might be a viable option." Jordan thought for a moment. "That might be an idea worth following up on."

"Pelican Pointe doesn't even have a library," Hayden pointed out.

Nick nodded. "A bookstore is a better bet."

"I was thinking a used bookstore," Hayden continued. "Nothing fancy at first, maybe a small area in front where people could sit and read, a couple of comfy chairs, something we might pick up at the thrift shop, or a little overstuffed loveseat maybe, where customers could drink a cup of coffee, work on their laptops, that sort of thing. We wouldn't need a retail counter when an old desk might work just as well, and again, we could find that at a thrift store for next to nothing."

"You know, I've got a ton of used books. And there are some shelves in the garage we could use. What do you think, Nick?"

He considered the pros and cons as he realized he'd collected quite a bit of books himself over the years that he kept in storage with all his other stuff he'd brought with him from L.A. when he'd married Jordan.

"It would depend on what kind of lease you could get, for say, no more than six hundred square feet. That might sound small, but you wouldn't feel so overwhelmed like you might if you had to fill up a larger size space. Six-hundred square feet is large enough to hold books from floor to, let's say, mid-ceiling, without biting off a huge chunk of space you'd have to struggle to fill up with inventory right away. Think about how tough it would be to fill up six hundred square feet of books, think how many books would fit in a space that size. Books don't take up that much room. Your displays might, and the sitting area you suggested might, but depending on the storefront, you could use the windows for display."

"You're right, start off small, work up. I like that. How many books do you think you two have?"

"A lot. Maybe not enough to fill up six-hundred square feet, but a start anyway."

"I'd say between the books Jordan has and mine we have enough to get you going. I could put the lease in my name for now."

Okay, that was the last straw. More and more, Hayden found she couldn't lie to these people. She shook her head. "Look guys, you've been so nice there's something I should probably tell you."

"Okay, shoot," Nick said mildly.

"My condo's up for sale in another state. It's taking longer to sell in this bad economy than I'd hoped. But when it sells, I'll have some money to put down on a place to live and maybe start that business, which was a good idea you had, Jordan. It's just that, I've had expenses lately and that's why I'm running a tad short.

"But the money from the Diner will help, even though it's less than thirty hours a week, I'll keep looking for another part-time position to make up for it. I could also help you out here when you need an extra pair of hands."

Hayden held up a staying hand. "You wouldn't need to pay me. I don't fluff off and I'm a hard worker. I haven't taken a vacation since college. I'm dependable. That's all I can tell you right now—about myself, about my past. If I could tell you more—I would. But no way do I want you to think I'm a deadbeat or a freeloader, or that I'm running from the law."

She looked first at Jordan and then at Nick, hopeful, trying to determine if they were disappointed or upset with her because she wouldn't divulge more.

It was Nick who asked, "Just tell me one thing, Hayden. Are you in danger? Is someone out there trying to hurt you?" Nick could see her swallow hard as if trying to gauge whether or not she should admit it.

When her eyes dropped to her lap and she didn't look back up, Nick had his answer. His first thought was that she was hiding out from an abusive relationship.

"Okay, you don't want to say, I get that. But promise me one thing. I've got Jordan and Hutton to think about, their safety, their security, you understand? I won't ask for references but you have to promise me to keep us in the loop. If it looks like there's any chance that this person might find you, whoever's out there, you have to be honest with me and give me a heads-up."

Hayden went white, the idea had her panic-stricken. This time she met his eyes. "Oh. God. Maybe I should move on. I didn't think about endangering anyone else by just being around other people. My plan is to keep a low profile. Or try to."

Nick rubbed his chin. "Unfortunately in this age of technology, a low profile isn't always enough."

Chapter Three

It didn't take long for Hayden to unpack the meager clothes she'd picked up along the way. She owned two pairs of jeans, one skinny, one Capri, a couple of tops, a silky white pocket shirt she'd worn with her interview suit, a berry-colored cashmere turtleneck, a green hoodie, the midnight-blue wool dress Katie had given her, the charcoal-gray suit jacket and matching pencil skirt she'd had on the night the beast had attacked her in the parking garage, and four pairs of shoes.

Good thing she'd worn her prized pair of Jimmy Choo, peep-toe heels to the interview that day, otherwise she wouldn't even have those, she thought miserably, as she set them inside the armoire next to her canvas sneakers, ancient hiking boots, and a pair of wedge sandals she'd picked up on sale at a shoe store in Missouri.

Now that she thought about it, maybe it was a good thing she had to wear a uniform to work every day because her wardrobe, limited as it was, couldn't handle a five-day challenge.

Looking at how out of place the black Jimmy Choo's were next to her other thrift store finds, she did her best to come up with a place in Pelican Pointe she could wear the heels. She decided it didn't matter. Those days of obsessing over footwear were over. She had other more pressing things to deal with than the best place to show off five-hundred-dollar pumps.

Her first night in her little studio apartment she didn't intend to spend dwelling on what she didn't have, but rather what she did. Thanks to Nick and Jordan Harris she had a place to live and it wasn't the backseat of her car.

When she spotted the stash of DVDs stacked in the little cabinet next to the old vacuumed-tube TV set, she decided to plant herself on the sagging green sofa and veg in her new space.

She flipped through the selections until she found one she liked, opened the plastic, and popped in the shiny disc. She couldn't go wrong with the musical, Mamma Mia. It offered plenty of lively songs and starred three hunks, Pierce Brosnan, Colin Firth, and Stellan Skarsgard. They didn't know it yet, but they were about to spend the night with her in little Podunk Pelican Pointe—singing and dancing their way through Abba's greatest hits.

What better way to christen her new digs than spending it with three hot celebs when you couldn't have the real thing? She settled back on the sofa, suddenly craving salty, buttered popcorn, pistachio gelato, and dark Belgian chocolate.

First thing the next morning Hayden drove into Pelican Pointe and picked up the uniform from Margie.

It wasn't the solution to her wardrobe problem she'd hoped it would be. The dress wasn't just pink, it was an ugly polyester thing with a wide, white, V-collar and a huge old-fashioned fake apron attached to the waist.

Not only did it look more like a Halloween costume than an actual uniform, it had some horrible stains spattered here and there, back and front. It looked like something Alice had worn at Mel's Diner and forgotten to wash decades earlier.

And luckily for Hayden, it was three sizes too large and didn't even reach her knees.

Margie wasn't sure what to do. "You could alter it," she suggested optimistically. "But then what if you don't work out? Maybe you could wear it with a belt or something."

Not in a million years, thought Hayden. "But I doubt I could alter it before my shift starts at four o'clock," she pointed out tactfully.

"Hmm, well, we've always worn pink here before. It's tradition, kind of like a 1950s thing. I don't have another one."

Thank God for small favors, thought Hayden. "I'll come up with something close, I promise," Hayden assured her, as she turned to leave, stuffing the pink thing down in her bag, hoping it didn't contaminate the contents.

"I've got a million errands to get done before work though. See you this afternoon." She didn't wait for Margie to approve or disapprove or add anything, she simply took off like a shot out the front door of the Diner and out onto the sidewalk on Main.

At a fast clip she walked down to Murphy's, the only place in town to buy groceries, hoping to pick up some food to stock in her little fridge and a few frozen meals she could heat up in her microwave, the one Nick had managed to dig out of an incredibly packed garage.

As she perused the narrow aisles, her mind on how she could make that hideous pink outfit work for her in less than six hours, she didn't see Ethan Cody amble up behind her.

"Good morning, Hayden-no-middle-initial-Ryan." She might be trouble with a capital T, Ethan thought, but she could fill out a pair of jeans with enough of a wiggle in her butt to make any male sit up and take notice. To make matters worse, he decided he found her hair sexy, the way it moved back and forth when she looked up at him. Those little gold specks in her incredible jade green eyes told him he'd surprised her.

Hayden laughed at his joke despite his pain-in-the-ass demeanor. "Low and behold if it isn't Deputy Dawg, on the job this early in the morning. I feel safer already," she joked as she tried to ignore the way his shoulders filled out his tan uniform. She refused to let her eyes wander down to his narrow hips and waist or to the taut look at the front of his pants.

"At your service."

"That's convenient since I might need someone to tote my groceries back to the car."

"I could do that once I pick me up some dog food. I'm out, or rather Grisham's out."

"Grisham?"

"My dog, a lab retriever mix that I swear eats me out of house and home."

"You live in Pelican Pointe?"

"Over by the pier. My grandmother's house. After she died my parents used to rent it out, but when I got assigned here for real a couple of years back, I moved into it." He shrugged. "It seemed the logical thing to do since work was here. Besides, I was ready to try some place other than Santa Cruz. How are things working out at The Cove?"

"Oh fine. It's beautiful there." She wasn't ready to tell him she'd rented the Harris's studio apartment. Or, that she'd landed a job at the Diner. Word would spread at some point and he'd find out anyway, but he wasn't going to hear it from her. "It's tough to be around Nick and Jordan though."

When she saw his face change with a certain level of disapproval she added, "Newlyweds."

"Ah. That does get a little old."

"It's incredibly sweet."

He shook his head. "Such a typical female thing to say. Women. What's with the groceries, you shopping for Jordan?"

Well, damn, she thought. Did the man ever stop being a cop? This guy had to be a step above Carnac the Magnificent or one damn fine, observant police officer. Not wanting to risk lying to him, she said without flair, "I'm picking up a few things for myself. I rented Jordan's studio apartment."

Ethan held his surprise in check. "What happened to Santa Cruz?"

"Nick and Jordan happened. They are the nicest, sweetest couple on the planet. Good people."

"Yeah, they are." And he sure hoped Hayden Ryan wasn't playing them or taking advantage.

As if she read his mind, she jutted out her chin and said with some heat, "Don't worry Deputy Dawg. I'm not planning to rob them and go on the lam. I'm not a grifter waiting for the first opportunity to take advantage of good people." And with that, she wheeled on her heels, left him standing in the frozen food section with enough of a chill to freeze ice cream, and headed for the checkout.

Neither Jordan nor Hayden could come up with any miracle to make the hideous pink uniform look any better. And besides, no amount of stain remover got rid of those oily splotches, or whatever they were, which in Hayden's book were a deal breaker.

She didn't mind wearing Pepto-Bismol pink, but she drew the line at wearing something that had belonged to someone else and looked filthy. And those stains wouldn't budge even with the half bottle of stain remover she'd used.

But by noon, from some buried trunk in that black-hole garage, miracle-worker Jordan dug out a pink outfit guaranteed to make Margie dance. Surely Margie wouldn't object to a Bobby-soxer-type, poodle skirt and sweater top Jordan had once worn to a Halloween party and looked like something Sandy Olson might have worn in the film, *Grease*.

"Make sure you point out that *Grease* took place in the '50s. Good thing we're about the same size," Jordan muttered, as she carefully ripped another section of black lace from around the bottom of the pink skirt.

"As ridiculous as I feel wearing this to a job, I honestly think it's better than wearing an oversized, fugly, stained dress. Please tell me I don't look as ridiculous as I feel."

"That uniform is downright disgusting. You can't wear that thing. And this won't look half bad when we're done with it. At least it will fit and fit well, if you know what I mean. You'll be showing a little cleavage what with the little sweater top that goes with the skirt, but if you add a scarf around your neck, it won't seem so—revealing. And it does look very '50s, plus it's pink. Margie won't be able to bitch about that."

"You are amazing, Jordan. I owe you so much for…everything. You and Nick have been wonderful to me. I didn't realize these past months how much I've missed talking to my sister, having friends around. Thanks."

Jordan knew firsthand how having family and friends could make such a positive impact. "You're welcome. I missed my family too when I first got here."

She tilted her head at an angle and gave Hayden the once-over. "I would have had you covered if Margie had wanted you to wear something black and white. In fact, I have tons of that left over from mom's catering days, even a pair of tuxedo-like shorts in black. But pink?" She shook her head. "That isn't exactly a common color they use in the food service industry."

"The saddle shoes are a nice touch," Hayden said as she stood in front of the full-length mirror. "Maybe if we took the skirt in so it doesn't flare so much it would look less like a—costume. You realize taking off the lace will bring the hem up to mid-thigh. I wonder if Margie is against showing skin, God knows she isn't against her waitress staff wearing dirty uniforms."

Jordan giggled at that. "We could take in the skirt but I think it'll be fine like this. Try to think of it as a role you're playing."

Oh Jordan, thought Hayden, if you only knew.

"Besides, with showing so much cleavage and plenty of leg, your tips should set a record."

Hayden arrived ten minutes early at the Hilltop to a shocked Margie who thought the costume was a terrific idea, better than the uniform.

"Now, why didn't I think of that? You look like you stepped right out of the '50s in that getup more real than the regular uniform," Margie gushed, after looking Hayden up and down and then nodding with approval.

"With that black hair, you and Betty Rizzo could be sisters. You look like you stepped right out of that movie Grease."

Hayden laughed. Except that Betty was this petite tiny thing while she was a good five inches taller.

"That's my fave movie. You know, I wonder if I could get one of those getups for Eileen and Abby?"

Great, thought Hayden. She wondered briefly if Eileen Faraday and Abby Pointer would ever speak to her after being saddled with wearing a costume right out of Grease.

But hey, the thing was better than the hot pink uniform and it seemed to make Margie happy.

And if the customers didn't laugh themselves silly without choking to death on their burgers and fries, maybe Hayden could manage to talk Margie into changing the uniform to something a little more dignified at some point. She could always hope.

For the next several hours, Hayden pretended she was at a costume party, slingin' hash. The toughest thing to get the hang of was the menu and the shorthand used to write down the orders.

And fortunately for her there was no complicated computer system or point of sale application to learn. Not with Margie. She and Max practiced their own system and it had nothing to do with technology. You either learned the lingo or you didn't let the door hit you in the butt on your way out.

Another thing she didn't have to worry about was running the cash register. As the owner and the hostess, that was Margie's territory, which was fine by Hayden.

Between waiting tables and waiting on those customers who chose to sit at the counter, she brewed coffee and tea, refilled ketchup and hot sauce bottles and salt and pepper shakers, wrapped silverware in white paper napkins and bussed tables.

The Hilltop Diner was different from the restaurant she'd worked at during college. That chain dining establishment had been much larger with a huge wait staff. At the Diner there was only one waitress for the entire place. And that was her.

The Hilltop Diner might have been old and ultra-casual, hence the paper napkins, but it seemed to Hayden everyone in town ate dinner there, which with one waitress, kept her hopping.

About seven-forty-five she looked up and saw Ethan Cody stroll through the front door, out of uniform, wearing tight-assed, stonewashed jeans and a tan T-shirt with the words "Save the Whales" on the front.

With a certain amount of resignation, she sighed. There seemed to be no way she could avoid bumping into the man every time she turned around.

She watched as Margie led him to a booth, handed him a menu, told him about the special of the day, which was meat loaf and mashed potatoes, and took his drink order, which was iced tea.

The drink order was then relayed to Hayden, who fixed the drinks. That's the way it worked. Margie played hostess and did the initial contact with customers while Hayden came behind her, took their meal orders, handed the order off to Max, and then she would pick up the food, serve the meal, making sure all the while they had everything they needed to make their Diner experience enjoyable and left tips like happy little clams.

She intended to do that with Ethan Cody, whether he liked her or not.

Hayden needed this job and she'd be damned if she'd let him ruin her first day here because he distrusted her. So much for the man's psychic ability, Hayden thought, as she took his iced tea over, set it down, and asked sweetly, "What can I get you tonight, Deputy?"

Ethan did a double take. He hadn't known she'd found employment. He looked her slowly up and down in her Grease poodle skirt and tight pink sweater and wanted to know, "Wait, isn't it a little early for Halloween?"

"Damn you." She took a deep calming breath, blew it out. "I had to wear something pink. Margie insisted. And this is all I had, or rather all Jordan had."

Amusement twinkled in his dark eyes. "I'm not complaining. It looks better than that ugly, pink waitress uniform especially the sweater and—" He cocked his head to get a better look. "That short skirt is a definite improvement." He put some extra time and effort into admiring the woman's long, tanned legs.

She lowered her voice. "Oh shut up. Do you want something to eat or not?"

He busted out laughing at the double entendre, biting back the urge to lick his lips. "Eat. Definitely…eat. Oh, you mean food?" He had the audacity to grin. "That too. I'll have a burger. Medium. No onions. Extra ketchup. And fries."

"Thanks." When she headed behind the counter to give the order to Max, she felt his eyes burn holes on her ass the entire way. Afterwards, she dropped off another customer's bill, refilled coffee cups, iced tea and water glasses, trying to avoid Ethan Cody's table.

When finally Max yelled out, "Order up," she grabbed the burger and fries and a bottle of ketchup, made her way over to Ethan, and asked pleasantly, "Anything else I can get you?"

"I owe you an apology. I'm sorry, Hayden. I had no right…"

"Don't worry about it." She had no intentions of giving this man the time of day. "Is your burger okay?"

"It's fine."

Great. Good. Then her job with Ethan Cody was about done. "Let me know if I can get you anything else." And with that, she took off for another table.

Ethan had to admit she took orders with an organized efficiency, engaged other customers with humor and wit, and filled out that damn pink sweater like a warrior goddess.

Her cold shoulder was nothing he didn't deserve, he supposed, as he sat there realizing Hayden Ryan must have really needed this job in order to go to work at the Hilltop. She didn't seem the waitress type and by that, he meant no disrespect to all waitresses on the planet.

But the woman had admitted to all of them the other night that she'd worked as an accountant. The question first and foremost in his mind was why would an accountant be desperate enough to take a job in a Podunk town like Pelican Pointe as a waitress?

He was afraid he already knew the answer.

The idea of her being in danger had him rethinking the last two days, which just showed how his ability could sometimes be way off the mark even downright wrong.

He'd thought that maybe she was hiding something, like a criminal past. But now, a blind man could see how wrong he'd been.

She was on the run from someone she obviously feared would find her.

He ate his burger and fries as if they were crow. When she wandered over to refill his iced tea glass, he tried a different approach. "Don't get so busy you forget to enjoy the cove while you're there, Hayden. It's a great little beach with nice surf. Have you spent any time there yet?"

"Not yet. Will there be anything else?"

"I could use a piece of blueberry pie."

"A la mode?"

"You bet."

She stormed off as if on a difficult mission to get the dessert. When she came back, she set the plate down, ripped the bill from her pad, and left it on the table without saying a single word.

Fifteen minutes later when he paid the bill, she still hadn't come back out from wherever she'd found to avoid him. Without meaning to, he'd spent more than an hour eating dinner inside the Diner, something he usually managed to do in half that time. Margie rang him up and seemed to notice it too. "Was everything all right tonight, Ethan?"

"Great. You've got a terrific waitress there, Margie."

"Yeah. She's not bad to look at either, is she, Ethan?" She asked with a twinkle in her eye.

"No ma'am. Not bad at all." By Ethan's calculations it was almost closing time. He guessed he could hang around and try to approach her on her walk to the car. But when nine fifteen came and went, when he saw her still inside scrubbing tables until almost nine-thirty, he realized she had to be bone-tired after spending nearly six hours on her feet. The last thing she needed now was him trying to make amends.

At nine-forty, after making sure she got to her car okay, which he knew for certain because he was sitting in Murphy's parking lot watching, Ethan decided to head home without confronting her again. After all, he'd just have to find a way to let her know he no longer considered her trouble with a capital T.

It was ten o'clock by the time Hayden pulled up to her studio apartment. Even though Jordan's borrowed saddle shoes fit, her feet were killing her. She couldn't wait to sit down, get her feet up and open up that mini bottle of wine chilling in the fridge.

She'd taken two steps out of the car when she saw a movement out of the corner of her eye. In the moonlight, she could see a man, wearing khaki shorts, and a blue open button down shirt, sleeves rolled up with a T-shirt on underneath, strolling casually through the middle of the courtyard like he was enjoying the walk in the night air. Hayden's first thought was that it was a little chilly to be wearing shorts, but then guys always seem to be ten degrees warmer than females, or so it seemed to her.

Her second thought was he didn't look cold but he did have his hands stuffed leisurely in his pockets like he didn't have a care in the world. The guy had to be a guest out for an evening walk enjoying the night air. Wondering when he checked in, Hayden began to make her way around the corner to the stairs at the side of the garage.

She must have made a noise because he stopped long enough to turn back around. When he spotted her, he sent her a wide smile and a friendly wave. Just as she raised her hand to wave back, the man vanished into thin air. Hayden's hand flew to her mouth. Without waiting another second, she raced up the stairs, fumbled with her keys in the lock, and fell inside the apartment.

She made certain the lock on the door was firmly turned behind her.

With a nine-hour time difference it was a little after seven in the morning in the French countryside, when Jeremy Dochenko sat down to breakfast on the sun-drenched terrace of his chateau, savoring his eggs Benedict.

Over the years the fifty-five-year-old Russian stockbroker and financier had gone to a great many lengths to hide his countless assets from the American IRS. After all, one would be foolish to declare every single dollar when it was so easy to do business with any number of offshore banks that specialized in that very thing.

But the twenty-two-room estate he was now living in, located in north central France, some one-hundred and forty kilometers southwest of Paris, might be his most treasured possession. He'd bought the villa because in order to make it to his front door a person had to negotiate not one, but two, hairpin turns on a dimly lit secluded road where he'd installed security cameras to keep track of meddlesome visitors. It was the perfect place to hide in plain sight since his nearest neighbor was three miles away.

Sipping a strong cup of espresso made from the coffee beans he had specially flown in from the Indonesian Archipelago at €125.00 a pound, he knew only one thing, or rather one person, stood in his way. Complete peace of mind from prosecution by the American authorities would elude him if his man didn't find Emile Reed.

Her lack of experience had been the deciding factor when he'd hired her as his CFO right out of college. Sure she'd been eager. But then he had played that to his advantage. After all, any decent conman worth his salt could fool a novice more easily than he could a seasoned, veteran bean counter. They tended to ask a shitload of questions.

In those early days of her employment, he'd simply overwhelmed the annoying go-getter with every task imaginable that kept her from prying into files she had no business seeing. She'd been easy enough to deceive; most people were, especially when it came to the master manipulator versus the average, trusting person.

After his associates took care of the naïve, little accountant, only then would he feel completely secure and be able to enjoy his freedom without looking over his shoulder every single day. With her no longer in the picture he could leave the estate, perhaps even make his way down to Tahiti, where he owned a nice little beachside cottage with a mere seventeen rooms.

The American courts might have thought they had won when they collected his passport after he'd been arrested. His lawyers had almost convinced him the judge would never go for bail. But Jeremy had learned a long time ago that the right amount of money could grease any number of palms if one were discreet enough. And getting a new ID could be had if you happened to know the right people.

Jeremy Dochenko knew the right people.

He motioned for the maid to bring him the phone. The minute she set it down on the glass table, he dialed a number he knew by heart.

"Has your work produced anything of interest to me yet?"

"No. But I've been inside her condo. It's on the market. I've found nothing to indicate her location, at least not yet."

"Then stake out the mother and sister. Emile is a creature of habit. She won't be able to stay out of contact with her family. And Luka, don't even think about screwing this up."

The SEC and the Justice Department might think their case against him was airtight. But if their key witness just happened to come to a gruesome end it was nothing to him, which is exactly why he kept men like Luka Radovan on the payroll. Luka was excellent at taking care of jobs like Emile Reed.

They just had to find her first.

Chapter Four

For someone who had seen a ghost the night before, Hayden woke the next morning early with renewed energy. She brewed coffee in her tiny kitchenette, even though she knew she could have walked across the quad to the main house where Jordan no doubt had some exotic blend going. But she wasn't yet ready to meet Jordan face to face over breakfast.

Hayden suspected the man she'd seen last night was Jordan's first husband, Scott, the friend Nick had described in some detail—the man they'd said had died in Iraq. But she'd need to see a picture of him to be certain. How did she intend to get a photo of the first husband without upsetting Jordan? Would asking her pointblank be a little too over-the-top and weird? Would it send her into a flurry of tears?

Hayden decided she had to consider Jordan's feelings in the matter. She couldn't very well blurt out the fact that she'd seen the ghost of her dead husband while eating a warm blueberry muffin.

She took down a box of Cheerios from the cabinet, got out milk from her mini-fridge. What she needed was to take a walk after breakfast and contemplate her approach.

If she upset Jordan, Nick would most certainly be none too happy about it.

Hayden had no desire to put her newly minted landlord relationship in jeopardy asking about a ghost. Besides, making waves wasn't Hayden's style.

After fixing herself two pieces of toast spread with Jordan's homemade blackberry jam to go with her cereal, she decided to take her first climb down to check out the cove everyone had raved about and see it for herself.

The scenery along the way didn't disappoint.

The trail was steep, but thanks to a set of wooden steps built into the side of the cliff and a pipe railing, she made the climb down with ease. She got a whiff of what she thought was rosemary and sage and realized the trail was lined with the stuff growing alongside ginger, beach grass and alfalfa.

When she reached the bottom, she dropped down onto a flawless stretch of sandy beach forming a half circle of inlet bay, perhaps forty yards long, where rocks jutted out here and there along the water line. She stared out at a sea of deep green water as it licked at a white pristine strip of sand. No tar balls here, Hayden noted. The sound of the surf lulled her into a blissful state while birdsong broke out from the trees on the cliffs above.

She was surprised Nick and Jordan hadn't given in to crass commercialism and disturbed the ecosystem by littering this perfect spot of cove with a bunch of beach chairs and other types of paraphernalia. But they'd chosen to leave it untouched, in its natural state so guests could appreciate the innate beauty.

That went a long way in Hayden's book. She had always loved nature, always loved spending time outdoors and had a passion for preserving the environment.

She'd grown up in Champaign, Illinois, and spent plenty of time trudging to school in snowy winters, as well as spending sweltering summers cooling off at the community swimming pool like all the other kids in the neighborhood.

But from the time she and her sister got their first summer jobs as trail guides at Prairie Valley Campground, Hayden had dreamed of becoming a forest ranger. Of course, she'd only been fifteen at the time, while her sister, Sydney, a year older, had wanted to be a nurse.

They'd grown up middle class, never spending too much time worrying about money or the lack thereof until a year later when her father had dropped dead from a brain aneurysm as he stood at the blackboard teaching a class full of fifth graders about plant cell structure.

After that, money had been tight. But despite the lack of funds for college, their mother, also a teacher, had made it clear she wanted both her girls to go to college. From that time on, both she and Sydney had buckled down and worked to get better grades. When it came time for college, Sydney had stayed local and pursued nursing at the University of Illinois at Urbana-Champaign while Hayden had received a scholarship to the University of Chicago, where she had also worked various odd jobs to help pay expenses.

By the end of her freshman year, Hayden had discovered that becoming a forest ranger wasn't all that practical. For one thing, all of her counselors had pushed her toward a more sensible career where she could make more money, like accounting. All of her evaluations had solidified that path toward finance.

How's that working out for you now? Hayden wondered, as she sat there on a rock, dangling her feet in the cold water of the cove, enjoying the surf lapping against her feet, and the warm sun on her face. Why hadn't she stuck to her guns and become a forest ranger? To hell with making more money, wasn't achieving happiness supposed to be the ultimate goal in life? If she had stuck with her original dream, every day might have been spent outdoors on days like this one, and she might never have crossed paths with the likes of Jeremy Dochenko.

After spending an hour at the cove, Hayden walked back up the trail, and went in search of Jordan. As usual, she found her in the kitchen with the baby.

"How'd your first night go?" Jordan asked as she cleaned up Hutton's face after the little girl had finished off a carton of yogurt with her own spoon.

Hayden watched a bit enviously as Hutton toddled off to play. It had been a long time since she'd been around a small child. Her career had always taken priority over everything else including a personal life, which she'd put on hold. And for what? What was she going to do without obsessing over her high-profile job? She looked over at Jordan and realized the woman was waiting for an answer.

"Last night was fine. Busy. I made over a hundred dollars in tips. I must have waited on half of Pelican Pointe. I'm pretty sure word got out that the new girl was in a pitiful costume and everyone stopped by to get a good look."

Jordan blew out a laugh. "Knowing the town, I don't doubt that."

"But Jordan, you've simply got to help me convince Margie to change that costume to a more dignified outfit. I can't wear the same thing five days a week, especially serving food."

"Maybe we could change it up a little. You know, pink poodle skirt one day with a black or white sweater and then black skirt with a pink top another day. I take it Margie didn't voice any objections."

"Are you kidding? The woman loved it." She sighed and shook her head. "Changing up the outfit every other day might work. My tips were better than I expected even if most of the town did come by to gawk. You know, if we do the bookstore thing, I could work on the place in the morning, fix it up, paint, set up the bookshelves, get the place stocked in the mornings and keep my job at the Diner in the evenings."

"You'd do that?"

"Are you kidding? Of course I will. Look I'll be happy to run the place, manage it for you and Nick, if you both agree that you'll take your percentage of the profits. I just don't have the money to invest my fair share yet, not until my condo sells. And besides, I have nothing better to do at the moment, might as well spend my time getting a business venture up and going for two of the best people I've met in a really long time."

"Hayden," Jordan confessed, "Nick and I don't really want to be in the used bookstore business."

She sighed. "I know. That just gives me more incentive to make a go of this. There's one storefront across from Murphy's, near the church that has shelves already on the walls and some movable bookcases. If the square footage is right it might be perfect. I could check into it before work this afternoon."

"Just make sure the sign doesn't say Springer Realty because half of those storefronts either belong to Springer outright or he's the broker handling the lease. If it doesn't say Springer, that's the one we want to deal with. Look for a realtor sign that's from out of town like Santa Cruz or San Sebastian."

"Gotcha. When will your guests arrive?"

"Probably around noon, depends on the traffic down from the Bay. There are two couples interested in spending a romantic weekend away from their kids. They stayed here over the Fourth, a family event. I'm so jazzed they decided to come back. Repeat business."

Hayden drummed her fingers on the counter, waited for an opening.

Jordan glanced over, took one look at Hayden's demeanor and said, "Okay, spit it out. What's on your mind?"

Hayden bit the inside of her jaw. Her fingers nervously flew to her mouth. "Jordan, I don't want to upset you, but your first husband, what did he look like?"

"What?"

"Scott, the guy Nick sees who died in Iraq. What did he look like?"

Hayden noticed Jordan's face go pale like maybe she knew what Hayden intended to bring up.

"Why do you ask?" Jordan finally blurted out.

Hayden hesitated. She really didn't want Jordan to start crying or get upset. "Do you have a picture of him—I could, uh, take a look at?"

Jordan went over to the desk in the corner of the kitchen, pulled open a drawer, and took out a small photo album, flipped it open. "This is Scott."

Hayden went over to study it, swallowed hard. "Yeah, I was afraid of that."

"You saw him." It wasn't a question.

"Yeah, I saw him last night when I got home from work. He was out taking a stroll in the gardens, walking in the courtyard, big as life."

Jordan slunk down into the chair at the desk because it was the closest place to sit. "I don't understand. Nick sees him. Now you. Why? Why not me? He never shows himself to me, never. I knew the man for four years, married to him for three. And I've never seen him, not once."

"Jordan."

"No, you don't understand. He moved me out here from San Francisco when we got married. It was his idea to come back here and get this house ready to open as a B & B. We spent six months like newlyweds, content, happy. Then his Guard unit got called up to Iraq. By that time I was pregnant. Just barely, but living out here alone. By myself. Get it?

"I spend a damned year here with just his letters, e-mails, a few text messages, and a couple of phone calls to keep me company. Then Hutton came along and we were alone here together. The two of us were living out in the boonies, no friends to speak of, in a town that didn't open its doors to newcomers, certainly not to us. Add in another year after learning I'd lost him in Iraq and I spent more time here without him than I did with him."

Jordan drew in a huge sigh before going on. "Scott's dream of turning this old house into a B & B is the only thing that kept me from just giving up and letting the bank have it. Turning this place into a viable business was what kept me out here during the worst time of my life. Losing Scott, I felt abandoned. I know it might've been ridiculous to feel that way. It wasn't his fault he had to leave to serve his country. But at the time, it was all so overwhelming, especially since this place was mortgaged to the hilt. I had to do something to keep from losing it though. So in the middle of grief and depression I tried to fix the place up enough to open.

"That's when Nick showed up. And during all that time, Scott Phillips sure as hell never bothered showing up to me in ghostly form or any other. If not for Nick, and the promise he made to Scott, we wouldn't be standing here. The house would be gone by now and developers would already be drawing up plans for a five-star resort courtesy of Kent Springer. If not for Nick..." She took a shaky breath. "I'm sorry. But I just can't get past the why. Why doesn't Scott show himself to me?"

Hayden wasn't sure what to say so she mumbled out, "I have no idea."

At that moment, the back door opened and Nick walked in. "Got the grass all mowed. This place is so huge it's a bit of a chore..." He glanced back and forth between the two women and then noticed his wife's pallor. He knelt down in front of her. "What's wrong? Did you faint? You're white as a sheet."

"Hayden saw him, Nick. Hayden saw Scott."

Hayden wanted to explain. "I didn't mean to upset her, Nick. If it's any consolation the man I saw looked completely at ease, happy even."

Nick sat back on his heels, glanced up at Hayden. "Let me guess, brown hair, wide grin, wearing khaki shorts, blue long-sleeved shirt, sleeves rolled up and a Tee underneath?"

"That's unbelievably accurate."

Nick shook his head. "It's odd. You're the first guest who's mentioned seeing him. I sort of thought someone might mention it over the summer. No one did. So far, it's just you and me."

Hayden placed a hand on Jordan's arm. "For what it's worth, I think Nick is right. The guy acts like he's watching over the place, acts at peace, without a care in the world in his own element. Although to be honest, he scared the crap right out of me."

"Welcome to the club," Nick said wearily.

Friday wasn't Ethan's usual day off. But because he'd worked a double shift during the storm, he'd sweet-talked his brother into giving him an extra day. That meant three days in a row he might get to sleep late, do a little house cleaning, okay a lot of house cleaning, maybe if he had the time he'd get in some surfing, and a whole lot of writing. Of course, he'd still be on call for any emergencies that came up in and around Pelican Pointe. But all and all, Ethan looked forward to a nice three-day escape, away from being a deputy, and heading into the world he loved, creating fictional characters.

He'd already accomplished the first thing on his list. He and Grisham had slept in until almost nine. Now if he could just do a little tidying up. He started in the living room shoveling out the collection of newspapers first, then moved on to the kitchen, where he transferred a week's worth of plates stacked in the sink to the dishwasher, which he had to empty out first. And since he couldn't remember the last time he'd changed the sheets on the bed, he took care of that too, which meant getting a load of laundry started.

If after all his chores were done he had any energy left, he'd reward himself and spend some quality time either in the surf or on the computer.

Wearing snug Capri jeans and a tank top under her green hoodie, Hayden set off to spend the afternoon investigating what Pelican Pointe had to offer in the way of viable bookstore locations. She had a couple of hours to kill before having to clock in at work, hours to stroll along Main or check out those little houses on Ocean Street, time she'd put to good use before she had to wear that atrocious poodle outfit and smile for the good people of Pelican Pointe to get more tips.

She'd brought a legal pad with her to take notes, write down each of the addresses of the storefronts, and find out which realtor listed the property. Surely they couldn't all be Springer's listings.

But just before getting to the city limits, she pulled the car to the side of the road at a spot she knew received decent cell phone service, and dug out her prepaid phone. She dialed a number on the east coast belonging to her mother's cell phone. It was almost five-thirty in Pellingham, New York, a good time to catch Laura Reed-Trenton just getting home from her job as a sales rep at the software company where she worked.

Three years ago her mother had met an economics professor at a teaching seminar in Chicago. She'd fallen in love with Rob Trenton, married him, given up teaching third grade, and moved with him to his home in upstate New York.

Although, Emile had been happy for her mother, she had missed making those trips back home to Champaign and the house where she'd grown up. She especially missed long visits with her mom when she could pour out the mess she'd made of her life. A phone call just wasn't the same thing. Of course, there was nothing stopping her from having those heart-to-heart talks with her sister, Sydney, an ER nurse working in a huge St. Louis hospital.

But Hayden had spent too many years immersed in her work in that crappy job she thought she had loved so much. She realized now the job had almost ruined Emile Reed's outlook on life. During the last four years, her mother and her sister had simply gone on with their lives. While she, on the other hand, had wasted those years in the pursuit of making money. Like an Ebenezer Scrooge character she had somehow managed to put work ahead of everything else. It hadn't brought happiness any more than it had brought her a significant other, or any close friends for that matter. Instead of spending her time getting a life, she'd sleepwalked through four years, unhappy with her job, and herself.

She could admit that now.

She tried to think back how long it had been since she'd had a date. Last year's Christmas party popped into her head. Ten months ago she'd brought a man to the event but for the life of her she couldn't even remember the guy's name or his face.

How pathetic, she thought now as she waited for her mother to pick up.

"Emile. Oh honey, it's so good to hear from you. Is everything okay? Are you all right?"

Her mother still couldn't get used to the name Hayden Ryan, and for the most part, Hayden let it slide. "Mom. Hi. I just wanted to let you know I've settled in someplace, although it's not Santa Cruz." For the next ten minutes, she told her mother as much about Pelican Pointe as she could in the short allotted timeframe, along with how nice Nick and Jordan had been to her.

The call ended much too quickly because Hayden always kept the calls to a ten-minute minimum. She knew it could be a pain to boost up the pay-as-you-go phone. And a hundred and fifty minutes went surprisingly fast when you needed to hear a friendly voice every so often. She was already down to a measly fifty-something minutes since she'd last bought cell cards in Nevada. Of course, she still had one or two prepaid phone cards she could use from a pay phone if she chose to do that. They always came in handy when she couldn't get cellular service.

With tears in her eyes, feeling more than a little melancholy, she pulled back onto the road and made her way to the business district of Pelican Pointe.

Her life was never going to be the same. But maybe, she thought as she parked the car, change was a good thing.

She left the ugly costume in the car while she wandered along Main Street peering into the dirty windows of each abandoned storefront, making notes on how large the places were and what kind of condition they were in. Most were way too spacious. Others needed too much work. And to her amazement Springer Realty owned most of the buildings including the one she had her eye on across from the church. Well, that sucked. It would have been the perfect location on numerous levels. Not only was it a high-traffic area right on Main, it was near the church which meant that people would most certainly drop in, if out of nothing else but curiosity. Plus, someone had already taken the time to build shelves into three sides and throw light blue paint on the walls. In addition, it fit Nick's idea of preferred square footage, which she estimated to be no more than 750 square feet.

But if Jordan said Springer wasn't to be trusted, who was she to question her judgment? She had to believe the woman knew what she was talking about.

Reluctantly, she moved on around the corner and started walking up Inlet Bay toward Ocean Street and the waterfront. She walked past The Pointe, an upscale dining establishment with white lettering on the side of the brick that indicated the place at one time had been an old fish hatchery. She had to admit this area of town, offered more local charm than the business district on Main.

Not only that, but there was one little Spanish style stucco house painted bright yellow that had caught her eye the other day. She wanted to check the place out. Actually, she thought it looked as if it had once been a business of some kind because there was an empty space where it looked as though a sign had once hung on an ornate overhang outside. Even though the flower beds and yard were a bit overgrown she wanted to take a look at the inside through the windows. If it didn't need too much work, the location would be ideal because it was smack dab in the middle of where the locals shopped, mingled and lived.

Getting into the thrill of starting a business, Hayden decided what this area of town needed was a good used bookstore.

When she read the realtor sign in the overgrown front yard that advertised a Santa Cruz phone number, Hayden pumped her fist in the air and did a happy dance. How Kent Springer Realty had missed listing this perfect little house she didn't know and didn't care. It had to be a good omen.

Since the house was one of those across from the waterfront, it had an amazing view of the ocean, as did all the houses along this street. In fact, she tilted her head and could make out the sound of the waves lashing about at the wooden pylons below the pier.

As she drew closer, intending to peer inside the windows, check the place out, she heard a woman's voice yelling as if in distress. No, the woman was screaming at the top of her lungs desperately trying to get anyone's attention she could, something about her child, a little boy.

"Please, someone help me. Help me! My little boy is out there. He fell in the water! Help me! Please!"

Hayden ran across the street to the wharf and scrambled to the woman's side. "Where?" Hayden was already toeing off her shoes, pulling off her socks.

"There. He fell in there, next to the pier. I can't swim. Please, please don't let him drown."

Sure enough Hayden saw movement off to the side of the pilings. Without waiting another precious second, she dived into the water, swam out a couple of feet or so before rounding back to the wooden pilings of the dock. There she spotted the little boy struggling with the undertow. It looked as if he was going down for what could have been the third time. Hayden caught him around the neck and began pulling the now limp, unconscious child toward land, all the while fighting the current. By the time she got him to shore, a crowd had gathered.

"Call 911," she screamed. Her lifeguard instincts kicked in. She immediately tried to get some response from the child by gently patting his small, pale face with her fingers. When nothing happened, she turned him on his side, swept his mouth to make sure it was clear. She lifted his chin to open his airway and covered his mouth with hers, blew in two quick successive breaths, waited for his chest to respond. After several interminable seconds when he still lay lifeless, she did it again. The minute she saw the boy's chest rise slightly, she repeated the process. As soon as his chest movement became more pronounced, she placed her palm in the middle of his breastbone, began compressions, and started counting to one-hundred.

She'd gotten to thirty-five when, all of a sudden, the boy coughed and threw up salt water.

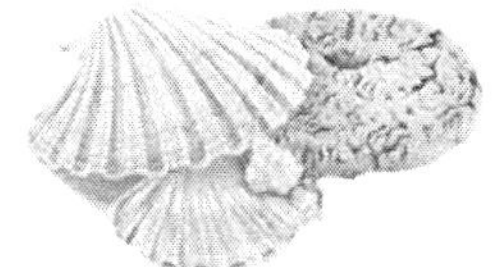

Chapter Five

Wearing his wetsuit, Ethan had just stepped out his front door onto his porch carrying his surfboard when he saw the throng of people gathered down on the beach near the pier. He leaned his board back up against the porch and took off across the street in a run toward the wharf. After making his way through the bystanders, he was shocked to see Hayden, soaking wet, giving CPR to a small boy of about five. He watched as the kid threw up a lungful of ocean.

"Has anyone called 911?" he asked, as he bent down to where Hayden worked on the boy and watched as she continued to rub his back, while a woman, he assumed was the child's mother leaned over and scooped him into her chest.

"I did," Flynn McCready, owner of the bar, offered. "They're sending an ambulance out of San Sebastian." When it looked like the boy began to shiver, Flynn took off a black and silver Raiders jacket and draped it around the little guy's shoulders.

"Good," Ethan said as he watched the mother grab Hayden around the neck and bring her into a bear hug.

"Thank you! Thank you! How can I ever repay you? One minute we were walking along the pier, looking at the boats and the next thing I know Justin had climbed up on the railing. I yelled for him to get down but before I could get to him he'd slipped and toppled over. I heard a splash and realized he'd fallen in."

"No problem," Hayden breathed out, as she hugged the woman back. "I'm glad I could help."

"You knew exactly the right thing to do," the woman announced, as she introduced herself. "I'm Jessica Hardin by the way. And this is Justin, my five-year-old son. We came over from Scotts Valley to visit my mom who had surgery last Friday. I didn't think it would hurt to go for a walk on the pier and show Justin the boats." She sobbed, "I've never been so scared in my life."

Her wet jeans and shirt made Hayden start to shiver. "That makes two of us. What time is it?"

Ethan looked at his watch. "Five after four."

"Crap. I'm late for work!" Hayden jumped up, ran back to the pier to get her shoes and socks and started to tromp off through the sand toward her car still parked down on Main.

After taking no more than three steps, Ethan grabbed her arm. "I'm just across the street, no more than forty yards away. Let's get you dried off."

She stopped to stare at him. "I'll dry off on the walk to my car where I need to get that pitiful outfit on and get to work."

Ethan didn't miss the glazed look in her eye. Was she in shock? "I'll call Margie." He patted his pocket for his cell phone and remembered he was wearing a wetsuit and his cell phone was back at the house. He'd been about to go surfing. He grabbed Hayden's arm and started walking back toward his house. "Come with me."

Hayden jerked out of Ethan's hold on her arm. "It's my second day. I can't afford to be late. Margie was very specific—"

"You saved a little boy from drowning out here today, Hayden. I'm pretty sure that entitles you to be late for work. Believe me, Margie will understand." He took her arm again and dragged her along through the thick sand. With every step, the sand stuck more heavily to her wet feet and her bare legs where her jeans ended. When he stopped in front of a Pueblo-style adobe house, he attempted to pull her up the walk and inside.

"Wait a damn minute. I need to wash off my feet. I'm a mess. I'll track sand all over your floor."

Ethan rolled his eyes. "Sit down on the steps then." He knelt down to brush off some of the wet sand from her feet and legs with his hands. Her legs were ice cold. The woman was freezing to death in her wet clothes and she wanted to spare his floor from a couple of grains of sand. "Believe it or not living at the beach, my floor has seen wet sand before today. Now get inside."

She followed, albeit halfheartedly. And was immediately attacked by a fawn-colored dog the size of a small horse. Grisham jumped up, landed on her chest with paws the size of pie plates. The force knocked her back a couple of steps.

"Down, Grisham. Sit," Ethan ordered, snapping his fingers while pulling on the dog's collar. "He's harmless. Get down, I said." He yanked a little harder and the dog reluctantly gave up the pressure of his front paws on her boobs. "Sorry about that. Grisham dropped out of obedience school, actually, that isn't true. It was more like he got kicked out."

"Like the dog in that movie, *Marley and Me*?"

"Exactly."

She laughed as she grabbed the dog around his neck. "Well, you're just a troublemaker then, aren't you? I like dogs. He just surprised me, is all."

Ethan went straight to his cell phone, dialed a number by heart. "Margie, this is Ethan Cody. We had a little excitement over here at the pier. Yeah, she did. She jumped right into the water, didn't hesitate. Right. She'll be a little late. Okay, I sure will. I'll see that she's all right before letting her come in to work. Give her about an hour, okay? Thanks."

Ethan took off to the bathroom, came back with several large beach towels.

Hayden stood where she was in the postage-sized vestibule. Her heart still raced, she felt a little lightheaded.

In the distance she heard sirens and couldn't help wondering about little Justin. She hoped he was okay. Before Ethan could catch her, she sunk to the floor in a heap, exciting Grisham even more. The dog took the opportunity to give her several licks to the face for good measure.

Ethan gently pushed Grisham aside and dropped down in front of her.

"All those summers I spent as a lifeguard. That's the first time I've ever had to save anyone. My knees are still shaking."

"We need to get you warm. That water had to be sixty degrees."

"I...I...didn't feel...a thing."

"Adrenaline, now your teeth are chattering," he reminded her, as he started drying off her hair first before wrapping the other giant towel around her shoulders. "Start taking off your clothes."

Hayden might have been in shock from the experience but she eyed him as if he had two sets of horns growing out of his head. "Yeah. Right. Sure thing, Deputy...Cody. I'll...just start...stripping for you."

His lips curved. "As much as I'd love for you to strip just for me, those clothes need to come off. Now be a good girl and go in the bathroom. It's just down the hall there and to the right, take off your wet things. I'll throw them in the washer and then dry 'em for you while you're at work. Do you need help getting to the bathroom?" He started helping her to try to stand.

She sucked in a breath, blew it out with a large sigh. "I can get there on my own."

"Good. There's a clean robe in there, put it on. Hand me out your wet things when you're done."

"I need my costume for work."

"I'll go get it. Where are your car keys?"

Just as she got to the door of the bathroom, she turned around, threw him the keys from her jeans pocket. "I'm parked in front of the flower shop."

"I'll be right back."

She heard the front door close and knew he had taken Grisham along with him.

She wasn't helpless for chrissakes. After she removed her clothes, she slid on his plaid flannel robe. Tentatively, she opened the door of the bathroom, peeked out. She walked around the house until she found the laundry room herself, which was right off the kitchen. Her jeans, top and panties went into the washer while she threw her bra into the dryer for ten minutes on delicate. She'd need the bra to wear under that stupid, thin pink sweater top and she didn't have time to wait for it to wash.

Remembering the socks on the porch, she ran outside to retrieve them. On her way back inside, she stopped to gawk at what she'd missed earlier. One end of the rectangular living room floor to ceiling was nothing but shelves filled to capacity with books. She walked over to study the titles. His tastes ran the gamut. Rows of history books competed with space for classic literature. He had books on architecture, astrology, geography, the paranormal, Native American spirituality, Middle Eastern foreign policy, ancient Egyptian art, true crime, thrillers, mysteries, and every John Grisham hardcover the man had ever written.

Realization dawned.

He'd named his dog after the author. About that time the booklover opened the front door.

Ethan found her standing in his living room perusing his books. "I thought you'd be taking a hot shower by now," he admonished. He handed off the pink poodle skirt and sweater top, the bag with her saddle shoes inside, and her purse, which felt like it weighed ten pounds.

"I went ahead and started the laundry. I forgot my socks though." She stood there in his bathrobe holding her damp, sand-gritty footwear.

"I'll put them in. Now, go on, take that hot shower. You'll feel better."

Ethan took the socks while she headed back into the bathroom and turned on the shower.

Ten minutes later, wearing the robe again, she emerged from the bathroom. The house seemed strangely quiet, no sign of either Ethan or the dog. She tip-toed straight to the dryer, grabbed her bra and ran back to the bathroom to get ready for work.

She blow-dried her hair using his brush, re-applied her make-up, adding a little eye shadow and mascara. But it wasn't until she started getting into that costume that she realized her mistake.

She should have put her panties in with the bra to dry instead of in the washer. The poodle skirt was thick enough fabric that you couldn't exactly see through it, but still… Should she stop the washer, retrieve her panties, and wear them soapy and wet? Ugh! She didn't want to do that. But then, how could she go to work without wearing underwear?

After a few minutes, she made her decision. Would anyone really notice she wasn't wearing panties under the skirt?

Decision made, sans panties, she walked out into the living room wearing her ridiculous poodle outfit and saddle shoes without socks, carrying her purse. The front door flew open and Ethan and the dog reappeared as if they'd been outside on the porch waiting for her. At some point, he'd changed out of the wet suit and into well-worn jeans and a blue sweat shirt that said "Spike's Bar & Grill." Then she realized that he and the dog must have gone back to the beach to check on the little boy.

"How's Justin?"

"They took him to the clinic to let Doc Prescott check him out. He's damned lucky you were there and knew what to do. He'll be fine." He suddenly looked her up and down, cocked his head to one side and sent her a wide grin. "Very nice, Hayden-no-middle-initial-Ryan."

"I'm glad you approve, Deputy Dawg, but I've got to go. Thanks for the use of your shower and for washing my clothes. Could you bring them—?"

He nodded, answering her without letting her finish. "I'll get your clothes back to you before you go home tonight."

"Thanks."

"I'll drive you to work."

"Don't be silly, it's not even four blocks. I'll walk."

As if he knew exactly which buttons to push, he said calmly, "Okay, but I thought you were worried about being late…"

"Fine then."

He locked up, leaving Grisham whining at the front door. Before they got to his truck though, he inexplicably took her arm and swung her around to his chest. He lowered his head and covered her mouth.

Lips seared together. White hot fire roared up between them.

Her breath backed up as she clung to his shirt, giving back every bit as good as she got. They fed off each other's mouths. Blinding arousal staggered her as she fought with his tongue. When they had to breathe, he released her. A gasp escaped as she finally stepped back just to keep from sampling more of him.

"Jesus, you taste good. I had to get that out of the way," Ethan admitted.

Her head reeled. She sputtered out, "You don't trust me, remember?"

As he opened the passenger door for her he pointed out, "I tried to apologize for that last night…twice. Remember?"

"So what are you saying?"

"I think you're running from something or someone who is dangerous. I think you're scared. I admit I thought the worst at first that you had something criminal in your past."

She sighed. "Well, that's blunt."

"It's honest," he contradicted, watching as she took great care to situate herself in the passenger seat just so, while making sure her skirt was tucked in around her thighs as if self-conscious about something.

He shrugged it off and crawled behind the wheel.

During the short drive to the Diner, they didn't say another word to each other. The minute he came to a stop in the middle of Main Street, he double-parked behind the tail-ends of the cars already lining the slotted spaces because there was no available place to park. He let the vehicle idle while he watched, once again, as she took great pains to crawl out of the truck, holding onto her skirt. Before he could utter another word, she politely thanked him for the ride and slammed the door shut in his face.

It wasn't until after he got back to the house and was loading her clothes into the dryer that it dawned on him. As he chucked her jeans, top, and socks into the drum along with a tiny slice of fabric that passed for panties, a light went off.

He chuckled, realizing she'd gone to work without wearing underwear.

And with that image pictured in his head, he couldn't stop grinning remembering how she'd felt up against him, how she'd responded.

Because that first taste had left him wanting a whole lot more.

Chapter Six

Even though Hayden had practically run from Ethan's truck like it had been on fire, once she crossed the threshold into work, she did her best to glide into waitress mode. After apologizing to Margie for her tardiness, she made a concerted effort to leave that lip lock behind, too.

It was difficult. Her lips still smoldered from that molten kiss. And what a kiss! She wasn't sure she'd ever felt anything so potent. Somehow she'd known Ethan Cody would be a pro in the tongue-exchange program.

Unfortunately, Margie and her chosen profession at the moment forced Hayden back to reality. Her boss didn't cut her much slack, either. "Don't think you can make a habit of being late," Margie snapped. But then to Hayden's surprise she added, "You did a good thing, girl, saving that little boy the way you did."

She conceded she might have to get used to Margie's gruff exterior, as well as the woman's brusque sense of humor, which bordered on crusty as a sailor.

"Believe me I don't intend to make a habit of jumping into the Pacific Ocean every day before work."

"Good. Because by the time we close tonight, you'll be dead on your feet. It's already all over town how you saved little Justin Hardin. And Friday nights are always busy anyway. But the locals will end up eating supper here just to get a good look at the girl hero. You watch."

Oddly, Margie's prediction turned out to be true. Hayden was busier than she'd been the night before. It seemed a steady stream of Pelican Pointe's upstanding citizens decided to come by to meet the woman who'd taken a dive into the Pacific Ocean.

She met the mayor and the owner of Murphy's store, who turned out to be a gray-haired man in his fifties, all five feet of him along with his steady companion, Carla Vargas, the petite, county social worker.

Drea Jennings, the owner of the flower shop, stopped by to introduce herself and officially welcome Hayden to the town by handing her a beautiful bouquet of fall mums.

Mr. and Mrs. Ferguson, owners of the hardware store, made a point of offering her a fifteen percent discount off paint any time she felt like redeeming it.

Wally Pierce brought Lilly and the kids by to see if she was all right and could finish out her shift. They even offered to drive her back to The Cove if she needed to go.

But it was the pharmacist, Carl Knudsen, whose visit left her slightly panic-stricken. According to Knudsen, the rescue story, such as it had been and always a popular feel-good news lead, had garnered the attention of all the Santa Cruz television stations, which meant there was a chance it might be picked up by the national networks.

If the story happened to go nationwide, what did that mean for Hayden Ryan aka Emile Reed? While she was certain there had been no news crews around with cameras rolling to catch Hayden on film, she knew in this day and age cell phones were as good as if not better than video cameras and everyone carried one. Had someone gotten the whole thing on video? God, she hoped not. And if so, would it end up going viral on the Internet?

Such a sad thing thought Hayden, as she went about serving hash to half the town. How a wonderful event like saving a life could be so easily turned into a three-ring circus she didn't know. But there was little she could do about it now. She could only hope Jeremy wouldn't recognize Hayden Ryan from Jane Smith, nor would his henchmen.

She had, after all, altered her appearance. Even though she'd been meticulous in making sure Emile Reed had disappeared, she couldn't get sloppy, no matter how small the town. She considered what Ethan had told her about his suspicions. Either she had been terribly transparent, or the man really did possess some psychic abilities. She was afraid it was a little bit of both.

She had never been a good liar, or a woman who manipulated others, or directed situations to get what she wanted. Right now, she wished she was better at both, like maybe being a better actress.

What with people taking the time to slap her on the back so to speak, her shift flew by in a blur. At nine-twenty-five she was running the mop over the floor one last time when she glanced up and spotted Ethan standing outside the locked door, waiting for her.

Her pulse jumped at the sight of him. She waved and held up her hand with her fingers splayed indicating she needed five more minutes. When he nodded, she went to dump the dirty water and get rid of the mop.

Once outside on the sidewalk, they began to walk to her car. Ethan held out a bag, shaking his head. "Your clothes, Hayden-no-underwear-Ryan. I can't believe you worked in the buff."

"I did no such thing. I worked without underwear, there's a difference. With all those books you have, you'd think you could crack open a dictionary."

"Bare-assed is what you are under that skirt."

"Bare-assed implies no clothes. As you can see, I'm fully clothed, decently so."

"I could amend that."

"Oh I've no doubt. You'd probably be smooth as silk while doing it, too."

"I rarely get complaints," he said jovially. "How about something to eat?"

"I just came out of a diner. What makes you think I didn't spend the last several hours stuffing my face every chance I got?"

"I figure working around food is kinda like working around law enforcement. Just because you're in the environment doesn't mean you want to immerse yourself in the flavor twenty-four-seven. A change of pace is a good thing. I made steak fajitas, got 'em warming in the oven. The smell is driving Grisham nuts."

Hayden stopped walking when she got to her car and stared at him. She looked around for his familiar county truck. Main Street was virtually deserted. "You're a constant source of contradiction, Deputy Dawg. Did you walk here?"

"I did. But left my dog behind over major protests."

She grinned. "Then get in. I'll drive you back to your place—for fajitas."

With guests tucked in for the night, Nick sat at the computer supposedly working on the B & B website they'd launched three months earlier. But he couldn't concentrate on the message he wanted to convey. Little wonder, after Hayden's disclosure that morning. Nick was worried about his wife and how she'd chewed on the news most of the day that Scott's ghost had once again been seen walking the grounds and not by her.

Nick wondered if he might be a little jealous.

And that was ridiculous. What sane man would be jealous of a dead man, a ghost? But there it was. While Jordan wondered why Scott never appeared to her, Nick fixated on why Scott was still hanging around.

He couldn't very well ignore the fact that this place had been Scott's childhood home. Just because he'd grown up here and brought Jordan back to start a family didn't explain why he still haunted the grounds.

He'd thought that after he overcame his survivor's guilt, after he'd married Jordan, Scott would see how happy they both were and leave him alone. But like so many other aspects over the past six months, it seemed as if Nick had underestimated the man's devotion to The Cove. Maybe Scott just didn't want to let go of this life.

When Jordan walked in and stood behind him, she wrapped her hands around his neck. Her presence did what it always did. It rocked his world, a sentiment that just six short months earlier he couldn't even have fathomed.

When she started trailing kisses down the back of his neck and then around to his jaw, he decided he really was being absurd focusing on a ghost. This woman was the reason he got up in the morning. The reason he'd left his life back in Los Angeles behind for the little town of Pelican Pointe. The reason he was so happy these days instead of the brooding man who'd served two tours of duty in Iraq.

He brought her around to face him. "You still look a little pale. Are you sure you're okay?"

"I'm fine. Better than fine. I'm wonderful as a matter-of-fact. It seems you managed to get one past the goalie." She waited for his reaction.

He sat up straighter. "What?"

"I'm pregnant."

His lips curved. His eyes lit up. He pulled her down into his lap, ran a hand over her flat belly. "Are you sure?"

"I just peed on the stick a second time. Believe me you're definitely going to be a father in about seven and a half months."

"I'm already a father," he pointed out proudly.

"And that, Mr. Harris, is why I'm crazy in love with you."

"When can we make an announcement? How long do we have to wait before I can tell Ben?" His best friend Ben Latham already had two kids and his wife was expecting a third in a little over six weeks.

"Since you look like you're about to burst, I think you can start sending out e-mails, start making phone calls right away."

Nick crushed his mouth to Jordan's. "I'll alert the media later. Right now, I'm taking my knocked-up wife to bed."

"So what's the deal with Kent Springer? Jordan tells me I should avoid the man like the plague," Hayden asked as she dipped the end of her fajita in the guacamole, took another bite of the tasty meat. Thankfully she'd rid herself of that hideous costume and changed back into freshly laundered jeans and her tank top. "I love Mexican food. You're a damn good cook, Ethan, for a deputy sheriff."

Ethan leaned back in his chair at the table, picked up his bottle of Corona, took a long pull. "I'm a man of many talents. As for good ol' Kent, avoiding him might not be that easy even though his trial's coming up next week. I see him around town now and again. He's been out on bail almost five months now. His lawyer's gotten his trial postponed a couple of times already. But next week is it; word has it the judge is fed up with any more delays."

He reached down and absently petted Grisham's head when the pooch rested his chin on his lap, stealthily eyeing his master's portion of meat.

"But what exactly did he do?" Hayden insisted. "Jordan is never specific."

"Well, for one thing, last spring he tried to set Promise Cove on fire. But Nick caught him in the act just as he was getting to it. He'd already poured gas out of one can. Something we didn't figure out until much later. All he would've had to do is light the match." At the time, Ethan had worked the crime scene and had been the one who had noticed that the area around the corner of the house had been saturated with gasoline. "Luckily Nick spotted him before he got the chance."

Hayden's mouth dropped open.

Ethan quickly explained, "He wanted the land for his own—to build a fancy resort in the area. He'd already missed a couple of chances to buy the property. Then when Jordan and Scott moved back here, I guess Kent thought he'd gotten a raw deal. Anyway, Scott had this dream of opening the house as a B & B. Those plans upset Springer's. Before that, he'd tried to bribe a county inspector to close the place down because the wiring wasn't up to code. We found out about that later, too. It seems Kent has a history of bribing county officials, beating up women, that sort of thing. He may have even killed one."

"Oh. My. God."

"It's just a suspicion. Brent, my brother, has spent almost a year investigating Springer in the disappearance of a Santa Cruz woman Springer had been dating last fall."

"Wait, rumor has it he and Sissy Carr are involved in a longstanding affair."

"Sure they are but if you think Kent's faithful to anyone, you don't know Springer."

"Okay, so he messed around on Sissy with a woman from Santa Cruz. What do you think happened to the woman?"

"She went missing, hasn't been seen for almost a year now. Kent was the last person to see her alive. But without a body we haven't been able to nail Springer for murder yet, just the attempted arson. If he gets convicted on the arson charge and is sitting in prison for nine years, it'll buy us some time to keep looking for more evidence in the woman's disappearance."

"According to the realtor signs, the man owns half the town."

"Kent and the First Bank of Pelican Pointe which if the rumors are correct, is in trouble. They've made some risky loans and bad investments, all seem to be connected to Springer. Feds are looking into the business practices of both even as we speak."

And didn't she know all about the feds, Hayden thought, sourly. She sipped the chardonnay Ethan had poured. For some reason it didn't taste as good as it had earlier. "Do you think he'll get convicted?"

"You never know what a jury will do. But yeah, I think there's a better than eighty percent chance of conviction. If they go by the evidence, it should be a slam dunk. But…juries can be fickle. And even though Springer is a scumbag, he has no shortage of friends in high places. If we don't get him locally for the arson and bribery charges, maybe the feds will reel him in for fraud. Either way, I think ol' Kent Springer's days of freedom are about done."

"So, he had it in for Nick and Jordan," she concluded.

"Jordan really, Kent hoped the bed and breakfast would never see the light of day and Jordan would lose the house. When that happened he'd be able to snatch it up at a bank auction. Springer didn't count on Nick Harris showing up though. Nick came along and he and Jordan pretty much got that place up and going in spite of the odds.

"At the eleventh hour when it looked like they wouldn't be able to open, Nick shamed most of the townspeople into getting them to help out with the finishing touches. As it turns out, one of the reasons the town had been so standoffish to Jordan was because of Sissy Carr. The woman had spent the past two years spreading nasty rumors about Jordan, rumors that turned out to be flat out lies."

By way of explanation, he went on, "Maybe because of the affair, Sissy said something, or in some way pushed Kent into taking matters into his own hands like attempting arson. Who knows? Whatever the reason, Kent decided to hedge his bets. A fire would have worked to his advantage and pretty much wiped Jordan out before she even got started. You can bet Nick is busting at the gut to testify against the bastard. He has a score to settle."

He picked up his beer again. When he took a look at her face and saw the disbelief, he added, "Hey, if you're going to settle in a small town, you have to know the dynamics of the place."

"Ah, I think I get it now. That's the rough time Jordan mentioned. She and Nick—together, as a couple, them versus the town." And thought Hayden, it would explain why they had been into the good neighbor thing. If the town wasn't that friendly—these two were bent on changing all that by getting new people in here. New friends, hence new chances. Second chances, Nick had said. She decided to test the waters. "Tell me, Ethan, do you believe in ghosts?"

"Of course. Hard to have Native American ancestry and not. Why?"

"Which Native American culture are we talking about?"

"Chumash. My father's people. They lived along the coast thousands of years before the Spanish ever arrived. They used plank canoes they called tomols to navigate the ocean selling and trading their goods back and forth between tribes. Even made their own currency from olivella shell beads. The kinds of shells still found all up and down the beaches here."

"I know. I picked up a pocket full of them just the other day. You have fascinating roots, Deputy Dawg."

"I do. But don't get my father started on how he plans to reawaken the Chumashan dialect. He's all about kiyiškɨhɨn a kiyiswana'n a siyatyatɨk." Eyeing the confused look on her face, he added, "kiyiškɨhɨn a kiyiswana'n a siyatyatɨk means keeping our culture alive. And paleontologists have found some serious cave paintings and tree carvings all along the coast they've attributed to the Chumash, if you're interested in that sort of thing."

"Really? That sounds fascinating. I'd love to see those sometime. Are they nearby?"

"South of here, around Santa Barbara mostly. Why do you want to know if I believe in ghosts?"

"Well, at the risk of you thinking I'm a nutcase, I saw Scott Phillips last night, walking the grounds." When he looked a bit perplexed, she added, "Yeah, Jordan's husband, first husband, the guy who died in Iraq. I know it sounds crazy…impossible even."

"Really? Maybe he's jealous of Nick, you know, because the guy married his wife."

"He didn't look upset, or jealous, or anything but blissfully content. Although to be honest I don't know much about spirits or ghosts. I noticed when I was here earlier you have a book that deals with the paranormal. I was wondering if I could borrow it. Jordan's kind of upset about the whole thing."

"I bet."

She eyed the gleam in Ethan's eye and added, "No, not like what you're thinking. Jordan said she'd spent months out there alone, a long time before Nick ever came, and that Scott never bothered showing himself to her. I guess that aspect is…problematic for her." She sipped her wine and studied the good-looking man sitting across from her. Out of uniform, with a beer in his hand, he looked the most relaxed she'd ever seen him. Unqualified warmth spread over her. She didn't think it was the wine, either. Damn it, she didn't want to be attracted to a cop.

"Are you saying she's upset because he shows himself to Nick, and now to you, but not her?"

She took another sip of wine to get her mind off the way his lips fit around the mouth of that bottle. "Well, think about it. She felt abandoned when he left for Iraq and didn't come back. Now, he's a ghost and doesn't bother appearing to his own wife."

"Okay. That's deep. Sure, take the book. But are you certain of what you saw. I mean…"

She nodded. "Jordan showed me a picture. Scott Phillips was as real as you are right now, walking through the courtyard in the moonlight, smiling, looking—happy. He was so real I thought he was another guest who had checked in while I was at work. And then, poof…gone! Besides, it isn't just me, Nick's seen him too."

"Nick seems pretty rock solid to me. You know he served in the same Guard unit as Scott. Memories of war might be responsible for Nick seeing him. But you?"

"Nick has a theory. And I've been thinking about it some. I have my own. That's why I want to read the book you have. See if it offers any new ideas."

"What's the theory?"

"Nick's idea is that he's watching over the people he loves and cares about."

"Sounds reasonable. But you don't agree."

"It's a noble thought, but if that were true, then why did he appear to me? Scott didn't know me let alone care anything about me. See what I'm saying? Anyway, I think the people who see him are troubled, unhappy for whatever reason, maybe groping their way through life looking for answers they don't have at the moment, or maybe looking for something they need—like help of some kind."

"Are you troubled, Hayden?"

She eyed him for a long time. "I thought you were psychic?"

His eyes darkened and became wary. "Who told you that?"

She ignored the question. "You told me yourself how you think I came to be here. I'm running from something, remember?"

"So, I was right?"

"In a manner of speaking. But I'm not running from an ex or an abusive relationship, if that's what you're curious about? It's a tad more complicated than that. And I don't have a criminal past."

"You're an enigma."

"It's a female's prerogative to be mysterious." She grinned and got up to clear the dishes.

After picking up her plate, he stilled her hand. "You don't have to do that. You're a guest, guests don't do the dishes."

"I ate like a horse. You cooked. I'll clean. That's the way it works." While she loaded the dishwasher Ethan filled the dog dish with water for the night, let Grisham outside in the small backyard to pee.

With the dog outside, he came up behind her, wrapped his arms around her. "What did you mean earlier when you said I was a contradiction?"

She stopped rinsing dishes, dried her hands on the towel, and turned to face him. "You're kidding, right? You seem restless, Ethan, like you aren't completely happy doing what you're doing. There's a guitar propped up in your living room." She cocked her head and purposely studied him. "But something tells me you aren't interested in pursuing a career as a rock star. You love the guitar as an outlet, for personal enjoyment, for fun. You get a kick out of performing on a lark. Then there's the fact that you own enough books to fill a small library. You name your dog after an incredibly talented author."

"So?"

His tone said it all. "Looks like I'm not the only one who has a secret they don't want to discuss."

Stunned at how easily she'd read him when no one else had ever gotten close to his furtive hopes, Ethan remarked, "Okay, I'd love to write, make a living at it, you know."

Her eyes went wide. That's the last thing she'd expected him to say. "Have you sent in manuscripts?"

He nodded. "All rejected."

"I read something on the Internet that said Grisham was rejected thirty times."

"I'm definitely catching up. There aren't even that many publishers willing to take a look at an unsolicited manuscript these days. The lousy economy is killing the hopes and dreams of the once-eager writer. And then there's the possibility that I'm kidding myself. Maybe I'm not that good and don't have what it takes."

When Grisham scratched at the back door, Ethan let him back into the kitchen. It was so rare to have someone to talk to about his writing. "You want another glass of wine." He knew he didn't want her to leave.

"I better not. I'm driving. And just because you get rejections doesn't mean you don't have talent as a writer. You shouldn't get discouraged. I read somewhere that publishers are so concerned about the profit-loss margin these days they're passing on perfectly good manuscripts. Advances are drying up to virtually nothing. Unless of course you happen to write about vampires, that's a really popular subject these days, especially with teenage girls." She grinned and glanced at her watch. "And I better get going. It's almost midnight." She touched both hands to his face. "If you thought you could ply me with alcohol and a good meal and then get lucky tonight, Ethan, you were wrong."

"I had to try," he said with amusement as he nibbled her ear.

She let him graze for a bit and then gently reminded him, "Two days ago you thought I was a criminal."

She let that sink in while she closed up the dishwasher before heading into the living room to pick up her work clothes. "You need to make up your mind just how rotten a person you think I am."

"I misjudged you. I told you that."

"You did. And I'm taking your apology under advisement," she said with mischief in her eyes.

"Ah, I get it now, you're making me suffer." He grabbed his keys off the sofa table. "And before you protest, I'm following you home. Once you leave the 101 the road out to the B & B's dangerous in the dark if you aren't familiar with it. You know the same road where I plucked you out of the rain. I want to make sure you get back to The Cove safe and sound."

All at once she grabbed his shirt, brought his head down to her mouth. "Now that gesture, Deputy Dawg, will definitely get you another fiery lip lock." She covered his mouth. The kiss was all tongues, attack and pursue, plunder and explore, nip and bite. It went on and on until they had to come up for air.

When they finally broke apart, he placed his hand on his heart. "You pack a punch, Hayden-no-middle-initial-Ryan."

"Damn straight," she replied as she all but glided to her car.

At five minutes after two in the morning, the music had long stopped drifting out of McCready's bar a good two hours earlier because the local noise ordinance shut everything down at midnight. That meant most of the neighborhood homes nearby had gone dark as well with their owners tucked into beds fast asleep.

Shadows hung over Smuggler's Bay as two figures made their way down Ocean Street toward the wooden pier pulling two huge trunks behind them. Once they reached the fifty-foot yacht, Easy Money, the two stepped onto the deck and began to ready the boat for sail. They worked quickly without a word exchanged between them, hoisting the main-sail then maneuvering the craft out of its slot and into the dark waters of the bay.

It seems Kent Springer and Sissy Carr had finally found a way to leave Pelican Pointe in their dust, so to speak.

It was four days before Kent's trial was scheduled to begin at the Santa Cruz County courthouse.

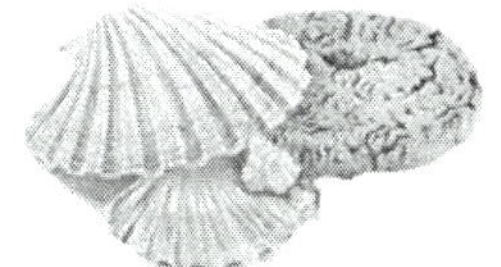

Chapter Seven

Ethan had trouble concentrating on his storyline. No matter how hard he tried to keep his mind in the moment, on his main character, he kept circling back to the real-life mystery that was Hayden Ryan.

If she wasn't running from an ex, then who had her in their sights and why? he wondered. How long had she been hiding, weeks, months? From what Ethan could tell it hadn't been that long. Only a few weeks earlier she'd gotten Nevada tags and a new driver's license. If he wanted, he could start from that point backward, find out more about her, a lot more.

But a background check on the woman he wanted to get into bed seemed like such a dishonest thing to do and just plain—wrong on so many levels.

Ordinarily he wouldn't have considered Hayden Ryan his type, especially since it was obvious there was a degree of the unknown surrounding her. A cop was usually none too happy with the idea of fuzzy facts; even vague could be annoying, which Hayden definitely was.

But he couldn't deny he liked her feisty side, throw in the long legs, the deep green shade of her eyes and the way she responded to his kiss and he could damn sure overlook the secrecy—at least until he couldn't.

He'd have to see what he could do about breaking through that reserved demeanor. Okay, so that side of her was an intriguing challenge. And it had been a long damn time since he'd had a challenge quite so gorgeous.

Momentarily at an impasse, he got up from his laptop to go to the kitchen, poured his umpteenth cup of coffee of the morning, strolled back to his computer and attempted once again to string two sentences together that made some sense. When his phone rang he grumpily got up to answer it. He hoped to hell it wasn't work.

It was Markus Cody, his father. He greeted him the way he always did using his Native tongue. "Haku, kʰoko."

"Haku, kwop, is this a bad time?"

"Never a bad time for you. What's up?"

"Brent's got a missing three-year-old girl out at Wilder Ranch State Park. Seems her parents got there early this morning to set up for a picnic, a birthday party for one of their other kids. Parents got distracted, spent a good forty-five minutes looking around for the tyke until they decided she was nowhere to be found. I thought if you weren't busy, you could lend a hand. Between the both of us…"

Ethan had worked with his father many times in the past but usually the elder man kept him out of the limelight, knowing how his son felt about bringing attention to himself. Ethan wanted no part of even the slightest hint of media attention in that regard, at least, not for his psychic ability.

If he ever got lucky and managed to get a publisher interested in giving him a book deal, he didn't want them getting wind that he was somehow different. He'd rather people knew him as a published author rather than a whack-job psychic, which is what he believed most people considered his father, or anyone else for that matter, who claimed to have a second sense about things.

What most people didn't know though, that as good as Markus Cody was at what he did, Ethan had always been better. "Sounds like she simply wandered off. That area's got plenty of things that would attract a small kid." At that point, he wasn't getting a vibe of any kind that she'd been abducted, but you never knew.

"That's what we're thinking. Brent's in the process of setting up a perimeter and a grid search."

"I'll meet you at the entrance." He glanced at his watch, assuring his dad, "I'll be there in less than thirty minutes." When he disconnected, he shut down his laptop, grabbed his jacket and keys and was out the door like a shot.

By the time Ethan pulled up in his truck to the entrance of Wilder Ranch there wasn't an available place to park. News vans with their satellite dishes already lined Highway 1, along with plenty of other cars belonging to the usual weekend park goers. He'd always thought the cars looked out of place here next to the rugged, rock-jutted coastline.

"Damn it," he muttered to himself as he double-parked next to one of the other deputies. He didn't want to end up playing traffic cop today. But just when that thought took hold, he realized that wasn't why he was here. He began to think in terms of what the little girl might be up against out in the elements.

The morning wasn't that cold, but for a child, alone, it had to be intimidating in unfamiliar surroundings.

Although the cliffs here were anything but steep, the landscape offered a ton of naturally occurring bridges, tunnels, coves and caves at beach level that might attract a small child. Maneuvering from one cave to the next, Ethan knew high tide could get you trapped or God forbid, swept out to sea.

Missing children and water were never a good mix.

But his senses told him, that had not happened to the little girl. At least, not yet.

Because Wilder Ranch State Park had once been a thriving ranch and dairy farm, it was a popular destination for field trips during the school year which made it one of the kid-friendliest parks around, a reason it attracted so many families on Saturdays and Sundays. The place was like a natural outdoor Disneyland. But instead of automated rides there were seven thousand acres of trees to climb, trails to hike, historic buildings to explore. The area was home to all manner of birds like snowy plovers, pelicans, and pigeons as well as countless small animals like cottontail that might attract a young child's attention.

As he looked around assessing the situation, it appeared to be a madhouse. Even though the fog had not yet completely lifted and the morning still cast gray skies overhead, the park had already gotten crowded. Everywhere he looked there were families with young children and parents unloading strollers, bikes and picnic gear for the day.

When he caught sight of his father, a neatly dressed man of sixty-five in a buckskin jacket with a pale-blue chambray shirt tucked into laundered black jeans, he ambled up to him, slapped him on the back.

The white-haired man with his long hair tied back into a ponytail, turned to greet his son.

"Haku, kwop. Thanks for coming," Markus Cody said before adding, "Brent's dealing with a pair of anxious parents."

"Haku, k^{h}oko," Ethan replied, greeting his father. He sent a look toward Brent strutting around in his sheriff's uniform. The brothers traded glances.

Brent stared at Ethan, disappointed to see that he'd worn his civilian clothes, an old denim jacket, a pair of well-worn jeans, and a white Tee, rather than his official uniform. Well aware Ethan often used any excuse to shed his uniform whenever possible for civvies, Brent sent him a knowing look. Because he also knew technically, his brother was still off-duty, doing this out of the goodness of his heart.

Ethan met his brother's stare. After all, they were as different as day is from night. And it wasn't just the five-year difference in their ages. Ethan, at thirty-three, was a bookworm, always had been except for a couple of years in high school when the baseball coach had made the mistake of thinking he had the same athletic ability as his older brother and drafted him into trying his luck at pitcher.

Back in his high school days, Brent had possessed a ninety-five-mile per hour fastball. He'd even gotten a baseball scholarship to UNLV. But instead of pursuing a baseball career, Brent had done a fifteen year stint in the army. He had intended to make it a career but with the Iraq war, Brent had completed three tours and called it quits for some reason. Back then when he'd announced to the family that he was leaving the army, no one had been more surprised than Ethan.

Ethan had always suspected that his older brother considered him somewhat of a slacker, particularly during his bartender/band days. Not that Brent had ever voiced anything but mutual respect for his younger brother, especially when it came to Ethan's special ability, which Brent didn't seem to have inherited. He had always gotten a vibe from Brent, that his older brother harbored a certain amount of ill will toward him for not following in his footsteps into the military, a career that did not appeal to Ethan on any level.

When Ethan caught his father eyeing him, he gave his dad a little head nod and said, "Let's see what we've got."

By the look on Brent's face, he suspected his father had called him before letting Brent in on the decision until well after the call.

"Dad's not getting anything, Ethan," Brent announced quietly. "I've got distraught parents, a park full of families. So far going trail to trail has given us jack squat, same with searching the buildings. We've got nothing. Deputies covered the strawberry fields, questioned the workers, no one's seen her."

"Show me where the girl was last."

Brent thumbed the air and pointed behind him. "This way."

It didn't take long to navigate the well-worn path to the picnic area. He saw a frantic couple run up to Brent. But it was the man who spoke. "We can't just sit here. Allison's been gone more than an hour now. She'll be getting hungry soon."

Then the anxious mother, wringing her hands, added, "She's so little. Please, you have to find her. What if...what if... someone's grabbed her? There are people running all over this place. She could be halfway to San Francisco by now."

"Mr. and Mrs. Wyatt, we can't issue an AMBER Alert unless we confirm she's actually been abducted but if we don't find her within the next hour…" Brent ran his hands through his hair. "Look, I know you're both worried sick but I have deputies spread out all over these grounds. Just sit tight for, let's say, another hour. Give me an hour. If we haven't found her by then, say ten-thirty, I'll organize an official volunteer search and rescue…put out the AMBER Alert."

Ethan closed his mind to the conversation and studied his immediate surroundings. Drawn to an area of meadow some forty yards beyond the picnic tables, he left his father and brother and began to trek east along the path. The ground cover here was sparse but once you reached the meadow, tall grass, easily over three feet high, could hide a small child from view especially from the picnic grounds.

When the wind picked up right off the ocean, lifting loose hair off his forehead and sent the grasses bending and swaying in the breeze, he squatted down at what he estimated might be a three-year-old's perspective. The tall grass looked a bit daunting. He didn't think she'd be tempted to venture that way. Looking right, off to the east, he noted the rows and rows of neatly planted vegetable gardens laden green with their produce. He ruled that area out as well.

He took off north toward the hillside dotted with an array of wild-growing white brodiaea and golden mariposa lily in the distance. The blossoms would surely attract a small girl who wanted nothing more than to pick a fistful of flowers for her mother.

He headed that way at a healthy pace.

With his long legs in a matter of minutes he soon passed the fields of flowers and reached the gentle slope of the foothills. Here the area was less bursting in bloom and covered more with thick underbrush lining the trails.

Coyote bush, thimbleberry, wild blackberry vines, California buckthorn, and poison hemlock grew prevalent here. The scent of eucalyptus was also strong. The smell might soothe a small child in distress who knew she'd wandered off too far and didn't know how to find her way back.

He stopped and cocked his head to listen.

And heard the faint sounds of a whimpering child. Heading in the direction of what he thought was a drainage basin, he tried to remember what the parents had called their daughter. Allison? Yeah, it had been Allison.

He decided to try that and called out, "Allison? Allison, are you out here?"

The whimpering became a wail. As Ethan drew closer to a pile of dirt, he saw a flash of pink and white and a bobbing head. He looked down into a simple drainage ditch, what must have been a cavernous deep hole to a small child of three but in reality was surrounded by little more than a four-foot pile of loose soil that would be impossibly difficult for a child of her size to climb out of without a great deal of effort. She'd somehow managed to fall into the ditch but couldn't figure how to get out.

Even standing up she was hidden to anyone who had been within a few feet. Wearing a pink top with a little princess graphic on it and a pair of dirty white pants, she sat in a puddle with her arms already outstretched in the air ready to be picked up. It looked as though she had wet herself. There was a huge stain around the front and bottom of her pants where the dirt was at its worst. Her brown hair, once tied neatly back in matching dog ears, had burrs sticking to several strands that had come loose and hung off to the side of her head.

She stuck an incredibly dirty finger in her mouth and demanded, "Ma-ma. Ma-ma, I want my ma-ma."

Ethan scaled the four-foot drop off, by mostly sliding down on his rear end to scoop her up. "Come on baby, come up to me and I'll get you to your mama. Your mama and daddy are waiting for you to have a picnic. They've been real worried about you. Are you ready to get yourself some lemonade?"

When she bobbed her head up and down in response, Ethan did his best to calm her down and get those big eyes to stop their flow of tears.

Brent was just about to organize the volunteer search and rescue when he spotted his brother walking through the grassy meadow toward the picnic tables. Relief swelled up inside as he saw what Ethan carried in his arms.

"Mr. and Mrs. Wyatt, would that be your little girl there?" When the couple looked up and spotted Ethan carrying their baby, they broke off in a run. "That's her! Oh my God you found her! Oh Allison, baby, mama's so glad to see you. Where've you been? You had us all worried sick."

Ethan relinquished the little girl to her mother. "She might have some poison oak, maybe a tick or two, but I think she'll be fine. If she were mine, I'd have the doc take a look at her just to be on the safe side though."

Ethan walked up to where his father and brother stood in the middle of the picnic grounds to applause from the other bystanders. His brother slapped him on the back. "Little brother, I don't know how you manage to do that, but I'm damned glad you do it. Where was she?"

"Drainage ditch about forty yards off one of the secondary trails. And I just tried to think like a three-year-old," Ethan replied, grinning broadly.

His father shook his head. "The little girl's soul guided Ethan to her. He had more of a connection with her than I had. If only the both of you would embrace your heritage without worrying about what others think, you'd be better off." With that, Markus Cody turned on his heels and headed to his car. Suddenly he stopped and turned, aimed a finger at his sons. "And your mother expects both of you for supper this evening. You better not disappoint her."

While Ethan played local hero, Hayden busied herself doing laundry in Jordan's enormous laundry room the same size as her kitchen back in Chicago. When her prepaid cell phone rang a little after eleven o'clock, the digital readout told her the number belonged to her sister, Sydney.

"Hey sis, the realtor called. She thinks she has an interested buyer for your condo. They've gone so far as to make an offer."

"That's great. How long does she think it will be before closing? I could really use the money. I've got my eye on a little house here."

"You're kidding. I talked to Mom this morning. She told me all about you settling down in Bird Pointe USA, wherever that is. You're really doing this then?"

"Pelican Pointe," Hayden corrected. "And I don't have much of a choice, Syd. I've traveled over three thousand miles, changed my name, got a new ID, all so I can fly under the radar. I'm in too deep now to go back."

"I know. But I wish you'd slow down a bit. You might not even like living in such a tiny little town. A move from Chicago to Podunk USA is a drastic change. You're as urban as anyone I know. All I ask is be careful. Small towns aren't quite what they're cracked up to be."

Sydney paused before adding the bad news, "And there was a man asking one of my neighbors about you this morning. She says he's been lurking around for several days."

Hayden's stomach dropped. "What did he look like?"

"I don't know. Sheila Somers, my neighbor, said he looked foreign, whatever that means, spoke with some kind of an accent. She said he'd been stalking around my apartment the past few days. I've been picking up extra shifts at the hospital, so I haven't been home much. Then when I'm here, I sleep. But this guy apparently caught up with Sheila coming out of the building and pointblank asked if I had anyone staying with me. It gives me the creeps to know someone is watching me to get to you. I'd call the police but what good would it do? They aren't interested in potential crimes, only ones that have already happened. If I make a report do you think they'd even take it seriously?"

"I doubt it. I'm sorry, Sydney. I never meant for any of this to affect you and Mom like it has. If I could rewrite history, you know I would."

"Don't be ridiculous. None of this is your fault. That slime bag Jeremy is the one to blame."

Hayden knew men weren't exactly high on Sydney's favorite people on the planet list right now, especially since she'd fallen for a doctor, a surgeon, who had no desire to stop his philandering ways in order to settle down with her sister.

Knowing that prompted Hayden to ask, "How are things with Stephen?"

"Stephen is a jackass. I'm not wasting any more time on a man who can't keep his pants zipped. I caught him nuzzling the new resident in the medicine supply room last week. The man hasn't a faithful bone in his body. Well, except for the bone he likes to use on new conquests."

Hayden snorted at that. "That's my girl. Don't give the jerk the time of day. He doesn't deserve you, Syd. He never did. I know your job's difficult being around him all the time, but you hang in there."

They talked a few more minutes before Hayden reluctantly hung up. She sadly checked the few minutes she had remaining on her phone. She'd have to boost it up before making or taking any more phone calls even though she more than likely needed to call her mother and warn her that someone might be nosing around, yet again.

She also needed to open a checking account. And get a California driver's license. And she wanted to show Jordan the little yellow bungalow and get her take on it. Why couldn't Jeremy leave her and her family the hell alone? Why did life have to be so messed up?

For Edmund Taggert life wasn't just messed up it was about to come to an end. He had just plopped down with a beer in front of the television set he and his wife, Ruby, had bought at Sears Roebuck in 1975, seven years before she had died. He'd lived alone ever since and never remarried, never even looked around after Ruby. Once you found the woman, the one you wanted to spend the rest of your life with, you didn't settle for a substitute even if the life you'd planned together had been all too brief. At least, Edmund didn't.

After a full day tending to his personal little patch of garden twenty feet from his back porch, he was flat tuckered out. It was one thing to produce enough organic fruits and vegetables and milk for half the county. That's why he had Will Foley to manage the farm. But he still took great pride in growing his very own plot of lettuce and tomatoes, even though doing so these days seemed to take everything out of him.

He ignored the tingling in his arm until the pain increased. When it moved to his chest and felt as if a vise gripped him there, he had difficulty taking the next breath. But when the pain tightened around his entire upper body, had a hold on him and wouldn't let go, he did his best to stand to get to the phone. He managed to take a few steps toward the end table not four feet away.

And collapsed in a heap on the floor, clutching his shirt.

How is it, Ethan wondered, that his mother, Lindeen Cody, could be such an angelic petite woman, so loving and kind one minute and so downright sneaky the next? He glanced across the room at the devious little sprite known as his mom, all five-feet-two inches of her and watched her busily whip up mashed potatoes for dinner.

He had little doubt the woman was up to her matchmaking tricks again. The minute his dad had opened the front door of the Craftsman-style house he'd grown up in, the second he'd spotted the effervescent Julianne Dickinson standing in Lindeen's kitchen helping her chop vegetables for dinner, he knew.

What he couldn't figure out was who Julianne was there for. With any luck, his sly, scheming mother had aimed her in Brent's direction.

Even though Brent had a failed marriage in his past, the one time in his life the guy had used poor judgment about anything; Brent was in fact just as single as Ethan—and was older. The way Ethan saw it since Brent was pushing forty and was the more desperate of the two in the woman department and as far as he knew wasn't getting any luckier on that score, he'd let Brent have good ol' Julianne.

In fact, he'd wager that Brent hadn't gone near a female in probably two years. Mainly, because the woman he'd been married to and divorced had done such a number on him, cheating on him while he had served in Iraq, getting pregnant with someone else's baby, and then lying about it. Throw in the fact that she hadn't even bothered telling him until he'd walked in the front door to surprise her, unannounced, excited about being stateside and home, laden down with flowers and caught her in the act, belly out to there, at least seven months gone, with another man in her bed.

Brent had understandably been devastated. And had refused to talk about the scene ever since.

Last Ethan knew Brent was still into abstinence, which made him all the more suspicious that Julianne was meant for him. If so, he'd just have to tell his mom that he'd met someone, someone he couldn't stop thinking about, and that when he kissed that someone, she had left him on fire for the next kiss. He hadn't felt like this before, not exactly like this anyway.

In fact, the only reason he'd come to dinner tonight was not out of heeding his dad's loose warning not to disappoint his mother, but because his someone had had to work tonight. So, it only seemed right that Ethan could rack up a few extra points with his mom for showing up for supper.

"Ethan, why don't you go in the living room and put on some music for Julianne? That group you like so much that Pearl Group. Better still, why don't you go get your guitar and play that song you love so much, the romantic one."

Okay, any time his mother requested that he drag out his guitar and play Black by Pearl Jam told Ethan he needed to take matters into his own hands—and fast.

The minute he saw Julianne point her dazzling smile his way, Ethan decided it was time to thwart the setup. He had nothing against the cute little brown-haired, doe-eyed Julianne. No, he liked her just fine. But the idea of his mother fixing him up with anyone at this point in his life put a ding in his pride. So when he spotted Brent heading into the kitchen, Ethan went to work.

Draping his arm around his brother's shoulders, Ethan stated, "Julianne, did you know this big guy here devotes his time off to helping underprivileged kids down at the Boys and Girls Clubs." Since Julianne had been teaching first graders for more than five years now, Ethan knew she had a soft spot for kids. The kid angle would definitely be the right button to headline Brent's stellar qualities.

"Yep, whether winter or spring, Brent's there making sure they have shoes for school, or a Christmas tree complete with a few toys he collects at the sheriff's department every year. Personally collects. Think of that, the sheriff here takes the time to make sure the kids have a great Christmas. And that's not all, nope not for this big guy, he sees to it each kid is safely tucked into an after school program, so they don't run wild and get into trouble."

For good measure, Ethan decided to go for broke. "Brent even makes sure Meals-On-Wheels never misses any of the elderly."

In the way of brothers, Brent eyed Ethan with enough disdain to show he was on to him and that he'd pay him back in spades, when he wasn't looking, even if the payback occurred in his sleep when he least expected it.

But then, Ethan's pager went off.

Brent, as dark and tall as his brother, gave him a wide grin full of smug satisfaction.

"Damn it, I'm off duty."

"Were," Brent reminded him quietly. "Technically, you're on call, little brother, there's a difference." He leaned over to whisper in Ethan's ear. "But if you've taken a shine to the lovely Julianne, I'll gladly sacrifice my Saturday night in the name of true love and take the call, make sure you and Julianne get to spend some quality time together."

Ethan rolled his eyes in a screw-you fashion. Some decision, Ethan thought, as he reached for the kitchen phone and dialed dispatch.

"Bite me," he muttered to his brother before the dispatcher could answer. He made a few notes and after a few minutes, hung up, his good mood gone. "I've got a DB at the Taggert farm. Looks like Edmund Taggert died this evening. His farm manager, Will Foley found him. Sorry, Mom, I'll need a rain check on dinner. I've got to head back to Pelican Pointe."

And with that, for the second time that day, Ethan Cody went to work.

It took over an hour for Pierce Hamlin, the forty-five-year-old coroner out of Santa Cruz to make the trip to

Taggert Organic Farms to tell Ethan what he pretty much already knew. It looked like Edmund Taggert had died of a heart attack. There was no sign of foul play, no sign of external trauma. The TV was still on. An open bottle of beer was left on the coffee table as if he'd just sat down for a relaxing evening in front of the tube.

"We'll do an autopsy if you want. But it's a safe bet he died of a heart attack. You'll notify the next of kin, or you want me to?"

"I don't think the old man had any family, at least none that I ever heard about. He and his wife never had any kids. But I'll get in touch with his lawyer, make certain. Edmund once told me that he and my grandmother went out once back in high school." The idea of Autumn Lassiter and Edmund Taggert dating had Ethan chuckling, remembering the conversation.

"Well, I guess that means you could've been his grandson. The lawyer would likely be old Aaron Hartley then. He's what, seventy-five if he's a day, older than the deceased that's for sure."

"And the only lawyer in Pelican Pointe." That brought him full circle. He just realized Nick and Jordan were right. This town was sorely in need of some new blood, since seventy percent of the residents were well over the age of fifty.

How long had the town been dying? he wondered, as he went outside in search of Will, who had been badly shaken up over finding Taggert dead. But as he explained to Will what would happen next, things like the autopsy, how he would take care of getting in touch with Edmund's lawyer, something about the old man's death sent him a reality check.

Maybe that was what Jordan had meant the other day. How much old blood had to die off before Pelican Pointe simply dried up and there was no town left at all?

His mother had a fondness for Pelican Pointe. She'd grown up here as Lindeen Lassiter. He'd visited her mother, his grandmother, Autumn Lassiter, countless times over the years. The town had been at death's door even then. He remembered how several of those storefronts along Ocean Street across from the house where he now lived hadn't seen an occupant in his lifetime.

One had been the old fish hatchery. It had sat empty for two decades. That is, until Perry Altman, a chef, swung through the area on his way to Napa Valley one weekend and decided he could turn the space into his own five-star restaurant. The Pointe had been open for three years now.

Ethan suddenly realized there were no hordes of people lining up to repopulate a little town that hadn't truly thrived since the sixties. It took people like Perry and Murphy, who had turned an old shell of a mercantile, into Murphy's Market so the town didn't have to go traipsing off to Santa Cruz or San Sebastian every time they needed butter or eggs.

Pulling out of the driveway of the farm onto the road, he knew he needed to make a stop next door to tell Nick and Jordan the news.

He couldn't help but think the two were on to something. Maybe a way to revitalize the town from the dead was to make it more attractive to newcomers. And this realization had come after he'd been so suspicious about Hayden's staying in Pelican Pointe.

When he knocked on the door of the B & B, it was Nick who answered and then led the way into the kitchen where Jordan was about to dole out dishes of ice cream. The moment she spotted Ethan she immediately wanted to know, "What's wrong? Is Hayden all right?"

Ethan took it from there and told them what had happened.

Sitting around the Harris table, Ethan noticed Jordan took the news harder than Nick.

"We got off to a bad start, him and me. When I first got here all he did was come over to complain, wouldn't even sit down and drink a cup of coffee with Scott or me. But last spring, thanks to Nick, the old man had a complete change of heart."

"The same time the rest of Pelican Pointe did," Nick finished. "But the last five months, Edmund was a fixture here and vice versa. For some reason, he bugged me to take an interest in his farm. I had to eventually tell him I didn't know squat about cows or farming. Which makes me wonder what the heck Will Foley is going to do now? He's been working on that farm since he was a kid."

Ethan nodded. "He and Francine both. You know, those two got married right there on the grounds, had the ceremony not far from the main house. Then held the reception outside in Edmund's garden. The whole town came. Hell, they still live in the original cabin Taggert's father built back in 1910. When I left just now, they were both pretty torn up."

"I hope Will and Francine understand how much Kent Springer will be chomping at the bit to get at that piece of property," Nick surmised.

"Everyone in town knew what Kent almost did to get hold of Promise Cove. Edmund was no dummy. He was fully aware Springer was interested in Taggert Farms. But Springer has his own problems. His trial starts on Tuesday."

"Yeah, I know and I can't wait for the DA to call me to testify against him either."

"Who will handle the funeral arrangements?" Jordan asked Ethan.

"I put a call into Aaron Hartley but no one answered. I'll take a run by his house after I leave here. He's always been Edmund's lawyer. But if you ask me, Taggert probably left the details to Will and Francine."

About that time, the three of them heard a car pull into the driveway.

"That'll be Hayden coming in from work," Jordan informed them.

Damn. Ethan had hoped to stop in at the Diner on his way home and get something to eat. Glancing at his watch, he realized it was almost ten o'clock. The night had somehow gotten away from him.

They heard a light tap at the back door. Through the glass, they all spotted Hayden at the same time.

It was Ethan who got up to let her in.

"I saw your truck in the driveway. What's going on? Is everyone all right?"

Ethan told her the news. All Hayden saw was pure grief on the faces of Nick and Jordan. Her heart went out to them. "Well, no one in town heard about it, that's for sure. Otherwise, it would've been all over the Diner. Instead they were all talking about Kent Springer's upcoming trial starting Tuesday morning."

Because of that gossip she'd gotten a dismal description of the guy's character, which pretty much rubber-stamped what Jordan and Ethan had said about the man.

Hayden watched as Jordan could barely keep her eyes open. But in spite of that fact, ever the hostess, she asked Ethan, "Have you had anything to eat tonight? I could fix you a sandwich."

But before Ethan could answer, Hayden laid a hand on his arm. "It's been a long day for everyone. Nick looks tired and Jordan looks like she's about to drop. How about we get out of their hair, Ethan?"

"Good idea. I need to take a swing by Aaron's place anyway before it gets much later." Or he might just have to wait until morning.

When they were standing outside along the garden path, Hayden turned to Ethan. "If you're hungry I have some of Jordan's leftover chicken upstairs. You're welcome to come up."

"I'd love to but..." Did he really need to stop by Hartley's place tonight? "If I could use your phone, I'll call..."

"I don't have a landline."

"What do you do for a phone?"

"I use a cell."

"You really need to have a landline out here. It's a ways from town. And cell service isn't always reliable this far out."

"So I've noticed. But if I need a phone, I can always walk across the courtyard and use one at the B & B."

His face creased into a frown. "But there might come a time when you need a phone up in that studio apartment."

Geez, thought Hayden, were they going to stand around all night and talk about telephones?

As if he read her mind he moved into her personal space, tilted his head down and took her mouth. At first, the kiss was just a light brushing of lips but then Ethan sought more and plunged deeper, tugging and nipping.

"You've got the lip lock down for sure."

"I'm not too bad horizontal, either."

"Why, Deputy Dawg, I do believe you're bragging. That's so—beneath you."

"No, beneath me is where I want you." He moved his eyebrows up and down.

"Brash, Deputy Dawg. But I'm not quite ready to do the bedroll boogie just yet. Besides, I'm starving. You coming up for cold chicken, or hoping to get a better offer?"

With his arms still locked around her, he replied, "Hmm, decisions, decisions. But if there's no chance in getting you horizontal, I'll have to settle for the food." He'd just have to make it to Aaron Hartley's place in the morning. Sunday morning. Another chunk of his weekend fell away, a part he'd hoped to spend at his laptop filling up blank pages with clever and witty characters of his own making. Ah well...

"Good because the invite has a short shelf life, probably shorter than the chicken."

Just then, past Ethan's left shoulder Hayden spotted a figure walking their way. She nudged Ethan around and pointed. "Take a look. Tell me you don't see that."

Ethan followed her gaze toward the other end of the quad, which was a good forty yards away. Sure enough, there among the cypress trees stood Scott Phillips, dressed in shorts and a long sleeved shirt rolled up at the elbows, he had his hands in his pockets.

Ethan had to remind himself that Scott Phillips had been killed instantly in Iraq some eighteen months earlier when an IED had blown up his Humvee. Yet, here he was walking big as life among the hollyhocks and hydrangeas.

Automatically, Ethan lifted his arm in a wave and watched as Scott miraculously waved back, all smiles. The hairs at the back of Ethan's neck stood up. Just because he had Native blood running through his veins and a strong belief in spirits didn't stop the shock and awe at the sight of watching a dead man stroll the grounds.

The cop in him wanted to grab a video camera for validation, evidence, even the camera in his cell phone would do. But the shaman in him wanted to grab the pipe and celebrate. He finally found his voice. "Doesn't it bother you, Hayden, to see that?"

"How could it bother me? Look at him, Ethan. He looks like a happy-go-lucky kind of guy without a care in the world, at peace. Now, if he were chasing me with a machete, I'd be screaming loud enough for them to hear me all the way to Santa Cruz. How about you?"

"I'm okay. But just so you know, after that," he nodded his head in Scott's direction. "I may need some form of alcohol to go with the chicken."

Chapter Eight

"**S**o what can you tell me about Scott Phillips before he started haunting the B & B?"

Ethan and Hayden were stretched out on the floor in front of the sagging green sofa eating cold chicken and pasta salad like they were on a picnic.

"You already know most of his background. Nice guy though, never heard him say a mean word to anyone. He grew up here, since he was five. If he's angry that Nick's taken his place here, it sure doesn't show on his face."

"I don't think that's it," Hayden said as she thumbed through the book about ghosts Ethan had loaned her. "It's more like he's here to protect, maybe offer advice to his family. But that wouldn't explain why he never shows himself to Jordan. She was his wife. If he loved her shouldn't he be bugging her?"

"That is kind of strange."

"For her, too. She's hurt because of it. I can tell."

"How far into the book did you get?"

"Enough to know that what happened out in the courtyard where both of us saw Scott at the exact same time is known as a collective apparition."

Reading the book over Hayden's shoulder, he commented, "You know, Pelican Pointe has its own paranormal expert. You should talk to him."

"You're kidding."

"Nope. His name's Wade Hawkins, retired history professor. Word has it he's writing a book about ghosts in general, not specifically those he's discovered inhabiting in or around Pelican Pointe, although he's found a few. He even invested in a couple of electronic boxes with all these sensors and gizmos he uses when he visits places he thinks are haunted. And he's been out here before."

"And found what?"

"Not sure. But I'll make a point to ask him next time I see him. Maybe I'll stop by his place after I see old man Hartley. You know, when I was over at Taggert's farm tonight it dawned on me that what Jordan and Nick are trying to do about getting new blood into this town is an excellent idea. The population of Pelican Pointe is starting to age. Considerably. It's actually a good idea to bring in some fresh faces."

"That's why I'm here. If not for Jordan— She's the one who convinced me. We're even trying to find a place to open up a used bookstore in town."

Ethan looked shocked at that. "You really are planning to hang around here? What if—? The person you're running from…shows up?"

"There's a good chance he won't find me."

"But there are no guarantees."

"No, there are none, I'm afraid."

To get that pained look off her face, he changed the subject. "And you'd run it? This bookstore? Did you find a place?"

"As a matter of fact I found a house across from the pier that might work. It's near where you live. The plan is to drag Jordan there to look at it on my day off, either tomorrow or Monday."

He wanted to ask her which house had caught her eye, but the cop in him took another path. "I don't want you to think I'm interrogating you, but…" He wouldn't know the answer until he asked. "Do you have that kind of money to start a business?"

"No. Not until my condo sells. And I told them both that right up front. But if I can find the right property, Nick's willing to put the lease in his name, pay some of the startup costs." She explained about all the books that Jordan and Nick said they had taking up space in storage.

"From what they tell me, some of the books are just gathering dust. When you stop and think about it, it's ready made inventory. The closest bookstore is San Sebastian. I looked it up online. Why should people in Pelican Pointe drive all that way there to buy their books? And there's no library in town. So a bookstore might—"

"This condo, it isn't in Nevada, is it?"

Hayden put down the chicken she'd been nibbling. This was getting eerily close to being a cross-examination. "No. Look, I promised Nick I'd keep him up-to-date with my situation. I don't want any harm coming to these people because of me, Ethan. The less any of you know about…things, the better. That's all I'm willing to say about it."

"So you think by not talking about it, by keeping things to yourself, you can keep whoever's after you at bay, keep them from finding you? Is that it? That isn't the way things work in the real world, Hayden. In fact, it's downright stupid to think like that. The bad guys will go to any lengths at their disposal to…to track you down."

"So, now I'm stupid? Well, thanks for your vote of confidence, Deputy Dawg, but you don't know a thing about it."

"That's right, I don't and whose fault is that? All you have to do is say the word, let me in the loop, and I'll find the guy who has you on the run."

Hayden got to her feet. "And do what? Put him in jail? Really? Just like that? The big, bad-ass Ethan Cody can do what the—" She'd almost said the feds but caught herself just in time.

"As law enforcement I have a slew of tools at my disposal, Hayden. I can find things out just by making inquiries. In fact, I could have run you through the computer but I held off—" Those words had slipped out and he couldn't take them back. The look on her face said she was way past boiling mad.

She wanted to belt him. "Make inquiries? Who's stopping you? Go ahead. That's all so convenient for you law enforcement types, isn't it? We're just considered collateral to people like you, a name and number in some computer database. You guys stake us out there in some fake world like lambs to slaughter as bait, making promises you can't keep, willing to say anything and promise everything to get us to do what you want us to do just to get a conviction, just to close a case. Well, I'm having no part of it. I'm not willing to give up my life just to help solve a stupid case. Now get out!"

When he continued to just sit there, she yelled again, "Get out, Ethan! I don't want you here." She whirled on her heels and ran into the bathroom and slammed the door hard enough that it rattled the panes of glass in the old windows.

For a guy who was supposed to have three days off duty, Ethan had spent the weekend cruising all over Pelican Pointe and then some. Come Sunday morning he'd already spent an hour at Aaron Hartley's place letting him know about Edmund Taggert and another hour with Wade Hawkins.

He'd been deluding himself that either stop could be done in less than fifteen minutes. But that was a small town for you.

Aaron Hartley had wanted to reminisce about his old friend. So Ethan had been forced to drink a half a gallon of coffee to wash down the canned cinnamon rolls Aaron had baked while he listened to the old lawyer walk down memory lane, which pretty much included thirty years of friendship between Aaron and Edmund.

With Wade Hawkins he'd gotten into a quagmire by getting him started talking about the paranormal. Ethan had listened to how each spirit was different and why it remained earthbound long after death. All of which was pretty obvious to Ethan. Without mentioning any names, though, Ethan had learned Wade was adamant about one thing. Most ghosts hung around because they had unfinished business on earth and weren't ready to leave for a range of reasons.

Ethan agreed. Scott Phillips definitely seemed to be patrolling the grounds of his childhood home with a purpose, guarding it for reasons of his own.

Before he left though, Wade had confirmed that he'd taken his sensors out to the cove's Victorian on two occasions and both times his electronic gadgets had soared off the charts.

Ethan didn't know anything about sensors, but he knew what he'd seen the night before. Scott Phillips wasn't giving up his life at the cove without a fight.

When he'd left Wade's, Ethan decided to make a trip over to Santa Cruz. It was time to use the county computer for official business and run the name Hayden Ryan through NCIC.

He had hesitated doing so before now. But last night she had pissed him off.

So now he settled back, got comfortable in his confining eight-by-eight, closet-sized cubicle. A tiny space, for which he was very grateful he didn't have to spend a lot of time in and waited for the results that would maybe explain why Hayden-no-middle-initial-Ryan was hiding from some asshole from her past.

When the search ended, he stared at the computer screen. Zero hits. Not in California or the other forty-nine states. Okay, she wasn't a wanted felon. That was something, he guessed. At least he wasn't attracted to a criminal.

But the woman was hiding something, on the run from someone.

Damn it. He scrubbed a hand over his face. She'd already hinted at that much. He was no closer to knowing her secrets than he had been before. So much for his psychic gift. She was giving off other more potent kinds of vibes distracting him.

That was the problem.

Or maybe he was just too attracted to this particular subject. Subject. She had accused law enforcement of thinking of her as bait, nothing more than a name and number. By running her through the system hadn't he just proved her right?

He was brooding into his third cup of coffee when he looked up from his desk and saw Brent leaning against the doorjamb, staring at him. "Glad to see you're such a dedicated officer, little brother. That you'd give up a Sunday and come in on your day off is—extraordinary." It wasn't like Ethan at all. Brent knew something was up, he just didn't know specifics, at least not yet. "What brings you into the office today?"

Did Ethan want to confide in his brother, the sheriff and his immediate supervisor, about the suspicious newcomer he had living in Pelican Pointe? Did he want Brent knowing he had gotten so cynical about dating, he was running criminal background checks on a prospective love interest? Hell, no.

Instead, Ethan went into the short version of how he'd spent the last two days.

Hayden slept late. After blowing up at Ethan the night before, she'd been so mad she'd tossed and turned and hadn't been able to settle down until after four in the morning. Looking over at the clock, it was almost ten.

She crawled out of bed to start a pot of coffee before jumping in the shower.

As the water sluiced over her skin, she refused to feel guilty for the argument. Since she'd first laid eyes on the man he'd been incredibly suspicious. Despite their attraction to each other, despite the heat-melting kisses they'd shared. Nope, there was no hope for them as a couple anyway as long as Ethan refused to accept who she was.

But who was she really? Emile Reed no longer existed. She'd morphed into Hayden Ryan. She was standing right here, essentially the same person. Damn it. She'd spent a good deal of money to make sure Emile disappeared. And yet, after all that, it had taken Ethan Cody two seconds on the side of the road for him to become her judge and jury and distrust Hayden Ryan on sight.

As she dried off she decided she should have stuck to the lie. She never should have admitted anything. Or clarified that it wasn't an ex or an abusive relationship for that matter. How the hell was she supposed to be good at this sort of thing? She wasn't the criminal here. Or a liar by nature. She was an accountant for chrissakes.

She dressed in jeans and a cropped sweater, poured herself a cup of coffee and got down the bread from the cabinet. She stuck two pieces into the toaster and got out the blackberry jam from the fridge.

Why should she spend a single minute more thinking about that blockhead Ethan Cody? Just because he could kiss better than any man she'd ever known was no reason to put herself at risk of making a mistake, a mistake that could surely cost her, her life. So she would just forget about Deputy Cody. She'd made the decision to start over here in Pelican Pointe rather than Santa Cruz. Look at the friends she'd made here. Nick and Jordan were the upside while Deputy Dawg was proving to top the list in the down column.

Since she had two days off, she mentally sorted through all the things she needed to get done by Tuesday. Priority one was to boost up her prepaid cell phone. Because Murphy's Market didn't carry the kind of card it used, she'd have to find another supplier or ask Murphy if he would order the cards for her.

But ordering the cards would take time. She needed to be able to make calls and receive them from her mother and Sydney in the event they needed to contact her. She decided to drive over to San Sebastian and look around.

Maybe while she was there she'd check out the bookstore she'd found over the Internet. She'd spent some time on Jordan's computer surfing the Web while waiting for her laundry to dry. The San Sebastian bookstore was the closest one to Pelican Pointe, which if memory served was a good forty-five miles away.

If she intended to follow through on seeing the bookstore become a reality here though, she needed to scope out the competition. Should she put that off until Monday since the bookstore might not be open on a Sunday? If her cell phone had more minutes on it, she'd phone them and ask. But then she decided the trip to San Sebastian could wait until Monday when she could also stop by the First Bank of Pelican Pointe on her way out of town and open up a checking account.

That meant she had all day to herself, a day to do with whatever she felt like.

She took her toast over to the little ice cream table and opened the windows on the ocean side of the studio to let in some fresh air.

The urge to get outside and take advantage of the beautiful day hit her twofold.

At the prospect of getting outside, she hurried to finish breakfast.

She dug out her backpack, crammed a power bar into the contents along with her small thermos filled with the leftover coffee, a couple bottles of water, and the romance novel she hadn't yet finished that she'd picked up in Reno.

Even though she was only headed down to the cove and the beach, she laced up the used pair of Asolo Styngers she'd found at a thrift store in Colorado. It was too chilly to wear sandals anyway and if the mood hit her to explore farther, she'd be prepared. Besides, she couldn't possibly walk very far in the canvas sneakers she had. She grabbed her sunglasses, making sure she had her digital camera and compass, and headed down the stairs and out into the brilliant sunshine.

Despite the fact guests had spent the weekend at the B & B, Hayden found the cove deserted, which suited her mood. Then she remembered that they would probably be checking out today to get back to the Bay. Suddenly she felt amazingly lucky to be here at this spot, enjoying this view, during this time of year. She was no longer a tourist where her time here was limited. If she wanted to she could stay parked in this same spot watching the tides for an hour, or six.

She got up to walk along the water's edge and wondered if any of the guests had seen Scott during their weekend stay. How would one approach a guest about that? Would seeing a ghost bring in more people or chase them away?

Just as she was about to make herself comfortable on a rock jutting out over the water, she spotted a dark opening to a narrow cavern. Curious, Hayden took off her backpack and wandered over, tentatively peering inside. The area was a naturally formed sea cave perhaps ten feet wide that snaked into the dark, damp space another twenty feet back.

A dinghy, moored with a rope and tied to a spiky natural stone, bobbed up and down precariously against the side wall of the smooth rock formation as it met the shallow inlet.

The longer she stayed here, the more enchanted she found this place. She made a mental note to ask Jordan if she could take the little boat out next week.

She went back to the water's edge to scan the horizon. For a few minutes she was tempted to untie the dinghy and take it out anyway to explore the dot of land in the distance. But when she realized it had been years since she'd rowed anything other than a machine parked in a gym, she decided her arms might not be up to the task.

Glumly, she went back to reading the novel. After forty-five minutes though, sitting on a rock trying to read, she gave up and climbed back up to the top of the cliff. It wasn't the author's fault she couldn't get into the book. The argument with Ethan still nagged at her.

But once she started back to the studio, she discovered she wasn't ready to spend her day off sitting inside four walls. She decided to check out more of the area. Following the natural curve of the cliffs, she walked along as close to the edge as safety allowed until she spotted a trail snaking off further south. She took out her compass and set off to do some exploring on her own.

It had been years since Illinois-girl-Emile-slash-Hayden had hiked anything other than the mall. After walking for almost an hour along a narrow sliver of path full of underbrush and some kind of wild tangled vines full of ripe berries, she realized she should bone up on what kind of vegetation grew in this part of the state.

If she was going to make this area home, if she planned on getting back into hiking and enjoying nature on a regular basis, she would need to know more about the flora and maybe even the fauna indigenous to this part of coastal California.

When she happened upon a field of wildflowers that looked to her like Indian paintbrush, she dug out her camera. Staggered by the sheer beauty and dazzling colors of what nature provided, Hayden took photos from every angle she could manage.

It wasn't until she decided to find some place to sit down and eat her power bar that she realized all the walking had caused her underused muscles to burn in protest. Good thing she hadn't dragged out that dinghy and set off trying to row through the tides. But as tired as her legs were, she was too excited about the prospect of being outdoors, about being a part of nature again to care much about her sore limbs.

Instead, she spotted a flat rock and sat down, peeled off the wrapper of her power bar. She drank, now lukewarm coffee, from her thermos. As she ate her meager lunch, she caught the scent of eucalyptus and began looking around for the source. She tried to remember what eucalyptus looked like but when nothing came to mind gave up and simply followed her nose. Sure enough, she found a field of eucalyptus trees where wild sage and fragrant rosemary grew waist-high in abundance. She took out her camera again.

After a while, after drinking all the coffee in her thermos, she needed to pee. So she began looking around for a place to take care of business.

Back at the B & B, Nick and Jordan had said goodbye to their weekend guests several hours earlier and there was still no sign of Hayden. Her car was parked in the driveway as it had been all morning. Knowing she had wanted to make a trip into town to look at the house for the potential location of the bookstore, Jordan was more than a little concerned. She had already tried knocking on Hayden's door three times but had gotten no answer, which is the major reason she'd opened the door and peeked inside. She'd checked the bathroom just in case Hayden had fallen in the shower and hit her head. But the bathroom had been empty. Jordan found her clothes still hanging in the armoire and tucked away neatly in the drawers of the chest. So she hadn't packed up and left during the night.

Jordan thought it looked like she'd made a pot of coffee and eaten breakfast. She wasn't sure what she should do. What if the person she was running from had found her here and taken her against her will?

Jordan flew out of the studio and met Nick in the courtyard. "She isn't up there. What if someone's kidnapped her?"

"Jordan, we didn't hear a disturbance of any kind. Maybe she's down at the cove," he reasoned. "You go back to the house. I'll go take a look."

But Nick hadn't found her at the cove.

Back in the kitchen, Nick and Jordan sat at the counter going over several theories. "Maybe she and Ethan hooked up." Nick took out a fat, apple-oatmeal cookie from the jar sitting on the kitchen counter. "After all, Ethan was here when we went to bed last night. Maybe they…"

"Then he would have spent the night here, Nick. There's a bed in the apartment."

"A very comfortable one, too." Nick's eyes lit up. "You know, now that I think about it, we never actually christened that bed."

Despite her worry, Jordan laughed and poked him in the ribs. "You're unbelievable. We've christened practically every bed in every room of this house and you're zeroing in on the one we didn't get around to?" She chewed on a nail. "Nick, do you think I should call Ethan in an official capacity? Should I let him know we haven't seen her? What if…?"

Knowing his wife, Nick knew Jordan wouldn't rest until they'd contacted Ethan. "Do you want me to call and tactfully ask him if she's with him?"

Jordan perked up. "Would you? That'd be great, you know, man-to-man."

Nick grinned and reached for the kitchen phone. "I'll call his house. Makes it less official that way." After the third ring, Ethan picked up. "Hello."

"Ethan, it's Nick Harris. Are you off-duty?"

"I'm never off-duty in a town this size, Nick. What's up?" He got a vibe that told him this call was somehow concerning Hayden. Sure enough, Nick's next comment confirmed it.

"Uh, would Hayden happen to be with you at the moment?"

"No, why?"

"It's strange. She and Jordan were supposed to go into town today. It's almost five o'clock and we haven't seen her or heard from her all day. Her car's still parked in the driveway. But there's no answer at the apartment. Her things are still inside." He wondered if he should mention that she might have someone after her. To cover all the bases, he decided honesty now should come first. "And… I think she might have someone looking for her, Ethan."

Ethan rubbed his forehead as his head began to pound. "Yeah. I know. She wasn't real specific and got very upset with me last night when I tried to get her to open up about it. Look, I'll be there in twenty minutes." With that, he hung up and went to get his badge and gun.

Even though her muscles ached Hayden was in her element. A good three miles into her hike, she discovered the back entrance to a cemetery called Eternal Gardens. Walking among the headstones, she came across some as old as a hundred years, some of the deaths dating all the way back to 1912. Fascinated, she began to stroll through the grounds at a leisurely pace reading the names and dates of each one. When she happened upon a plot marked Phillips, she looked around for the one she wanted. It didn't take long to locate it. Five headstones down from what looked like the final resting place of his grandparents and parents, she found Scott's. She ran her fingers across the marble and sat down on the grass at the base of the marker that read:

David Scott Phillips
Beloved Husband and Father
Died In Service to His Country

Standing tall and sleek in the urn, fresh long-stemmed, yellow hibiscus seemed to guard the gravesite.

"Jordan brings Hutton out here every week for a visit. They never come empty-handed. They usually bring me all kinds of flowers. Nick comes too but not always with them."

Hayden wanted to jump out of her skin at the sound of the male voice. Instead, she did her best to try for calm. Scott stood less than four feet away wearing the same clothes that he'd had on last night. Her heart did a double beat. He didn't look scary from this close. He looked like any other man, flesh and blood, with light brown hair worn military-style, sparkling blue eyes, about six feet tall.

"There's no reason to be scared. It's broad daylight and besides I'm not that kind of spirit. What are you doing here anyway?"

Hayden laughed. "Me? What are you doing here? You're—not alive."

"True. But dead is relative and boring. So, Emile Reed what brings you here to Pelican Pointe?"

"How…? You know about Emile?"

"I know about a lot of things now that I didn't know when I was alive."

"I'm sorry."

This time Scott laughed. "Oh believe me, I am, too. Truly sorry for many things, for many reasons. Unfortunately there's no changing the past."

Hayden sighed. "I know something about regrets. I guess you could say my life is a mess."

Scott stuck his hands in his pockets. "Be grateful for life, Emile. Or do you prefer Hayden?"

"Hayden's my name now. I miss certain things about Emile though. My blonde hair most of all, the dyed hair makes me feel like such a phony sometimes. But let's face it, Emile's life was far from perfect."

"Back in Chicago, huh? Life isn't supposed to be perfect. It shouldn't be. Stop looking for perfection and start seeing the possibilities in a new place. Was Emile happy in Chicago?"

She shook her head. "Not really. I thought I was but…"

"Then maybe there's your answer. Even though Dochenko fled the country you shouldn't let down your guard because he still has his henchmen looking for you."

"I didn't do anything criminal."

"I know. Look, it'll be dark soon. You need to start back to the cove now, Nick and Jordan are worried. And Ethan's looking for you."

For the first time Hayden noticed half of the sun had dipped below the horizon. She glanced at her watch. It was almost five-thirty. When she looked back up again, Scott had vanished.

Hayden heard Ethan's voice a good thirty yards before she found her way to the trail out of the underbrush. He was speaking to Nick in short, clipped tones.

Damn it. She realized they were looking for her like she was a five-year-old. Well, she hadn't been lost for chrissakes. Maybe nearly, but that didn't count.

She picked her way along the narrow path and finally emerged from the woods. As casually as she could Hayden asked, "What are you two doing?"

Ethan looked up and saw a disheveled Hayden. She had twigs in her hair. Her clothes were dirty. Her face was tender pink from either exertion or too much sun. Damned stubborn woman looked sunburned as hell. He'd bet a twenty she hadn't even bothered to wear sunscreen either. "Looking for you, where the hell have you been? It's almost dark."

Ethan's angry tone had her snapping back, "There is no need whatsoever to take that tone with me, Ethan Cody."

"Yeah, well, Nick and Jordan were worried about you. When you didn't show up for your planned trip into town, she and Nick thought you might be in danger. Did it ever occur to you if you wanted to wander off in the woods and get yourself lost you could have let someone know where you'd be?"

She'd be damned if she was going to stand here and let him chastise her. "You go to hell, Ethan Cody. I went for a hike." She drew out her compass, held it up. "What does this look like? I've hiked before today, Deputy, and I can guarantee you I will hike in the future. I used to be quite good at it. And I did not get lost. I simply enjoyed being outside and lost track of the time."

Ethan put both hands on his hips. "Let me ask you this. Do you or do you not have someone chasing you for whatever reason, a reason you refuse to share with anyone?"

She let out a loud audible sigh but refused to answer him. This man, the cop, was going to throw that up to her every chance he got. She listened as his lecture went on.

"The fact that you have chosen not to divulge the identity of the person hunting you doesn't make the situation any less dangerous. So when you disappear for hours without a word, people have a tendency to worry that perhaps you might have been abducted, taken against your will." Ethan turned to Nick and declared, "I think I'm done here, Nick. I'll call Brent and cancel the search."

With that, she watched him storm off through the grove of trees, through the courtyard, and disappear around the side of the house.

"I'm sorry, Nick."

Nick raised both hands in self-defense. "We're just happy to know you're okay."

By the time she'd showered and made her way over to the main house it was almost six-thirty. She slipped in the back door and found Nick and Jordan sitting at the kitchen table where a laptop computer sat between them.

Hayden stood just inside the kitchen. "I think I owe you both an apology. Once I calmed down I realized it must have looked like something happened to me. I didn't even think to let either one of you know I wanted to explore the area. So I set off on my own. I am so sorry for the trouble I caused you both, sorry I forgot about taking the trip into town and looking at the house. It's just that once I got outside, once I started walking I got caught up in the scenery, all the wildflowers, and taking a slew of pictures. I found I wasn't ready to spend my afternoon off cooped up inside." She finally took a breath.

"It never occurred to either one of us that you'd gone off exploring on your own. Have you eaten?"

"I fixed myself a sandwich. Look, for the first time in a long time, I'm seeing that there's a definite upside to starting fresh in a new place, especially one as peaceful as it is here."

Jordan took a closer look at Hayden's face. Had she been crying? "You look like crap," she told Hayden before she got up from the table and pulled the woman into a hug. "Want some tea?"

"I'd love some. You must be a good friend, Jordan; otherwise you'd lie and tell me how wonderful I look."

As she put the kettle on to heat, Jordan said, "Sorry, but you look like you've been crying. The puffy eyes gave it away. Did something happen with Ethan?"

"Ethan is an asshole."

Nick couldn't help it, he laughed. "Hayden, the guy was right there with us trying to figure out what had happened to you. He was really worried about where you had gotten off to."

That made Hayden feel small for all the terrible things she'd silently voiced about him during her shower. "So what you're saying is I should apologize to him, too."

"It's up to you, but it couldn't hurt. Ethan has a good heart and he genuinely cares about people."

Somehow she knew that was true. It only made her feel worse. "Look, I need to tell you guys something about my hike." She glanced at Jordan standing at the stove and then Nick.

"Then you should sit down," he offered. "We pretty much get all of our confessions out around the kitchen table."

Hayden took a deep breath. "The reason I was gone so long is because I took a lot of pictures, covered a lot of ground. I must have walked close to eight miles. During my hike I stumbled upon the back entrance to Eternal Gardens."

Nick eyed her warily and very much feared what she was about to say.

"I found Scott's gravesite. I also had a conversation with him." Hayden saw Jordan's mouth fall open, saw Nick chew the inside of his mouth. A gesture she suspected signaled he was annoyed. But she had to get this out. "I thought about keeping this to myself. Maybe I should. But in light of what happened earlier I decided if you were worried about me, trusted me with so much, given me a roof over my head, you deserved to know. I don't want you to think I'm holding stuff back from you. You two are the only friends I have here. And I didn't have that many friends before."

"What did Scott say to you, Hayden?" Jordan finally squeaked out.

Hayden looked from Nick to Jordan. "I want you to know I'm not trying to upset either one of you by sharing this."

"Implying that this will indeed upset us," Nick said as he stood up, squeezed Jordan's hand before making her take a seat at the table. They exchanged places while he waited for the kettle to heat and remained standing to hear what Hayden had to say.

"It may. It wasn't a long conversation. But Scott knew things about me, the real me, the one someone is looking for."

When the kettle whistled, Nick poured the water over a couple of teabags and brought the cups over to the table. "That's…"

"Crazy? I know. Scott spent a few minutes philosophizing about my mess of a life. When I asked him about how he knew, he said that there were a lot of things he knew now that he hadn't known while he'd been alive. I have to say it was almost like he talked in riddles."

Nick watched Hayden and felt a measure of sympathy. He'd spent a year of his life with Scott's ghost haunting him every step of the way. Even after he'd shown up at Jordan's front door with the intent of unburdening his guilt, he remembered that time he'd spent in hell when he had believed Scott's death had been his fault. Nick knew firsthand survivor's guilt could be an impossibly heavy burden that you had to eventually unload. But that didn't explain why Hayden was seeing Scott.

"Yeah, Scott was always good at that," Nick finally confessed. "Since you seem to be in the loop now, no one loves to talk more than Scott. What else did he say to you, Hayden?"

"Just that he was sorry about how some things had turned out. And that I should get myself back to the cove." Hayden finally took a breath. "He knew you guys were looking for me. The whole thing was surreal."

"I take it Scott hit the nail on the head when it came to the real you," Jordan finally said with a look of dread.

"Yes," was all Hayden said, as she sipped her tea. "But he made me feel better about things while he was at it. How can I make it up to you about missing the trip into town, Jordan?"

"We'll go tomorrow," Jordan promised her. But Hayden noted Jordan seemed distracted. She finished her tea and got up to go.

"Well, I guess I'll head out. If I have to eat crow, I need to get it done before going to bed."

After Hayden left, Nick turned to Jordan and asked, "You okay? You're awfully quiet."

"Hey, I'm just fine. If the son of a bitch would rather talk to everyone and anyone but me, why the hell should I care?"

Chapter Nine

Hayden pulled up to the curb in front of Ethan's house. She noticed the Honda Ridgeline parked behind his truck which told her the man wasn't alone. Fine, she thought, I'm not here to interrupt his evening with whomever he chooses to spend it. Reluctantly, she got out and marched up to the front door on a mission. She rang the bell.

When the door opened Ethan filled the door frame. Music drifted from behind him. The Foo Fighters' *Learn to Fly* echoed from his speakers. Between his fingers, he held a bottle of Corona.

"Well, well, well, Hayden-no-middle-initial-Ryan, what brings you to my front door tonight? Here to file a misconduct report on me?"

On the drive in she'd rehearsed her spiel. "Not at all. This won't take long. I owe you an apology. Earlier you responded to an official call from a concerned citizen. You had no way of knowing whether I was in real danger. But you were worried about my safety, concerned about my well-being, and acted accordingly as a public official. I'm sorry I acted like such a jerk earlier when you were simply doing your job." With that she turned on her heels and headed to her car, leaving him standing on his porch with his mouth open.

Brent leaned over his brother's shoulder and cocked his head, watched as the woman's long legs ate up the sidewalk, striding back to her Mini like a rocket propelled her along the way.

"So that's who has you all knotted up?"

"Screw you. I'm just fine, thanks."

"Sure. Whatever you say. Is that why you ran her through NCIC?"

"Shit. Come back inside and I'll tell you all I know."

After listening to Ethan list Hayden Ryan's issues, Brent wasn't impressed with the woman. "And nothing came up in NCIC?"

"I can read a damned report, Brent," he snapped. But then he ran a hand through his hair and calmly added, "Sorry. No. No hits."

"Then Hayden Ryan isn't her real name."

"Who says you don't have psychic abilities, Brent?" Ethan scoffed.

"Okay, so you'd already figured that much out. Who says you aren't a good cop?"

"Let's not go down that road tonight. How do I find out what she's hiding from or from whom? Did she witness a crime? Did someone try to force her to do something illegal and she panicked and took off?"

"You know Ethan, just because the name didn't come up with a hit, doesn't mean she's innocent."

"I'm not so gullible that I haven't considered that possibility. But every vibe in me, along with everything I've learned from you in the last four years as a cop, tells me the woman doesn't have a criminal bone in her body."

"And what a body. Her legs aren't bad, either. Not to mention, you've always been a sucker for green eyes."

"Not that you got a look up close."

"Yeah, it wouldn't be a hardship to get a lot closer to that, though."

Hayden blew out a breath of relief, glad that little scene was behind her. As she drove down Ocean Street past the wharf, ear-splitting rock blasting out from McCready's drifted through the open windows of her car. Scott's words blinked into her head. "Stop looking for perfection and start seeing the possibilities in a new place." She couldn't see possibilities if she didn't experience her new surroundings. On impulse, she decided to pull into the lot designated for bar patrons only and check out the bar.

Inside the dimly lit pub she recognized the bartender as the big man she'd seen on the pier the day she'd pulled Justin Hardin out of the bay. For a Sunday night the place was packed, standing room at the bar and every table taken. All three pool tables were busy with what appeared to be some kind of friendly competition. She looked around for a place to stand and squeezed between a woman in her forties and a man who looked eighty standing at the end of the ancient, scarred mahogany bar.

Hayden ordered the house red and tried to concentrate on the music coming from the juke where Bruce Springsteen wondered what it was like in the back of a pink Cadillac. All the while she kept thinking about Ethan's face when she'd apologized. Those dark brown eyes of his hadn't been warm tonight, they'd been stone cold. He hadn't even invited her inside. He'd definitely had company, which was none of her business.

Ethan Cody could do whatever he wanted and with whom. She didn't give a rat's ass.

The friendly pool game started getting less friendly as someone complained about the other bumping into an arm as they'd lined up to take their shot.

When a seat at the bar opened up, the old man standing next to her nudged her and gallantly offered, "Come on, pretty lady, have a seat."

But when the fortyish woman balked at his gesture, Hayden motioned for her to take the stool instead.

"Thanks, honey, don't mind if I do. I'm Janie Pointer. I own the Snip 'N Curl. And you're the newcomer hereabouts they call Hayden. What kind of name is Hayden anyway? You one of those lesbians? It's okay if you are. I'm not judgmental that way."

"Uh, no. Is your sister Abby, the one who works at the Diner Sundays and Mondays?"

"Yep. That's my baby sister, practically raised that girl when our mama ran off with a cook working out at the Denny's on the interstate. Got me a little three-year-old niece, too. Wanna see a picture?" Janie automatically reached for her purse, dug in her handbag until she pulled out a billfold, slid out a photo of an adorable, red-haired, little girl.

Knowing how she'd once hoped for nieces from Sydney, Hayden commented, "She's beautiful."

"We named her Colleen what with all that red hair and all. Look at those freckles. Takes after her daddy. He's in Afghanistan now, on his second tour."

Hearing that, Scott Phillips popped into her head. "I hope he stays safe."

"Paul Bonner is Colleen's father. But he had to join the military, couldn't find any work around here within a good sixty miles. He and Abby plan to get married as soon as he finishes this tour though."

By this time, the pool players were working up to full tilt and getting louder. The verbal insults ratcheted up a notch. The banter flew back and forth with some heat. Someone accused the other of cheating.

Before Hayden knew what was happening fists started pounding on faces, glass shattered, pool cues broke, and arms jabbed in all directions.

Then someone yelled for Flynn to call the cops.

When Ethan's phone rang practically across the street from McCready's he'd just taken two steaks off the grill. Ethan had already downed three beers. But Brent had thrown back four. "Yeah," he barked into the phone as he held the receiver between his ear and his shoulder.

Brent watched the scowl form on Ethan's face as he listened to the call and knew when Ethan slammed down the phone he was on the clock.

"Damn it, the Turley brothers are tearing up McCready's again." Ethan was already reaching for some breath mints, as well as his badge and his gun.

"Hey, don't look at me. You're more sober than I am. Plus, I had to bust them two weeks ago over in Scotts Valley. It's your turn."

"Shit." Since there was no jail in Pelican Pointe that meant Ethan had a trip to Santa Cruz in his immediate future. "Can't you at least do the booking for me? You're going back to Santa Cruz anyway."

"Been drinking, bro. I was planning on bunking here tonight." Brent turned a deaf ear to his brother as the curse words spewed forth like Mount St. Helens.

As he watched Ethan stomp toward the front door, Brent reminded him, "And watch out for that little bastard Sal, he likes to sneak up behind people."

When Ethan walked into the bar he was in no mood for pleasantries. His three days off had been a joke and damn it all, his steak was getting cold.

Looking around at the mess, all hell had broken loose. Tables were overturned. Chairs were still flying. Broken glass littered the ancient linoleum floor.

Ethan didn't take the time to ask questions about who was to blame. History and Flynn McCready's phone call told him the Turley brothers had picked another fight, probably over losing a pool game.

Why Flynn kept allowing them back in the bar was anyone's guess?

Ethan grabbed Derek Stovall and pushed Lenny Jacobson out of the way to get to Sam Turley who was sitting on top of Mel Stubbs beating the crap out of the guy's face.

Ethan jerked Sam off Mel and threw his forearm across Sam's chest long enough to hold him in place while he slapped handcuffs over his wrists. "You're under arrest, Sam. Again."

Out of the corner of his eye Ethan saw movement.

But it was too late. Sam Turley's brother, Sal had already come up behind him holding a broken beer bottle, the jagged edge pointed toward Ethan.

"Let go of my brother, Ethan. You take those cuffs off him right now."

Ethan straightened and yelled, "Sal Turley, if you don't drop that bottle right this minute I'll consider it a lethal weapon and you'll be in more trouble than drunk and disorderly. I'll lock you up for assault with a deadly weapon and throw in the attempted assault of a police officer."

Drunk, Sal ignored the warning. Sal lunged at Ethan anyway. And dropped like a rock when a whiskey bottle came crashing down on the top of his head.

Nothing could have prepared Ethan for the sight of turning around and seeing Hayden Ryan standing over Sal's crumpled body, gripping a whiskey bottle in her closed fist.

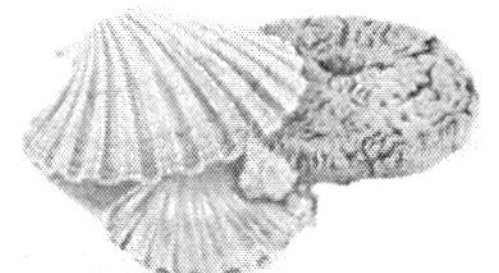

Chapter Ten

Monday morning Hayden brought Jordan along with her to Pelican Pointe where she opened up a bank account. Afterward they drove over to Ocean Street and to the little Spanish-style bungalow with the red-tiled roof.

While Hayden walked around the house several times peering in every available window, Jordan remained strangely noncommittal. Since leaving the bank, she acted as though she knew something about the house Hayden didn't.

"The front porch is a little small but since we intend to have a business here rather than a home it will do nicely, don't you think?" Personally, she preferred a big porch like the one out at Promise Cove. But she had to remind herself that up until five months ago she'd lived in a high-rise condo without so much as a four-foot front stoop.

"The good thing is the outside doesn't need painting. Of course the yard needs work. And it doesn't have a garage. But that just means it's more geared to a business than an actual place to live."

Finally Hayden's enthusiasm rubbed off on Jordan and she broke her silence. "That front room could use a couple of fresh coats of color on those walls no matter what the owner decides to do with it," Jordan concluded. "That plaster has holes in it." She pointed to the flooring through the glass. "But the wood floor's in good shape. You can tell that from here." All of a sudden she blurted out, "I should probably mention that this house used to belong to Autumn Lassiter."

When Hayden didn't show any sign of recognition at the name, Jordan knew she hadn't made the connection to

Ethan Cody. And after listening to Hayden's tirade about the deputy sheriff during the ride into town that morning, Jordan wasn't sure how the news would go over.

She hated to burst Hayden's bubble but… "Autumn ran a candle and gift boutique here, Hidden Moon Bay Gifts. She made her own line of scented candles using all kinds of herbs she grew herself. She made her own gift baskets for years and delivered them around town until the day she died."

"Really? That explains the missing sign. How cool is that? Did she live here, too?"

"Not exactly."

"When did she die?"

"Not long after Scott deployed to Iraq. I remember because I was pregnant at the time. I ventured into town one day to do a little exploring. I was lonely. I think Autumn could sense my moodiness. Anyway, I walked into her shop that day. She fixed me a cup of tea. We had a nice chat. She was perhaps the only person who was friendly to me at the time besides Murphy. And then about two weeks later I stopped by and there was a sign on the door. She'd passed away. Autumn was gone and so was the shop."

"How sad."

"It was incredibly sad. I don't think anyone's lived here since. Look Hayden, I don't know how to tell you this so I'll just say it. Autumn Lassiter was Ethan Cody's grandmother."

Hayden's face fell. Her shoulders slumped. "Oh. Perfect. Just perfect. That figures. So the man owns two houses in this little town."

"They both belonged to Autumn. We could talk to him. I'm sure he might…"

"Forget it, Jordan. It wasn't just the argument Saturday night. Ethan and I are just too different. The cop in him is never going to trust someone like me. I'll start looking for another place."

But just then, Hayden spotted Ethan walking toward them. "Ladies, how's it going this morning?"

"Fine," Jordan said. "Heard about the fight you two were in last night." Jordan all but snickered. "Nick's elated that Sal finally got thrown in jail and that Hayden had the foresight to wield a whiskey bottle as a weapon." Jordan turned to Hayden and added, "Nick and Sal have tangled before. Last spring in that very bar Nick broke Sal's nose."

"Well, Sal won't be tangling with anyone for a while, at least not on the outside. Judge refused to set bail. He'll be locked up until his hearing."

Ethan stuck his hands in his pockets, rocked back on his heels. "So you're interested in Autumn's house?" Even though he was staring at Hayden when he asked, she said nothing and seemed content to let Jordan do the talking.

"We're thinking about it," Jordan said after a lengthy silence.

"It's available to lease. You know Autumn ran a business out of here."

"I was just telling Hayden the story about your grandmother's boutique, the gift baskets she made."

"I think she'd like knowing someone was making use of the house. A bookstore, isn't that what you were thinking about, Hayden?"

This was silly, Hayden decided. She'd have to talk to the man eventually. "That's the plan."

"I appreciate what you did for me last night. Picking up that bottle probably saved me from a gash. Bashing Sal's head in took seventeen stitches to close up."

"Good. The man deserved it, sneaking up on you like that. He was going to jab you right there in the bar with that broken beer bottle."

Ethan grinned. She really was a fascinating woman with so many sides to her he couldn't keep up. "That's one of the reasons he's looking at two to five years courtesy of the state. Two dozen witnesses or thereabouts will testify to his attempted assault on a cop." He stared Hayden squarely in the eye and asked, "Are we okay now, Hayden? I'd like to go back to the way things were."

Hayden smiled, too. "Sure. We could do that." She held out her hand. "Friends?"

Ethan reached out his hand, tilting up her chin. "That's a start." Then when he turned to leave, he added, "You let me know about my grandmother's house. I guarantee I'll make you a good deal."

After dropping Jordan back at Promise Cove, Hayden took the directions she'd downloaded off the Internet and headed over to San Sebastian.

She had errands to run.

Almost an hour and one wrong turn later, Hayden crossed into the city limits of the little town which was twice the size and population of Pelican Pointe. It took her three stops before she was able to locate a store that sold the cell cards she needed to boost up her phone. And when she found them, she purchased four more just in case she couldn't persuade Murphy to stock them. After taking the time to key in the card info, she felt better knowing her phone was good-to-go.

When she got hungry she stopped at a sidewalk bistro café that reminded her of one back in Chicago off Lake Shore Drive and ordered the special of the day, half a club sandwich and a cup of vegetable soup.

After lunch, she spent two hours perusing the shelves at the San Sebastian Library, wishing she had a card so she could check out some of the books, especially a few on making your own candles and growing herbs in containers. For some reason, Jordan's story about Autumn Lassiter kept rolling around in her head. Maybe adding homemade candles to her book inventory would give the place more of a boutique/gift shop feel.

Before leaving the rows and rows of books behind, Hayden asked the woman at the front desk for directions to the bookstore and was shocked to learn it had gone out of business in August. Not a good sign, thought Hayden as she asked the librarian what she needed to provide in order to get a library card.

When the woman told her she needed proof of residency, she asked for directions to the nearest DMV. Luckily there was one four blocks away.

After placing a phone call to Jordan to get the exact address of the studio apartment so she could fill out an application for a California driver's license, she sat in a room with a ton of other people for forty-five minutes waiting for them to call her up to the counter.

Once she took and passed her written test, had her vision checked, gave her thumbprint, surrendered her Nevada license, they took her picture.

When they handed her the paperwork for her brand-new license, even though she'd have to wait two weeks to get the real piece of plastic in the mail, she whooped and hollered and did a happy dance right there in the DMV.

Within minutes, she made her way back to the library where she applied for a card, and checked out all the books she could carry on candle making and growing herbs in small spaces including container gardening and apartment balconies.

Loaded down with books, she headed back to her car. From the moment she'd learned about how the San Sebastian bookstore had failed after only a short time in business, Hayden began to have serious doubts about the bookstore idea.

As she drove back to Promise Cove, she considered the fact that if a store couldn't make it in a town the size of San Sebastian with a good five thousand people, how successful would it be in an even smaller market like Pelican Pointe in a bad economy. Pondering the question, she wondered if everyone ordered their books online these days. Surely there was still a need for a local bookstore where one could walk inside four walls, browse up and down rows and rows of books, flip open the pages, read the book covers, and weigh the storyline.

When she got back to the B & B she'd have to look up the statistics on how many people were going digital these days and buying ebooks.

She racked her brain to think of other business possibilities. It brought her to what Scott Phillips had said about new beginnings. On some level she had Dochenko to thank for this new beginning. But then he was also trying to kill her.

For some reason she couldn't let go of Autumn Lassiter's candle shop and gift boutique. It kept spinning around in her head. She glanced at all the books on the front passenger seat and wondered how hard it could be to learn how to make candles and grow herbs.

It hit her then. Her thought process was all over the place. So much that she had to laugh at herself.

By the time she reached the turnoff to the cove, she decided to go over the ideas with Nick and Jordan and get their take. Maybe the three of them would be able to come up with a few fresh "possibilities."

It took Hayden less than two minutes in the house to determine that Jordan looked exhausted and could use an extra pair of hands in the kitchen. Hayden got to work peeling potatoes and carrots and making iced tea, all things she could do without fear of ruining something.

While she watched in awe as Jordan rolled out pie dough from scratch for pot pies, she told her about the San Sebastian bookstore closing.

"I'm wondering if we should go another route."

"How about becoming a tour guide?"

"What? Where did that come from?"

"You said yesterday you liked to hike, liked spending time outdoors. You were asking me this morning about taking out the dinghy. Maybe you could start some kind of tour business taking the guests we get here on nature hikes. In the past they've expressed an interest in seeing the local sights, such as we have. Last summer we had a young couple from Ireland who came to California to hike the area around Big Sur. I'm sure they might've stayed longer if we'd offered some kind of tour of the area."

Hayden opened her mouth to speak but didn't know what to say. That was actually not a bad idea. But she hadn't told a single soul here or anywhere else about her early desire to be a forest ranger. And how stupid was that idea at this late date. For chrissakes, she'd be twenty-seven years old in six months, a little late to start thinking about the forest ranger angle. But a tour guide? That might be doable and not a bad idea.

"You could take people out to Treasure Island."

"What's Treasure Island?"

About that time Nick came in carrying Hutton. "Treasure Island is the nickname Scott gave a small island due west of the cove about half a mile offshore. I'm sure you've seen the little dot of land in the distance. And local legend says there's a shipwreck south of there. Do you dive, Hayden?" He asked as he settled Hutton into her high chair.

"No. Why?"

"For starters we could use someone to motor guests out to Treasure Island during the spring and summer months. Maybe as we grow we could include taking the guests out to dive and explore the shipwreck. It was Scott's original plan for this place."

"That sounds great for spring, but what about now? I need a viable plan now."

"True. Well, we'll keep brainstorming until we hit upon the right thing for you. Don't worry something will pop. You'll see."

Over dinner, Hayden told them about getting her driver's license. "They mail the actual piece of plastic out within two weeks. So, now I'm legal." Then she told them about getting a library card and all the books she'd checked out.

When she noticed they were staring, she thought it was because she'd monopolized the conversation.

"I guess that means you really are planning to stay then?" Jordan asked, a bit emotional.

Hayden smiled. "I am. And it feels good to decide that." Eyeing Jordan's hormonal state, she didn't want to make her cry or upset her further, so she changed the subject. "Do you guys ever get tired of having people underfoot? I mean, do you ever resent having to share your house with so many strangers?"

"Sometimes. I don't know about Nick but after having spent such a long time out here alone, it's nice having other people around to talk to."

"Some people," Nick agreed. "But then you get the ones who are difficult the minute they step through the door and make demands at every turn. Like the group from Cincinnati we had here in June for a retreat. They had both Jordan and me running ragged for them, insisting on a particular kind of cheese, fussy about the wine, particular about everything from soup to the main course. Personally, I was glad when their five days were up."

"They were a challenge," Jordan admitted. "I doubt we'll see them again, anyway. They thought we were a little too remote for their tastes."

"And bitched about it for five days. What I couldn't figure out is the woman in charge of booking the whole thing had checked us out the month before. When it was just her and her husband, she didn't seem to mind the accommodations then or the food."

"I bet I know," Hayden offered. "When she was here before with her husband she didn't have an audience to impress. But with the group, she hoped to impress them, wanted them to ooh and aah over every little thing. When they didn't..."

"Now that I think about it, you're probably right."

"Oh, I've seen it time and time again with Jeremy. He'd try to impress his clients, people around him, wait for their reactions and when he didn't get it he'd throw a temper tantrum and—" Hayden stopped talking when she realized what she'd said.

Jordan patted her hand. "It's okay, Hayden. We aren't going to run to Ethan and tell him you slipped up."

"I'm terrible at this."

"You mean you aren't good at pretending?" Nick offered. "Or lying?"

"I'd say that's a plus, not a problem," Jordan finished.

"It would be," Hayden said, before adding, "If it weren't so important."

After supper, Hayden cleaned up the kitchen and did the dishes. She'd dried the last pan, when she looked over and found Jordan staring at her.

"Thanks for cleaning up."

"You cook, I clean. Do you think it's crazy that I would want to learn how to make candles, grow herbs, and learn to cook at this late date?"

Jordan laughed. "You're young yet. Before I met Scott, my major was education. I planned to be a teacher like my dad, maybe cater in my spare time if I needed some extra cash. Then Scott swept me off my feet and I ended up here. You can plan and plan all you want, but life has a way of throwing you a curve. Life is all about change. You have to be willing to look at new avenues. Learning to cook isn't that difficult. You follow a recipe, use the right tools, terrific ingredients, and before you know it, you've got yourself a meal."

"You make it sound so easy, so simple. In fact, you and Nick both do."

Jordan smiled at that. "Stop being so hard on yourself, Hayden. Everything will work out. You'll see."

Luka Radovan had worked for his boss as a loyal employee for almost twenty-five years. He had begun his illustrious career as an errand boy at the age of sixteen and was now Dochenko's right-hand man. He'd moved up in the ranks because he was an unrelenting, ornery bastard with a deadly aim. And it helped that, like any paid hit man, he had absolutely no conscience. He liked what he did for a living. After a quarter of a century in the business, he was good at it.

It had fallen to him to locate the whereabouts of one Emile Reed, the straight-laced accountant who had taken off after his lackey had dropped the ball in that parking garage and sent her running.

Luka shook his head. He should have taken care of the problem himself. But he'd sent one of his up-and-coming underlings on a simple job. Taking care of Emile Reed's demise should have been a piece of cake. The plan had been to make it look like a random mugging. The robbery angle had worked before. Eliminating Saul Raymond had been a walk in the park. He'd slipped inside the man's condo that night and—no more business partner to worry about spilling everything he knew to the feds.

Because of that screw up, Luka had personally taken care of the underling. The man who had failed to get rid of Emile Reed had been disposed of that very night. Failure wasn't an option. Dochenko would never tolerate the inability to contain the government's key witness. Even Luka knew that. He'd sent his minions to stake out her sister, Sydney Reed, in St. Louis, and the mother in Pellingham, New York.

Time would tell if either produced results.

So far, they'd turned up nothing. But in his line of work, patience, as well as a certain amount of persistence were qualities you could never have too much of, especially when you were in pursuit of someone who didn't want to be found.

Luka knew in order to be successful you had to be thorough.

There were all manner of ways to locate Emile Reed. Dochenko seemed to think she'd stay in contact with her family, either by e-mails, texts, or phone calls. As soon as he could get inside the homes of her sister and mother, he intended to find out which.

He'd already arranged to get inside the woman's condo, to fool the real estate agent into thinking he was interested in purchasing that little cracker-box. Of course, he would string along the agent as long as he could, maybe until she gave up whatever information she had on Emile Reed. If that turned out to be nothing, then he'd drop the buyer angle.

Because when it came to locating the accountant, Luka Radovan would leave no stone unturned.

Chapter Eleven

On Tuesday morning Hayden discovered she hadn't lost her ability to get along with a two-year-old, at least one in particular. After agreeing to babysit Nick and Jordan's daughter, Hutton, while they attended Edmund Taggert's funeral service, she could admit now she'd been nervous at the prospect of being alone and solely responsible for a toddler. Another something she hadn't done since her college days when she'd picked up extra money at the university day care center taking care of other people's kids.

At first it had been a challenge to figure out what Hutton was trying to say to her. As good as Hayden had been at learning college French, after twenty minutes she'd discovered that two-year old-speak was a good deal more difficult to grasp.

As she sat on the living room floor reading Hutton her fifth story book, she realized mothers should come equipped with mindreading capabilities or built-in translators. The little girl was trying to add her two cents to the storyline. What it was exactly, Hayden could only guess. But it didn't take her long to realize Hutton possessed the same easy-going personality as her mother. Or perhaps the little girl had gotten her even-tempered nature from Scott. She certainly had her father's eyes.

And wasn't it weird that Hayden knew that firsthand. But after having a conversation with Scott the other day, she figured she could make the comparison.

If anyone had told her six months ago, she would willingly sit and talk to a ghost, she'd have laughed them into oblivion. But the truth was something about Scott pulled at her. While his spirit seemed content enough, it also hinted at an undefined restlessness. There were issues at play, she was sure of it. She just wasn't certain what they were.

Either way, she turned her attention back to the little girl, who continued to babble on about the pink polka-dotted rabbit in the storybook they were reading. For a few brief minutes the colorful, furry little thing had come to life for Hutton, mainly because it was so different from all the other bunnies.

Hayden couldn't help but make the comparison. For a span of minutes out in that cemetery, Scott Phillips had been real to her. She could only wonder why and what it all meant.

The Community Church at the corner of Main and Inlet Bay overflowed to capacity for Edmund Taggert's funeral service.

Dressed in his official uniform, Ethan stood at the back of the chapel near the double doors in case he got a call and had to make a quick exit. Surveying the crowd, it seemed as though the entire town had turned out to pay their respects. He looked around at the sea of faces, faces as familiar to him as his own family.

Murphy and Carla Vargas had shown up. Nick and Jordan were here. Will and Francine Foley had tears in their eyes. Wally Pierce had brought Lilly Seybold. Margie Rosterman sat in the front row with Max and Flynn McCready, who seemed to be with Janie and Abby Pointer. No doubt about it, old Edmund would have been pleased at the turnout.

If Ethan had expected to see Hayden he was sorely disappointed. But then why would she show up? She hadn't even known Taggert. He gave in to his curiosity and couldn't help wondering what she was doing at that very moment. Like a kid in middle school, he thought miserably, focused on a woman with a mysterious past was never a good sign.

He couldn't help going back over the argument they'd had Saturday night. He was certain that she had talked about law enforcement as if she'd had dealings with them. And it hadn't ended well. Of that he was certain.

The fact she didn't have a very high opinion of his profession was just one more reason to steer clear of Hayden-no-middle-initial-Ryan. Yeah, like that was going to happen. The woman had hit Sal Turley over the head without a backward glance because she thought he was in danger. Not many women would have the balls to do something like that. But then, Hayden was different than any of the women he'd known.

For one thing, the enigma angle kept pulling him in. Whether he wanted to admit it or not he loved a good puzzle. Hayden, or whatever her name had been, was a challenge. For another, he couldn't ignore his attraction to her. To do so, would be ridiculous on his part. That sleek body and green eyes were keeping him up nights. He shook his head at his own bad pun. Any decent writer should be able to come up with something better than that.

When the choir began to sing the first chorus of Amazing Grace, it brought Ethan back in time to his grandmother's funeral. Autumn Lassiter had lived to seventy and died peacefully in her sleep. Sometimes he thought he could still hear her voice, especially her singing. She'd always loved this song, he thought now.

He wondered how it would feel to have Hayden opening a bookstore in his grandmother's bungalow. Would she stick around Pelican Pointe for good if she started a business? Or would she take off at the first sign of trouble?

And those questions were another reason he needed to keep his distance.

After several more songs and a brief eulogy by Aaron Hartley, people started to file past the open casket for one final look at Edmund.

At the sound of one of the double doors creaking open behind him, Ethan turned to look into the serious face of his brother, Brent. Ethan watched as he motioned for him to follow him outside.

Once they were standing on the steps, Brent asked, "How's it going in there?"

"Good turnout. What's up? You didn't drive all the way from Santa Cruz to ask about Taggert's funeral."

"Kent Springer didn't show up for court this morning. Before coming here, I took a swing by the pier. His boat, Easy Money, is no longer moored in the bay." He patted his breast pocket. "Got me a search warrant for his house here in Pelican Pointe."

Ethan scrubbed a hand over his chin. "So the bastard ran. I'm surprised he waited this long. What's next?"

"The judge issued a bench warrant for his arrest. I need you to go with me to Sissy Carr's place over on Landing's Bay. If anyone knows where he is, it'd be Sissy."

"What about the search warrant?"

"I already have deputies tearing his house apart for a hint at where he's headed."

Just as Ethan was about to crawl into the passenger seat of Brent's cruiser, Frank Martin, second in command at the First Bank of Pelican Pointe came running up to the car. "Ethan, we've been robbed."

"Come on, Frank, settle down. The alarm didn't even go off."

"There's money missing from the bank, a lot of money, over and above what the feds were looking into with the fraud issue."

"Define a lot," Ethan asked.

"At least $600,000, maybe more. We just found out this morning when Milton Carr discovered the funds missing from his business account. It had to be an inside job. No one else had access to that money."

Brent and Ethan exchanged looks. It was Ethan who said, "Oh, that's just perfect, six hundred grand missing, Kent's boat no longer in the bay. Something tells me Sissy finally decided to put Pelican Pointe in her rearview mirror for good."

"You think Sissy lit out with Kent?"

"I know her better than you do. That's exactly what I think. She's been looking for a way out of here for years."

"Okay. Then we get a search warrant for Sissy Carr's house and hope like hell we find something that tells us where they're both headed."

Aaron Hartley, Edmund's lawyer, spotted Nick and Jordan Harris headed to their SUV. He made his way across the church parking lot and caught up with them just as they were about to get in. "If I could have a word with both of you."

"Sure," Nick said. "I'm sorry you lost your friend, Mr. Hartley."

"Thanks for that. Such is the way of getting old I fear, you start losing people right and left. Before you know it you're the only one left standing. As you well know, Ed could be a cantankerous cuss when it suited him. Knew his wife Ruby. Had the most beautiful golden hair I ever laid eyes on. She used to make the best sweet potato pies, too. Got the cancer in the breast. Died within seven months of getting the diagnosis. That was back in '82. Ed never did quite get over losing his Ruby. Anyway, I was wondering if I could have a minute of your time?"

"Do you want to talk right this minute or follow us out to the cove?"

"If you wouldn't mind I'd just as soon do it now. My house is two blocks over on Landings Bay. Just follow me home."

When Nick got settled behind the wheel, Jordan turned to him and asked, "What do you suppose he wants with us?"

"I have no idea. But we're about to find out."

They followed Hartley to a two-story Tudor-style house with an arched doorway and a bay window. Once inside, Hartley's housekeeper, Alice, led them into Aaron's study and office where the lawyer took a seat behind a desk. He motioned for Nick and Jordan to sit down in matching wing chairs. "Make yourselves comfortable. Alice, I think our guests would like some refreshments."

"Of course. I'll be right back."

"What is this all about, Mr. Hartley?" Nick asked. "We left our daughter with a sitter and she's expecting us back shortly."

"I promise this won't take long, Mr. Harris. It's about Edmund Taggert's will."

"I'm sorry, Mr. Hartley, but what does Edmund's will have to do with us?" Jordan asked, truly baffled as to why they of all people had been asked to follow him here.

"You may or may not know that Edmund and Ruby had no children. And his older brother died some nine years ago from pneumonia. Edmund had no other living relatives."

About that time Alice came through the door carrying a tray with coffee and cookies. Aaron waited patiently until Alice served the coffee, handing off their cups in perfect hostess fashion.

"Thank you, Alice."

Once Alice had closed the door, Aaron got back down to business. "Edmund's will generously provides for his long-time foreman Will Foley and his wife, Francine. Everyone hereabouts knows Will and Frannie worked their magic on the farm for almost thirty years. Edmund's given both of them a sizeable cash endowment. But the farm and the land, Mr. and Mrs. Harris, Edmund left to both of you. You two now own Taggert Organic Farms."

"What?" Nick and Jordan exclaimed at the same time. "That's impossible," Jordan added.

Aaron shook his head. "I assure you it isn't. It's what Edmund wanted."

"What about Will and Francine Foley? Why us?"

"As I said, the Foleys will receive a sizeable cash bequest, a retirement package if you will, for their long and loyal service to Edmund. But Will and Francine have other plans. It seems last spring they approached Edmund. April, I believe it was." He shuffled some papers around on his desk. "It seems the Foleys explained to Edmund they wanted to leave Pelican Pointe for good so they could spend more time with their children and grandchildren in Tulare, where Will's son and his daughter-in-law are apparently trying to get an organic farm up and running there, not as competition mind you, but for a co-op.

"Anyway, as a result of that conversation, Edmund changed his will on May one of this year, a little over four months ago. I assure you, Mr. and Mrs. Harris, the will is up-to-date and legal. I have all the financials here, which we will go over at your convenience. The farm, which consists of forty acres, is quite a profitable business venture, one of the most successful small organic farms on the West Coast, as a matter of fact."

"I still don't understand. Why us?"

"Because, Mrs. Harris, the Foleys have already made plans to pack up and move. Knowing that information, Edmund decided you and your husband would benefit the most from inheriting the farm since it is adjacent to your property. Although you own it now, Edmund was certain you wouldn't want to see the property sold off to unscrupulous developers. He felt certain, Mr. Harris that you and your wife would keep that from ever happening. Although as I said before, you own the property outright so legally you are free to do with it what you wish. However, I can tell you that Edmund was very hopeful that you both would continue to run it and keep it in your family for generations to come."

Jordan got tears in her eyes. The pregnancy hormones were on overload. "I don't know what to say. I mean... I didn't even think he liked us all that much."

Aaron smiled. "I believe, Mrs. Harris, Edmund had a change of heart last spring where you and your husband were concerned. I believe he started stopping by Promise Cove, as it's now called, regularly beginning last spring for coffee and dessert and continuing to do so during the summer months. He got to know the two of you rather well. And he mentioned that at least twice a week you had him to supper. He was quite moved by your willingness to forgive him for his abominable behavior before last spring."

"Before that, all he stopped by for was to complain about the noise," Jordan added as she dabbed at the tears in her eyes.

Once again, Aaron merely smiled. "As I said before, Mrs. Harris, Edmund could be an ornery cuss without trying too hard."

"Of course we'll keep the land from falling into the hands of anyone like Kent Springer, but neither one of us knows a thing about running a dairy and growing organic vegetables," Nick explained.

"Then I suggest you and your wife plan on spending as much quality time with the Foleytas before their departure for Tulare. In fact, I would go by the farm as soon as possible and make the arrangements."

Outside in the driveway, Nick and Jordan were still in shock. It was Jordan who spoke first. "Do you think we could convince Will and Francine to stay on and manage the place for us?"

"I don't know, but we're sure going to try. I'd consider dangling a sizeable bonus offer in front of them because I don't know a thing about running a farm."

"I certainly don't. I'm just now getting the hang of running a B & B. I'm not sure we can take on this added responsibility, Nick. This is huge. And in less than eight months we'll have another child. What with a toddler and a newborn and the bed and breakfast, how will we manage?"

"Okay, first we don't panic. Don't panic, Jordan. I don't want you to stress out what with the pregnancy. We'll figure this out." He reached over and wrapped his arms around her. "The first thing we're going to do is stop in and talk to the Foleys. Maybe they'll take pity on novice farmer owners and be willing to stay."

But even though they spent a good thirty minutes trying to convince the Foleys to abandon their plans for Tulare, the older couple had already made up their minds. What they wanted to do now was spend more time with their grandchildren. And no amount of persuasion would convince them to change their plans. They wanted their remaining years to be spent around their family. But the couple did agree to give Nick and Jordan three weeks to learn everything they could about running an organic dairy and vegetable farm.

As they drove off toward the cove, Nick and Jordan could only hope three weeks would be enough time.

Hayden was just coming out of Hutton's bedroom after putting the baby down for her afternoon nap when Quake let out a friendly little bark and headed straight for the front door, pawing at the wood. She heard the key fit into the lock and sure enough one of the double doors opened wide. Nick and Jordan walked in looking harried and tired.

"Uh-oh, you guys look frazzled. What happened?"

"How was Hutton?" Jordan asked as she made a mad dash down the hallway and straight to the bathroom without waiting for Hayden to answer.

Okay, something was up, thought Hayden. "Surely, she wasn't that worried about my babysitting skills. Hutton is fine. She even ate all of her lunch and went down for a nap without a hitch. I think I wore her out."

Nick shook his head. "She isn't upset with you. We've had a rough morning."

"That doesn't sound good. Funerals are always emotional. Anything I can do?"

"You wouldn't happen to know anything about running a dairy farm, would you?" Nick asked absently as he started going through the mail on the hall table.

"Huh? Uh, no. Sorry. I'm just now beginning to read up on how to grow herbs in tiny containers. Why?"

"Edmund Taggert left his farm to Jordan and me. We found out after the funeral."

"You're kidding?"

Jordan reappeared holding a wash cloth to her mouth. "Unfortunately, he isn't. And the couple who've managed the place for more than a quarter of a century has decided to move away. That's why we were so late getting back. We stopped, tried to beg them to stay on. Because what Nick and I know about running a dairy farm and raising organic produce would fill a tiny thimble. We have exactly three weeks to spend with the Foleys to learn everything we always wanted to know about running a farm but were afraid to ask."

"Are you okay, Jordan?" Nick asked taking his wife's hand in his. "Morning sickness?"

She nodded.

Hayden was no dummy. "Morning sickness equals pregnant. I take it all that trying has finally paid off?"

Jordan smiled weakly. "Like a winning slot machine!"

Hayden laughed. "Ah, well congrats. No wonder you've looked so tired these past few days. You didn't say a word yesterday when you let me drag you all over town. If you weren't feeling up to it…"

"I felt fine yesterday. The morning sickness has apparently kicked in because of all the strain of everything else. Nick and I decided to keep the news quiet for another week or two, you know, just in case. We haven't told anyone yet. You're the first."

"Then I feel privileged and will keep the secret locked in the vault until you give me the green light."

It was Nick's turn to laugh as he wrapped Jordan up in a hug. "I'm thinking about sending out an e-mail to everyone I know. I'm about to burst with the news but this Taggert thing has been a little over the top for both of us. I think we need to focus on the pregnancy right now and forget about the organic farm thing for a couple of days."

"Wait a minute. Did you say you have three weeks to learn how to run a farm? What if I went with you? I could spend mornings there, afternoons at the Diner. That way I could help you run the place. Look, I used to be an excellent accountant. I can give you references…" She stopped again in mid-sentence. "Damn. I hate this secrecy thing."

Nick and Jordan exchanged looks. "It's a deal. We'll take all the help we can get. Between the three of us we should be able to spend enough time with the Foleys learning the ins and outs of running the place. Short of milking cows and spreading manure we should be fine."

"Speak for yourself Nick Harris," Jordan said patting her stomach. "I'll have you know I did not get pregnant so I could spread manure and milk dairy cows."

Hayden laughed. "Wait. I'm trying to picture Jordan sitting on a stool milking a cow. Nope, can't do it."

"Oh, shut up," Jordan said with amusement twinkling in her eyes. "Just for that, I'll make sure I bring the camera the day you have to spread your first load of manure around, how's that?"

"Life must be all about change. Otherwise, I'm fairly certain I'd never consider tossing out the word manure so easily in a conversation."

Nick laughed. "Well, over the next three weeks, we all may be tossing it around."

Without an official sheriff's substation in Pelican Pointe, the deputies made do with one of the Sunday school classrooms at the Community Church where they assembled for their daily briefing before their shift started.

In a town that didn't see a lot of hardcore crime, the Springer-Carr case had generated the most excitement since last spring when Kent had been arrested for attempted arson out at The Cove. Before he ever got to the lectern, Brent sensed the adrenaline coming off the dozen or so deputies, both male and female, gathered in the room.

"Kent Springer and Sandra 'Sissy' Carr have been added to the NCIC database," Brent informed them as he read from his notes. "With the boat gone, my guess would be they're on the run south to Mexico or north to Canada. Ethan and I canvassed the pier and no one remembers seeing the boat moored in the bay after Friday night. The Coast Guard's been alerted but with a four-day head start…"

"They could be anywhere," Ethan finished for him. "If they wanted to, Easy Money is a large enough yacht to make the crossing all the way to Hawaii." He shrugged his shoulders. "It's a thought."

Brent agreed. "A good one. Even though it's likely they're out of the country, we don't stop looking, or stop making inquiries to other law enforcement agencies in other jurisdictions. We make our own calls, send out our own faxes. We don't let up."

"Maybe they want us to think they've left the area," Ethan offered. "What if they're sitting ten miles offshore someplace? I say we get the choppers airborne, fly up and down the coast, cover as much ground as we can, ASAP."

"Good idea. Unfortunately, the feds have forced their way into this case because of the half a million dollars missing from Milton Carr's business account and the fact they're investigating Springer for bank fraud. As of two hours ago, they're calling the shots. But as far as capturing these two, this is local and therefore, our problem. Having said that, I'll see if I can persuade them to get the choppers in the air and make a sweep within a fifty-mile area over the water."

And Ethan knew his brother could be a stubborn cuss when the guy wanted to argue his case. "Since Pelican Pointe is my territory, I'll brief everyone on what the feds found when they executed the search warrant at both the Springer and Carr houses." With that, Ethan took over while his brother left to meet with the federal agent in charge of the case.

Chapter Twelve

Before starting her shift at the Diner, Hayden drove through the gates at the cemetery. This time, she brought flowers, a cluster of Indian paintbrush from the field of wildflowers she'd found on Sunday.

She walked among the headstones until she got to the Phillips' plot where she took the time to arrange the stems in the urn, which strangely sat empty, unlike before when it had been full of yellow blossoms.

She breathed in deep, inhaled the air right off the ocean. Nothing more peaceful than a cemetery thought Hayden as she plopped down on the grass and spread her arms behind her. She looked up to study the sky. Purple clouds hung low to the ground. In the distance, a marine layer built up. There would be fog by the time she got off work tonight.

She waited a few minutes to see if he showed himself. When nothing happened, Hayden started talking to the headstone. "Well, if you're here, Scott, I just wanted you to know…uh, Ethan loaned me this book about ghosts. I've been reading up on…the paranormal. Some of what I've read doesn't pertain to you because contrary to popular belief, I believe you've accepted the fact that you are dead. And since I don't think you're violent—"

"I love this place. Not the cemetery, I mean Pelican Pointe and the cove. I used to roam this entire area when I was a kid. I played in those woods and climbed those rocks along the cliffs until my grandmother would come looking for me to call me in near dark for supper."

Hayden jumped a little at hearing Scott's voice, so calm, so reflective. She sighed when he took up a sitting position across from her on the lawn. "Why did they change the name, the cove, I mean?"

"New start, I guess, new beginnings for Jordan and Nick. Change. Life is all about accepting change. Nothing stays the same. Ever."

"Jordan called it exploring new avenues. Why are you so angry with her? Because she's with Nick?"

"You have it all wrong. She's the one hoarding the anger, keeping it bottled up inside, won't let it go either."

"Hurt. She's hurt—you haven't bothered—showing yourself to her."

"I've been in that house almost every day since I died. But Jordan's anger keeps pushing me away. I had no idea how unhappy she was here, alone for so many months. I mean I knew, because I got her letters, her e-mails, one or two phone calls, but I didn't realize how deep it went and that it would simmer into full-blown depression before Nick showed up. Part of that turned into hostility, all directed toward me."

Hayden sat up straighter. "Really?"

Scott laughed. "Do you plan on being the go-between, Hayden? Carrying messages back and forth from the dead to the living?"

"If that's what you two need to straighten out this misunderstanding."

"It doesn't matter now. She's with Nick. She loves him."

"She's pregnant, Scott."

"I know. Life goes on, Hayden. It may be difficult to understand this, but I'm happy for Jordan. She deserves every ounce of joy she can squeeze out of life."

"You must have really loved her."

"Oh, yeah. I certainly did that. I'd give anything if I could've held Hutton just one time after she was born."

Hearing that, Hayden got tears in her eyes. But when she reached out to touch Scott's hand in response to comfort him, her fingers slipped through air, landing softly on the blades of green grass.

The big news at the Diner was no longer Hayden's unorthodox method of helping Ethan Cody out of a jam when he arrested Sal Turley. After all, she had been off on Monday and missed all the talk her bottle-wielding incident had caused.

She hadn't been the least bit disappointed when she'd clocked in today and discovered that her heroic save no longer headlined the town's news. The bar fight had been replaced with brand-new scandal, talk that made her whiskey-bottle-knockout pale in comparison.

It was Margie who hit Hayden with the news about Kent Springer and Sissy Carr and the missing half a million dollars from the bank. While rumor had spread by five o'clock that the bank auditors were staying out at the cove until they'd finished their investigation at the bank, a fact Hayden could have confirmed but chose not to, it was her conversation with the ghostly Scott that gave her pause to think.

Hayden didn't give a whit about missing bank money or the two fugitives. What she did care about was the dynamics between Scott, Jordan and Nick and their well-being. Maybe including a ghost when worrying about someone's well-being would have been a stretch for some people, it wasn't for Hayden. At least, not now.

She genuinely liked Scott, or rather Scott's ghost. And she would do anything for Nick and Jordan to see that conflict didn't bring heartache to either one of them. If she could help in some way by being the go-between as Scott had called it, then so be it.

If she had been on better footing with Ethan she would have loved to talk to him about all of it. But even though they had agreed to be friends, being friends wasn't exactly the first thing that came to mind when she thought about the deputy.

But having the guy that got you all hot and bothered mistrust you so openly wasn't exactly a good sign of a stable, future relationship. And because of that , she needed to move on.

At seven-forty-five Hayden looked up from taking an order, and saw Ethan coming through the door of the Diner. She sighed. The man had to be a creature of habit. And ignoring each other wasn't a viable option at this point.

After finding out from Margie he wanted iced tea, Hayden poured a tall glass and took it over to his table. The man looked exhausted.

She smiled and said, "Hello, Ethan. What can I get you?"

When Ethan's eyes landed on Hayden all he could think was that the woman looked good enough to eat. Her eyes glinted a mossy green. Her smile seemed genuine and warm. Even the way she said his name generated sparks. As tired as he was she seemed to brighten this otherwise miserable day he'd had.

When you started the day with a funeral and it got worse from there, the only place to go was up. He'd had to handle a lot of paperwork to get two search warrants, as well as interact with a couple of stone-faced federal agents. Dealing with the feds had never been at the top of his list. "If it's Tuesday the special must be chicken-fried steak."

"Max's specialty. He says it comes from his Texas roots. Of course, he also says that about his barbequed ribs and his fried catfish. The steak comes with your choice of fries or mashed potatoes and fresh string beans. So fries or mashed, Deputy Dawg?"

"Fries."

"You got it." She walked off to put in the order.

The minute she left the table Ethan made a decision. If he was being honest with himself all of it hadn't mattered from the moment he had first met her. Not the flashes or the vibes. The bottom line tended to get blurry when emotions entered into the equation anyway. But one thing was clear. He hadn't felt attraction this fierce since he'd been a randy, sixteen-year-old and buxom Katie Bennett had ventured within reach of his teen hormonal radar.

When she brought his food, the minute she set down the plate, he reached for her wrist. "Go sailing with me Sunday, Hayden."

"Ethan, this isn't the time or the place."

He leaned over and whispered, "I know Hayden Ryan isn't your real name. And I don't care. It no longer matters to me. My birthday is Sunday. I want to spend it with you out on the water. Come sailing with me."

She took his hand in hers. "We'll discuss this later, Ethan. Eat your food now. It's getting cold." She touched her fingers to his cheek. "And then go home. You look as though you could sleep for a week."

"Okay. But we aren't finished. I'll be back at closing."

"Ethan, don't push this. Eat your dinner now before it gets cold."

By closing time a storm had blown in and brought with it a brisk wind off the water. While Hayden dragged the mop around the old stained floor, thunder rumbled overhead. Fat drops of rain began to batter the windows in earnest.

"Quit daydreaming there, Hayden. Finish up. I want to get home. The radio says we're in for a good soak tonight. Floor's clean enough," Margie reasoned as she pulled an umbrella from under the counter. "Take this and head on home. You be careful on the roads. They're slick tonight."

Hayden put the mop and bucket away, got her jacket and handbag down from the peg and headed out the door. She heard Margie flip the lock behind her.

She made a dash for her car and jumped out of her skin when Ethan stepped out of the shadows. "Jesus, Ethan. You scared me into the afterlife."

"Sorry. How about coming to my house for some hot soup?"

"You just ate chicken-fried steak not two hours earlier."

"But you haven't. My mother sent it over. Lindeen Cody makes a terrific vegetable beef soup."

"Do women ever say no to you, Ethan Cody?"

He grinned. "Why would you want to say no, Hayden? We're standing here cold and wet while you could be sampling some of my mom's delicious homemade soup and cornbread."

Soup did sound good. But who was she kidding? Food wasn't the reason she wanted to follow Ethan home. "Okay. Feed me, Ethan."

As he got down bowls from his cupboard, Ethan told her about his busy weekend. "I haven't seen so much happen in Pelican Pointe in a seventy-two-hour period since Delia Sanderson found her husband in bed with Sally Jensen, which set off a three-day chain reaction." He ladled soup into bowls and set them on the table.

Making herself at home in his kitchen, Hayden got out two beers from his fridge and twisted off the tops. "Chain reaction?" she asked as she took her seat across from Ethan.

"It was a domino effect from the moment Delia knocked Sally off her hubby from where she uh, sat on top, if you get my drift. Delia and Sally duked it out some. There was hair-pulling of major proportion until Bill, Bill was the cheating husband, called the cops, which is where I come in. I get to the scene and pull Delia off Sally, who by this time is bleeding profusely from various scratches all over her naked body. Did I mention Sally was naked as the day she'd been born? Did I mention Delia was quite a bit larger than Sally?"

"No. But I'm rooting for Delia. Did you arrest Sally?"

"Arrest Sally? For what? She was the one beat up. Remember Delia had attacked Sally. But Sally was so embarrassed she refused to press charges." He paused as he tasted a spoonful of soup before continuing. "Anyway, everything was fine until the next day when Sally's husband, Jim, went looking for Bill. Found him too, down at the docks where he was waiting for him to come in from his catch of the day. A fight ensued. Jim beat the crap out of Bill."

"So you arrested Jim?"

"I could have, but I didn't."

"Bill didn't press charges."

Ethan grinned. "Now, you're getting the hang of the dynamics in a small town. But the next day the vandalism started. Sally wanted to get back at Delia so she keyed her car—several times. She was caught in the act. And Delia pressed charges. That's when I arrested Sally. But then Bill, wanting to get back at Jim in his own way for the punches he'd taken, punctured all four of Jim's brand-new tires. Jim caught him in the act, pressed charges. I arrested Bill."

Hayden laughed. "So after cheating and getting beaten up by each other's spouses, you arrest Bill and Sally for vandalism? What happened to them?"

"They appeared before the judge, got probation and a fine, and then ran off together leaving Delia and Jim to take care of four kids between them."

"Wow. Life in Pelican Pointe. What happened to Delia and Jim and the kids, or do I want to know?"

"As soon as they got divorced from their respective cheating spouses they married each other a year later. I guess all that crying on each other's shoulders paid off."

She chuckled and spread butter on her cornbread. For a few minutes she sat there enjoying the taste of the soup and then said, "Ethan, if I could tell you about how I ended up here, I would. Would you settle for knowing something about my past, something real about my mother and sister?"

"Only if you want to tell me. I really don't care anymore who you were. I'm more interested in who you are now."

"Somehow I doubt that, Ethan. You're a cop. Cops are cynical and distrustful. I'm not sure how we'll ever get past that."

"Have you lied to me about anything major?"

"Lied to you?" She thought a moment. "No, not outright. I just haven't told you details."

"Then I can deal with that. Even though I wish like hell you would just tell me his name and what happened and be done with it, I know you won't do that."

"And how long will it take before you can't get past that?"

"We'll take it slow. I understand I have to earn your trust. You've been burned by cops, haven't you?" When she looked surprised, he added, "You aren't very good at this deception thing, Hayden. I thought back to what you said Saturday night."

"I wouldn't say burned, maybe more like skeptical of the hollow promises they make. Okay, here's what I can give you from my past. When I was sixteen my dad passed away. Aneurysm. He taught fifth-grade science. He was standing at the blackboard in his classroom when he just dropped like a rock and was gone. They had to go tell my mother what had happened. She was in the same building in another classroom teaching third grade.

"Money was tight after that, but as tight as it was my mother insisted her girls go to college. My sister and I both found part-time jobs, not just for spending money, but for college. We saved every dime. After Dad died, we both buckled down at school to get good enough grades in hopes of getting a scholarship. The next year, Sydney nailed one for nursing. She works in the ER. A year after that, I managed to get one. I earned a degree in accounting. A mistake I think now."

"What did you want to be?"

"Don't laugh. I wanted to be a forest ranger."

"The hiking and being outdoors thing."

She smiled. "Anyway, my mom kept teaching until she met and married again and then followed him to another state. She works for a software company now. Look, I'm just a regular person, Ethan, who found herself in a dangerous situation. Hayden Ryan is my legal name now. Although my mother hasn't accepted it." She smiled again. "I've broken no laws, Ethan, not even to get here."

"Thank you for that." He squeezed her hand, brought it to his lips to kiss her palm. "I want you, Hayden. I meant what I said earlier. It isn't your past that bothers me. It's the danger you're in from someone who is unknown to me, knowing someone is out there who wants to hurt you doesn't sit well with me. You understand that, right?"

The tenderness she saw in his eyes did her in. "Now that, Deputy Dawg will get you another lip lock. And one more reason why I really like you."

He came around to where she sat, leaned down and started nibbling her neck. "That's good because I really like you, too, especially this spot right here on your neck." He kissed her throat with his open mouth, began a sucking motion before turning her around so he could nibble her lips. Tilting his head, he deepened the kiss.

He had a skilled mouth that worked to send quivers through every fiber of her body. Her fingers latched on to his long, thick hair as he continued the assault on her mouth.

He dropped his arms down to her rear end and yanked her further in. Body to body, all she could think about was lying beneath him, surrendering to him.

But sanity jerked her back to reality. "It's getting late. I need to go, Ethan."

"I was afraid you were going to say that. I'll follow you back to The Cove."

"That's just plain silly. You look exhausted."

He ignored her. "Look, I don't mind taking it slow but there are a couple of reasons you don't want to argue with me about this."

"Oh really. That bossy attitude may work with some women, Ethan, but not me. I'm perfectly capable of driving to The Cove without a police escort. I know the way now. I'm a good driver even in the rain. I don't need you to—"

"I'll worry about you if I don't see for myself that you get there. Okay?"

She blew out a breath and dug in her bag for her cell phone. "I'll call you as soon as I pull in, how's that? Should I worry about this controlling side to you?"

"Controlling? I'm trying to protect you from some unsub who wants to—" He blew out a frustrated breath. "You're really stubborn, you know that?"

"Same goes. I don't want to fight with you, Ethan. Is Sunday really your birthday?"

He pulled out his wallet from his back pocket, slid out his driver's license, handed it to her. "Satisfied?"

"Thirty-three? Wow, you're a lot older than I thought." She snickered. "Okay, Sunday it's a date, we'll go sailing, see if we don't manage to throw each other overboard in the process."

"Good. Now I have a question for you. That date of birth on your Nevada license. Is April 30 real or fake?"

Exasperated at his persistence, she dug into her bag again and brought out the paper representing her brand-new California license that she'd have in two weeks, held it in front of his face.

"First, the Nevada license is history. Did you know once you move to California you have ten days to get a new license? I'm within the law, Deputy Cody. Second, April 30 is off by two weeks, just two weeks! And I'll be twenty-seven next May 15th. Third, the only other lie on that license is the color of my hair. But that doesn't count because women change their hair color all the time. Satisfied?"

"Really? What's your real hair color?"

"Trust me, Deputy; you aren't nearly ready for that kind of top-secret detail."

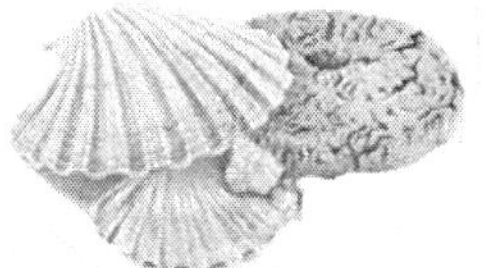

Chapter Thirteen

As the days grew cooler, the nights chillier, as trees dropped their leaves, the fall tapestry of browns and golds dominated the landscape around the grounds of the old Victorian. The walkways, the courtyards, the front flower beds, exploded in an array of fall buds. Hearty marigolds and coreopsis blossomed alongside dazzling firecracker and colorful ice plants.

Because of Jordan's pregnancy and the fact that she still had the B & B to run, guests to tend to, and a toddler to care for, Hayden took on most of the day-to-day instructions from Francine Foley at Taggert Organic Farms.

Taking on the additional responsibilities, Hayden stayed busy.

Early morning could find Hayden spending time with Fran, following her around like a baby chick, taking a tablet full of notes, or hanging out in the vast vegetable garden dutifully trying to tend to five acres of kale, spinach, carrots, broccoli, sweet corn, and various kinds of lettuce.

If she wasn't pulling weeds in the vegetable garden, she could be found tracking the growing stages of two different kinds of melons, marking the progress of the ripening gourds, or helping pick pumpkins they would sell down at Taggert's roadside stand, which he kept open rain or shine, April through mid-November.

If she got bored there, she could wander up and down the rows and rows of McIntosh apple and cherry trees in the orchard, doing her best to recognize the early stages of the dreaded powdery mildew, the enemy of so many farmers and put an end to it by pruning out any infectious buds.

Each day she learned something different, something more fascinating about the farm than the day before.

It seems old man Taggert hadn't certified his farm organic until sixteen years earlier when he'd decided to do away with using high concentrations of pesticides. Going low impact and using the minimum application of the stuff meant his farm would be recognized as the finest organic supplier in the area.

The old farmer had relied heavily on his right-hand man, Will Foley, over the years to come up with the healthiest ways of producing the best varieties of fruits and vegetables. Will believed strongly in good cultural habits, like plenty of air circulation and limiting the use of fertilizer. According to Will, both practices made for healthy plants.

With four outbuildings, complete with tidy refrigerated facilities used for packing, they could ship the freshest produce to the immediate surrounding markets without relying on an outside source. With their own greenhouse, which housed all kinds of baby seedlings, they could ensure a steady crop rotation while keeping production at a premium.

She'd never seen fat black-and-white cows up close and personal, certainly never watched them plod along to graze in pasture land on grass high above cliffs that offered some of the best views of the Pacific Ocean she'd seen yet.

The day she got her first peek inside the milking station, she realized she might as well be living on another planet. How fifteen cows could produce so much milk twice a day was nothing short of amazing!

While Hayden scribbled all pertinent info and instructions down on her pad for future reference, she looked over at the boss and found Nick deep in conversation with Will about when and how to apply the natural fertilizer he had developed.

The look on Nick's face had said it all.

They had a lot to learn and a short amount of time to do it in. The task at hand, running a farm they had no experience running, was proving to be a challenge for both of them.

She felt bad for Nick because he seemed to be overwhelmed at the prospect of taking on a new business venture he knew very little about.

In his previous life, in addition to serving in Iraq, he had been an investment banker. The knowledge hadn't been all that surprising to Hayden. Nick appeared to be extremely savvy in all things technical and corporate. But she suspected he was nervous about taking over the farm. And who could blame him?

Taggert Organic Farms was a complex operation and new territory.

It was a new life for Hayden as well, one Emile Reed could never have imagined.

Knowing she was helping to relieve the burden for Nick and Jordan though, two people she not only cared about but also admired, brought a great deal of personal satisfaction to her. She'd never once experienced such a sense of achievement during the four years she'd spent as Dochenko's accountant.

Personal fulfillment aside, her job description read like a gigantic to-do list. That is, until Nick brought on a full-time farm manager. But until that happened part of the responsibility fell on Hayden.

She should have been nervous. But her devotion to Nick and Jordan refused to send Hayden into panic mode.

After all, keeping the books she could handle. But filling Will and Francine Foley's shoes was a huge undertaking and a different matter entirely. Thank goodness they could still rely on the two full-time brothers, Silas and Sammy, who harvested and tended the crops, as well as their two cousins, Marty and Ben, who were dedicated to overseeing the packing, shipping, and delivery. All four were young, not even twenty-five yet, but had been working the farm for a couple of years and all seemed to have excellent work habits.

Because she took the job seriously, her mornings belonged to Fran, learning the farm routine and schedule as well as Nick did.

Before clocking in at the Diner though, Hayden made sure she spent at least two hours either in Fran's kitchen or Jordan's, soaking up as much info about the ins and outs of how best to utilize all the fresh fruits and vegetables they grew in abundance. The way Hayden saw it, she could take what she learned and pass it on to customers at the roadside stand whenever they asked about the seasonal crops.

Even though Jordan was the more professional cook of the two women, Hayden learned everything she could from both.

From Jordan she got proficiency and a skill that tended to lean more on the expert side, more like what you'd get from a five-star chef. And although Frannie's way was considerably more downhome, the "throw it in the pot and see how it all turned out" approach, Hayden couldn't argue with the delicious results, especially when it came to Frannie's cornbread, or her cherry or apple cobblers.

What she discovered was that both women might create pot roast from two different angles. But both angles made for mouth-watering meals.

One thing both women agreed on though was that to be successful in the kitchen it all started in the garden. To make great dishes, you had to have the freshest ingredients and nothing could be fresher than from the garden to the table.

And growing anything seemed to be Fran's specialty. The woman had a green thumb to envy. Hayden found Francine a genuine delight to be around. Fran was bubbly and energetic, a contrast to what she had expected from a woman who had been doing the same chores for over thirty years. Her enthusiasm it seemed never waned. Fran's love of the farm seemed to show through everything she did. Hayden admired the way the woman tended the garden, the way she babied her seedlings along in the greenhouse, even the care she gave the mulching and weeding.

In a matter of a few short days, Hayden discovered a side to herself she didn't know existed, the creative side of working with her hands. As exhausting as the physical work was, it was also rewarding. Imagine, being able to put a seed in some dirt and watch it sprout with a little TLC and water.

Hayden couldn't wait to grow something of her own. So when Fran gave her rosemary and basil seedlings, she rushed out to The Plant Habitat to buy containers to set on the little landing outside her apartment door.

But thanks to both Jordan and Fran, Hayden's confidence kicked in for real when she started learning how to cook for herself. Jordan had insisted they replace the stovetop in the studio, which allowed Hayden to try out a few simple pasta and rice dishes on her own, like homework assignments. The results turned out to be actual home-cooked meals.

But as much personal fulfillment as Hayden got shadowing Fran and Jordan, she still had to wait tables Tuesday through Saturday evenings down at the Diner which left her Sundays and Mondays to do with as she pleased.

Like today, she and Ethan were out on the water, celebrating the fact he turned the big three-three. They were spending time together like a date, like a couple, on the deck of his sleek, twenty-two-foot sloop, sailing to an unknown destination because he had refused to tell her where they were going.

As the boat rocked and swayed, she stood at the railing getting used to the motion of the boat. As it made its way farther out into the choppy water of the bay leaving behind the shoreline, Hayden scanned the smattering of people sitting along the strip of sandy beach. Soon the beachgoers grew smaller and smaller as the wind caught the sails and the boat picked up speed. The people stretched out on beach towels or blankets became dots until all she could see were the colorful assortment of umbrellas, sticking up out of the sand.

She turned to look at the birthday boy and his dog. Grisham, at the moment, stood next to his master, content to thump his tail happily back and forth on Ethan's leg. Meanwhile, Ethan steered them farther out onto the open sea.

"How long have you been sailing, Ethan?"

"Since I was maybe eight or nine. My dad always believed in taking his sons out on the water, to fish or snorkel. We always had a boat of one kind or another. Taking us out on the water was one way he could spend some alone time with us telling stories about our roots. It was a great way for him to make sure he got and kept our undivided attention, making sure we kept our Native past alive in here." Ethan placed a hand over his heart.

"What kind of stories?"

His face crinkled with amusement. "How did I know you were going to want to hear one of our legends?"

Her lips curved. "Using your intuition on me already, Ethan, and we aren't even thirty minutes into our sail. Come on, tell me a story."

He gave Grisham's head a rub, giving him time to think. "Once there lived a beautiful, but headstrong, young maiden with long raven hair, named Nahala. Her beauty attracted many suitors in her own village. But Nahala would have none of them. As it turned out, she had already given her heart to the young and strong Manaku from another settlement nearby, a man her father did not approve of.

"For some time they were able to keep their love a secret. But as often happens, the young lovers became impatient to start their life together. So on the night of the full moon, Manaku and Nahala decided to pack up their belongings and run away. She hadn't been gone long though, when Nahala's father and brothers discovered her missing. They immediately set out to find her, only to learn to their surprise there was not one set of tracks, but two. Fearing she'd been taken against her will by one of their enemies, they were determined to find her and bring her back.

"Letting the full moon guide their way, the couple walked fast and far, far away from both of their villages, far away from Nahala's family who sought to bring them back. Their journey brought them to the Bay. But by that time, in the distance, they could hear the cries of her father and brothers. As Nahala's family grew closer, the lovers became frightened that if found they would be separated forever and never see each other again. When they spotted a giant condor flying overhead, Manaku called out to him for help. The huge bird heard the man's pleas and took pity on the young lovers.

"The condor spread its wings and soared upward, up high into the night sky, so high his wings blocked out the light of the full moon, giving the young lovers enough time to find a cave overlooking the bay where they could hide.

"With the condor hiding the moon, without its light to guide them, Nahala's father and brothers might as well have been blind, for even though they searched and searched well into the night, they found no sign of them. Inside the cave, Manaku and Nahala shared their smoked fish with the condor and promised to feed him forever and always if he would continue to hide the moon so they would be safe and be able to live together for always.

"And to this day, Nahala and Manaku live by the bay with the condor, hidden from all who seek them. That is why my people took to calling the bay, 'initap'i' a nimeyesh a 'awa'y, or the bay of the hidden moon."

Hayden smiled into his warm brown eyes, felt that familiar tug in the belly. "You're a good storyteller, Ethan. Tell me, do you play the guitar as well as you spin a yarn?"

"The guitar is a hobby, although I do love music. And the story is centuries old." He really had no interest in sailing today or telling stories. No, what he wanted to devote his full attention to at the moment were Hayden's long legs, which he could see because she'd worn a pair of low-riding, hip-hugging white shorts. He'd been hoping for a bikini, a red one, but knew it was the wrong time of year to wear such things on the bay to go sailing. Even though the sun felt warm the wind had a bite to it. So he blessed his good fortune for the sight of those legs in the shorts and didn't complain.

When she caught him staring at her legs, she offered, "Good thing I picked up these cargo shorts at that little touristy shop in town. My wardrobe is rather limited these days. There aren't many places in town you can shop for clothes, especially if you want the latest fashion. And I went the entire summer without indulging in a pair of shorts, can you imagine that? You don't think they're out of style do you?"

"I think they're fine, more than fine. Once we get out into the open sea, I'll be glad to show you—exactly how fine I think they are."

She giggled. "Ethan, where are we going?"

"Someplace private, someplace where we can be alone. I threatened Brent with bodily harm if he so much as thinks about calling me out on my day off."

"No news on Kent and Sissy?"

He shook his head. "I'm not talking shop today, Hayden." To make his point, he changed the subject. "What's in the cooler you brought?" He did his best to keep his eyes on the horizon and not on those points of interest under the green hoodie she wore. The woman had a stunning body and didn't seem to know it. She certainly didn't obsess on clothes like other women he'd known.

"A birthday picnic. Jordan helped me put it together. There's lobster salad to die for, shrimp salad, a melon fruit salad with strawberry vinaigrette, and fudge cake."

"Jordan's fudge cake is superb."

"I creamed the butter and sugar for the icing," she added proudly. "And I put together the melon salad and mixed the vinaigrette."

"Did you now?" He grinned. "Thank you. I know cooking's not your forte."

"Not yet, but I'm determined to learn. I made an omelet this morning for breakfast. Okay, it turned into really tasty scrambled eggs, but the point is I tried."

"Really? Why?"

"Because I've always wanted to learn and now that there is no sixty-hour work weeks keeping me chained to a desk, I can enjoy taking the time to do it right. Although, I am swamped out at the farm. But if I cook, there's no need for takeout, unless you count what I take from Jordan's, which I don't. No fast food either unless you count the Diner—"

"Which you don't," he teased.

"Might as well learn to fix my own meals. Besides, I won't be living in the studio forever."

"Still thinking about Autumn's house for a bookstore?"

She sighed and took a seat on the deck. "I'm afraid that idea was a little premature. I found out the bookstore in San Sebastian went bust. I don't see how Pelican Pointe could support one. Besides, now that Nick and Jordan have given me the task of learning everything I can about the farm, keeping the books, I'm determined not to let them down."

"You always this loyal to your friends, Hayden?"

She thought about that for a minute and answered with certainty. "I haven't had that many since college and I didn't really go to the trouble of keeping in touch with them after I graduated. But when you're starting over in a new place with nothing and you happen upon such terrific people like Nick and Jordan, it makes you realize that with everything bad in the world, it reaffirms your faith that there are also good people out there."

"So the bookstore thing is off."

"Pretty much. I've put the business idea on hold for now anyway because I'm too busy out at the farm to think about anything else. How far out on the water are we going?"

"We'll sail out to Treasure Island and back."

"Really? The water's beautiful today. I wouldn't mind learning to sail. You know Jordan mentioned they might need a tour guide in the spring. Taking people out to Treasure Island and back, maybe explore the shipwreck while they're at it."

"Ah, the shipwreck. Scott mentioned that a couple of times."

"You knew him, didn't you, when he was alive?"

"Some. He was older, maybe by three years. I'd see him around town every now and then with his grandfather whenever I was over here visiting my grandmother. And of course everyone knew he'd lost his parents when he was little."

"I think I would've liked having him as a friend—in real life, I mean."

Ethan couldn't help it, he laughed. "Scott could talk your ear off if you let him."

"You know he thinks Jordan is angry with him."

Ethan's brows drew together in a frown. "Hayden, are you seriously telling me you're having conversations with Scott, for real?"

She drew in a breath, slightly embarrassed for having mentioned it. "What if I told you I've had several? The first time that day I went for a hike and you thought I'd gotten lost. I found the cemetery while I was walking. Curiosity had me looking for his headstone. And there he was. Big as life. The second time I went there looking for him one day before work. And I don't care how silly it sounds talking to him makes me feel better about things. I can't explain it anymore than that."

Ethan scratched his chin. He'd never known anyone outside of his father and a few of the tribe's shamans to admit to having conversations with spirits. "Maybe knowing you're troubled about—things, he is—trying to help you. You need someone to talk to and Scott's providing the venue."

"I'm sure that's it. He knows the real me, my real name." She let those words sink in before she changed direction. "I think I might like the tour guide idea."

So she could talk about her troubles to a ghost, unburden herself to a dead guy, but not to him. How insulting was that? Good Lord, was he jealous? Ethan had to laugh at himself. He shook his head. "You're all over the place, Hayden. Come here."

She looked guarded for a moment before moving into his chest.

"You think I'm crazy."

"No, I think you've found an outlet that's helping you deal with the stress you're under. And it's cheaper than a shrink."

She snickered. "Then I need to lengthen my appointments, make the most of him as a sounding board."

He lowered his mouth to hers. For a moment he simply enjoyed grazing and nipping at her lips before hungrily devouring her in a mouthy kiss.

Hayden felt the stirring in her belly, felt her blood heat. She dragged the kiss out as long as she could before they had to come up for air. "You've got a first-rate tonsil-dive there, Deputy."

"You're not so bad yourself. I want you, Hayden."

She sighed. "We're getting there, Ethan. But I'm still not sure it's wise for me to get involved with anyone, least of all someone who has issues—with my honesty."

"Think about how good we'd be together and forget about issues." He covered her mouth again, brought her into his body.

Hard male met soft female.

His body throbbed with need. He wanted her horizontal, under him, the sooner the better. But for now, he let her go and had to blank his mind to get the buzzing in his ears to stop. The woman flat out packed a punch.

When he spotted the little dot of land known as Treasure Island, he focused on steering toward the postcard-sized strip of rock and dirt in the distance.

He prepared to come about, lowered the mainsail, and then sought out Hayden's hand, helping her go through the steps to work the jib.

Without the sails, the wind seemed to die as the sloop's progress dwindled to a stingy sway and give. The boat bobbled feet away from the tiny strip of land. "Picnic on the deck of the boat or Treasure Island?" Ethan asked. "Ladies' choice."

"I'd love to look around the island."

"Land it is then," he said, as he prepared to wade through the water, carrying the cooler. "I'll come back for you."

Hayden looked insulted. "You think I'm afraid of getting wet?"

Ethan watched Grisham spring off the deck and into the waves like a dolphin as the dog paddled the short distance to shore and was already shaking off the water.

"There's no need to get huffy, or wet. Besides, it's an excuse to wrap my arms around you again."

"Aww, well then, I'll stand here all damsel-in-distress-like and wait for you to carry me across the water, even though, I could just as easily traipse over there myself."

"And get those brand-new shorts wet? No way. And there will be no traipsing, my lady," he said in mock fashion. He scooped her up, planted his mouth on hers. Little tugs of need flared between them.

He took a measured step into the water. As the shallow tide swirled around his knees, he made like he was going to drop his hold. "Are you going to be nice to me today, Hayden?"

"Ethan, don't you dare drop me or…"

"Or what?"

Those playful eyes drew her in. She grabbed his head between both hands and went with instinct. She brought his lips down to meet hers. Desire bloomed. Doubt melted away. "I want your hands on me, Ethan."

He grinned and plopped her down on the rocky slab of beach. "I was hoping I'd wear you down. I'll go back to the boat—get the blanket I have stowed on board and—a few other things." He thought of the box of condoms he'd conveniently picked up at the drug store in Santa Cruz.

Before turning to go though, he looked at her and said, "Don't change your mind before I get back, okay?"

Hayden laughed. "I won't. But hurry." She watched him stride back through the water, watched as his muscles bunched and he pulled himself into the sloop, disappeared below deck.

She looked around at the little slice of island no more than a half a mile long and even less than that across in width.

The beach sloped upward, more rock than sand, before leveling off into various patches of vegetation and knee-high bunchgrass. Aromatic white sage dotted the landscape as well as eucalyptus. She recognized flowering California sagebrush from the books about native plants she'd checked out at the library.

Across the inlet in the distance, she could make out Promise Cove as the old Victorian seemed to cling to the side of the cliffs. She narrowed her eyes at the swath of cove beneath and recognized the same jagged rocks she'd stood on to look out over the water.

Ethan came up behind her, smelling like sea and man. His hair was damp. His shorts wet. He dropped the blanket he carried on top of the cooler and took her by the hand, tugged her up and over the rise. "Let's see if we can find enough wood to build a fire."

"A fire? But the sun's out. It's not even that cold."

He took the time to peruse her long, lanky frame, making no secret of his intent. "Without clothes a fire will come in handy. See that circle of stones over there in the clearing. Ready-made fire pit. That pit's been used to build a fire since…probably forty years or longer."

As she trooped behind him, gathering up sticks and small branches for kindling, she listened while he checked off the merits of fire safety. Something about contained areas versus wind direction. After a couple of minutes, she couldn't help it, she laughed. "Why do I get the impression you were an excellent boy scout?"

"Once upon a time," he said with a grin. "But I never once wanted to be a forest ranger."

She rolled her eyes at him. "Oh, look at those chubby birds over there with the funny plumage on their heads. They look like small chickens."

Hayden pointed to a cluster of knobby sagebrush nearby where the colorful blue and gray fowl nested together, seeming to burrow into the soft sand. As she stood there admiring them, she'd swear they were talking to her, repeating Chicago, Chicago, over and over again. Weird.

"California quail." Ethan explained. "The state bird. They're native to the coastal shrub."

With his arms laden with wood, he squatted down in front of the fire pit, dumped the logs on the ground, and began to stack the assortment of branches as if building a small tower.

Hayden knelt beside him, tempted to run her hands over his broad shoulders, feel the strength there. He took the kindling from her and their eyes locked. "We'll get this show on the road and then start our own fire, how's that?"

He took out matches, set the logs to flame. As soon as he was satisfied the fire caught enough not to die out, they walked back over the rise and down to the beach to retrieve the blanket and the cooler with the food.

Ethan plunked down the cooler, flipped it open, studied the label on the bottle of chardonnay while Hayden dug into the picnic basket and handed him the corkscrew. As he uncorked the wine Hayden brought out two glasses wrapped in cloth napkins. She held out both and waited while Ethan poured.

They sipped the wine and Hayden asked, "Are you hungry?"

He busted out laughing. "You keep asking me that. Oh yeah, I am, but not for food. I'm about ready to show you." He picked up her hand, tugged her closer where he could nibble her ear. "It seems Hayden-no-middle-initial-Ryan has been making me crazy since that night on the side of the road, on purpose I think."

"Who me?" She lifted her glass in a toast. "Happy birthday, Ethan." She turned her mouth up to his. After gnawing and nipping at each other. They set the wine down long enough to spread out the blanket near the fire.

The ground was hard and unforgiving, but they got as comfortable as they could on the hard-packed sand. It was a nervous Hayden who leaned over, placed her lips against the side of his face. "This is where I'm supposed to say, I should go change into something more comfortable."

He brought her into his arms, skimmed his hands up and down her back then began to graze along her throat. "Uh-uh. For weeks I've visualized you without clothes, especially getting you out of your panties."

"I'm not wearing any. Panties that is," she confessed as she watched how hard he swallowed.

"That's kind of a habit of yours."

She snickered at the long look he gave her. "I've never made love outside before either."

"Ever? Well, we're out to change that." He reached to unzip the hoodie she wore, discovered she had nothing on underneath. Rose-tipped points stared back at him.

His breath hitched. "God, you're beautiful. It's a wonder we made it to the island." He slid the hoodie down off her shoulders as she snaked her arms around his neck, offered her mouth again.

He dipped his head, drew in a nipple, suckled one peak before going after the other.

Her head fell back, lolled onto her shoulders as she lost herself, content in the pleasure. He slid her cargo shorts down and off. She kicked out of them, leaving her completely bare. He caught sight of a few blonde wisps, a sexy little landing strip of natural hair, before finding her mouth again.

She pulled his Tee up and off, tossing the shirt aside. She worked on the zipper to his shorts. Once he'd kicked out of his clothes, he lifted her onto his lap. Finally she could run her hands along the muscles of his chest.

She draped her arms around his neck, listened to the crackle and pop of the fire. The sound of the surf a few feet away, lapped in rhythm against the rocky shore. Nature, she decided, was the perfect backdrop for making love.

Ethan got a kick out of the flutter of anticipation he felt emanating from her. He'd barely touched her, and yet, there was already a prelude to lust, a yearning building up.

He covered her mouth with his. Playful tongues slicked to taste and tease. Probing strokes turned hungry, greedy. They explored each other, fingering along folds, discovering all kinds of sensitive peaks and valleys.

It might have been broad daylight, but Hayden saw stars. Purple and red bursts of color blurred her vision as he took her higher, his long fingers working toward that white-hot light. Large and small rockets went off in every direction. After such a long drought, Hayden fractured into the palm of his hand in an explosion of silky heat, breathing out his name.

She'd never felt so uninhibited before. It had to be making love outdoors, underneath the sky, so near the ebb and flow of the ocean. Why hadn't she ever made love outside before now? she wondered. She felt like a warrior goddess and mother earth blended into one.

That combo had her feeling powerful, bolder. She lowered her head and sought to touch Ethan in every way she could reach. She sleeked along his body until she could straddle him, guided him into her in one fluid motion.

From above, pools of mossy green speared deep chocolate. She discovered when aroused his exotic brown eyes took on an even sharper molten quality, their purpose meant to arrow straight into her soul.

From below, Ethan kept his eyes locked on hers. He toyed with her breasts, letting her set the pace. But before long, he eagerly latched on to her hips as he shifted to accommodate her tempo.

Anticipating each other's movement, they began to build on thrusts, slow, fast, slow, fast. Beat and pulse soon gave way to need, urgency.

In a blast of heat that burst from both of them, they shattered into each other.

Still inside her, linked, Ethan was bombarded by flashes.

Initially he saw a darkened parking garage, then a golden-haired woman with Hayden's face, pushed up against a concrete wall. He caught the silver glint of a knife as a man held the weapon to her throat.

His jaw tightened. His gut clenched. He tried to shake off the picture in his head, did his best to get back into the moment.

Hayden fell on his chest, breathless. He heard the sigh escape her lips, felt her breath against his skin, watched as she raised her head and those green eyes pierced his.

With the image of the man with the knife still in his head, Ethan heard her say, "That was…amazing."

She sent him a dazzling smile. "I like being on top." Her head went back, eyes focused on the bright blue of the sky. She spread her arms out wide. "I feel so powerful, so emboldened. Is it always like that…making love outside, I mean? If it is, then we should make a point of doing this outside as often as we can."

In spite of the vision, he chuckled. He shook off the dregs of what he'd seen, determined not to let it ruin this moment. "Good thing. I'd have crushed you on top. Even with the blanket this ground is like concrete. But I'm not complaining," he added quickly, as he toyed with her hair. "Let me guess, you're a natural blonde. A green-eyed blonde."

Her eyes grew wide before she choked out a laugh. "Observant, aren't you?"

"It's a shame you had to dye it. When will you be able to put it back?" A blur of lanky blonde with longer hair running in high heels through a parking garage flitted through his head. He swallowed hard, torn between wanting to keep the images coming and making them stop.

The cop in him had questions and wondered if the man with the knife had come after her specifically or had it been a random attack?

"Ethan, don't spoil this," she warned as she reached over and found her hoodie, zipped it up. "It's just hair." She blew out a nervous breath and veered the subject into safer waters. "Worked up an appetite yet, birthday boy?" she asked, shimmying into her shorts.

"I'm starving," he answered, watching her get dressed. He gave her a wink, trying for casual, even calm, though he was anything but. "We should probably eat first, keep up our strength."

Once they set out the food, Ethan made fast work of the lobster and shrimp salads before moving on to the fruit. Then, as if rewarding himself for a job well done, he ate his piece of chocolate cake and half of Hayden's.

But the images were there along the fringes of his vision and wouldn't go away.

Stretched out on the blanket with his hands locked behind his head propping it up, his legs crossed at the ankles, Ethan sighed audibly. He wondered if he was pulling it off. Was he acting casual enough? "I feel like a nap," he said after a moment. But when he caught Hayden staring at him he asked nervously, "What?"

"I'm trying to remember the last time I saw a grown man eat so much in one sitting. Where do you put all that?"

"High metabolism. I work it off." He suddenly sat up and snatched her around the waist, bringing her down on the blanket beside him. "Let me show you how."

Nipping her lower lip, he coaxed a kiss out of her before slowly unzipping the hoodie again. "How about we get you out of these shorts too?" he prompted as he tugged them down her long legs.

The things he could do with his mouth, thought Hayden as she held his head in place, while he tugged and nipped at her breasts. But she wasn't prepared when the man began moving lower, licking and tasting his way past her belly. Making his way further down, he went after her center, telling her, "Ah, you are my real dessert."

As his tongue played, she squirmed and writhed to the motion until finally she begged, "Now Ethan, now."

He quickly got rid of shorts and shirt, collapsing back down on the blanket again. He settled her on his lap, began an assault on her mouth. With her arms and legs locked around him, he completed the link as one and slipped inside.

Hard male chest leaned up against soft female curves. Ethan began moving, fast, hard, slow.

Hayden let Ethan take her under again as waves of delight continued to lap at the edges. White bursts of light distorted her vision. In a blaze of heat he brought them through the flowing current while a gigantic riptide carried them under, finishing together.

As they lay there connected, Ethan rested his head on Hayden's forehead. The snapshots were still there if he looked. It was difficult not to. It was definitely Hayden in that parking garage, fighting with a man who held a knife to her throat. Because she'd fought, she'd been able to get away, to run.

And she was still running, he thought miserably.

He looked up into her face. She was eyeing him curiously.

"I don't think I'll ever see this island the same way again after today," he forced out.

Hayden gave him a tight belly laugh. "We didn't even take time to explore every inch."

"Mmmm, I was too busy exploring more interesting inches, like this one right here." He nuzzled her throat. "And this one." His long fingers trailed along a breast.

"I could stay like this forever," she said, still wrapped up in his embrace. "Making love outside is exhilarating."

Damn. He was going to have to end this peaceful solitude and not in a good way. He wasn't sure how she'd react. He set her off his lap, breaking their connection, and watched as she self-consciously reached for her shorts.

As they began to gather their clothes, the sun dipped a little lower in the afternoon sky. Time on their little slice of island was about to run out.

In a quiet tone, Ethan wanted her to know, "I'm expected at my parent's house tonight, Hayden, for a birthday supper. I want you to come with me."

After pulling on her hoodie, she opened her mouth to object, but nothing came out.

He watched her for any sign she was pulling back away from him figuratively. He expected resistance, was even prepared to go into stubborn mode to nudge her toward accepting the invitation.

She zipped up her top and finally managed, "Do you think that's really wise, Ethan? Your parents won't be expecting me." It was way too early to meet his parents, knowing they'd surely put her under a microscope if she got within ten feet, asking questions about her background most people took for granted when they were simply trying to get to know someone, especially a someone their son is—dating.

Were they dating? They were doing a helluva lot more than dating now.

Would she ever be ready to answer those kinds of invasive queries from people who just wanted to know something real and true about her? At the prospect of having to lie to his parents, her stomach tensed.

Ethan didn't have to be intuitive to recognize unease when he saw it. "I've already told them to expect I'd be bringing a date." He certainly hadn't wanted to risk his mother setting him up with the first-grade teacher again either. "It'll be all right, Hayden. I'll be there to run interference, keep them from getting too nosy." Although he couldn't guarantee his father wouldn't pick up on her guarded demeanor. "What do you say?"

"Okay. But I need to go home and change clothes. I can't go like this. Besides, I smell like sex."

"You do," he agreed amicably. He nibbled her jaw again and smiled. "And it just makes me want to eat you up all over again."

Chapter Fourteen

The Santa Cruz home of Markus and Lindeen Cody, a beach bungalow Craftsman built in the 1920s, turned out to be filled to capacity with a lively bunch of family and friends who had gathered there to make sure Ethan had an unforgettable thirty-third birthday.

Hayden decided a little smugly she'd done a pretty good job of taking care of that herself. But as she snuck another glance in the direction of his parents, who seemed to be giving her a rather wide purposeful berth, she was more than a little anxious around all these people, who were obviously relatives and close friends.

Ethan had failed to mention that he was bringing her to an actual party rather than the sit-down conventional dinner she'd been expecting with just his immediate family.

Good thing she'd had the presence of mind to listen to him when he'd suggested she dress casually in her skinny jeans and turtleneck instead of the dress she'd wanted to wear. At least Ethan had steered her away from dressing up because here every partygoer was in jeans or beachwear.

Because of that, she couldn't blame her uneasiness on the fact she'd broken some dress code.

As she looked around the deck where a buffet had been set up, she was bombarded by a sea of faces belonging to his numerous aunts and uncles and cousins, all of whom paraded past her in a haze of names attached to all kinds of humorous anecdotes about Ethan as a boy. These people seemed friendly enough as if they hadn't gotten the memo that Markus and Lindeen were advocating a standoffish approach where she was concerned.

When Hayden spotted Ethan's brother, Brent walking her way, her stomach automatically tightened as if a hundred knots were twisting inside. She hoped the lobster salad she'd eaten that afternoon didn't make a sudden reappearance.

She tried to summon up courage and reminded herself that she wasn't a wanted fugitive. Why couldn't people like Brent concentrate on finding the bad guys like Jeremy, instead of acting as though she had something to hide?

But then she reluctantly realized she did have something to hide, like who she really was.

When Brent handed her a plate filled with an assortment of appetizers, almost like a peace offering, she fixed a smile on her face. "Thanks. I was just listening to Ethan's uncle tell me about the time Ethan had to pull his dog, Snap, off the postman."

Brent actually smiled. "Yeah, I think Ethan was probably seven at the time. He and Snap were pretty much inseparable back then. And the postman was old man Bitters. The guy loved to torment Ethan's dog every chance he got. Ethan took exception and decided he and Snap should teach Bitters a lesson. They waited in the bushes and when old man Bitters got close to the porch, they jumped out, yelled, 'boo.' But Bitters was looking for any chance to go after the dog. He started hitting Snap with the night stick he always carried with him. Ethan reacted like a wild boy trying to separate the two. Here was this little guy trying to get a grown man to stop hitting his dog."

"And got whacked with the damn night stick right across the back of the head," Ethan added as he came up behind Hayden, locking his arms around her waist.

"Took twelve stitches to close him up. Didn't do a thing to dent that hard head of his though," Brent said, before taking a bite of a rolled taco. Out of the blue, he asked, "Are you planning on staying put in Pelican Pointe, Hayden?"

With Ethan at her elbow, she felt suddenly bolder. She turned to face Brent. "I am. I'm settling in just fine, thank you. Learning to cook, even, learning how to grow veggies, as well. Francine knows everything there is to know about growing organic."

"She should, she's been there for thirty years. You really think you can learn how to grow stuff like kale? If I could make a suggestion, why bother? That stuff tastes as bad as Brussels sprouts if you ask me."

Hayden muffled a laugh. He sounded like a twelve-year-old boy who didn't care for eating green veggies. "I'll be manning the fruit stand starting next week. Why don't you stop by? I'll make sure you get a nice big pumpkin to decorate your front porch. Even the top cop in Santa Cruz needs a little Halloween spirit."

Ethan laughed and had to tamper his urge to nibble Hayden's neck right there in front of his parents. "Brent here hasn't had any Halloween spirit since Tara Dettinger picked up a bowl of spiked punch at the community center dance and dumped the entire thing over his head."

Brent placed a hand over his heart. "Tenth grade. Tara always did have a feisty streak. But that's what I liked about her."

"He was sixteen at the time and head over heels in lust with red-haired Tara."

"Yeah, it might have been the red hair that did it."

"Whatever happened to Tara anyway?"

Brent sighed. "Last I heard she married a doctor, a plastic surgeon in Santa Barbara, had three kids. She and the doctor are probably rolling in dough from all the Botox he dispenses."

Hayden appreciated the razzing between brothers. With an older sister, she could relate to a little harmless banter among siblings. But Brent surprised her when he asked, "You're really happy out at Taggert's farm?"

She smiled at him. For the first time, it was relaxed and genuine. "I am. Who knew a bean counter could find such contentment in the middle of a bunch of cows?"

After the crowd of well–wishing relatives thinned out, Ethan managed to get his parents alone for five minutes in the kitchen without Hayden around to hear. He'd been a little put off by the way they had both treated Hayden all evening. It wasn't like either one of them to be so frosty to an invited guest either. But the fact that both of them had ignored her told him something was wrong.

But as soon as Ethan met his father's eyes, he had his answer. Markus Cody had already apparently passed on to his wife everything he'd "read" from Hayden.

Markus cautioned, "The aura of danger surrounds her, enough for me to worry about my youngest son. You've fallen for her, have you not?"

Ethan couldn't have denied it even if he'd wanted to. "Then why did you and Mom keep your distance tonight?"

"She's trouble, Ethan," his mother added. "After all the women I've set you up with over the years, you pick someone with such a difficult past." She shook her head. "What about Julianne? She loves children, she's—"

Ethan didn't let her finish, even held up a staying hand. "We've been over this. I'd much prefer to find my own women, okay? And you don't know a thing about Hayden. If you'd have bothered to say more than two words to her tonight you might have—"

But Lindeen Cody was just as adamant. "Ask questions she doesn't want to answer truthfully? Give us answers that mean nothing, that are probably little white lies? I don't think so. Will you deny she's hiding something?"

Ethan shook his head. No way was he going to tell his parents about all those flashes he'd gotten that afternoon. His dad would want specifics, like how he'd gotten such a powerful connection so quickly. He wasn't about to share those kinds of details with his father. Hell, if Markus Cody was in top form though, he could probably pick up on the how of it anyway. And that had Ethan ready to leave.

"Look, it isn't what you think. If you'd give her half a chance, get to know her even a little, you'd find out she's a terrific person." He laid a hand on his heart. "Here. Inside. Her heart is true." He pointed a finger at his father. "And you of all people should be able to read that as well as the dangerous aura. She has her reasons."

"She doesn't even use her real name," Lindeen Cody pointed out stubbornly.

"No, but I'm working on it. Do you trust your own son?" He saw the concern warring with reluctance in their eyes, but waited until he saw them both nod before he added, "Then rely on my instincts where she's concerned. Because I'm telling you, you're both making a mistake by not getting to know her."

Ethan had left it like that with his parents, but he wasn't happy about it. He wasn't angry with them, exactly. No, more like frustrated. He'd known when he asked Hayden to accompany him to their house his father would pick up on her issues. And despite that, he hadn't wanted to drop her off back at Promise Cove without including her in a family gathering, especially after what they'd shared that afternoon on the island. Yes, the sex had been incredible, but it wasn't just the physical. Somehow, they'd managed to connect on a level he hadn't known existed with anyone else, as if her past had melded into his. He'd never gotten flashes that strong, that quick, while inside another woman before in his life until this afternoon. Ever.

Right now, he was tempted to chalk up how he felt to the flashes he'd gotten and nothing more. But he was lying to himself if he tried to deny how he felt. And that left him feeling a little downhearted at his parents' reaction.

As soon as they got into the car, he turned to Hayden and asked, "How about stopping for a drink?"

"Ethan, we just left a party where there was enough beer to float a boat." Even though they hadn't drunk that much, she knew because true to his word, he'd pretty much stayed glued to her side all evening.

"Then how about some music?"

Puzzled, trying to gauge his mood, she agreed, "Sure. Are you upset with me about something?"

He picked up her hand, brought it to his lips. "Not at all. It isn't you."

She frowned. "Ah, something happened at the party then?"

About that time she watched as he pulled into the pot-holed, parking lot of a dive along the wharf, not five minutes from his parents' house. The bar, called Spikes, was a seedy little place in worse shape than McCready's.

"I used to tend bar here while I went to college. The band on Sunday nights are friends of mine from high school," he shouted over the din of music blasting from a stingy six-by-six-foot stage, where four guys belted out what sounded like Green Day's *Boulevard of Broken Dreams*.

But the minute the guy behind the pock-marked counter spotted Ethan, he sent up a friendly wave and Ethan waved back.

He led her to the only available table the size of a postage stamp near the stage.

"I'll go get us some drinks," he yelled in her direction as he set off toward the bar.

Not sure what they were doing here after the birthday party, Hayden decided to sit back and study this whole new side to Ethan Cody. This wasn't the uniformed-deputy, or the birthday boy, or the eager lover she'd spent the afternoon wrapped up in. No, this Ethan seemed moodier than she'd ever seen him, troubled maybe or distressed about something. She could only wait and see where the evening went from here and which one of his moods accompanied her home.

When he brought the drinks back, two sodas with a hint of vanilla rum, the band vaulted into an easy rendition of Barenaked Ladies' *If I Had a Million Dollars*.

The place was too loud to have an actual conversation, so she watched Ethan's shoulders relax layer by layer and could tell the minute he let go of whatever was bothering him once he got into the music.

But when the lead singer spotted him at the table, he motioned with his head for Ethan to join them on stage. Seeing him hesitate, Hayden nudged his knee with hers and bellowed, "Go on, show me what you've got."

She got a kick out of watching him strut on stage with all the confidence of someone who'd been there before. He picked up one of the extra guitars leaning against the back wall, slipped the strap over his head, and immediately dived into The Black Crowes' *Hard to Handle*, lead vocals and all.

The guy had a killer voice. Rock star good looks. And by the time the song ended with a round of applause and whistles, it seemed he also had a following. Every female waitress in the place, as well as most of the women in the audience, had their eyes on dark-haired, good-looking Ethan Cody.

When the band riffed into the first chords of the heart-tugging, *Let it Be Me*, Ethan's sultry vocals hit every range, blending with backup like he belonged there.

The minute their eyes locked—Hayden's heart reluctantly plunged—into a place she didn't want to fall. She didn't need complications. Her life was messed up enough. But by the time he harmonized his way through Snow Patrol's *You're All I Have*, seemingly singing the song just to her, she'd lifted off like a rocket again, deciding to enjoy every moment of the ride.

After that night, the days ran together as Hayden kept up a brutal pace. She did the bookkeeping at the farm on automatic. She might have been in her element with accounting, but she discovered little satisfaction in it. Certainly not like before, before she'd found this backwater little town with its slice of ocean, beach and sand, before she'd found Ethan Cody.

Five nights a week when she worked at the Diner, she usually stayed over at his house, practicing a new kind of schedule, a new kind of rhythm. At least for Hayden it was new.

After her shift ended, he would always be there to walk her to her car. Then they'd head to his house, have a late bite to eat, talk until they fell into bed where they'd make love into all hours of the night.

Even though they didn't get a lot of sleep, Hayden found a joy in having someone to share things with, things she'd never thought to share before. They never lacked for conversation. He seemed to always have something interesting to talk about, some amusing anecdote from his beat around town, or some passage from a book he'd read, or was currently reading. He went everywhere with a book under his arm, whether it ranged from classic literature like Steinbeck, or Jack Kerouac, or to rereading one of John Grisham's novels.

If he had to get up earlier than she did to make a police call, and they didn't eat breakfast together, he'd leave her little notes on his pillow that said things like, "enjoy your day," or "maybe we could meet for lunch."

She wondered how she could have been so self-absorbed in her career that she put having a personal relationship on the backburner. It didn't take a genius to figure that one out, though. She'd never known anyone like Ethan before. Ever. Or anyone who could make her bones melt in the sack for that matter.

Before Ethan, sex had been just sex. That is, when she had bothered with it. But spending time in Ethan's bed, she now fully understood the difference. Just thinking about their time together, and how they'd spent the night before doing things to each other, had her cheeks flushing.

She glanced around to see if anyone in the Diner had caught her lustful day-dreaming before letting her eyes drift to the wall clock. Eight-forty. Like a kid waiting for the final bell to ring at school, she couldn't wait for closing time to get there, couldn't wait to get her hands on Ethan. She sighed, and started cleaning up a good twenty minutes before it was time to put the Closed sign on the door.

Over the next several days every time Ethan made love to Hayden, the images of what had happened to her in that parking garage got stronger, sharper. The snapshot of the man with the knife was sometimes so clear he no longer had to wonder why she was on the run since he could clearly make out the perp's steely gray eyes and determination beneath the ski mask he wore.

But without a name there wasn't a helluva lot he could do with the description. He sure couldn't run an image of a ski mask in his head through NCIC.

Each time, he'd wanted to grill her about the incident. The temptation had been so great he'd all but had to stuff his mouth with the bedding not to ask her twenty questions about it.

The fact that he hadn't was a testament to how much she meant to him. They were just getting to a good place in their relationship, a place that spoke comfort and trust.

Even though he knew damn well Hayden Ryan was not the name of the woman he was sharing his bed with, he didn't really care.

And the cop in him had difficulty accepting that. Any other time, with any other woman, he wouldn't have hesitated to question her at length. But each time something held him back. Maybe it was the sheer terror he saw in those big green eyes that night in the garage, or maybe it was the helplessness he saw there. Whatever it was, it was keeping him in a constant state of frustration. And that had him feeling more than alarmed for her safety.

But then again, it might have been something simpler, like the woman's body and the way it responded to his.

That man in the parking garage had tried to rape her. A random attack? Ethan didn't think so. She wouldn't go on the run, change her name, because of a random attack. Even though he saw the images clear enough, he knew the man had threatened her; he just couldn't make out the words.

With every flash inside his head, Ethan had also gotten a sense that the man had been intent on taking her life that night, as if he had been sent there for that very purpose.

But why? What had she done? What had she seen? The questions nagged at him.

Ethan was fully aware that even if he did break down and confront her with all of his questions and suspicions, she'd simply pull away.

It would put an end to their easiness together.

And he found, he simply couldn't do it. The cop in him was tempted.

But the man just wanted the woman. Period. Any way he could get her.

Chapter Fifteen

One day after Hayden and Nick had spent the entire morning poring over the farm's books, Nick ran his fingers through his hair and said, "A dairy farm isn't as easy as it looks. In fact, this is a lot more complicated than I originally thought. To stay organic we have certifications we have to maintain."

"I know. Fran told me there's a long list of specifications we have to meet. I had no idea there was so much to growing organic vegetables," Hayden said with a laugh. "Are we making progress here, Nick? We only have ten more days before Will and Fran abandon us."

"It's like cramming for an exam. But we can still rely on Silas and Sammy. And thanks to Marty and Ben, they have the packing and delivery schedules down to an art. They've been working here almost two years now and Will has shown all four of them the fertilizer methods, as well as the limit on the pesticides to use. You know, Will and Francine did agree that if we had questions after they get to Tulare, we can always call or e-mail them."

"That's fine, Nick, but a garden isn't going to grow because of anything I find out in an e-mail." She sighed audibly. "What if I don't possess the slightest hint of a green thumb? What if I kill every plant you own, in spite of Silas and Sammy's direction? Have you read up on that powdery mildew stuff? It's scary. Even Sammy said it's tough to get rid of once it takes hold."

Nick chuckled. "I see I'm not the only one with a huge chunk of doubt. We'll do the best we can, okay? This is new ground and we're sure to make a few mistakes along the way."

"Jordan seems to think it's going well."

"Jordan is an eternal optimist. Speaking of Jordan, I was wondering if you'd mind babysitting Hutton for me. Jordan's birthday is the week before Halloween. I'd like to take her to San Francisco for an overnight trip, get her away to a five-star hotel where she can relax, do nothing but indulge herself. That way, she won't have to think about guests for twenty-four hours. If you'll agree to take care of Hutton for us, I'll see to it you don't have to worry about guests staying that day."

"Sure, I'll babysit. But why don't I ask Margie for a Saturday night off. That way you guys could leave Saturday morning and make a weekend out of it. You could even stay until Monday night or Tuesday morning. Your choice. Give you more time alone together, more downtime for Jordan to unwind. I don't have to be at the Diner until Tuesday afternoon."

"You'd do that?"

"Nick, if you don't know by now, I'd do just about anything for you and Jordan, then I'm a failure as a friend."

Nick laughed. "Aww, I like you too. But Margie might be upset."

"Margie will get over it. Besides, despite the woman's gruff exterior she's a marshmallow on the inside. She's a bit of a romantic. She goes through more romance novels than a junkie goes through crack. Who would have thought? But it's true. She and Max have been together as a couple for at least a decade. That's longer than some marriages last."

"Margie and Max? This town is a continuous source of surprise in the couple department."

"Isn't it though? Murphy and Carla Vargas can't keep their hands off each other whenever they come into the Diner for lunch. Same goes for Wally and Lilly. And Janie Pointer is sweet on Flynn McCready."

Nick's eyes went wide. "Janie, the hairstylist, and Flynn?"

"Yep, hot and heavy."

"Look, I'd appreciate it if you wouldn't mention anything to Jordan about the trip. I'd like to surprise her."

She put her thumb and forefinger together and held them to her mouth, gave a little twist as if she were turning a key. "Not to worry. It's in the vault. If you plan to leave that Saturday you'll miss the Homecoming parade though. It's all the high school girls can talk about, that and the Homecoming dance."

"Let's see, I've only been in Pelican Pointe since last winter and already I've seen more parades than I ever did in my entire life. Hutton gets a kick out of them though. But she'll never know she missed the Homecoming parade."

"I could take her. If you remove her car seat from the SUV, leave it so I can put it in the Mini, we could go."

"That'd be fine. And just so you know, I plan to mention the trip to Ethan. It's okay by me if he stays out here while we're gone. In fact, I'd prefer it. Leaving you and Hutton here alone, I don't think is a good idea."

She laughed and playfully punched him on the arm. "Why Nick, it's like you're the big brother I never had."

He shot her a brief grin before turning serious. "I love The Cove, but it's a long way from town. If Ethan can't stay out here at night while we're gone, then I may have to rethink leaving you and my daughter alone."

"Look, I won't say I don't think of the guy who wants me dead every now and then, but I think I'm off his radar. You really think of her as yours, don't you?"

He didn't have to ask to know she meant Hutton. "Absolutely. I mean I know she's Scott's, but she couldn't be more mine." But then he caught what she'd said. "Did you say dead? Hayden, I really wish you would tell Ethan who it is. I realize you're trying to..." He scratched his chin. "I'm not sure what you're trying to do, but isn't it better to be honest with Ethan? I know you two are...involved with each other."

She grinned at the way he phrased that. "And you? You want me to be honest with you?"

"Frankly, if you told me, I'd go straight to Ethan with the details." When he eyed the hurt on her face he explained, "Out of concern for your safety, Hayden. Not only that, I believe that honesty between two people is first and foremost. Without that you have nothing. In this case you're keeping something that could be detrimental to your safety. Look, when I first got here, I wasn't upfront with Jordan about a lot of things. I had issues, mostly dealing with Scott. I wasn't honest and it could have cost me Jordan. When I think about that now, about how I could have screwed up the most important relationship I'd ever had, I don't want to see this person put some kind of a wedge between you and Ethan down the road. I speak from experience. I got lucky with Jordan, she's the exception. I just don't want you making the same mistakes I made."

"Well, when you put it like that, I'll think about it. I've been talking to him, you know." When she saw the confusion in his eyes, she corrected the misconception. "Scott. Not Ethan. I go out to the cemetery whenever I can spare a minute. We have long talks. If someone passed by, they'd more than likely think I was insane, sitting there in front of his headstone on the grass talking to myself. But going out there, talking to him is somehow—comforting."

Nick shook his head. "You've obviously made a connection to him."

"Yeah. I haven't told Jordan. It upsets her. And what with her being pregnant and all, I think it's better if I keep this to myself."

"She's upset that Scott doesn't bother with her."

"I know. He says she's blocking him because she's so angry about being out here so long alone. Despite how crazy that sounds, I like him, Nick. It's hard not to."

"Well, Scott always did like to talk. Think of it this way, if nothing else, it's cheap therapy."

Later that morning, Hayden caught sight of Will Foley sitting on the tractor pulling a load of newly picked pumpkins down the long driveway to the roadside fruit stand. Suddenly a light bulb went off. She decided they might do a lot more business if they turned the fruit stand into a pumpkin patch like she'd seen a lifetime ago back home.

When she mentioned it to Will, he took off his ball cap, scratched his head, and said, "Not a bad idea. Might increase sales at that. I'm surprised Frannie didn't think of that before now."

After talking Will into delivering more bales of hay and all the wooden crates he could find, Hayden set to work. It took most of the morning, but by noon, she'd made a couple of life-sized scarecrows out of the old jeans and tattered shirts she'd found among the boxes of Edmund Taggert's clothing Fran had planned to donate to the Salvation Army. As Hayden stuffed hay into the jeans, she decided that maybe using his old clothes, in some eerie way Mr. Taggert could still feel part of the place while Nick and Jordan took over running it.

She shook her head. She couldn't help wondering what was with her lately. Since meeting and talking to Scott, she'd definitely gotten sentimental about the dead lately.

Once she got the scarecrows set up on each side of the front counter, she started to work on arranging the pumpkins on the ground and then on the various levels of hay bales. Realizing she needed flowers to make the display pop, she wondered if Jordan would mind if she cut some of her sunflowers to use for decoration.

She had just decided the entire plants would work better when her prepaid cell phone rang. One glance at the digital readout told her it was Sydney. "Hey, Syd."

"Hi ya, sis. Got a few minutes between patients to chat. How're things out west? Still playing farm girl?"

"You are so cruel. And yeah, right now I'm setting up the roadside fruit stand for Halloween." She wasn't about to update her sister with the details of sleeping with the local sheriff's deputy. That knowledge might send Sydney completely over the edge.

"Geez, Em, oops, I mean Hayden, you're really settling in there. You know, back in your teens you used to be so creative. It wasn't until you got to college you left that side in the dust for good to go for the moneymaking side of life."

"Most of the time life requires the moneymaking side."

"Don't I know it? Look, I bugged the real estate agent a couple of times this week before I got an answer. It seems the interested buyer has up and disappeared. He's not returning her phone calls and it seems the number he gave her is no longer a working number. I thought I should let you know the deal fell through."

Hayden's heart sank. "Somehow, I knew it was too good to be true."

"I'm sorry. I know how much you want to get rid of that place, bad memories and all. Look, I've got to run, a guy just came into the ER with a screwdriver stuck in his head. Construction worker I bet."

"Ouch."

"You hang in there and stay out of trouble. Okay?"

Hayden ended the call more than a little bummed. She had counted on the sale going through. Getting back to setting up the pumpkin patch, she decided The Plant Habitat would have plenty of sunflowers already growing in good-sized pots this time of year. She needed several with giant stalks at least two or three feet in height to put some definite pizzazz into the whole fall look. What her scarecrows needed other than a bunch more pumpkins and gourds were the flowers to balance out the total presentation.

Heading back up the path to the farm to get her car, she put the bad news behind her. Instead she needed to take a run into town and buy Halloween decorations.

Wheeling her cart up and down the aisles at the nursery, she weighed the selections of blooming fall flowers. Who knew there would be so many more choices than simple sunflowers or chrysanthemums? Drawn to the four-inch pots of orange and yellow daisies, she checked the little plastic tag stuck inside the dirt to see what kind of plant it was and how difficult it was to keep alive.

Deciding she could take care of the drought-tolerant Helenium, she added three to the sunflowers already on the cart and was in the process of picking up a tray of crimson-spotted toad lilies when she looked up and saw Ethan heading her way.

Her heart did a little flutter at the thrill of seeing him in the middle of the day.

"Saw your Mini in the parking lot." The woman was buying herself enough flowers to decorate a float in the Rose Parade. Why hadn't he thought to do that for her? Isn't that what a good boyfriend did? Was he the boyfriend? When was the last time he'd been anyone's boyfriend? They were sleeping together. They were a couple. Every time he went anywhere in town lately someone invariably always stopped him to ask something about Hayden. Was she settling in all right? Was she working that night at the Diner? Wasn't she learning how to cook? They always assumed he had the answers. And of course, he usually did.

Hell, half of Pelican Pointe already treated them like a couple. He could certainly crack open his wallet once in a while to give the woman in his life a bouquet of flowers.

At that moment, he realized he wanted to be the man in Hayden's life. Without waiting for an opening, he moved in, covering her mouth with his, right there in the middle of the trailing clematis.

"What do you say after you get off work Saturday night I take you over to Santa Cruz for some dinner and dancing afterwards? Go out on a real date." And he would stop by the florist and pick her up a dozen roses. "At one time you mentioned you wanted to see the area, the boardwalk, and the beaches. We didn't get to do that on my birthday."

She ran her arms up his back. "That sounds great. But we've already been out on a real date." She thought back to the hours and hours of making love on the island. "And look where that got us."

He shot her a grin. "As I recall, I got into you is what I did."

"And bragging about it too."

"Absolutely. So what do you say? There's a fantastic restaurant that sits out over the water. We'll get there too late to watch the sunset, but the place serves great seafood and it's upscale enough so you can wear that blue dress, the one that shows off your legs."

"What, no seedy dive this time where all the waitresses happen to be fans of yours?"

"Hey, I grew up there, it's my stomping ground." No way did he intend to revisit his bartending days at Spikes.

"Okay, it's a date. Pick me up at nine-thirty. I'll bring a change of clothes. That way, I can get dressed at your house."

As he nibbled her ear, he said, "If you do that we'll more than likely never leave the bedroom."

"Oh no you don't, no getting out of a real dinner date. I'm holding you to eating out at a nice restaurant."

Walking behind Hayden, he kept his eyes locked on the sway of her hips. He pondered how much time they had before she had to start her shift at the Diner. One glance at his watch told him they had forty extra minutes—for a lunch break. "Let's get this show on the road. Time's wasting," he muttered as he grabbed the cart and pushed it toward the checkout.

Even though Hayden didn't spend as much time at Promise Cove as she had before Ethan, she still paid rent and wanted the grounds near the garage apartment to look as tidy and neat as the rest of the place. In her opinion, the walkway leading from the studio to the courtyard needed some color. And she wanted to surprise Jordan.

This morning, she'd brought over two trays of lavender seedlings and almost as many marigolds from the greenhouse at the farm. Before starting her gardening though, she went back to her car, pulled out the tray of purple blue-eyed daisies she'd found yesterday at the nursery and carted them over to the bare patch of dirt next to Jordan's still-blooming periwinkles.

She hoped the purple would not only complement the blue pearl of the already flowering beds but also fill up the space where the summer bachelor's button had long ago succumbed to the chilly nights of fall.

Pulling on her gardening gloves, she took out her little spade and started digging in the loose soil, something she'd lately discovered extremely cathartic.

"You don't have to do that, you know."

Hayden forced herself to take a calming breath. She hoped she hadn't jumped at Scott's voice. It had been several days since she'd "talked" to him and that had been out at the cemetery. Today was the first time he'd plopped down anywhere near her while at the B & B. But then she hadn't been spending that much time out here.

"I liked picking them out. I might even like growing them if given half the chance. I spent so many years unhappy in my job. I think I'm learning to like myself again. Flowers are part of that, so is the farm, settling into a new place, a new job. My sister reminded me that when I was younger I had a creative side and gave it up once I got to college to make money."

"We all have to give up things we enjoy doing in order to earn a living, make money."

"It seems I went in that direction and lost myself though. That's how I ended up with Jeremy. I remember going on probably twenty-five interviews right out of college. He was the only one who made me an offer. Six figures right out of college. I remember wondering at the time why he would offer me so much. I guess now I know. I admit the money went to my head."

"Then find yourself again. Find what makes you happy. Ethan makes you happy."

Her lips bowed. "He does. But I was talking about money and careers and jobs. None of which made me happy. Nick says I should level with him, tell him about Dochenko."

"Honesty is always the best policy. Most people won't put up with dishonesty in a relationship."

"Did you ever lie to Jordan?"

"Not outright. At least not that I remember. I might've exaggerated a few things though. I see that now. Might've put an overly optimistic spin on the town, too. But then I wanted to come back here and raise my family, live in the house I grew up in, make the house into a business where I could stay home with my kids. I wanted Jordan to share in all of that and be as excited about this place as I was."

Hayden snickered. "You're good at putting a positive spin on things, Scott. In fact, you get an A+ at spinning."

Scott guffawed. "I hope Ethan appreciates your sense of humor. You should ask him about the summer he was ten and visiting his grandmother, right here in Pelican Pointe. Ask him about the time he went down to fish off the pier. A bunch of older boys, I counted five at the time, was already there, fishing poles in the water. They told him he couldn't fish next to them, to go find another spot."

"Why?"

"Kids don't need a reason to be mean. But in this case it was because he was Native American. Now me, I thought being Native was about the coolest thing that summer. In fact I was thirteen and tagging along after his older brother, Brent. Brent got all the girls back then, even here in Pelican Pointe it was no exception. The two of us, Brent and I, were hanging out at the beach that day, surfing, trying to impress a group of girls." He still remembered what the waves felt like as the water sluiced over his body that day, a body he no longer had.

"I bet you were," Hayden smirked. She saw him shoot her a grin.

"At any rate, we saw these boys, oldest was probably fourteen and a big son of a gun, giving Ethan a hard time. Turns out, it wasn't the first time this group of boys had picked on him that summer. Anyway, we went over to help him out."

"But not because you were still trying to impress the girls."

"No, of course not, we were playing the swaggering heroes out of the goodness of our hearts. So what if Sally Kennerman and Brittany Baker just happened to stroll by, see us playing hero defending a ten-year-old from a bunch of bullies. If it got us noticed that would be okay too.

"The thing is I thought when they caught sight of badass Brent, who towered over most of these guys, I thought when they saw him, they'd back down, you know. But I guess they weren't that smart because they decided the best offense was to attack as a group. As soon as the punches started flying, we heard this gun go off behind us." Scott roared with laughter. "I look back and see tiny Autumn Lassiter, all four foot eleven inches of her, standing there holding this big-ass shotgun, pointing it up in the air, yelling for those boys to leave her grandsons alone."

"That shotgun must have packed a punch."

"Oh, it did. But I guess she'd known these boys were picking on Ethan for awhile and she decided to follow them that day, put a stop to it right then and there."

It was these kinds of talks with Scott that made her enjoy seeking him out. Besides, he was the only "person" who knew the real Emile Reed, the only one who knew about Dochenko and the mess she'd left behind. She found solace in that.

At that moment though, Hayden noticed Jordan standing not two feet from her, eyes as big as saucers, boring holes through her. How long had she been standing there? Hayden had been so engrossed in Scott's story she hadn't heard Jordan walk up along the pathway.

"Hayden, what are you doing out here talking to yourself?"

Okay, she'd been standing there long enough to see that. "Uh…" Why on earth couldn't Jordan see Scott sprawled on the lawn next to the bedding plants? "I didn't see you there, Jordan. I decided to replace your bachelor's buttons with these purple daisies. The color's almost the same. I brought marigolds, too. Did you know marigolds keep aphids away? That's why they keep them at the farm. They plant them among the vegetables." She couldn't seem to stop the drivel from tumbling out of her mouth.

"He's here, isn't he? Scott's right here. That's who you were talking to?" Jordan accused as she looked around, wringing her hands, inspecting every blade of grass, staring long and hard at the flowering plants, as if that would make him suddenly appear.

"Uh…he's sitting on the grass, Jordan. I was just, uh…uh…he was keeping me company while I plant these flowers, telling me this story about the time Ethan was a boy…and..." But Jordan wasn't listening. Hayden saw tears stream down her face then watched as she turned on her heels and stormed back into the house.

"Looks like, I'm in trouble," Scott concluded.

"Why doesn't she see you, Scott?"

"I have no idea. I thought it would pass. I thought—"

Hayden sighed. "Well, you aren't going anywhere."

Scott shook his head. "No, I'm not going anywhere."

Saturday night came and went but Hayden and Ethan never made it to Santa Cruz. Right after Hayden's shift ended at the Diner, just as Ethan had predicted, they'd tumbled between the sheets and hadn't come up for air until hunger got the best of them.

Around midnight they'd ended up eating cold leftover lasagna in bed.

Ethan lay stretched across the rumpled covers, naked. "I'll make it up to you. Tomorrow night I'll take you over to The Pointe. I promise."

Sitting cross-legged, with a plate across her lap, she leaned back on the headboard and patted her stomach. "Hmm, I'm not missing a thing, here, Ethan." She dished up another fork of pasta and almost purred, "Your mother makes excellent lasagna. I'm not sure we're doing it justice by not heating it up. Even cold though, it's delicious. Do you think she'd give me the recipe?"

A touchy subject, Ethan decided since his mom still held out hope his relationship with Hayden was a passing phase. Good thing she hadn't gotten wind the woman had been interested in renting Autumn's house.

"By the way, tell me about the time your grandmother, Autumn Lassiter, took out her shotgun and ran off a group of boys who'd been tormenting you all summer long."

Ethan choked on his pasta. "You've been talking to Brent."

"Nope. Scott told me. He was there. He told me the whole story about how they'd picked on you because you were Native."

Ethan's mouth dropped open. He remembered that summer day. His brother and Scott had been fierce in defending him. In fact, after that day, those boys had left him alone. Not only that, but the same day, he'd also seen another side to his diminutive grandmother. She'd shown a feisty streak he'd never known existed.

"Was she really only four-feet-eleven?"

Ethan stared at her in disbelief. "Okay. Scott's story was fairly descriptive. These talks with him are real then."

"They are. I didn't know you doubted it." She took another bite of the cheesy concoction. "I'm thinking about paying Wade Hawkins a visit, having a conversation with him about ghosts. Want to come with me?"

After cleaning his own plate, he started forking over lasagna from hers. "Sure. But what do you think you'll find out from Wade? I told you everything he told me."

"A different perspective maybe. I've read all the books you gave me. Maybe talking to Wade will give me some clue as to why Jordan can't see her own dead husband's ghost." When she said it out loud, it sounded fairly ridiculous. "I don't know. Something. He's the local expert. And you aren't the only one who has mentioned Wade's strange pursuit of the paranormal."

"Wade hasn't exactly been secretive about it. A lot of people think he has a screw loose." Ethan went over once again what Wade had told him about taking his electronic sensors out to the cove.

Hayden fidgeted with the fork she held. "Jordan caught me talking to him. Of course, it looked like I was talking to myself. But she knew he was there. She just couldn't see him."

"You do realize that talking like that the whole town will start thinking you have a screw loose as well."

"You don't let on that you believe in ghosts and spirits and stuff like that, do you, Ethan? You keep that to yourself, don't you?"

"Being Native has always been enough of a challenge without me babbling on about that, too. I leave the subject of shamans and ghosts to my father."

"That bothers him, doesn't it? The fact that you haven't fully embraced that part of your heritage, so to speak, upsets him?"

He arched a brow, wondering how she read those kinds of things in him that no one else seemed to pick up. "He's always wanted me to be more out there when it came to reading things, talking about what I do with the world, or so it seemed."

"And you like being more private about it."

"A lot more private. Are you sure you don't have a little psychic ability in your background, Hayden-no-middle-initial-Ryan?"

She giggled like a ten-year-old. "Not that I'm aware of, Deputy Dawg."

Pulling her back down on the bed beside him, he ran his fingers through the ends of her hair. "What with all this fake black, maybe you have Native blood running through your veins and just don't know it?" he teased as he found the curve of a breast, nuzzled a pebbled point, and started grazing down the length of her body.

"Mmm, maybe."

For the time being their interest in ghosts faded. And once again, it was hours before they fell asleep.

Sunday afternoon they stopped by Wade's house, a rambling, western-style ranch, located about two miles north of town. The place reminded Hayden of a rustic ski lodge complete with a massive stone fireplace, log-paneled walls, and vaulted timber-plank ceilings.

The man with the wild head of white hair, ushered them into his study where he'd already set out a tray filled with a decanter of coffee and homemade chocolate chip cookies.

Hayden and Ethan got settled in winged chairs while the long-time council member and retired history professor went through his files and dug out his notes on the readings he'd taken out at Promise Cove.

Wade adjusted his glasses and held up his electromagnetic field meter. "This is the little gizmo that gave me such a strong indication out at Jordan's. The needle blew off the chart, especially in two locations, the courtyard and the kitchen."

"I don't dispute your findings, Mr. Hawkins, I know Scott's there on the grounds. What I'm really trying to get at is why he appears to Nick and to me, even to Ethan here, but not to his own wife, uh…former wife. Jordan spends the majority of her time in that kitchen where you say your meter showed the strongest indication, and yet, Jordan doesn't see him. And I totally understand why he's still around there because the cove is his childhood home, he grew up there. His happiest memories are right there in that house, on the grounds."

"It sounds like you've gotten to know him quite well over a short period of time."

She glanced at Ethan, waited for an indication to go on. At the nod of his head, she began telling Wade about all her "talks" with Scott.

Wade sat there contemplating the situation, taking it all in, before surprising them both. "Had a poker game out here last summer, the town leaders try to make a point to get together and play about once a month. Doc Prescott, Murphy, Bran Sullivan, Wally Pierce, Carl Knudsen, even Joe Ferguson, they were all here. The subject of Scott came up. It was right after Nick and Jordan tied the knot. I won't say which ones, but half of those guys I just mentioned said they'd seen Scott—in his ghostly form, seen him strolling along the dock near the pier, walking behind McCready's, even hanging out in the parking lot of Murphy's Market, more than once I might add."

Ethan pointed out, "There's an old Native legend that speaks about what happens after the leader of a village passes on. The shamans believe his spirit is restless because it needs to watch over, to become that village's protector, keeping it safe from outsiders, making sure his family and the people he cared about in life are taken care of after he's no longer with them. In other words, his spirit guards his family and friends. The legend calls it, the guardian spirit."

Wade nodded. "I'd say that fits what Scott Phillips does to a tee. We aren't talking about getting rid of him, are we?" He shot a troubled look at Hayden.

"Absolutely not. Scott deserves to be here as much as any of the rest of us. He isn't scary, or a menace. He's more—"

"Benevolent," Ethan finished for her.

"Exactly. But you've just proved my point. If all those other people see him, why doesn't Jordan?"

"I'd say she doesn't want to," Wade answered.

Ethan agreed, "My father would say Jordan is not yet at a place in her life where she's open to seeing Scott. Once she opens her heart and mind, my guess is she'll see plenty of the guy."

Chapter Sixteen

Margie Rosterman had been less than enthusiastic about Hayden taking a Saturday night off. But when Hayden explained her reasons, her boss couldn't very well turn down her request. It seems Hayden had pegged Margie after all; the acerbic woman had a romantic side.

After Hayden got the go ahead from Margie, she persuaded Abby Pointer to cover her shift, and then made everyone involved swear an oath of silence they wouldn't let the cat out of the bag.

With enough secrecy to make the CIA proud, when Saturday morning rolled around, Hayden helped Nick stage the scene. While Jordan and Nick ate breakfast, Hayden stealthily snuck in the front door and into the master bedroom to pack Jordan a bag with enough stuff in it to last a good three-day weekend. When she was done, she tip-toed out the way she'd come to their Ford Explorer and placed the bag in the back under a blanket.

Even as Hayden played out her clandestine role, Nick got into character. It was his job to get his wife in the car without her suspecting anything was up. As he cleaned up the breakfast dishes, he announced, "I was thinking maybe we should go over to the farm and spend a couple of hours with Will and Fran. If you're feeling up to it, that is. You'd just be taking notes and making sure we go over everything before they take off for Tulare. Hayden offered to look after Hutton for us. Then if there's time, while we're out, we could grab some lunch at the Diner." It was a tribute to the whole scam that he kept a straight face.

"I'm feeling pretty good this morning. Now would be a good time to go over there and sort out what we should expect once they're gone. It's hard to believe that place is really ours."

"I know what you mean. Inheriting this farm has meant a lot more work for both of us."

Ten minutes later, they walked out to the SUV as if they were simply going next door. But at the end of the driveway, instead of making a right to go south, Nick made a left turn and swung north.

When Jordan realized they were headed in the wrong direction, she looked over at Nick and asked, "What's going on?" The minute she saw his lips curve, she knew something was up.

"How about a nice long weekend at the Hotel Vitale?"

"In San Francisco? You're kidding? What about Hutton? Am I dreaming?"

"Not yet. But you will be with three days of room service and spa treatments at your fingertips. Hayden is babysitting until Tuesday morning."

"Three days! Really? Oh Nick, you always know what I need, when I need it. I feel like I've been run ragged lately, stressed out. And I haven't even been involved that much with the farm. I've left you and Hayden with that burden. I'm sorry for that."

"Hey, don't be. You've had the B & B to take care of while I've been swamped next door. But this weekend I'll have you all to myself. We check in at three this afternoon, check out Tuesday morning. With a baby coming who knows when we'll get to do this again."

"I'm so excited. I should call Hayden and thank her for keeping Hutton for us." She reached over and picked up their cell phone, but there was no service. "I'll call her as soon as we get to the highway. I can't believe you did this for me, Nick. I'm so ready for a getaway. How did you know?"

He grinned, picked up her hand and brought it to his lips, placed a kiss on the palm.

"I pick up on things because I love you. And we've both been under a lot of stress lately. Happy birthday, Jordan."

With Nick and Jordan out of the house, the huge old B & B was silent as a church except for the energetic two-year-old and the almost full-grown puppy they called Quake. To Hayden, the dog and little girl seemed to have bonded like glue sticks to paper.

Just as Nick promised there were no guests scheduled to arrive. The place had emptied out two days earlier when the feds had finally packed up and headed back to their Bay Area office.

But Hayden had already decided that if someone did show up unexpectedly, like she had done weeks earlier, she would gladly offer them a room and take their money. She might not be able to offer them Jordan's excellent cuisine, but she could do more than boil water these days.

And thinking about meals had her coaxing Hutton into the kitchen so she could keep an eye on her while she dragged out Jordan's Crock-Pot.

"I get the food started and we'll head out to the Homecoming parade. How's that sound, Hutton?"

"Parade," the little girl repeated as she clapped her hands together.

"That's right, Hutton. We'll see the bands march and play music."

Hayden ran cold water into the slow cooker, dug out chicken breasts from the fridge. Peeling off the plastic wrap, she dumped the meat into the pot, turned the dial up to high.

She got down a bowl from the cabinet, checked her list of ingredients from the recipe Jordan had left. She drizzled what looked like two tablespoons of honey into the bowl, added soy sauce and ketchup. She threw in fresh ginger, chopped up garlic, and then poured all of it over the chicken.

Six hours from now she could only hope she'd have an edible meal that was supposed to taste very much like ginger chicken cooked in a Crock-Pot.

Satisfied she had supper well in hand she picked up Hutton, and headed off to get a two-year-old toddler dressed to watch a parade.

Hutton had insisted on wearing a hat to accessorize her purple outfit. Light lavender shirt, over a darker pair of purple overalls. It seemed the girl was crazy about purple and—headwear. She'd picked the cutest little knitted purple cap out herself because it had long curls at the very top of the crown that spiraled downward. Every time she moved her head from side to side, she could feel them bounce back and forth.

At least that's what Hayden thought she had said in two-year-old-speak. As she glanced over at Hutton, the little girl started clapping her hands together as soon as she spotted the county patrol car rolling past with its lights flashing, kicking off the start of the Homecoming parade. From their perch sitting on the back of Max Bingham's pickup truck, parked in front of the Diner, they had a front row seat. As soon as Hutton heard the band, as if on cue, she came over and plopped down onto Hayden's lap.

At the first notes from the high school marching band, Hutton began to bounce to the music, a rendition of *The Contender*, a song probably chosen to gear up the fighting spirit of the football team in anticipation for their game later that evening. But Hutton could've cared less what song they played as long as it was loud. The girl loved music, loved to dance and for a little bitty thing, had rhythm.

For the first time in almost ten years, Hayden listened to a fight song played by a group of kids dressed in their white shirts and jeans as they marched down Main Street. It took her back to another time and place to Champaign, Illinois, when she and Sydney had participated in a similar event. Both had played the clarinet and both had done plenty of marching.

She thought back to the night Ethan had played guitar and she'd discovered his incredible vocals. How long had it been since she'd picked up a sheet of music? He'd pursued what he enjoyed doing. She'd followed…what? Her love of money? Her bliss certainly hadn't been in accounting.

Rather emotional at the memory of her old self once upon a time, Hayden's vision blurred with tears.

Ethan came to a stop from a good twenty feet away and watched Hayden as her eyes grew moist and tears leaked down her cheeks. He saw her wrap her arms tighter around Hutton as if she might need the little girl as an anchor.

He stood there more than a little perturbed wondering where exactly she had gone during those few minutes. Wherever it was it had made her cry. That alone didn't upset him. What did was the fact that he couldn't ask her about it. She'd made it clear, more than once, she didn't want questions about her past.

The minute she looked up and spotted him, wearing his tan official uniform, she began to wipe at her wet face. He recognized the moment she went on alert and resented it. But those images in his head of a parking garage had him tamping down his annoyance. Instead, he walked over, leaned down and brushed his lips against her forehead. "How's it going, Hayden? Who do we have here?" he said to Hutton.

Hutton went into her shy mode, burrowing closer to Hayden's body.

But when Hayden pointed out that the cheerleaders on the flatbed trailer being pulled by a Dually were throwing out candy, the little girl went from reticent to talkative in a heartbeat. Hutton forgot about her shyness and scrambled to pick up as many pieces of candy that were now landing in the back of the truck aimed there just for her. Soon she had her fists full of Tootsie Rolls and Starbursts.

Hayden laughed at Hutton's exuberance. "I think, Deputy Dawg, you've finally found a female who doesn't fawn all over you."

Next to her ear, he whispered, "I'm hoping, come tonight, you'll fawn over me, Hayden. Whaddya say?"

"I might. But first we have to get our babysitting chores out of the way, which includes bath time and reading her a story."

Before Ethan could respond, Harold Boedecker called out to get his attention. "Hey, Ethan. A couple of kids over at the pier are tossing firecrackers into the water. You better get over there."

Ethan rolled his eyes, leaned over. "I'll be finished here around five, sooner if I can manage it. You call me though if anyone shows up looking for trouble out there, okay?"

Hayden snickered. "The only person I know looking for trouble is you, Ethan Cody. Fortunately for me, I have your number though." She brushed her lips quickly against his mouth before whispering, "I bought a black teddy online a week ago. UPS delivered it yesterday morning."

"You've got a mean streak, you know that, Hayden. I still have five hours to think about that image."

"Probably longer, what with babysitting duties and all. Anticipation is half the fun."

She watched him reluctantly stroll off to his patrol car until she finally turned back to Hutton, chuckling at the look of lust she'd left on his face.

By the time a classic Camaro convertible rolled past carrying the Homecoming queen, who sat atop the back seat waving at the sparse crowd, Hutton was already bored and restless. She needed lunch and a nap.

Hayden climbed down off the truck as she followed Margie and Max into the Diner, where she intended to take care of getting Hutton fed.

Hayden was in the kitchen a little after five o'clock when she heard Ethan's truck pull into the driveway. Anticipation had her belly fluttering. But when the sound had Hutton for the tenth time in an hour asking about mommy and daddy and where they were, Hayden's heart went out to the little girl. Even though the toddler had spoken to both mommy and daddy earlier on the phone when they'd called after checking into the hotel, Hayden still wanted to reassure her.

"That's Ethan, Hutton. You remember Ethan from the parade. He's here for supper. You want to help me set the table?"

Luckily, that took the baby's mind off missing mommy and daddy at least for ten minutes.

Hayden's Crock-Pot chicken had the house smelling like Chinese takeout, which in turn had her feeling a certain amount of pride at making a meal from scratch. She set the rice in the cooker to steam.

When Ethan came through the back door, she felt the immediate harder pull to her lower belly and wondered if she would ever get used to that little pang of desire she felt every single time she set eyes on the man.

And just like that, from across the room their eyes zeroed in on each other.

He was holding a garment bag draped over his shoulder, a reminder that he was spending the night. She watched as he hung the bag on the peg by the door, unstrapped his weapon, and placed it inside the top shelf of the kitchen cabinet, well out of reach of the baby.

When Hutton toddled up to him, he bent down and picked her up. "Well, what have we got here? Look what I found, Hayden, a gorgeous little bundle with big blue eyes waiting for me."

By mouthing to him without words, Hayden let Ethan know, "She's missing mommy and daddy so do not mention Nick and Jordan at all."

"Ah, got it. Why don't you show me your doll, Hutton? Where's your doll? Go get your doll so I can see if she's as pretty as you are."

As soon as the baby wanted down and took off to get her doll, Hayden breathed a sigh of relief. "That was thinking on your feet. Thanks. She was so close to crying when she heard your truck pull in. She thought it was Nick and Jordan. And it isn't the first time today she's gotten weepy. I'm not sure what I'm going to do for two more days when she's missing them this much."

He came up behind her at the counter and kissed the back of her neck. "Have you heard from them?"

"They called from the hotel, got there safely. She talked to them for over five minutes. But then she went room to room looking for them. It broke my heart. I was able to get her mind off of them long enough by playing some music and dancing with her, but I'm not sure it'll work every time."

Not knowing a whole lot about kids, he said the only thing he could think of. "I guess we'll have to take it day by day. Get through tonight; keep her busy tomorrow and the next so she won't think of…you-know-who. All quiet out here?"

"Nothing but peace and solitude in the country. How about you? Did you arrest anyone today, Ethan?"

"Nope. If I had I'd still be doing paperwork in Santa Cruz."

"Hmm, not fond of paperwork, huh?"

"No cop I know likes paperwork." He nibbled on her ear. "What smells so good?"

"Ginger chicken."

"No kidding?" He picked up the lid on the pot, inhaling the aroma. "You make this yourself?"

"No, the food fairy delivered it about an hour ago." She rolled her eyes. "I'm getting a little tired of everyone thinking I'm totally brain-dead when it comes to the kitchen. I told you, I've been practicing."

"Aww, I like it when you get all indignant. It smells delicious."

"Thanks. Now if the rice turns out as well as the chicken…" About that time Hutton came running back in with her doll. Both of them focused their attention on the baby. While Ethan made a game out of playing hide-and-seek with Hutton, Hayden threw a salad together and put the finishing touches on supper.

By the time they sat down to the table, the toddler was in a better frame of mind. And thinking ahead, Hayden had fixed chocolate tacos for dessert which provided that extra incentive to get the baby to finish her rice and chicken.

They cleaned up the kitchen together, even Hutton helped load the dishwasher.

But later, when Jordan called around seven-thirty, even though Hayden did her best to sound upbeat, she had to eventually explain to the worried mother how much the baby missed them and how hearing her voice over the phone earlier, had sent her looking into every room downstairs for them.

"She's fine now. She's had her bath and Ethan and I are about to read her a story."

"This is the first time I've left her alone with a sitter for this long. Nick and I didn't even have a honeymoon because we were just getting the B & B going. I didn't realize how hard this would be on both of us. I was so excited about the trip in the car, but now…"

Hayden glanced over to make sure Ethan had the baby occupied with one of her dolls before explaining in a gentle tone, "Listen, Hutton is just fine, more than fine. I'm just trying to tell you that hearing your voice right now may set her off again. The next two days, Ethan and I will keep her busy so she's not asking about you and Nick every five minutes." She tried to redirect the conversation. "Are you and Nick having a good time, Jordan?"

Jordan's voice cracked. "We were."

"Then keep doing what you're doing, keep enjoying this time alone together. Think of it as your long overdue, but fairly abbreviated honeymoon. With another baby on the way, who knows how long it will be before you get this opportunity again. If it will make you feel any better, it's okay if you call fifteen more times tonight. But I bet in thirty minutes she'll be fast asleep and she won't know you're an hour and a half away."

Hayden heard Jordan sniffle. "Okay, but call me if she so much as wakes up, no matter what time it is."

Hayden chuckled at that. After another five minutes of assurances, she finally managed to get off the phone.

From the sofa Ethan looked over and grinned. "That was some nervous mother."

Hayden put her fingers to her lips and shook her head. "Shhh. No mention of m-o-m-m-y. She was crying about not being here. That is so sweet."

After getting Hutton to bed, they settled in front of the fire with a glass of wine to watch a movie. Ethan dug out the *Casablanca* DVD, the film they'd both agreed on during dinner.

As the credits rolled on the flat-screen TV, Ethan told her, "You did a good job with the food. You've come a long way in a short amount of time. The chicken was great, the chocolate taco an inspiration."

"That was out of necessity. Jordan clued me in that Hutton loves them and can be bribed. Besides, I'm a quick study."

"Me, too." He nuzzled her ear, nibbled on her jaw. "Whaddya say we make out to As Time Goes By?"

"Is that all you ever think about?"

Ethan busted out laughing. "I'm pretty sure it is. I've had that image of you wearing a teddy on my brain since this afternoon. As I see it, it's really your fault."

Glancing down at the bulge in his pants, Hayden snickered in his ear. "Hmm, I don't think you need much incentive."

He started sucking on her neck. "How many times have you seen this movie?"

"About two dozen."

"Me, too. What are we still doing on the couch when there's a nice bed upstairs where we could get horizontal? Besides after patrolling Pelican Pointe and keeping law and order all afternoon, I need a shower."

"Then what are we waiting for?"

"Now you're talking, which room do we get? Point me in that direction and I'll take my stuff up."

"The infamous Sand Dollar Room. The one I stayed in the first night I got here. You remember that, don't you? Back when you thought I aimed to plunder and steal from Nick and Jordan first chance I got."

His lips curved at the memory. "Yeah, well, I had a change of heart."

"Change of heart my ass, you were wrong Ethan Cody. Admit it!"

"I love it when your green eyes fire up." He moved closer to her on the sofa, teased her lips apart to deepen the kiss. Her mouth felt warm, the taste a mix of dark chocolate and red wine. He drew the kiss out, need springing up between both of them.

"That's it! I'll grab the baby monitor, check on Hutton, and meet you upstairs in five minutes."

He shot off the couch, grabbed the remote, putting an end to the movie, and switched off the TV. He headed to the kitchen to get his garment bag still hanging by the back door. "It won't take me five minutes to lock up. And don't forget to put on the black thingy," he reminded her over his shoulder.

When he heard her laugh, he added, "On second thought, don't even bother with it."

"Are you kidding? I paid a day's worth of tips for that tiny scrap of lace, I'm wearing it—eventually."

"Fine. Then I'll just have to rip it off."

"Promises, promises," she challenged as she headed down the hallway to check on Hutton, chuckling to herself all the way.

The minute Ethan set foot in the kitchen, he went about checking to make sure all the doors were locked, including the one in the laundry room. He grabbed the change of clothes he'd brought, and on instinct, took out his .45 from its hiding place in the cabinet. With naked thoughts of Hayden running through his head, he didn't linger. Instead he dashed upstairs via the back staircase, taking the steps two at a time and set out to locate the Sand Dollar Room.

Thanks to a little gold plaque on each bedroom door indicating which room was which, Ethan stepped inside. He went to the closet, hanging up his garment bag on the rod and stowed his gun on the top shelf. Heading into the bathroom, he quickly began to shed his uniform. He turned on the shower. While the water heated, he took out his shaving kit.

By the time Hayden strolled into the room, she heard the shower running. She set the baby monitor on the dresser, and began pulling off her top, jeans, and underwear. When she opened the door to the bathroom, she stopped to listen. Ethan stood behind the curtain—singing the song, *As Time Goes By*.

With the tune drifting in her ears, she stretched back the curtain enough to step into the tub. Seeing his skin wet and slick, her heart did a little extra bumpity-bumpity. And they hadn't even touched each other yet.

All singing ended in mid-tune. Ethan narrowed his eyes and pulled her to him. Around steam and swirling mist, he took her mouth. It thrilled him to see the green of her eyes darken with sheer lust. He backed her up against the wet slate and was inside her in two seconds.

"Hang on," he said as he grabbed her hips and hoisted her up. She wrapped her long legs around his waist.

Plunging, diving, Ethan took them both up and then over, driving slow and then fast. She rode out the pleasure in all its glorious heat.

Afterward, Ethan could feel her body still quivering and pulsing.

"Well." She dropped her head to his chest. "We got that out of the way pretty quick."

"Hmm, sorry. It's just…I've wanted you all day."

Her fingers stroked his face. "Not complaining here."

He laughed, telling her, "I think you're clean from the inside out."

"Since you're so thorough, why don't you wash my back?"

"Hmm, how about if I start right…what is this on your hip?" He turned her around to stare at the little cluster of freckles in the shape of a bear. "How come I didn't see that before?"

"It's a birthmark."

"I'll be damned. It looks like a bear. Are you sure you don't have Native blood somewhere in your gene pool."

She chuckled. "I'm pretty sure I'd know if I did."

Later, they were sprawled in the king-sized bed, working up to round two when Hayden looked over at him and saw questions form in his dark eyes. It had been happening a lot lately, especially after they made love.

She took a deep breath, blew it out. "Come on, Ethan, something's been bothering you. I see it on your face. I saw it again today at the parade and now…what's wrong?"

"Hayden, you know I said it didn't matter about your past."

Her belly tightened. It felt like her heart might drop out of her chest. She'd been afraid of this moment, the moment when the secrets she kept would be too much for a cop to handle. "But it does, of course it does," she finally managed to squeak out.

"Some. Keep an open mind though, okay? Remember, I accepted the fact you were having conversations with Scott Phillips, didn't I?"

Her brow creased, wondering where he was going with this. "So?"

"I've been getting flashes, almost from the beginning. That night you were on the side of the road until…when we started making love, they got a lot stronger."

A sinking feeling hit the pit of her stomach. "Flashes?"

"Who was in that parking garage with you that night?" He saw her go white. Lose all color in her face. Her eyes were as big as quarters.

"Oh, God! Before I answer that, I want to know which hat you're wearing right this minute. Is this an official conversation with law enforcement, or am I confiding to the man I'm sleeping with, my lover?"

"Hayden, that isnt fair and you know it."

"Maybe not, but I want you to answer the question."

"Fine. I'm worried about the woman I…care about. Don't try to put this on me. That man tried to rape you."

She shuddered and closed her eyes, remembering that ski mask, how his breath had smelled like stale cigarettes, how he'd held the knife to her throat with fingers that bore little prison tattoos across his knuckles. "The guy who wants me dead sent him. The man who wants me dead is a very bad man, Ethan."

"Why? Why does he want you dead? Do the cops know about him?"

"The feds, and yeah, they know."

"Feds? This isn't a witness protection situation then, is it? You took off on your own."

She wanted to crawl out of bed, move away from him, but couldn't get her legs to move. "Do you know when you enter the witness protection program you have to give up all contact with your family, leave them behind for good as if they didn't exist. You can't contact them, Ethan. Ever. This way, my way, I at least get to call them every now and then."

Dread moved over him. Ethan took a calming breath. "Hayden, please tell me you use a pay phone to make those calls." But he knew. How many times had he seen her take out her mobile phone? "If you still call your sister and mother, those calls can be tracked."

"No. I use a prepaid cell."

He shook his head. "Listen to me, they can still be triangulated, they have to know your carrier, but that's easy enough to find out. There are only a dozen or so. If you know the right carrier…" Without finishing, he watched the fear snake into her eyes.

Oh. My. God. That's why they've been hanging around Sydney's house!"

"Who's Sydney? Start at the beginning," Ethan demanded.

She took him through all of it, from the time she'd left Chicago, her detour through the Midwest, where she had changed her name to when she ended up on the side of the road in Pelican Pointe.

By the time she finished he was pacing up and down in front of the double French doors, the warm afterglow of sex as cold as the freezer section in Murphy's Market. He'd thrown on a pair of jeans but kept looking at her with what she could only think of as the three D's—disgust, disappointment, and despair.

Why didn't he say something?

After a few minutes of stony silence, he finally blurted out, "Jeremy Dochenko, I remember that son of a bitch. He stole millions from his investors. They arrested him, but the judge set bail and he took off, skipped the country."

"Uh, Ethan, it was more like billions. As his very naïve accountant I can attest to a fairly accurate amount of just how much he bilked from his clients."

"Billions?"

"The guy's a sleaze and a killer. He had Saul Raymond murdered."

"Wait a minute, you left that part out."

She was about to go into a detailed account about how her co-worker had ended up with a bullet to the back of his head when he held up a hand.

"Never mind, I need a computer."

"What're you going to do?"

"I'm Googling this stuff," he explained as he grabbed a shirt and left the room as if he needed to get as far away from her as space allowed.

A fairly decent researcher when it came to the Internet, Ethan had made a pot of coffee and sat at the little desk in the corner of the kitchen, tapping out search after search on the keyboard of Jordan's desktop computer.

Over the past six weeks he'd imagined quite a bit about Hayden Ryan's past. Nothing could have prepared him for finding out she'd been associated, worked for, and knew the sleazebag, Jeremy Dochenko, personally.

Website after website confirmed that Emile Reed had been the government's key witness. He'd found photos taken of a blonde Emile as she'd left Dochenko Investments surrounded by reporters and cameras after the man's initial arrest by the feds had essentially put an end to his investment firm. The place hadn't opened its doors for business again after that.

He discovered photos of her that went back to her college days at the University of Chicago. At one time, the press had dug up everything they could find about her, going back to her high school graduation and plastered every piece of that knowledge all over the Web. The fact that the case and Emile Reed had been so prominently reported on for the past nine months, it was a wonder someone hadn't recognized her.

He learned that without her, the feds had to rely on the complaints of all Dochenko's individual investors, the ones he'd ripped off. According to one news source, the case had stalled because the government literally had to pore over thousands and thousands of documents to ready themselves for a trial.

There was just one problem. Dochenko, the sleazebag, and Emile Reed, the witness, had both fallen off the face of the earth.

Ethan put his head in his hands. His eyes burned. Emily Reed. E-R. That explained all the E-R flashes he'd been getting. They'd been driving him nuts ever since that night in the rain on the side of the road.

Just then he looked up to see Hayden staring at him from the doorway as if she were afraid to walk into the room.

"Is there anything you want to ask me about…about what you found out online?"

He held out his hand. "Come here, baby. It'll be all right. You must have been scared to death."

The minute she sat down in his lap and started to cry, Ethan broke. "It's okay. I'm not mad. I understand why you left. Think of it this way, if you hadn't left, if you hadn't gone on the run, this entire mess wouldn't have somehow brought you to me."

"Ethan, I'm so sorry. Nick was right, I should've told you. But I was afraid—for a variety of reasons." He didn't bother asking what those reasons were. She stared into his eyes. "What happens now?"

He'd thought about that. But for now, he evaded her question. "Since we've pretty much kicked open this door, honesty from here on out. Deal?"

"Of course."

"Tell me something, if you just up and left the way you did, am I to understand you weren't in a relationship? You don't have a husband out there somewhere I should know about, or a boyfriend you've pined over these past months, do you?" The information on the Internet hadn't mentioned either one but he had to know.

For the first time in an hour, she laughed. "No. No husband. No boyfriend."

"What's wrong with the men in Chicago?"

"It was me. I realize now I might have been a little too work-driven, never taking the time for myself, not really doing anything that made me happy. I forgot how to be happy, Ethan. That is, until you." There she'd said it. Put it out there on the table for discussion. "I didn't tell you because I was afraid of losing you."

But instead of a verbal response, Ethan lowered his head, took her mouth. "Let's go back to bed, Hayden. I'm suddenly feeling very tired."

Three hours later, Ethan was still having difficulty sleeping. Once or twice, he'd glanced over at Hayden curled up beside him in bed. Realization had hit him in the kitchen. He was in love with a woman who couldn't have been in a more dangerous spot if she'd written herself a role in a Lifetime movie of the week. For the first time in his life he'd taken the fall and now he had to figure out how best to get her out of this Dochenko mess.

After several more minutes, he got up, pulled on a pair of jeans and grabbed a blanket, wrapping it around his shoulders. As quietly as he could, he opened the double doors to the balcony and headed outside where he could pace and think and breathe.

Barefoot, he didn't even notice the cold air as he walked up and down the landing. When movement caught his eye, he looked down at a shadowy figure below in the courtyard. His first instinct was to run back inside and grab his .45 from the closet. But then, he recognized Scott Phillips, who lifted a hand in greeting as if he were on sentry duty, patrolling the grounds.

Leaning over the railing, Ethan lifted an arm in welcome. Oddly, Scott's presence gave way to a sense that he somehow knew the danger Hayden faced and was on her side.

Ethan stared up at the full moon hanging low over the glistening water of the cove. Dochenko was out there somewhere, or rather his paid lackeys. The man wouldn't get his hands dirty, wouldn't bother coming after her on his own. But he would hire people to do it.

They were after the woman he loved. Of that he was certain.

Now the question was, what did he intend to do about it?

Chapter Seventeen

For the first few hours the next morning, Ethan and Hayden were too busy taking care of a rambunctious, energetic two-year-old to openly discuss Emile Reed.

The pair soon found out if you kept Hutton busy enough during breakfast, then afterwards, helped her with putting together enough puzzles, put on her favorite dance music, it kept her mind off asking about mommy and daddy every five minutes.

It was almost ten o'clock when Ethan's cell phone rang. He'd already decided that if it was an official police call, he planned on taking both Hayden and Hutton with him. For the next two days, until Nick and Jordan returned to the B & B, he didn't intend to let Hayden out of his sight.

He stepped outside the back door to take the call.

But the phone call was from his father with a problem of his own. "Haku, kwop. Ethan, there's a woman down in San Diego who has been missing since Friday. Her family wants me to come down there today to see what I can get about her disappearance."

"Haku, kʰoko. What do you want me to do?"

"Yesterday your mother hurt her back. I took her to the emergency room, they gave her a shot for the pain. She's been a little loopy ever since. I'm not leaving her alone unless I know you'll check up on her this afternoon and tonight, maybe even tomorrow morning depending on how she's getting around."

"What about Brent?"

"Brent has to drive to Sacramento for a law enforcement conference that starts tomorrow. In fact, he's already left. I promise to try and be back by Monday afternoon."

For as long as Ethan could remember, his family had been all important to him. "Go ahead and take off for San Diego, Dad. I'll see that Mom is taken care of."

Official call or not, knowing about Dochenko, Ethan wasn't leaving Promise Cove without Hayden and Hutton coming with him. For one, Nick and Jordan were out of town and had left their daughter in Hayden's care. He would talk to Nick the minute he got a chance, bring him up to speed on the situation. But until then, Hutton was his and Hayden's responsibility. And both of their safety was first and foremost to him.

Now that he knew her history, she couldn't live in fear day after day wondering when the bad guys would show up on her doorstep and put an end to her existence. Somehow, he needed to buy time over the next two days because he needed to think how best to move forward. Whether they wanted to or not, at some point, they had to come up with a way to deal with Dochenko's henchmen. If that meant going to the feds then so be it.

And his mother might be able to help him out in that department. Especially, if he handled it right. At least for the next two days anyway.

The closer Ethan got to the home where he'd grown up, the edgier he became. Knowing Hayden wasn't Lindeen Cody's favorite person at the moment, he pondered how best to pull this off. He looked over in the passenger seat of the Mini at Hayden, glanced back in the rearview mirror at Hutton sitting in her car seat in the back, playing with the doll she'd brought, and decided there were worst ways to spend a Sunday afternoon.

"How'd your mother hurt her back anyway?" Hayden asked, genuinely interested.

"I forgot to ask. She's always been active though, could be any number of ways. Maybe she tried picking up a heavy box, or maybe she was babysitting one of the neighbor kids, strained her back picking one up."

Turns out, Lindeen Cody wasn't the least bit interested in discussing how exactly she'd pulled the muscle in her back. Even though she couldn't get out of bed, after taking Percocet just fifteen minutes earlier, she was delighted to see her son. At least she had been until realizing he'd brought that woman with him.

But that woman stood at the foot of her bed holding an adorable little two-year-old girl on her hip. Eyeing the diminutive towhead, Lindeen got misty-eyed. "Since I have no grandchildren of my own, thanks to my two selfish sons who refuse to cooperate in that department, I have to latch onto any kids that come my way. Pathetic, isn't it? I have to make do with neighborhood children, but neighbor kids aren't the same thing as having my own, now are they?"

She sent Ethan a disgusted look before going on, "Wouldn't you think as many times as I've set this one up with absolutely delightful, young women over the years that just once he could oblige me and find a first-grade teacher attractive enough to marry her, give me a few grandkids in the process?"

"And how many times have I told you to stop fixing me up," Ethan admonished. "You're making Hayden uncomfortable by saying that kind of stuff." His mother might be outspoken, but drugs or not, she had no right to say such things in front of Hayden, especially since he knew how his mother felt.

Hayden listened to the byplay between mother and son. Understanding dawned on her then. Mrs. Cody didn't find her the least bit suitable for her youngest son. That's why she and Markus had kept their distance at the birthday party.

For some reason, Hayden found that incredibly awkward and funny. Recognizing she was in a position to have a little fun at Ethan's expense because his mother was obviously on a slew of painkillers, her eyes twinkled with amusement. "Now I ask you, what kind of man wouldn't be attracted to a first grade teacher? Who in their right mind wouldn't want to fall in love and settle down with someone like that who so obviously adores children? Plus, a woman like that has devoted her entire life to educating them. Why, they should have at least six, don't you think?"

Sensing an ally, Lindeen was a little too far gone on the meds to realize the joke. "Exactly. See, a sensible woman knows a good match when she sees it." Giving her full attention to the little girl now, Lindeen asked, "Who is this little angel anyway?"

"This is Hutton; she's Nick and Jordan's little girl. You know the couple who own the Promise Cove B & B out near the cliffs." Hayden went on to explain, "I'm watching her for a couple of days while they take a break. Did you know they never even got to go on a honeymoon before they had to open up last spring? They've been swamped out there ever since. And now that Jordan's pregnant if they don't take some time off now, who knows when the opportunity will come up again?"

Picking up on the one bit of new information she hadn't known, Lindeen zeroed in. "Jordan's pregnant. Isn't that wonderful?" She eyed Ethan. "Everyone's getting married, having babies these days, except my own two sons. Brent's given up on women and Ethan—" her voice trailed off as she realized she'd wandered a little too close to quicksand.

"I had no idea you were so deprived," Ethan teased his mother. "Nor did I suspect you were so obsessed over having grandchildren."

"Lord knows I've dropped enough hints over the years. My oldest is knocking close to forty and this one here isn't getting any younger. Short of hitting you and Brent over the head with a brick, neither of you obviously took the hint." But one more glance at the stubborn look on her son's face had Lindeen reluctantly deciding to abandon the subject of grandchildren. "There's some beef stew in the refrigerator, enough for everyone to have some for lunch."

"Are you hungry, Mrs. Cody? I'd be happy to heat the stew up for you, if Ethan will keep an eye on Hutton that is, while I'm in the kitchen. You're such a good cook. If it's half as good as your lasagna, I bet it's delicious."

"You liked my lasagna?"

Ethan watched his mother's set jaw relax a little at the praise and had to admire Hayden's tenacity. She seemed determine to get on his mother's good side with that chatty demeanor he recognized. The same one she reserved for a few of her harder-to-please customers at the Diner.

If anyone could win over his mother, it was Hayden.

"I loved your lasagna! I'm trying to learn to cook. Francine Foley and Jordan have been giving me pointers. And I've been practicing on Ethan."

Lindeen caved a little when she learned Francine was acting as the woman's mentor. Francine had always been such a good judge of character. She looked up at Hayden and suggested, "You might as well sit down, no sense standing there holding that baby."

"Tell you what, you stay here and entertain my mom, I'll go take care of lunch," Ethan offered. He shot a glance at his mother who seemed to realize she'd taken the bait and was now neatly boxed in by her own son.

Hayden took a seat in the chair at the side of the bed. The baby wanted to get down and walk around and explore the new surroundings. "Hutton, why don't you show Mrs. Cody how old you are? We've been working on this. She isn't even two yet. And still—"

As if on cue, Hutton held up two little fingers. And then two more on the other hand.

Once Lindeen went into a detailed conversation with Hutton, praising her for being such a smart girl, her harsh veneer seemed to soften, even Hayden noticed the difference. By the time Lindeen drifted off to sleep, whether it was the meds putting her in such a mellow mood or not, she seemed to have accepted the fact that Hayden was now part of her son's life, albeit temporarily.

That afternoon from his mother's house Ethan placed a call to Nick to explain why they weren't spending the night at the cove. "We locked up the B & B. We'll be back there tomorrow afternoon when my dad gets home. Hutton's fine. But I should also tell you Hayden finally told me about her past. And I think you might want to have her stay at my place until we get this mess sorted out." He listed the details of Emile Reed's background to Nick.

"Jeremy Dochenko? My God. If even half of what I've read about him is true, she has reason to be scared. Everyone knows he has connections to some really bad people. That man's heartless."

"That's why I think it's a good idea to keep her off the phone to her family and keep her here in Santa Cruz until you guys get back in town."

"Look, Ethan, if Hutton's in any kind of danger, we'll cut our trip short. With traffic, we should be back in two and half hours, be back at the cove by tonight."

"That's entirely up to you, but I think she's safe here at my mom's house as is Hayden if you want to stay another night. Once you two get back in town, though, I think it's a good idea if Hayden stays at my place at least until I talk to Brent and figure out which way we go from here. No sense bringing Dochenko to your front door when Hayden can stay with me. Do me a favor though, when you guys get back, if you have a single male book a reservation, or show up unannounced for a lengthy stay, let me know. If he's looking for the last known ping on Emile Reed's cell phone, my guess is it will bring him to Pelican Pointe sooner or later."

"You got it. And Ethan, thanks for letting me know all this. You be sure and take care of Hayden. Despite all this with Dochenko, she's a good a person."

Ethan glanced over at the woman in question as she sat, legs crossed, playing dolls with Hutton on the floor of his mother's living room. His belly tightened. "Yeah, she is."

He just hoped he could convince his parents of the same thing. But even if he couldn't, he'd already made his decision on the drive to Santa Cruz in the car.

Ethan Cody intended to marry Hayden Ryan aka Emile Reed even though, at this point, there seemed to be a helluva lot standing in their way.

Markus Cody walked into his living room Monday afternoon and couldn't believe his eyes. His wife, Lindeen, sat on the sofa with the mysterious Hayden Ryan having an honest-to-goodness conversation with the woman.

"Markus, it's about time you got home. How'd it go? Did you find any sign of the missing woman?"

He gave his wife a curious glance, but shook his head. "Once I got down there, I got nothing. Maybe I'm losing my touch. Maybe Ethan should have been the one to go."

And maybe his son had been right. Maybe he needed to take a closer look at this woman to find out the true nature of her heart.

About that time Ethan came through the door from the kitchen carrying a little girl on his hip. Markus did a double take. He stared at his youngest son holding the toddler. Ethan was a nice enough man, but Markus hadn't seen a domestic side to his youngest son. He couldn't help wonder what had changed that put that look in his eyes. A look that said he might be thinking about settling down with this woman, making her a part of his life in the long-term. Had he missed that on his son's face during the birthday party or just conveniently ignored it?

Markus shook his head. Just one more sign life had dramatically changed over the short amount of time he'd been in San Diego.

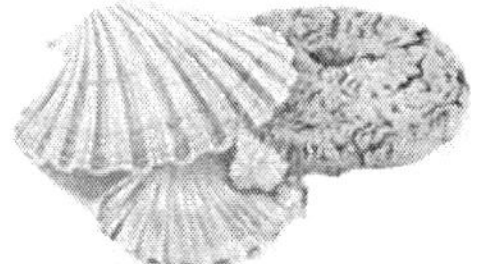

Chapter Eighteen

After a long twelve-hour shift in the ER, Sydney Reed, dragged her weary body out through the automatic doors of the ER at Saint Louis General Hospital and headed to her car parked in the employee lot.

It was twelve-twenty a.m.

Once she got outside, she breathed in the night air, grateful she was done with work for the next forty-eight hours.

She was about thirty feet from the car when she noticed what she thought looked like a man crouched in between her Chevy and the vehicle immediately to the left. She stopped her forward progress and hit the panic button on her car key, engaging the alarm. The noise of the horn going off brought the man from his hiding place. He started sprinting toward her.

Sydney took off running back the way she'd come, screaming at the top of her lungs across the lot. After what seemed like several long minutes, one of the on-duty residents who had been standing outside the ER doors, smoking a cigarette, heard Sydney's calls for help. He left his position at the entrance and ran out to meet her halfway into the lot, already on his cell phone dialing the cops.

Eight hundred miles to the northeast, in Pellingham, New York, Luka Radovan waited until the Trenton household was tucked in for the night before heading around to the back of the house and jimmying the lock on the sliding glass patio door.

He stepped inside a tidy kitchen in the dark, waited for his eyes to adjust, hoping he could locate what he was looking for without having to resort to violence. But if someone decided to investigate any noise in the middle of the night, he certainly wasn't above using the untraceable .38 strapped to his shoulder.

He took out his penlight, thumbing it on and shining the beam around the appliances and counters. It didn't take long for him to realize what he wanted wasn't in this part of the house.

Trying not to make too much noise, he moved on, going out into the connecting dining room. He spotted a woman's purse sitting prominently on the table. After digging around in the handbag and not finding what he was after, he moved on. Probably on a charger somewhere, he decided as he headed for the living room. There on an end table next to the sofa he spotted a cell phone cradled in its charging station. He picked it up, turned it on, and worked the menu around until he found the call history.

Taking out a pad and a pen from the inside pocket of his jacket, he began listing names and numbers from the screen. Luka could have just taken the phone, any other time he probably would have. But in this case, taking the phone might raise suspicion, maybe alert someone that he was in pursuit and getting closer.

This way, they would never know he'd been in the house, never know he'd gotten a look at the call history.

He didn't have to scroll down far until he found several possibilities. Deciding that jotting down every potential number might take too long, Luka took out his own cell phone, began snapping pictures of the entire list of phone calls going back several weeks.

When he'd finished, he left the way he'd come, out the sliding glass door. As he made his way through the dark neighborhood back to his car, Luka wondered if his associate in St. Louis had gotten as lucky as he had.

With Sydney Reed's cell, they could compare numbers rather easily. If a number had been called by both the sister and the mother, then he would get the word to his counterpart who kept track of such things.

Luka put the car into gear to head back to his hotel room in a better frame of mind. After six months on the run, the search for Emile Reed might be coming to an end.

The next morning it was a hectic time at the Trenton household as Laura loaded the breakfast dishes into the dishwasher. As soon as she finished that chore she turned to the roast defrosting on the kitchen counter and absently dumped it into her Crock-Pot for dinner that night.

She checked her watch, decided she and Rob were both running late. Heading out to the dining room she grabbed her purse off the table, headed into the living room to grab her cell phone from its place on the charger.

She bumped smack into Rob in the hallway as he picked up his briefcase to head out the front door to make the eight o'clock economics class he had that morning.

"Professor Trenton, if you don't get moving I'll have to write you a tardy slip," she teased her husband.

"I know. I know. Had to go back and retrieve my wallet. I'm meeting that cheapskate Roy Shaughnessy for lunch and he never picks up the tab."

Without thinking, Laura snatched up the cell phone and grabbed her coat from the hall closet, never realizing in her haste to get out the door, her cell phone battery had gone dead. The thing hadn't charged because it had been left off the charging station.

Since his associate had failed so miserably in St. Louis to get Sydney Reed's phone, comparing contact numbers was taking forever. Luka had to eliminate phone numbers the hard way, one call at a time. Going through the list he had already tracked most of the calls back to friends and relatives of Laura Reed-Trenton.

None had turned out to belong to Emile Reed.

But when he zeroed in on the seven-seven-five area code indicating a Reno location, he sat up a little straighter in his chair. It was the only number on the phone with such a distant area code, two thousand miles to the west of Chicago. Knowing the Reno number had potential, Luka placed the call to his friend enlisting him to track down the carrier assigned to that particular cell.

"How long before you retrieve the data?" Luka asked.

"Give me twenty-four. If my manager comes back on duty though, it might be longer."

"Fine, but I want every last known call from that phone."

"Why don't you just call the number, see who answers?"

"And tip her off that I'm closing in? No way. I've been spending twenty-four-seven on this woman for months now. No way will I give her the chance to take off."

Because once Luka had the last known calls, he could triangulate the phone's location, once he had the last known location, he would catch the first plane out west and wherever Emile Reed had last used that phone.

Chapter Nineteen

It was almost six o'clock when Nick and Jordan arrived back at the cove Monday evening to the enthusiastic applause of their own baby daughter, who couldn't stop clapping her hands and offering them kisses.

As ecstatic as Hutton was to see mommy and daddy, her babysitter was a bit more subdued, apologetic even.

Hayden stood a couple of feet back from the car parked in the driveway waiting to offer an explanation of sorts. "I would never have intentionally put Hutton in danger, not for anything. You have to believe that," Hayden told them. "And except for a brief time on Saturday, when Ethan was on duty, he never left us alone. Not once. We had a member of law enforcement right there beside us the entire time you were gone."

Jordan put an arm around Hayden's shoulders. "If we'd known your circumstances, I doubt we would've gone anywhere."

"I know. I'm sorry."

Jordan glanced at Nick who was unloading their bags from the back of the car. "We had a wonderful time, Hayden. I missed Hutton like I missed my right arm. But Nick and I needed to get away, if for no other reason than to have some time to ourselves to relax, to talk."

Hayden snorted. "Is that what they're calling it now?" She bumped Jordan's shoulder in a playful gesture that had the other woman laughing.

"Oh, we did that plenty of times, too." She sighed. "We ordered room service, ate breakfast in bed Sunday morning, then again this morning. Nick ordered a masseuse to come to the room for a soothing massage. I swam laps in the pool. It was fantastic. I feel so—rested."

She looked Hayden in the eye. "We talked about you on the drive back. We aren't mad at you, Hayden. In all these months, you were the only one who offered to look after Hutton for us, to keep an eye on this place. It's really good to be home though. I feel as if I've been away for years instead of just two measly days."

"You do look rested."

"Oh, I am!"

At that moment, Jordan grabbed Hayden's arm in a death grip. "Oh. My. God. It's him! It's Scott!" She took two steps toward Nick, captured his arm as well. "Look, over there, by the front porch. Do you see that? I see him, Nick." Tears formed in her eyes and spilled down her cheeks.

As everyone followed her gaze to the long front porch, Jordan yelled out, "I'm not mad anymore, Scott. I'm not mad. I was missing you so much, that's all. I was lonely out here by myself without you. But I have Nick now. I'm sorry, I was so mad at you for leaving me. But I'm over it."

Hayden looked over at Ethan then at Nick to catch his reaction to Jordan's epiphany.

Nick had tears in his eyes as he watched his wife's animated conversation with his best friend's ghost.

But soon all three of them noticed the transformation that came over Scott's face. Joy maybe. Certainly elation at the prospect Jordan had opened up enough that she could finally see him.

The knowledge had his lips curving into a wide smile.

Hayden looked over as Jordan took Hutton out of Nick's arms and smiled back.

"You're here, Scott, in Hutton, each and every day. I never gave up on this place, not even when things looked so awful." She picked up Nick's hand and dragged him closer to the porch, closer to Scott. "Neither did Nick. We worked ourselves silly doing this—for you." Jordan's hand flew to the top of Hutton's head. "And for her. She'll grow up here, Scott, just like you did, just like you wanted."

Her hand went to her flat belly. "And she'll have a brother or sister to play with soon. We all love you, Scott. We all miss you so much!"

They watched as Scott's arm lifted in a wave and then, like every other time before, he was gone.

Later, after Ethan and Hayden had moved her few belongings over to Ethan's house, she was hanging some of her clothes in his closet, when she asked, "Do you think he's gone for good? Do you think that was why he was hanging around all this time, waiting until Jordan finally saw him?"

"I don't know. I guess we'll have to wait and see. That's the damnedest thing I ever saw, though. If I hadn't been right there, I might not have believed it."

Hayden sunk down on the bed. "I know. It's amazing how Scott is so—accepting of Nick, you know, being with Jordan. It's so obvious he wants her happy. If you ask me that's gotta be the ultimate way of showing how much you loved someone in life, to want them to be happy without you. And knowing she's having Nick's baby has to hurt on some level. Can a ghost hurt?"

"Watching them together has to be tough on him, no doubt about that. But hey, he's chosen his role in the afterlife, or whatever it is you believe happens after a person dies. He doesn't have to hang around there so aware of what's happening."

Ethan turned to her then, took a seat next to her on the bed. "Look, there's something we need to talk about. Brent will be back tomorrow. We're going in to see him, sit down face to face, get all this out in the open."

Her face fell. She sent him a sulky stare. "That means he'll contact the feds. Ethan…"

"No, don't look at me like that. This is the only way, Hayden. What do I call you now anyway? It's bothered me now for a couple of days. Do you prefer Emile or Hayden? Which is it?"

She sighed and picked up his hand. "Hayden. This is my new life, use my new name. It's legal by the way. A lawyer friend helped me change it. And the other day Sydney used it for the first time. Now, my mother's a different story. It's taking her longer to leave Emile in the dust. But for some reason the name feels right."

She eyed his face for any lingering doubts and then asked, "What else bothers you, Ethan? I don't want you spending another two days holding back. You might as well get it all out now."

"The phone calls you've been making are a problem."

"I just don't see how. I was careful. Are you saying I can't even use my phone to check my messages? I bet my family's tried to call me." She was itching to get her hands on the device and make certain her family was okay.

But one glance at Ethan had her realizing how serious the phone issue really was.

"Making calls on that phone is one sure way to bring Dochenko's men right to your front door. It might as well be an open invitation, Hayden."

"But you won't even let me turn it on."

"That's right, turning it on pings the nearest cell tower, which we don't want to do. If you want to call your family, then I'll take you to a pay phone over in San Sebastian. Caution is our byword from here on out." But he didn't even want to bring up the fact it might already be way too late for that.

Hayden was nervous. Sitting in Brent's office the next day with the door closed gave her a feeling of déjà vu, even claustrophobia. The walls were closing in. The room wasn't all that large to begin with and with three people crammed into the closed-up space, it felt confining.

She'd been answering Brent's questions all morning. But according to him and Ethan, a federal agent was on his way down from the Bay at this very moment, scheduled to arrive any minute to take yet another official statement from her.

At the prospect of having to go over all of it again for the umpteenth time, her throat tightened. Just thinking about the federal agent had her stomach cramping. She knew what was coming. A lecture about how she shouldn't have taken off.

When the door opened and Brent's assistant showed a well-dressed, suited, forty-something man into the office, Hayden knew this was the federal agent.

The cocky demeanor was a dead giveaway.

"Well, well, well, Emile Reed. I'm Matt Russell." He turned to Brent. "Nice work, Sheriff. Collaring this one will get you some attention from the director."

Brent simply shook his head and angled a look at his brother, who was all but ready to snap at this man's smug behavior.

It was Ethan who sneered, "He didn't collar her, you idiot. No one collared her. She came in of her own free will to make a statement." Ethan didn't mention that he had practically had to drag her out of the car and through the front door to get her inside the building. But the fact was he didn't like this guy's attitude one bit and could detect Brent's derision on his face, as well.

"Is that so?" Russell put his focus back on Hayden. "There are plenty of people at the justice department hoping you'll do the right thing this time around and stick it out."

"First of all, I didn't take off because I didn't want to do the right thing. I took off because someone tried to kill me in a parking garage. I'm not used to people wanting me dead. I was scared, okay? And not just for myself but for my entire family. The lack of faith wasn't in me, Agent

Russell. It was in you and the federal government for not being able to protect what you called, 'your star witness.'"

"Come on, Miss Reed, how do I know you didn't make up that attempt-on-your-life story just to get yourself a new name and start over someplace else in that little backwater bird town?"

Ethan didn't like Russell badgering her.

Hayden shot an accusing glance at him, then at Brent, before standing up to face off with Agent Russell. "I guess it's just a coincidence that Saul Raymond, your other witness by the way, just happened to conveniently take two bullets to the head, execution-style, the day before that thug showed up in the parking garage after me. I didn't even know about his murder until my mother told me about it a week later."

She crossed her arms over her chest, defiant now. "You guys are unbelievable! You demand cooperation, but then won't take any responsibility when things go horribly wrong and people get killed. Where was Saul Raymond's protection? Where was mine?"

She paced two feet toward the door and then back again, chewed on a thumb nail, thinking.

"You will testify to what you know though, correct? You will testify that you saw Dochenko falsify financials, testify you overheard him make false statements about the financial condition of the company to the bank?"

"That and a few other things about Jeremy that might hold your interest for longer than five minutes, things I've remembered over the last few months, things the agents back in Chicago didn't ask me about. Yes, I'll tell them everything. But first I want to talk to my mother and my sister. I'm not saying another word until I get to talk to my family, a long conversation at that where they take the time to assure me they're safe and doing just fine."

She pointed a finger at Russell's chest. "And I want round-the-clock protection for Sydney Reed in St. Louis. I want the same for my mother Laura Trenton and my stepfather, Rob in New York. Without that, we have nothing to discuss. You might as well lock me up right now, throw away the key because I'm not saying another word until I know my family is protected."

The swagger seemed to go out of Agent Russell.

Ethan knew she was pissed at him for putting her through this. He could see it in those green eyes that seemed to flame gold around the edges each time she shot a daggered look his way.

As he watched her in Brent's office, standing almost toe to toe with the brash federal agent, he couldn't have been more proud of the woman he intended to make his wife. It didn't go unnoticed by him that she asked nothing for herself. She simply wanted to make sure her sister and mother would be safe.

Five and a half hours later though, Emile-slash-Hayden emerged from an interrogation room, exhausted. After answering questions, after giving them every tidbit of information she could drag out of her brain, she wasn't just tired, but furious.

How had her life gone so horribly wrong?

When she looked up and spotted Ethan waiting for her on a bench in the hallway, she resolved to close this chapter of her life once and for all. The minute she saw him heading toward her, she dragged in a breath and prepared to wage a different kind of battle.

Like she had earlier with Agent Russell, Hayden pointed a finger at Ethan's chest. "Get away from me, Ethan Cody. I want you to get away from me now. Go home and box up all my stuff from your house. Pack it up! It won't be that difficult, there's not that much to bring back. But I want what few things I've managed to scrape together over these last few miserable months on the run. I want you to bring it back to me before I leave. I'll be staying in a hotel tonight under lock and key with a guard posted outside the door."

Ethan let her rant, even knew he deserved some portion of it. But after she finally wound down, he said quietly,

"They aren't taking you anywhere. You're coming back to Pelican Pointe with me. Tonight."

"Oh, really? Is that what you thought would happen when you dragged me in here today, Ethan? You might want to check with the agent in charge of this case now. That would be Matt Russell, the man calling all the shots."

"I know you're upset. You have every right to be. But think of it this way, that initial questioning, that part is over."

"Are you really that naïve? They're taking me to San Francisco first thing in the morning, Ethan."

"They aren't taking you anywhere. I'm taking you back to Pelican Pointe—with me."

Hearing the argument, Agent Russell swept out into the hallway looking as energized as he had when he'd first arrived hours earlier. "She's right, Deputy Cody. I'm afraid her cell phone usage has compromised her safety. I've just learned that the other day, her sister, Sydney, had an encounter with a man in the hospital parking lot where she works. Might've been random, but..." He shot a glance at Hayden. After spending so many hours with her, his opinion of the woman had changed. "And her mother thinks someone got in the house and messed with her cell phone. From here on out, we take no chances."

Ethan ran his fingers through his hair. This time it was Ethan who stepped into Agent Russell's personal space. "I can protect Hayden. There's no need for you to take her to the Bay or anywhere else for that matter. I'm a trained member of law enforcement. And whether or not you think this is Bumfuck, California, or not, she stays with me where I know she's safe."

"You can't possibly watch her round the clock."

"That's where you're wrong. Bring your guards and put them outside my house." He grabbed Hayden's hand. "Because that's where she'll be staying until you guys find Dochenko."

Once they got to his county vehicle, Ethan turned a pissed off Hayden around to face him. "I'm sorry. You have every right to be mad at me but remember I'm on your side. I'm not the one who got you into this mess."

Knowing that was true, some of the fury drained out of her. "Thanks so much, Deputy. But I tried to explain what I went through back in Chicago. You members of law enforcement think you know so much more than the rest of us. They could have killed Sydney in that parking lot. They could have killed my mother and stepfather in their own home in their sleep. And what did any of you do about it?"

The tears started to come for real. After a long miserable day, the waterworks opened up and allowed the frustration of the past few months to pour out of her.

Because she needed the contact, she let him put his arms around her, nuzzle her neck, run his hands up and down her back.

"I know you're scared. You'd be crazy not to be. But sitting down with the feds was the right thing to do."

He rested his forehead on hers. "I've never been more proud of anyone in my life than today when you stood up to that asshole Russell. I love you whether your name's Emile Reed, or Hayden-no-middle-initial-Ryan. It doesn't matter much to me because…" He put his hand over her heart. "I know what's real in here."

It took a couple of seconds for those words to pierce her tired psyche and find their way to her heart. She sniffled. Her arms stretched around his neck. "You love me? Say it again."

"I love you." He covered her mouth with his.

After the kind of day she'd had, it didn't take much for her to sink into the kiss. "Mmmm, I love you, too."

"Still want to move out?"

"Oh, shut up. You might've mentioned you loved me before today. I felt like you were throwing me to the wolves to further your career, get that pat on the head from the director."

"I know. I'm sorry about that. But I'm new at this being in love with someone thing."

"Then you need to get better at it—and fast—because from here on out this is going to be a rough ride."

"Nothing we can't handle."

"Your mother doesn't like me."

He opened her car door, gave her another hard kiss. "That's okay. I have every belief in your ability to break down her resistance the same way you did mine."

She grabbed a fistful of his shirt. "What are you talking about, Ethan Cody? Once I made up my mind, you were mush in my hands."

He grinned. "That's exactly right. And I've no doubt my mom will fall the same way I did. But remember the woman desperately wants grandchildren. If I were you, I'd use that to your advantage."

Hayden laughed. "I guess I could handle a couple of little brown-eyed toddlers that look exactly like their father."

Ethan's breath hitched. He picked up her hand and kissed the palm. "A couple? I was right there when you promised her six."

She looked over at him sitting behind the wheel of the car and got that familiar tug in the belly. "Suggested six, not promised, there's a huge difference. I guess I'll just have to work on bargaining her down to four."

"See, that's how much you know. I'm pretty sure she'd easily settle for three."

Chapter Twenty

Over the next several days, Hayden insisted on returning to her schedule. Despite a federal agent tagging after her wherever she went to keep her safe, she refused to disappoint Nick and Jordan and give up her duties out at the farm. Nor did she intend to quit on Margie at the Diner, either. She'd made a commitment to people that counted on her each and every day and she intended to follow through. No amount of Ethan's pestering or arguing could change her mind or make her alter her routine or her duties.

Once she'd tallied the day's receipts, caught up on her bookkeeping, and paid invoices she wandered down to the roadside fruit stand to help out the new girl Nick had hired, Mona Bingham, Max's eighteen-year-old daughter from Texas.

While she'd been grilled by the feds, it seemed life had gone on in Pelican Pointe. Mona had needed a job and Nick had provided one.

In between waiting on customers, Hayden found out Mona had come to California from Texas to reconnect with her father, whom she hadn't seen in five years. She'd also been persuaded to help out at the Diner this past weekend when Abby Pointer's little girl had become ill and had to be rushed over to see Doc Prescott.

As Hayden and Mona worked together replacing the fruit and vegetable baskets and pumpkins as customers purchased them, Mona went on about how she'd only been in town since last Thursday. "My relationship with Max has always been rocky at best. But after I lost my job at the

Dairy Queen a week ago, I decided I needed a change of scenery, a new start in a new state."

"There's a lot of that going around," Hayden said with a smile. "Besides, being here will give you an opportunity to get to know Margie, as well as, Max. Margie's not as brusque as she lets on. Beneath that rough exterior is a good person who knows what it's like to struggle."

"She's been nice enough, I guess. But I'm already missing my friends back in Texas."

Uh-oh, thought Hayden, another restless soul.

That opened the door for Mona to expound on her take on Margie. Listening to Mona gave Hayden the distraction she needed to finish out her day before heading over to the B & B where she planned to meet Ethan for dinner.

An hour later she glanced over at her bodyguard, Agent Troy Dawson, who looked bored out of his mind. Studying the six-foot-tall man with toffee colored skin and deep chocolate eyes and just out of the Academy, Hayden said, "You know, Pelican Pointe isn't as out of step as it seems."

In a soft-spoken voice, Troy said, "Are you kidding? I grew up in a tiny little town of less than two thousand people in eastern Alabama. That's why they gave me this assignment. Well, one of the reasons. The other being I'm low man on the seniority pole."

"Really? So that southern accent is real?"

He grinned. "Yes, ma'am. Genuine southern-speak as my mother would say."

"So you aren't missing having a slew of fast food joints around here and no pesky urban noise at night?"

"Let's put it this way," he said patting his stomach. "I can do without the high-calorie fast food, although Max's cooking is giving me cause to take up jogging again. His food's addictive. That chicken-fried steak and mashed potatoes he serves up are damn close to what my grandmamma used to make. As far as I'm concerned he's a genius in the kitchen."

"He is that. Let me guess. Meat and potatoes man? Am I right?"

Troy grinned. "And the rural setting is fine by me, reminds me a lot of the countryside where I grew up."

"Good. Because you're about to spend the evening with two of the best people on the planet. One of whom just happens to make terrific meat and potatoes that melt in your mouth."

The next day Nick and Jordan sat at the kitchen table eating leftover roast beef sandwiches when the phone rang. Nick got up from his lunch with his mouth still full and glanced at the digital readout on the desk phone in the corner. It told Nick it was his old Guard buddy Ben Latham calling. He swallowed his food and picked up the phone. "Hey Ben, I've been meaning to call you and tell you voice-to-voice, Jordan's pregnant."

"What? That's great. How far along?"

"Eight weeks now."

"Congratulations, buddy. It didn't take you guys long to go on stork watch, did it?"

Nick laughed. "Hey, I kept giving it my best shot." He looked over at Jordan and winked.

"How's she feeling?" Ben asked.

"Tired mostly, but we just got back from a three-day trip to the Bay for her birthday where she got in some serious R & R, away from the grind of running this place. And the last couple of weeks have been considerably rough since Edmund Taggert passed away and left us his organic farm, the adjoining piece of property. The whole thing's been stressful for both of us."

"Geez. Well, I hate to add to what sounds like a bad time, but we've got us a problem, Nick. I just got off the phone with Colonel Marks." Marks had been their commanding officer in the National Guard unit in which they'd served together for years. "Remember Cord Bennett and what happened to him back in Leesburg last year? To say the guy's having a tough time is an understatement. Right now, he's locked up in a Houston jail for drunk and disorderly and misdemeanor assault. Bar fight. I don't doubt he's guilty as hell but I think he needs someone to go down there and get him, bring him back to California."

"What about the assault?"

"He'll probably get off with a fine, probation maybe, as long as someone is there to speak up for him."

"What do you want me to do, Ben?"

"Go down and get him out of jail. I'd go, Nick, but Sheryl is about ready to pop any day."

"You can't leave Sheryl now to go to Houston."

"I know, but it sounds like you have your hands full there, too."

"I won't lie to you, inheriting the farm has been a major headache. Taking three days off was a godsend but I'm not sure I can be gone from Jordan and Hutton long enough to jump a plane to Houston and sit around waiting for Cord to get his act together."

It occurred to Nick then he didn't want to leave home right now when Hayden had God knows who out there looking for her. He couldn't very well ask Ethan to park himself here at the B & B for who knew how long either until Cord got squared away in Houston. It might be days before his hearing came up.

"Look, if it were a simple twenty-four-hour turnaround trip to get him out of jail, I'd do that in a heartbeat. But you and I know there's more involved here. We don't know what Cord's situation is like. We know for a fact he's had a drinking problem the past year. I'm not judging him after what happened, but I'm just telling you, it's gonna take more than twenty-four hours to sort out Cord's situation and get him on a plane and back to California."

Nick glanced over at Jordan. "Look, I don't mind giving him a place to stay once he gets out of jail, once he gets back here. How about if I call Jarrod Collins? The last time I talked to him he hadn't been able to find work. If he has time on his hands, he could catch a flight to Houston out of L.A., be there to post Cord's bail, and then bring him back here. I'll pay for the airfare to and from Texas. But I don't feel comfortable leaving Jordan and Hutton here alone just now."

"There's something else you aren't telling me."

Leave it to Ben to pick up on his hesitation. "Suffice it to say, I have my reasons. We were able to leave for three days because a friend was generous enough to babysit Hutton for us. But the friend is having some problems of her own right now. I don't think it's a good idea to tempt fate and take off for Houston and leave Jordan and Hutton alone."

"If you can talk Collins into it, I'll go half with you on the roundtrip tickets. Someone's got to go help Cord, Nick. He's self-destructing and if something doesn't change in his life pretty soon, he's going to end up in jail for worse than drunk and disorderly. That guy is a ticking time bomb. He hasn't had a break in over a year."

"Okay, I'll call Jarrod and get back to you."

Thirty minutes later, after talking to Jarrod, it was agreed that Nick and Ben would split the cost of the airline tickets so that their fellow Guard buddy, Jarrod Collins, could fly down to Houston, pack up Cord and his things and drive him back to California in Cord's pickup.

What San Diego native Cord Bennett had been doing in Houston all the way from Leesburg, Virginia, was a mystery in itself. Since Cord was the only one with the answers, they would have to wait until he arrived in Pelican Pointe to find out.

The very afternoon Nick had contemplated leaving for Houston, Luka Radovan arrived in Hicksville. That was the kindest thing he could say about the pathetic excuse for the little town known as Pelican Pointe. There wasn't a fast-food chain within fifty miles of the place he had quickly deemed, 'the bird sanctuary.' The tallest building was a three-story house. The town itself looked as if it had dried up in the '80s and someone forgot to tell the residents life had bypassed them for a real city.

The pings from Emile Reed's cell phone had brought him here. Thus, he was determined to find out which part of town had been her haven for the past five months. But first he had to get his bearings. Driving up and down each street searching for a BMW 323 might not prove resourceful. More than likely she no longer owned the vehicle. But scanning the streets gave him an opportunity to look for anyone who resembled the woman's features, a description he had branded on his brain.

After all, he had been at this for months. He had to remember the element of surprise was on his side.

The first time Ethan had spotted the rented SUV with the fleet license plate, it had been sitting at the light at Main and Beach Streets. Now, the GMC Yukon seemed to be patrolling up and down Ocean Street near the wharf area.

They got tourists in town, sometimes a lot during the summer. But since today was the end of October, Halloween to be exact, and definitely the off-season Ethan doubted the car belonged to a tourist. For some reason, Ethan was drawn to the vehicle like cobalt to a magnetic force field. Following gut instinct, he ran the plates.

With any luck it might come back as stolen. But that idea went up in smoke when dispatch confirmed it was a rental out of the San Francisco airport. Ethan went a step farther. He asked for them to fax the name on the driver's license and a description of the renter who leased the car. Knowing the results would take some time, he watched as the Yukon pulled into the slotted street parking in front of the Diner.

Ethan placed a call to Brent, told him what he suspected and to look for the fax from the airport rental agency. With that done, he bided his time, sitting behind the wheel of his patrol car, thrumming his fingers on the console.

Sudden images of how he and Hayden had made love that morning jammed his brainwaves. He shook off the sexy imagery and decided he needed to focus on the job at hand. He knew Troy Dawson to be a capable agent he could trust. But that didn't mean Hayden couldn't be caught in a vulnerable situation under the right set of circumstances.

As soon as the driver climbed out of the car, Ethan took out his cell phone and snapped a picture of a very tall man, six-four at the least, and watched as he made his way inside.

Glancing up and down the street, he realized he might possibly be overreacting. The guy had more than likely veered off the Interstate, gotten lost and ended up in Pelican Pointe. It had happened before. The guy was probably no more than a businessman taking advantage of the situation to get something to eat before heading back to the highway.

At least, Ethan hoped that was the case.

Even though it was three hours before Hayden's shift started, he punched her number into his cell phone, hoping she got service at the roadside stand. But she didn't pick up and the call went straight to voice mail.

Thirty minutes later the door to the Diner opened. Ethan was surprised to see the six-four man reappear carrying a sack in his hand. So the man had gotten his food order to-go. Another good sign he was headed out of town and back the way he'd come.

But once the Yukon backed out of the slotted space, it headed north out of town in the direction of Promise Cove.

Ethan emerged from his truck and made his way into the Diner. Before his butt took a seat at the counter, Margie came around from the kitchen in a hurry. "Ethan, there was a stranger with an accent in here not five minutes ago asking about Hayden, had a picture of her too, with blonde hair."

"What did you tell him, Margie?"

"He said he was her brother, but I'm not stupid, Ethan. In all the time she's been working here she's mentioned having a sister, but not once did she ever say anything about having a brother."

He really wished Margie would get to the point.

"So, when he wanted to know if she lived around here, I told him I didn't know where she lived, but if he wanted to talk to her, she had a job out at Taggert's Farm this time of day."

Ethan sucked in a breath and sprinted out the door. The guy had a five-minute head start. At that moment, he could only hope Troy Dawson kept her safe until he got there.

Luka Radovan ate his greasy club sandwich and fries on the way out of Bumfuckville. He couldn't get out of town fast enough. As he drove past nothing but countryside, a bunch of trees and crap, he briefly wondered if maybe that bitch at the Diner had been pulling his leg.

It was difficult to believe Emile Reed had a job working on a farm. The woman he remembered sitting in her corner office on the twenty-fifth floor of a high-rise office building had been immaculate, perfect nails, perfect hair. She had expensive tastes in clothes. He remembered her wearing four-hundred-dollar suits and shoes to work, practically every day of the week.

What could a woman like that possibly find the least bit interesting to do on a farm? If this is where she'd ended up after leaving Chicago, no wonder it had taken months to locate her.

On his first pass by the roadside stand, Luka missed the turn into the entrance to Taggert Organic Farms, largely due to the fact he was doing close to fifty-five. One glance at the fruit stand though told him a female stood behind the counter. But then he couldn't make out the features other than dark hair. In fact, he'd bet five hundred dollars there was more than one person standing behind the counter. How on earth could there possibly be that much interest in a vegetable stand at this time of day?

Luka knew Emile Reed was a platinum blonde, or had been. To Luka, women pretty much changed their hair color as often as they changed men.

A hand-painted, bright orange and white banner waved in the wind and stretched across an open three-sided structure that resembled a shack he'd seen once in rural Chicago. The sign read, "Pelican Pointe Pumpkin Patch." Luka shook his head. He'd never seen so many of the orange fruits in one place.

He'd clearly landed in Oz.

He went another mile before he found a place on the shoulder to turn around. This time when he came to the Pumpkin Patch, he pulled the Yukon into a gravel parking lot along with four other cars and shut off the engine.

He studied the dark-haired woman behind the counter. Even from twenty yards away, he recognized Emile Reed. The dyed black hair wasn't much of a disguise. Who was she kidding? The dark hair didn't even look natural.

Luka gauged his surroundings. After all, he had a job to do.

The woman had customers, including a bunch of kids, perusing the fruit, walking up and down the rows of pumpkins, searching for the perfect one. He counted at least half a dozen women milling about, another three or four noisy rugrats who did nothing but run around the display and one more trying to clamber up the scarecrow.

Removing the automatic Beretta .380 from its carrying case on the floorboard, Luka screwed on the silencer. Opening the door of the SUV, he stepped out onto the gravel, heard the crunch of pebbles under the soles of his fifteen-hundred-dollar Russian calf-skin shoes.

With his gun lowered to his side, hoping no one would notice, he made his way toward the counter. He wasn't here for a mass execution. All he needed was one clear shot of Emile Reed and an escape route. Like any assassin worth his salt, he'd already mapped that out ahead of time. He'd head northeast keeping to the back roads until he reached the 880, switch cars in San Jose, take the 680 north and he'd be home free.

So intent was he focused on his target Emile Reed, Luka didn't see the old woman sneak into his line of vision until it was too late. He felt a thud against his back like someone had shoved him. He heard the old crone scream, "He's got a gun. He's got a big-ass gun."

Myrtle Pettibone threw her whole body into another blow, hitting the gunman again with her handbag right across his back.

At that moment, Ethan Cody screeched his patrol vehicle to a stop, skidding a good ten feet on the black top. With his brother Brent as backup, Ethan pulled his .45 and threw open the driver's side door.

Troy Dawson heard the brakes squeal to a stop from where he'd gone to help a couple of seven-year-old boys pick up and carry the biggest pumpkin in the patch back to the counter for purchase.

At the sound of Ethan hitting the brakes, Troy looked up and spotted a tall man with a gun making his way toward the woman he was supposed to be protecting. He dropped the gourd to the ground, ignoring the cries of the two little boys who watched as it bounced several times on the pavement before cracking open near the driveway leading to the farm.

By the time Troy pulled his revolver, Ethan had leaned across the hood of his truck, taken aim at the unsub with his .45 and yelled, "Drop the weapon. Put the weapon down now! Now! Take one more step and it'll be your last."

Brent circled around from the side with another .45 pointed at the man's back. By this time Troy had the man in his sights as well. "You heard the Deputy, drop the gun."

Ethan made his way from the car, gun pointed at the unsub's chest. He never took his eyes off his target. Moving closer, getting within several feet, he said, "Myrtle you step back, now. Get away from him." Myrtle did as she was told, and Ethan shouted again, "Drop the gun and get down on the ground. What's it gonna be?"

Just in case Ethan didn't see what he was up against Myrtle pointed out, "You watch it, Ethan, that gun's got a silencer on it. He means business. I watch TV shows, too, you know. He could've shot us all."

The Russian took stock of his situation, alive he might be able to cut a deal, shot full of holes, no chance of a deal. Three guns to one, he supposed he'd make a deal. Ever so slowly, Luka dropped the Beretta and put his hands in the air. He knew the drill. After all, this wasn't his first time to the circus.

Once the gun was on the ground, Myrtle tried to run up and kick it out of the way, but Ethan grabbed her arm just in time, pulling her back. "I've got this Myrtle. Go stand over there by the scarecrows. Round up those kids for me. Go on, now."

Brent was in the process of cuffing their unsub when Ethan asked Hayden, "By any chance do you recognize this guy?"

Voice trembling, Hayden's knees felt like jelly. "His name is Luka Radovan. I saw him come into the office lots of times. He works for Dochenko. I was never sure what exactly he did though."

"I think it's safe to say, we now have a good idea of his job description."

Once Luka was in handcuffs and sitting in the back of Brent's patrol car, Hayden finally turned to Ethan. "Are you okay? He could have shot you. You could've been killed."

"Me? What about you? That guy was three steps away from taking you out."

But realization hit him when he realized she'd been as concerned for his safety as he'd been for hers. He'd have to get used to this love thing he decided. "I did my job, Hayden. I pulled up, saw the bastard holding the gun not ten steps from you, and my heart dropped out of my chest at the thought I might lose you."

"I didn't even see him walking my way until Myrtle called out. Then I saw you pull up, get out with a gun and was scared to death he'd shoot you."

"Well, he didn't."

"My knees are still shaking."

"Mine, too."

"Oh, please. You looked cool as glass."

"Adrenaline. Remember the day you saved Justin from drowning? You didn't slink down on the floor until it was all over."

She ran a shaky hand down the side of his face. "Somehow I don't see you slinking down on the floor."

"Maybe not but where you're concerned, my knees wanted to buckle."

"Maybe it's because you love me."

"Maybe it's because I want to marry you."

"Oh, Ethan, you pick the damnedest time to say stuff like that. You're proposing to me right here? Yes, the answer's yes." She threw her arms around his neck.

"You'll marry me even though I'm not a famous author yet?"

She laughed. "I'd marry you even if you were a lowly deputy sheriff. You know, you could always self-publish your books. But there's something I want to do. Not sure how you'll feel about it though."

"Please don't tell me you want to move back to Chicago."

She let out a nervous giggle. "Go back to those freezing winters? I don't think so. I want to open that used bookstore in Autumn's house. In fact, if you self-publish I'll guarantee to give your books top priority and display them prominently about the store. I'll even hold your first book signing. How's that? I know the shop may not make much money at first. But money isn't everything. Of course, I know Pelican Pointe isn't exactly begging for a bookstore. It'll probably go under in sight of six months. But—"

He grabbed her and covered her mouth. The fiery kiss went on until they came up for air. Resting his forehead on hers, he pledged, "Whatever you want, Hayden. Whatever you want."

Epilogue

Seven weeks later
Christmas Eve

Inside Autumn Lassiter's little golden-colored Spanish-style stucco house with the red-tiled roof, Hayden busily unpacked another carton of used books. Nick and Jordan hadn't been exaggerating when they'd said they had a "bunch" of books.

After Nick had cleaned out a storage locker and that black hole of a garage, the tally had totaled some twenty plus boxes of various hardcovers and paperbacks that covered every genre from romance to true crime. Ancient children's books from Scott's childhood were mixed in with his college textbooks, along with a surplus of how-to programming manuals.

So far, Hayden hadn't been able to discard any of them, which made her wonder how she intended to handle opening for business and actually parting with them via a sale.

This past weekend she and Ethan had put the finishing touches on painting every room of the nine-hundred-square-foot house and installing bookshelves in what would soon be Hidden Moon Bay Books.

To keep from putting any more holes in the wall though, Hayden had acquired six rolling carts that could easily be wheeled from room to room. They'd buffed the hardwood floors to a shine, brought in a few thrift-store chairs she'd already recovered, and restained an ancient desk she planned to use for a checkout counter. Even now there were still drop cloths spread around everywhere to keep the damage to the floor to a minimum while she got things squared away and prepared to open the doors for business the first week of January.

A knock on the front door had her yelling, "Come on in, door's open."

Jordan walked in carrying a couple of to-go containers full of steaming coffee. Looking around the small front room she said, "Wow! This place is really coming together."

"Thanks to you and Nick."

She handed Hayden one of the cardboard cups of the aromatic liquid. "Thought you might need a pick-me-up about this time of the morning. Now I want you to stop and look around at all the hard work you've done. You've taken cartons of old books that were otherwise gathering dust in storage now you're making them inventory, so stop this habit you have of thanking Nick and me every time you see us. We want this town to come back from the dead. You're part of that plan now, Hayden."

"I know. I'm so excited I can hardly sleep at night waiting to open up."

"I just love the bright blue walls."

"Thanks. We're hoping the color says buy, buy, buy!"

Jordan laughed. "I think you'll be pleasantly surprised at how many people are hungry for a place to buy books here in town."

"I hope so. It'll be such a kick when I make my first sale."

"I ran into Ethan at Murphy's getting the coffee. He told me the good news. Thanks to Interpol and the information you provided about Dochenko's villa, the French police were able to arrest him trying to board a plane to Tahiti."

Hayden smiled. "I know. He's been in custody four days now. They reassigned Troy Dawson. He's left town to spend the holidays with his family back in Alabama and then he's off to Ohio to babysit another government witness."

"Did you get hold of Lilly?"

"I did. She gave me a terrific price, should have my sign ready to hang next week right on schedule."

"Need anything else?"

"Nope, I think I have everything covered. How's Cord working out at the farm? Just say the word and I'll fill in any time you need me. I got pretty good at recognizing powdery mildew so I can help out in that department."

Jordan snickered. "He's a good worker. But..."

"Still drinking?"

"Off and on. He'll stop for a week and then fall off the wagon."

"Well, since I'm still doing the books I've got to make sure Taggert Organic Farms thrives, plants, cows, and employees alike. I love that place. Look, I have something to ask you. It's about the wedding. I want you to be my matron of honor. I already told Sydney I'd ask you. She understands the reasons why I feel the way I do."

Jordan's eyes misted over. "Me? Are you sure you don't want your sister? I mean, by Valentine's Day I'll probably weigh two tons. I'll waddle down the aisle ahead of you big as one of Taggert's cows. Are you sure that's what you want?"

"Oh, please. You're barely showing. Why is it pregnant women think they're huge by four months?"

"By your wedding day, I'll be six months along. You just wait. I'll remember what you said when you're knocked up and don't fit into any of your clothes anymore."

Hayden chuckled. "Deal. And Sydney's fine being my bridesmaid. She knows if not for you I wouldn't have gotten this far. I wouldn't be marrying Ethan in February. I wouldn't be opening this place either. If not for you I'd have gotten up that next morning after Ethan found me and headed for Santa Cruz."

To prevent from getting teary-eyed, she purposefully glanced around at all the boxes. "Jordan, do you realize most of these books belonged to Scott at different stages of his life?"

Jordan let out a huge sigh. "Yes. But he'd want you to have them, don't you think? He loved this town, Hayden, almost as much as he loved The Cove. He'd love nothing more than knowing his books helped bring about getting the town a bookstore. He used to dream about this town's rebirth. Nick and I are out to make sure it happens."

About that time Hayden picked up a well-worn hardcover book from the carton. "Look at this, Treasure Island. How many times do you suppose Scott read this?" She ran her hand across the collector's edition of the beloved classic.

"Probably a hundred. It was his favorite."

As Hayden thumbed through the pages, a piece of paper fell out and drifted to the floor. She bent down to snatch it up off the drop cloth.

"What's that?" Jordan asked.

"I don't know." Hayden unfolded the piece of paper. "Oh. My. God."

"What is it?"

"It's a note. Read it, Jordan. Tell me I'm not hallucinating what it says."

Jordan took the piece of paper from her trembling hands. Hayden watched as her eyes went wide before growing wet again.

The note read, "Welcome to Pelican Pointe, Hayden. Relax. You've come this far. Don't give up now. Take care of Ethan. Take care of my town and the people in it."

Dear Reader:

If you enjoyed *Hidden Moon Bay*, please take the time to leave a review. A review shows others how you feel about my work. By recommending it to your friends and family it helps spread the word. If you have the time, please Tweet/Share that you've finished *Hidden Moon Bay*.

If you do write a review, by all means let me know via Facebook or my website.
I'd love to hear from you!

For a complete list of the author's other books visit her website.
www.vickiemckeehan.com

Want to connect with the author to leave a comment?
Go to her Facebook or blog
www.facebook.com/VickieMcKeehan
www.vickiemckeehan.wordpress.com/ blog

Go to the next page for a preview of
Dancing Tides

Dancing Tides

Prologue

Eighteen months earlier
Leesburg, Virginia

Decked out in his Sunday best, a tux no less, he stuck his index finger between his sweaty neck and the collar of the scratchy, white shirt he wore, and nervously gave the fabric a tug as he waited at the altar for his bride to make that walk down the aisle where she would become Mrs. Cord Bennett.

Even though the stifling heat of Indian summer had the crowded church feeling airless, Cord tried to loosen his tie about the same time his best man, Paul Angleton, bumped his shoulder, and batted his hand away to put an end to the fidgeting.

Cord shot a thumbs up in the direction of Paul indicating he was A-OK, even though he was anything but.

Not even close.

His gut felt like the drummer in the band had gotten an early start and set up a steady beat in his stomach. The rehearsal dinner party the night before had gone on too long. He'd indulged in too much wine and woke up this morning with the hangover from hell.

But if he puked now, Cassie would never forgive him. So he swallowed down his bile and tried to ignore the sickening smell of all the flowers lining the altar.

In fact, it might have been the powerful combination of all those fragrant blossoms coming together along with the sweet-smelling blend of perfume from the hundred or so guests, packed like sardines into a chapel meant to hold no more than seventy-five, that had his upchuck reflex on overload.

Whatever it was, it had him wishing they'd get this show on the road.

He supposed every groom was nervous before uttering those two little words that would cement a bond for life. Thinking like that, his queasiness got worse.

Not because he was having second thoughts. No, he'd given his heart to Cassie three years earlier and knew for a fact no other woman would do.

For him, Cassie Spearman was it.

At that precise moment though another whiff of magnolias hit his nostrils and almost brought him to his knees. The pungent odor had him wishing they'd eloped to Virginia Beach in a quickie service without all the fuss. He knew a buddy there who had taken up preaching since coming back from Iraq. Knew for a fact he could've had them married without a frill or a piece of lace. But Cassie had wanted to tie the knot in front of her entire family wearing the dress, the one that had cost her parents a small fortune.

And that, too, was apparently what regular families did.

Family.

Cord didn't have a clue what it meant to be a part of that kind of a unit. He'd grown up in San Diego in the system, a ward of the state.

At first, around eight or nine he'd thought that somebody might come along and adopt him. But by the time he'd celebrated his tenth birthday that notion had died on the vine and he'd accepted the reality of his situation. No one wanted him. And too many didn't even care, not even the foster families he'd repeatedly tested to the limits. They'd taken him on, albeit briefly, and passed on making him a permanent part of their unit.

By the time he'd hit thirteen, his teen rebellion had kicked in for good about the same time he'd realized no family felt like taking a chance on a kid that never seemed to measure up to their expectations.

There had simply never been a good fit.

He had stayed stuck in the foster care system until he'd struck out on his own at sixteen. He hadn't even graduated high school, at least not until much later when he got his GED in the army. In between his military stint and joining the California guard unit, he'd managed to sandwich in two years of community college.

But Iraq had put an end to anything beyond that. His unit had been called up and, once again, he'd served his country.

So, if Cassie wanted to say "I do" in front of a bunch of relatives she loved and who loved her back, then he could damn well stand here in his Sunday best and breathe in the smell of a bunch of flowers, even though they made him slightly ill.

It had to be the lilies, that array of buds representing the tried and true language of love and tradition only a bride could fully appreciate that smelled so freaking strong. They stood tall and straight, lining the dais in so many different shades of pink and white he could hardly keep them all straight without conjuring up a bottle of Pepto Bismol.

But the lilies were Cassie's favorite. And because of that he had no doubt she knew every blessed variety of petal or bud. The woman kept track of every stem and shade of color that had been delivered to the church that day. He would bet money on it. Because she had spent hours and hours with at least a half dozen different florists in town picking out just the right shade of pink—for the flowers alone. The ones she had bugged him about, the ones he'd barely given a second glance or given a second thought—because let's face it—he hadn't cared a whit about what kind of flowers she carried or what genus decorated the church.

As long as she said "I do" when the right time presented itself, as long as he could manage the same without choking or stammering or forgetting that one important line, he didn't give a good crap about a bunch of flowers.

But Cassie Anne Spearman did.

He scanned the small chapel and its sea of faces, checking out the rows of pews where family sat alongside friends and co-workers waiting for Cassie to take center stage.

His lips curved into a wide grin. These people had shown up to spend their Saturday afternoon watching the two of them tie the knot after a long courtship, a courtship that had included three tours of duty in Iraq for him, as well as numerous separations. Cultivating a long-distance relationship with a soldier during a war was never a good bet. But he and Cassie had weathered the storms, cut through the pitfalls and come out the other side better for it.

Here today, they were about to exchange vows and prepare to spend the rest of their lives together.

They'd been through a lot. So it didn't really matter to him about her choice of flowers or the dress or any of the details that had seemed to drive his bride-to-be crazy over the past several months.

He'd spent that time watching Cassie's careful planning, saying "yes" when it was expected, nodding his head in agreement whether the topic had been about napkins or the choice of caterers, or how many place settings they would need for the dinner parties they would surely give.

He'd let her choose whatever bridal registry was the best, let her be the deciding factor as to whether they served chicken or fish at the reception.

No, up to this point, he had been all about getting to the church and to this day when he would cease his bachelor existence and become husband material for all time to "the one."

Cassie Spearman was the one. At barely five-foot-three, the little blonde had managed to capture his heart, his mind, his soul.

And for him, she had been the first one to do so. Before Cassie he'd made sure he kept his heart from ever suffering any kind of major rejection or defeat in that department.

Good thing she had agreed to become his wife. Otherwise what Iraq hadn't been able to do to him, a broken heart surely would have.

And at six-four Cord Bennett wasn't an easy man to take down. Nor was he a pushover. At least not until Cassie had come into his life.

Not half an hour earlier his best man had reminded him that no matter what Cassie looked like in her dress, he was to make absolutely certain that the expression on his face told her, in no uncertain terms, that he was blown away by her appearance, by her dress, by her presence.

But when he spotted Cassie at the end of the aisle, about to take that step toward him in her soft white gown with her hair swept up off her shoulders on the arm of her father, there had been no need for pretending.

He had simply been blown away by the sheer beauty Cassie innately showed to the world. Her face lit up, standing there in the gown she had so carefully chosen with the bead and pearl bodice, the way the skirt showed off her curves and full figure.

He fell in love with her all over again. The nerves fell away. All of his unease subsided.

Staring at his soon-to-be wife, his mouth gaped open; he would have bet money on it. He was that awestruck.

But then, it all changed in a flash of gunfire.

By the time Cord realized what was happening, the uninvited guest had already fired a series of fatal shots. His eyes zeroed in on the man holding the Luger. Cord started running down the aisle toward Cassie. But he couldn't get his legs to move fast enough.

Bullets flew. People screamed.

Boom, boom, boom—the man kept firing.

Cord saw the shooter turn, take a few steps toward him, and aim his weapon.

That's when he felt the burn in his chest.

As he went down, Cord saw Cassie's dress turning from the silky, shimmering gown of white to a blood-red splatter born of rage and hate and jealousy.

The last thing he remembered was the sickening sweet smell of blossoms as the air around him changed to the putrid iron odor of blood.

He'd survived three tours of duty in Iraq. But a gunman had taken him down in a suburban church in the middle of a quiet, residential neighborhood.

And with it, had ended the life he'd dreamed of spending with Cassie Anne Spearman.

Don't miss these other exciting titles by bestselling author

Vickie McKeehan

The Pelican Pointe Series
PROMISE COVE
HIDDEN MOON BAY
DANCING TIDES
LIGHTHOUSE REEF
STARLIGHT DUNES
LAST CHANCE HARBOR
SEA GLASS COTTAGE
LAVENDER BEACH
SANDCASTLES UNDER THE CHRISTMAS MOON
BENEATH WINTER SAND
KEEPING CAPE SUMMER (2018)

The Evil Secrets Trilogy
JUST EVIL Book One
DEEPER EVIL Book Two
ENDING EVIL Book Three
EVIL SECRETS TRILOGY BOXED SET

The Skye Cree Novels
THE BONES OF OTHERS
THE BONES WILL TELL
THE BOX OF BONES
HIS GARDEN OF BONES
TRUTH IN THE BONES
SEA OF BONES (2018)

The Indigo Brothers Trilogy

INDIGO FIRE
INDIGO HEAT
INDIGO JUSTICE
INDIGO BROTHERS TRILOGY BOXED SET

Coyote Wells Mysteries
MYSTIC FALLS
SHADOW CANYON
SPIRIT LAKE (2018)

ABOUT THE AUTHOR

Vickie McKeehan's novels have consistently appeared on Amazon's Top 100 lists in Contemporary Romance, Romantic Suspense and Mystery / Thriller. She writes what she loves to read—heartwarming romance laced with suspense, heart-pounding thrillers, and riveting mysteries. Vickie loves to write about compelling and down-to-earth characters in settings that stay with her readers long after they've finished her books. She makes her home in Southern California.

Find Vickie online at
https://www.facebook.com/VickieMcKeehan
http://www.vickiemckeehan.com/
https://vickiemckeehan.wordpress.com

29419411R00185